"I'm █ █ █ █ Being your.
Disc█ █ █ for duty.

T█ █ █ █

L█ █ █ █ generous and patriotic of
you. █'d really like to take █ ready we can get, but █'re
already overmanned. We took some of the crew of another
vessel that got seized, and some transients on leave. It's ass to
nose aboard now."

I decided to improve the odds. "I have other shipboard
skills," I told the lieutenant.

"You realize we may be in combat as soon as we hit the Jump
Point? We don't have a fleet carrier, so there's no phase drive.
We go where the Points dictate. They're probably waiting."

"Sure. But I don't want to stay here and wait to be pulled
by the UN. I just want to get to the Freehold."

The sergeant grabbed his phone and called aboard. "Can
we ID a vet from seven years ago?"

It turns out I was actually safe in that regard. Any records
there might have been were at HQ and probably scrambled
already. The ship's archive didn't have anything. So the UN
would probably have never IDed me that way.

It got uncomfortable. They didn't want to take a possible
spy or wannabe. I didn't have much to offer. I had my old ID,
but that could be faked.

"Weapon in my bag," I said. "Can you date the issue
number?"

"Probably," the sergeant, Bandan, said.

"Five seven niner six five four one. M Five with the Second-
Gen upgrade. My training company was . . ."

Someone on the phone said, "Yeah, that's her. Screwy
spelling on her name."

I didn't recognize them, but once I was in view he said, "I
was in Fourth Regiment Personnel Section. I remember seeing
you, and your name is unique."

"Thanks," I said, sounding stupid. What else should I say?

Lieutenant Broud said, "Welcome aboard, Medic."

Baen Books by
Michael Z. Williamson

Freehold Series
Freehold
The Weapon
Angeleyes
Rogue
Contact with Chaos
Forged in Blood (Edited by Michael Z. Williamson)

Better to Beg Forgiveness . . .
Do Unto Others . . .
When Diplomacy Fails . . .

Other Baen Books by Michael Z. Williamson
The Hero (with John Ringo)
Tour of Duty
A Long Time Until Now
Tide of Battle (Forthcoming)

To purchase these and all Baen Book titles in e-book format,
please go to www.baen.com.

ANGELEYES

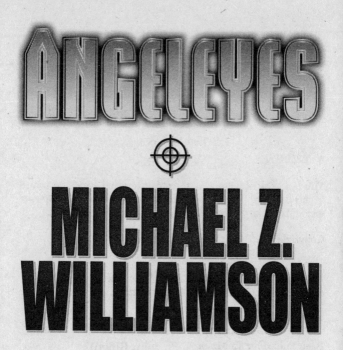

MICHAEL Z. WILLIAMSON

BAEN

ANGELEYES

This is a work of fiction. All the characters and events portrayed in this book are fictional, and any resemblance to real people or incidents is purely coincidental.

A Baen Books Original

Baen Publishing Enterprises
P.O. Box 1403
Riverdale, NY 10471
www.baen.com

ISBN: 978-1-4814-8295-0

Cover art by Kurt Miller

First Baen paperback printing, March 2018

Distributed by Simon & Schuster
1230 Avenue of the Americas
New York, NY 10020

Printed in the United States of America

10 9 8 7 6 5 4 3 2 1

For the hardworking staff at Baen Books:
Marla, Hank, Danielle, Laura, Corinda, David A.,
Christopher R., Christopher C., and Carol.

ANGELEYES

CHAPTER 1

⊕

My name is Aonghaelaice. It's pronounced "Angelica." My parents are freako alt-agers. That's part of why I left home early. They did a lot of fairs and festivals, and that's why I wanted stability. I never got it, of course. I'm too much of a butterfly. I tried marriage. I lasted a year.

During the War, I was a spy.

I actually didn't notice when the War started. I mean, I saw the news mention it. I didn't really pay any attention. There'd been several attacks between forces, with a handful of deaths and no real followup. I watched reports on those. I'm a veteran, so I kept wondering if I'd see any of the medics I served with show up. Second Legion never got involved in those, though, so no.

I wasn't homeless. I was transient. I paid my way, and I had savings in several systems in case I needed them. It's hard to travel interstellar without either a roll of money or some kind of business, but I managed. I made myself useful as needed. Sometimes I was a ship's cook. Sometimes I was a medic. Usually I was just a cargo

1

handler. If need be and I felt like it, I was somebody's girlfriend.

A lot of the time I was in Grainne's Outer Halo. It's a good place to go to—and from—anywhere. Of course, Station Ceileidh and Station Breakout are damned near thirty light-hours apart. It's often easier and cheaper to hop around through Caledonia, Novaja Rossia and Earth than try to grab in-system transit.

But I hadn't been on dirt in about five Freehold years when the War started. That's eight Earth years.

As I said, there'd been a couple of shootouts between Earth and Freehold. After each one, nothing happened. So I figured it was some chest-thumping stuff for the public, and the governments would do something behind it to clear things up. I was much more concerned with getting back to the Halo from the Prescot's mining system of Govannon. It's all minerals, covered in domes, with resorts for the stupid rich. If I wanted to land, the flight in would cost fifty K-marks, then I'd need ten K-marks per night for lodging, and I heard food was about two K a day, minimum. Stupid rich.

I was twenty—thirty Earth years. I looked pretty good, and I give killer head, but you can't see that. No one was going to hire me as their girlfriend unless I had about 50K in wardrobe to get to the right parties. Even then, chicks with a lot of biosculp surgery, who were full-time escorts and looked younger even if they weren't, were going to be top call. And I don't mind being a girlfriend to some rich guy, but I'm not in it strictly for money. So I was never going to see the indoor ski slope, the indoor lake and beach or the indoor jungle cave.

But there was a lot of work in the stations. They'd been moving a meshload of processed metal a week out of there for a couple of centuries. I can't do advanced math, but I can do a bill of lading and count mass ratios, I know how to operate a forklift, tug sled (gas jet or chemical), and can move pretty good loads. Cargo loads, I mean.

I'd seen what I needed to, and wanted to clear out of my bunkie, load up my backpack and get back to the Freehold for a bit. After that, I might try Alsace or Salin for a change. Money goes a long way in Salin.

It can take months to find transit, and sometimes you take what you can get, traveling around six sides of a square, to get there. I hung around the scheduling office in the mornings, and spent the afternoons visiting shipping offices personally and flashing my assets at them.

No, that did not involve dressing down. I'd rather work my way than bitchhike. Quite a few ships have a professional sex worker, or at least simulacra. I don't show cleave or wear lips when asking for a job. I keep my hair longish but ship style, natural red-tinged gold, and wear a clean shipsuit with just enough wear to prove I work. Some people wear a qual badge of some kind, but I don't bother. Your quals should be on file, or readily provable. A badge can be bought anywhere. If you want to look green, hang crap off your work clothes. Professionals generally don't.

I had a file on archive for any interested parties, and was on the rolls with a hiring agency. I scurried into the station office lounge every morning to see what was available. I'd decide which ones I'd consider, and go from there. I won't go on a ship if I'm the only female. I won't go with Earth Arabs, but Ramadanis are usually okay, and most Mtalis, but not the Shia from there. New Indians I need to interview with to decide if it's safe.

From there, I'd see which ships needed crew. I was hoping for Wednesday to be good. That was the big load day. There was always a processed ore load leaving for Sol system, with minimal facilities for passengers. I thought of that as my last-ditch nasty route. There were two luxury cruisers scheduled, but they were unlikely to need crew. They ran extensive background checks and paid well, and if they happened to wind up a body or two short would rather just run that way than take local hires. Their passengers were billionaires.

Billionaires had nothing on the three private yachts who wouldn't be interested in me for anything, although there was a slim chance one of the crew would want a playmate and be allowed a courtesy guest.

But in the last twenty-four, a tramper had come through, en route to Caledonia. I couldn't afford the M10K or so transit fee, but they might need labor or have other openings.

A couple of their crew were hanging out jabbering with the woman at the Support cubicle. They might have been fueling or transshipping some local stuff. I didn't need to know that right now. What I did know was they were flirting with her, badly.

I toed over in the low G, letting it do wonderful things for my chest, which was fully restrained inside my professional coverall. They could see my figure, however, and that got their attention.

"Good morning," I said. "Are you with the *Kubik*?"

"Yes," said the one to my left. Not bad looking. Fit, clean, neat. That told me they kept a good ship. "I'm Ted Kubik. Purser." He held out a hand and I shook it, going for a firm grip.

I stepped back and to the side to give some distance from the Support tech. "Angie Kaneshiro. Pleased to meet you."

"You're trying to crew?" he asked.

"If you have space, I'm ready to work," I said.

"We have space, but it got quiet. We're not going to need a full complement."

Damn. I'd been afraid of that. I pitched anyway.

"Then I'm your man. I can handle cargo loaders, lading charts, lashing plans, and I'm trained as a cook and medic."

"Certs?" he asked. He was still interested.

"Paper for the loaders, I can demonstrate the rest. Military for medical."

"Colonial military?"

"Freehold of Grainne."

He suddenly shied away.

"Yeah, if you're a Graunna vet," he mispronounced it, "we can't have you aboard. Too complicated with the invasion starting."

"I have Caledonian ID," I said. "Landed immigrant."

He looked unsure. Gods dammit, why had I been so honest? I should have just said I was a Caledonian resident.

I lowered my voice, and said, "I don't even care about the money that much. I just want to get back home."

Caledonia wasn't home, but I did have legit ID and kept a drop box there.

He looked at the other one, who hadn't been introduced, but I was pretty sure he was an officer, too.

They looked at each other.

"Got a scan?" he asked me. "I can show it to the captain-owner."

I drew a stick from my pocket and passed it over. It had my face, "Able Spacer" and "Multisystem" on it. My name was listed as "Angie," not the awful spelling. It listed my quals and some of the ships I'd transited with, for reference. As big as the universe is, most spacers know someone who knows someone. I'd be "Oh, yeah, that girl," to most of them, but that could be enough.

I figured the captain-owner was his father. Quite a few family companies plowed all their assets into spacecraft to get off Earth, or struck resources in the colonies and used it as capital.

If they didn't bite, I'd try again in the morning. It was better if there were two or more ships. If they needed crew and thought they might have to compete, they made option offers. As it was, I was running out of local funds. I didn't want to dip into my emergency money.

There weren't any other choices, but I hung around until lunch just in case. I had lunch with me, prepared cold in the minikitch at my bunkie. Tuna salad and rice crackers.

Nothing happened by noon.

With that, I went looking for station work. If there was any, it wouldn't pay much, but I needed to keep my balance up as best I could. I had already decided I wasn't coming back here. The Prescot family owned it outright, and ran a closed shop. It was a good shop, but unless I wanted to ground and work in the mines for a year or two, there was little to offer. Working in the mines, or even in HQ, wouldn't get me into the resorts. So there was no reason for me to land in domed habitats that were just like space habitats but on the surface.

Unless I wanted to sling hash as backup hash-slinger in a crew dive, there weren't any station jobs listed, either. At least, if I ran out of funds, they'd give me a "free" trip to Sol system. Some systems are reported to have spaced vagrants, meaning anyone without air money.

I decided I'd take a walk around the station. I had nothing else pending, and I needed to decide if I wanted to take the fry cook job for a few days, or lower my standards and be an entertainer. Not that there's anything wrong with being an entertainer, but it's not what I wanted.

It also has its own risks. You'll get seen by crew. If you show up the next day looking for work, you'll be, "That stripper chick who wants to play in space." If I decided to do that, I'd have to raise money fast, stash most of it, live super austerely, and wait for all ported ships to rotate. That wasn't going to happen here.

Govannon's station is called "The Highlands." The perimeter passage is called, "The Zodiac Walk." It's roughly in the ecliptic, with large view ports, but the Earth constellations are badly beaten because of the distance between stars.

It's an attractive walk, made to look like cobbles. There's an electric trolley for faster travel and ambience, and it's actually free.

The Prescot family is oddly conservative. You can't buy

most recpharm. You can buy tobacco. I went past a tobacco shop and stopped to look.

I don't smoke. I'm fascinated by the delivery methods people have. Cigars, cigarettes, cigarillos, pipes, tinglers, hookahs, censers, holders, cutters, lighters. They had everything. And it smelled delicious. Why does it smell so good raw, and so revolting burned?

"Good afternoon, ma'am," the clerk greeted me. "Can I help you find anything?" Behind him were tubs and bins and cans of various mixtures, a sign offering custom blends, and more signs listing types and origin.

"Just browsing," I said. "I don't smoke."

"Not an issue. I don't want to be rude, but I'm going to have to close for an hour. I have a shipment waiting on the docks and it has to be moved. My wife is sick today, so I've got to get it."

I slipped a card out of my thigh pocket and slid it across the counter.

"I'm Angie Kaneshiro. I've got certs on loaders and tugs. I do have a bond on file." It was in Caledonia, but I figured he wouldn't check that hard. What would I do with a pallet of tobacco and accessories?

"Okay?" he asked, looking at it.

"I could get it for you so you don't lose sale time."

Just then a couple walked in, and I stepped back out of the way. I busied myself looking through the glass of his small walk-in humidor.

He helped the man with a blend of something lychee and apple for a hookah, apple-scented charcoals for it, and some little tools that were used for maintenance. They took a glance around, came near me and I heard him say,

"Seeing those humidors almost makes me wish I smoked cigars."

He sounded Earth Canadian.

They left, and I looked back at the owner.

"How much?" he asked.

I asked back, "How much stuff is it?"

"Two standard cubes."

"You have a dolly?"

"Yes." He gestured toward the back.

"I'll leave my ID. Fifty marks and a meal." I figured that was up-end of average for this station, based on what I'd gotten elsewhere.

"Fifty flat," he countered. "I don't have any food handy."

"Done," I said.

He pointed to the storeroom, and I found the dolly. It was a manual type. He handed me a Landed Cargo slip, and off I went, out the rear and into the service passage, which was much less pretty, but a lot more interesting. I might find more work back here.

I skated the dolly down to the dock, found his cubes, strapped them on, shoved them back and got a bit sweaty. The whole task took me about an hour. He handed me a L-note and my ID.

"Thank you," he said. A party of four had just left.

Well, that would feed me cheap for a couple of days, and pay for my bunkie for one more. But I'd found a couple more places needing general labor, so I went back down the service passage, now that I had a reason, and made another M76 by day's end.

Their definition of a bunkie is pretty roomy, too. I had

a double bed, drawers mounted at the head and foot, a shelf on one side. The other side had enough room to stand and change. That was offset with the one above me, so they managed with about twice the width, but no more height than what most places offered. The soundproofing was good. The upright end near the bed head had a micro/induction heater/minifridge. There was more storage under the bed, too. My backpack and rolly were there. The bathroom down the passage had five stalls and usually at least one open. The showers were clean and roomy enough for a friend or toys. I took toys. I felt a lot refreshed after that, and slept well. I like it completely black.

The next day I was back at the station office. If you're reliable on searches, you are seen as reliable for work.

I was in luck. Ted Kubik was there again, with the captain-owner.

"Ms. Kaneshiro," he said, and offered a hand. He was old, gray, didn't smile, but seemed to be in good shape and alert. "I'm told you can work cargo manifests and some various duties?"

"Loading, cooking, yes."

"Engines?"

"No, sir. I don't know anything about them. I can watch a gauge while someone takes a head break. That's it."

"Fair enough," he said. "What do you think about the Hevi Six dash Four vs the dash Three?"

That was a loader on my qualification list. "I think they made it too complicated instead of doing an actual upgrade. Most of the display choices aren't needed, and the controls for that are hard to reach while actually gripping anything."

"You'll be happy with our dash Threes, then."

"Oh, good." I'd work with either. I just left the monitor screen cold on a dash Four, and drove it by eye.

"We're tight on funds," he said. "I can offer two K flat for the trip. But, I'll give you point five percent time saved on loadup and loadout charge as a bonus."

Yeah, that wasn't much. But the bonus would help a little. And it got me from here back to Caledonia, where I had some funds and some gear I could sell if I had to.

"Private berth?" I asked. I was hoping.

He said, "Yes. We don't have any passengers this leg."

"Deal," I said. Good. Private berth, locking door, transit where I needed to go, and credits. I wasn't going to find anything better.

Govannon wasn't a bad place, but it wasn't a place for my skillset.

"I have your berthing number. When do you need me?" I asked.

"We start loading at twelve seventeen local."

That was in three hours.

"I'll be there. Thank you very much, sir."

He gave me a pass authorization for their ship. I took that to the office, and they crosschecked my ID, added my bond number and image, and handed it back. That would get me through dock control and customs.

I got to my bunkie, stuffed my clothes in my backpack, and my dress outfits in a garment carrier. My pocket tools and "lock adjustment tool" went into an outside compartment. My rolly contained my coveralls and tension vac suit. I punched for the rolly to evacuate and it sucked everything down for maximum compression. I had nothing that Earth stations could consider a weapon, but I could sure as hell adjust someone's attitude with that wrench. I had three other tools in case I needed them, but I wouldn't here.

I logged out, slipped the key, recovered my deposit, and was ready to go. I took another walk around the Zodiac. It really was impressive, and there was no way I could afford any of it. There was a Gio Leather shop, with shoes starting at Cr1000. They were fantastic. I could get handmade mechanical watches, very retro. There were engraved pens. There were more practical things, like licensed stun batons dressed as walking sticks, and handmade backpacks that were almost reasonable—M500. There were casinos, but most were above anything I could afford, and the luck games are for suckers, and I stink at placing bets on cards. I never went in them.

I stopped at a kiosk for food.

"Morning, ma'am," the cook said. He was Turkish, of course, with gyro meat roasting behind him. "Donor kabob?"

"Chicken, please," I said. "Veggies, tzaziki sauce, banana peppers and a Coke."

I don't eat mammals. I rarely eat birds. It's a personal thing. I wasn't sure what they were serving aboard *Kubik*, but it shouldn't be more than twenty days, and I can manage on salad for a while. And I had some canned tuna and salmon.

I paid, and sat at a table watching people as I ate. It

was good. The chicken was raised in-system, actually in microgee. It was very tender, and nicely seasoned. The poor things probably *wanted* to die, as tight as they were penned.

I succumbed to temptation and bought some Austrian chocolate and authentic Italian cheese as I headed for the docks.

At the dock, it was like being home. There were lighted walkways, traffic lights, warning lights, loader lights, people in reflective suits shouting at each other, the throbbing of rams. It meant work and travel. I was happy.

Kubik was much like other ships I'd been in. The drive section was aft and none of my business. The command deck was forward, and something I hoped wouldn't be my business. In between was crew quarters and holds, and the davits that held towed cargo. The co-owner and first officer was the wife of Mister Kubik, Sr. She greeted me at the ramp, which reassured me a lot.

She was slightly soft from a lifetime in space, but reasonably fit and shapely. Spacers get more arm and less leg from pulling stuff around. She had gray hair pulled back in a short tail, and a shipsuit with *Kubik Deep Space Transport* embroidered on it.

"Ms. Kaneshiro?"

"Yes. Ms. Kubik?"

"Yes!" she grinned as we shook hands. "Frame four zero starboard is your berth."

"Four zero starboard, got it," I said.

"If you want to stow your gear, we'll be ready to load in about twenty minutes."

"Roger," I said with a nod.

I found the stateroom easily enough. It was a bit larger than a station bunkie, and included a comm and phone terminal. That's not a courtesy aboard. It's necessary communication for emergencies. I checked that it worked, established an access, dropped both my bags and went below.

The ship was old but maintained. It might be half a century and change. As long as they fly and can transit a Jump Point, they'll stay in use.

They had three loaders, and Ted and someone I hadn't met were on two of them. I took the third, flipped it on, checked all the op lights, and got to work.

I think I impressed them. They had twelve haulers delivering containers from the holding sally. Each one got imaged from all six sides so damage in transit could be accounted for. Each one pulled up, released the container, which dropped sides and exposed the cubes. We'd each grab one, back to the ship's flank, spin, elevate on the loader's scissor jacks, and stuff the cube into the hold, where two others snagged them with davit harnesses and swung them into stow. The haulers were scheduled five minutes apart.

After the second one, Captain Kubik called and told them to make it four minutes. He couldn't go any faster, because they couldn't position stuff internally any faster.

In fifty minutes we were done, so I'd earned .5 percent of whatever they saved on undocking. If you don't pay flat rate, you pay by the minute. That matters for tramps.

On the last load, Ted and the other guy swung out, ran

along their forks, and jumped aboard to help wrangle in the hold.

"Park 'em and stow 'em," he called while pointing. I nodded, dropped mine to the deck, and drove it up into the lower hold. There were three slots. I noticed my lock fob was labeled "Kubik #2," so I parked it in the middle, and ran back for each of the others. Ted was waiting on the hatch as I rolled in the last one, nodded and hit the release. I grabbed all three fobs and handed them to him.

"Thanks," he said. "We're shoving off. You've seen your couch?"

I nodded. "Yes. I'll go there now."

He said, "We'll update over phone."

I placed my bags in underbunk stowage, rolled into the bunk and pulled out the gee harness. I checked my earbud and my phone itself. You pretty much never remove the earbud, and I know some people have them surgically implanted. I just wear mine. The phone itself has better reach but isn't always needed.

No one wastes mass or money painting a ship. Everything is bare extrusion or alumalloy. But sleeping spaces are the exception. Mine was a cool blue, which I liked. I'm not a fan of pink or puke green. So I had a bit of color for my space.

Mister Kubik's voice came over intercom. "All hands, I show green. Any delays or alibis, let me know now." Thirty seconds later he said, "All green, stand by for undocking and external loading."

Departure wasn't a problem. Hydraulics pushed us out, the maneuvering thrusters came on, then retroed.

They hadn't told me anything, so I assumed the towed

containers were being attached by station crew. I felt some faint vibrations, and a couple of slight shoves to the ship's orientation. That meant they were attaching stuff. Trampers typically carry as close to safe margin as they can, anything that can be stuffed in or hung on the outside. Any gram of capacity not used is a gram you're not being paid for. Cargo is easier to find than passengers, but they'll take passengers, too.

Kubik warned us about thrust again, and I felt it hiss, then rumble. He moved us slowly, making sure the latchlocks on the davits were tight, the cargo secure and oriented. I knew he was satisfied when the screen over my rack warned me he was going to gas it. Thrust and G increased, adjusted, then main power came online and we were outbound for the Jump Point. It was seven and a half Earth days from here to there. In the meantime, I'd do any shipboard routine they needed.

"All hands may undog and start spaceside duties. Dinner at eighteen hundred in the mess."

Ted's voice came over, "Angie, you're welcome to relax until chow. There's nothing pending."

"Thank you, sir," I said. "Call if there is."

Dinner was baked longtrout, and not bad. The crew was all family and inlaws. I'd flown on ten or more ships like it and they were in my log if I needed reference.

"Where are you from, Angie?" the engineer asked. He wasn't ugly, but definitely not my type. Fit enough, but just, no.

Being discreet, I said, "Caledonia, but I've spent my life traveling."

"I bet. Your accent doesn't sound Caledonian." He slid

over the food dish, and I decided he was just being conversational.

"Probably not anymore," I said. He didn't press the issue. "It's what my passport says, though."

"Have you been on land?"

"Not really. My parents did the wandering thing."

"That's not common."

"No, and look how I turned out. I can't stay anywhere more than a year." I stuffed fish into my face to avoid more convo.

They didn't push me for more details, and I sat out of their family convos. They were friendly enough, but this ship was their world. It was just a job and a cubby for me.

I spent the time until jump, and after jump, doing routine shipboard maintenance—flushing compartments for pests, checking seals, checking batteries on the loaders. Much of it was automated, but it still called for eyes on to make sure the automation was connected.

When we docked at Station Orkney in Caledonia system, we raced to pull the cargo. We were done in thirty-seven minutes. The terminal hadn't finished with the external pods.

Mister Kubik came down as we stowed the loaders.

"Thanks for crewing with us, Ms. Kaneshiro."

"You're welcome, sir," I said.

"I could use one more leg to Earth if you're free."

"I appreciate it, but I have things to do here," I said. I didn't want to go to Earth again, unless I knew I had passage back out.

"Very well. Possibly we'll cross flights again."

"Possibly."

He handed me a draft for M2000 and the bonus of almost eight hundred. That would keep me going a couple of weeks, and I had accounts here I could draw on.

Ted and his mother came by. We shook hands and parted as professionals. I'd definitely keep their info in case we did cross flights. It does happen.

I found a bunkie off-dock, stowed my gear, then went to a small stowage I keep in a traveler's locker. They're meant for personal belongings that might violate code as you change systems—drugs, weapons, porn. I keep all those, and some valuables, and clothes.

With better clothes, I was ready to go clubbing and see who I could find. A girl can only deal with toys for so long, and as I said, crew are off limits.

I took the case to my bunkie, and pulled out magenta hair dye, and a straightener. I gave it a quick brushing to neaten it up, then grabbed a blue catsuit and white bolero. I didn't bother with underwear. I did wear boots with low heels that gave me a little lift but had plenty of support. Gravity at the club level was mid, so I chose a bra with a little lift, but not the superstructure I used back on Grainne at 1.18G. Now I had cleave, and I painted my lips for fullness. That was a hint.

I hadn't been here in six months, but Club Eden was still open.

The guy at the door might have recognized me. He squinted slightly, scanned my chit and nodded. I smiled a little and walked in, with just a trace of strut. I wanted to look confident, not arrogant.

It was dark, with flashing colors. There was even a

magenta flood similar to my hair. They had a gym of chromed bars, and four dancers were weaving through it. They were in very sheer skintights. I'm not much into women, but I eyed the brunette. She was slinky but lush. Her cheeks were fantastic. All four of them.

Much of the crowd were younger. Some military, some crew, some station, and probably some corporate, either interns or adult children of execs. I was probably one of the poorest ones in the place.

I got a cola with just a dusting of Sparkle in it. I wanted to heighten things slightly, not affect my judgment.

I don't know much about music, but I know they can tweak the waveforms so they're constantly shifting and basically resonate in the brain. They were doing that. The beat was hypnotic and sexy, and whatever was playing lead was complicated and oddly classical.

I got out on the floor, under the cage, and just started moving. I noticed the lights were running in sequences, and followed them with my eyes, and my feet. I occasionally bumped someone, and most of the dancers were couples, but there were some other singles.

I danced with three guys, and decided two of them were worth considering. The other one just felt desperate to me.

One was younger, fitter and had fine maneuvering technique. He twisted me between the other couples and gripped me with a firm touch I appreciated.

The other one was older, probably had more money, and was still in good shape. He had green eyes, hair shot through with gray, and I got a veteran vibe from him. I liked how that added up.

The most important question was: Did I want this man crawling over my naked body for several hours?

Oh, Gods, yes.

The Sparkle had worn off enough I was sure I was thinking straight, and I filed a pic of him in case I needed to ID him.

"I'm Angie," I said, giving him a card that had a throwaway contact in case I needed to dump him.

"Darren," he said. "You've got a lot of energy."

"A lot more," I said, and half-winked. "Want to buy me a drink?"

"Sure."

This time I took a rum and Coke, light on the rum. I could get plowed after . . . well, after I got plowed.

Yes, he was the one. We finished our drinks, got back out to dance, and I said, "It's too noisy here."

He nodded, took my hand, and led me out the door. His timing was perfect. A train had just pulled up across the passage.

The shuttle whipped us around the perimeter. We kept casual but interested hands on each other's legs as it traveled. We got out at Perimeter 90, and I wondered where his lodging was. Some people prefer low gee, others standard, and there are rentals at all levels, at all price ranges.

We took a lift not far down to .7. I felt bouncy and light, and my boobs were higher on my chest. The boots turned into slippers despite the heels.

"This way," he said, and led me down a passage that was owned by Noble Lodges. Not bad. They were an upper midrange chain.

He swiped the door and ushered me in.

I placed my pouch near the door, just in case, but I was sure he was decent. As I stood up, his hand ran down my spine and I shivered. I turned to face him, and I could see he wanted to kiss me, so I moved the process along and kissed him first.

He was good, and warm, and wrapped his arms around me, and slid them down my back.

His hands cupped my ass and he realized I had no underwear. He paused for a moment and I said, "Step back."

He did so, and I dropped the jacket and peeled the catsuit. Sometimes you want to tease them along. Sometimes you just want them to get to work.

Gods, could he work.

He had me on the bed and went at me with hands and mouth, while I tried to get his clothes off. When I succeeded, I returned the favor. He had firm muscles and moved smoothly and had lovely texture against my tongue. Between gasps I managed to say, "Bend me over," and tossed my legs off the bed. I liked his weight, and his strength, and his motion. I was stretched and stuffed, and clenched until my knees cramped. I about blacked out.

I got more sleep substitute than sleep, but I think we decided we were both very happy with the night. I was actually a bit stiff when looking for work the next morning. I did keep his info. I had no idea how long I'd be on station.

CHAPTER 2

Back in the main colony circuit, I did okay on legs. I found a NovRos transport heading back that way paying M3000, good enough for the trip, then M1000 for an in-system leg to planetary orbit. It was the *Sorokin*, and I'd crewed on her a couple of years back. The owners remembered me. Two of the crew thought I looked familiar. One of them hit on me and I politely told him I wasn't available until I debarked.

He wasn't bad, but I could probably find someone closer to what I needed. He was on the "maybe" list.

My only issue was they liked their ship cold. I wore a liner over my briefer and under my suit, and an ear band. I had lightweight gloves but couldn't wear them much.

They had valuable indoor cargo—wine, liquor and caviar that had come from Earth. It had to be checked every few hours. I'm not sure why. The hold container was conditioned, but I had to eyeball it, and once a day the purser did as well.

They also had a passenger pod. I helped the cook with labor and delivered it to the passengers.

The cook was fantastic. Iliana actually had attended a formal school in Italy on Earth. She was taller than me, very solid, and could chop food by hand for hours, it seemed like. She never got tired.

"Food is art and science," she said. "Getting it all ready at once is science. Making it good is art. So stir this."

I did. She had two pans stirring themselves, me stirring another, while she hand chopped herbs and tossed them into the gravy she had me holding.

She even had a chicken stroganoff aside for me and another crewmember who didn't like beef.

She reached past me and swapped pans, replaced a cutting board, grabbed a different knife, and just moved nonstop, items going past me and into serving containers.

The containers all went on a rolly, which I hauled down to the pod. There was a housekeeper assigned to them who took it and thanked me.

It was fifteen days from station to station and then in-system. NovRos has one of the spacewheel transfer stations the Freehold has. We dropped down in-system, latched on, and it threw us down the gravity well. We spent most of the trip at low-thrust retro to brake. I'm told you don't use any more fuel, you just arrive faster since all you're doing is braking, not accelerating.

"We're legging out in three days," Captain Mirovich told me. "Back to Caledonia. I can take you on standard pay for the jump transit, deadhead from here to there."

"Okay," I said. I wanted to look about their orbital station. I hadn't been there in four years, and that had been about three days, too. I didn't have a reason to stick around, so back out was fine. I stamped a contract, left my work gear aboard, and took my personal bag stationside.

I had friends here, but I got a message that they were both away on contract. Bob and Ray were my go-tos in this leg. I'd hoped to avoid lodging and have fun with friends. No luck, and it was a short turnaround.

Instead I found a lead on a place with roomy bunkies. They were actually almost bach rooms. Private bath, bed and chairs, and a unitized kitchen machine. It was slightly larger than a crew stateroom. They cost about twice what a bunkie does, but I could get spread if I wanted to.

I figured to try the Ice Palace, so I used blue and white makeup down to my collar, glitter out from my eyes, a long ice-white wig with blue ticking, and a blue unitard. I found a store with a white icicle skirt and paid to have it delivered by tube to the kiosk in the lobby.

Like a lot of older stations, this was an inflated planetoid. They have open trains because it's only three kilometers in diameter and length both. It's not quite a cylinder, but close enough. There's a raised "hill" on one side and a lake on the other. They're okay recreation, but more for families.

I took the train down the axis and out between the lake and hill. That's where the Ice Palace is, across from the Sun God.

I really did dance, with Electroade cocktails in between. Blueberry Electroade, a splash of vodka and a dusting of Sparkle, over a solid cone of ice. It's refreshing, and I got into a great dance trance. I could feel the music and rhythm, and just gyrated with it. Inside I felt like I was squirming. It's hard to describe. If you've sparkled, you know what I mean.

Then it all overlapped with the music and low G and I got dizzy. I ordered a hit of straight O2 to clear my head.

The bar had some snacks, so I grabbed a chicken beet salad and some vat-raised roe on toast. I watched the other dancers from a corner table.

There was one amazingly fiery couple. They both had olive skin, ripped muscle and moved in perfect synch. I'd swear they'd had years of practice, but they were young. Back, forth, angles, sides, turn, hands on hips, step, twirl out. He was amazing, and if he'd been alone . . . then I wondered about the two of them. I knew I'd enjoy it, but I had no way to know if they went that way, or if I could fit into their mix well enough.

But it wouldn't hurt to ask. If not them, who else?

That was when a handful of uniforms came in.

Military, UN, undress, which they wouldn't do in Earth but I guess would here. Most of them were pretty average. It's not just the difference in gravity. They just don't push fitness in the UNPF the way we do. Three of them, though, were in good shape.

I stepped out and smiled at one of them. I gestured, he nodded, and we got to dancing. He was nice to look at, definitely showed interest, but his rhythm was only okay. He had olive skin that shaded well with his uniform shirt.

His buddy was a bit better. He was gorgeously coffee-hued with a very sexy grin full of naturally perfect teeth. I worked between them, let them get on either side and guided their hands in so they knew it was okay to touch me.

That was possible. I thought I might do that as a second option.

I smiled my way out from them, and turned to where that couple had been. They'd moved over a few meters, so I jig-stepped that way. The lights kept shifting, the bass rumbled and some sort of waveform whooshed in and out of phase.

They were still moving back and forth, sometimes locking eyes and grinning, sometimes watching their feet, sometimes closed and arching. They were just perfect. I can do a woman if a man is involved, and he had a great ass and shoulders.

I got alongside, waited until they noticed me, and open-handed to them.

She gave me this gorgeous smile, and it was such a beautiful turndown I couldn't even be disappointed. She was amazingly expressive.

That one look said, "I'm so sorry, but we're alone this evening. You're definitely pretty and interesting, but I can't share. He's got to do some serious work on me before I sleep. Another time perhaps."

Actually, I could have done her alone, based on that smile.

I bowed back and turned enough to show I understood and would move away as the dance took me.

But my soldiers were still free. They were dancing with a couple of other girls, who I could tell were only there for the dancing. I moved around the outside, until the flow of the floor moved the girls a bit back.

I ran fingers up each of their spines, smiled and shimmied back between them. Dale and Jacques, I found out, and they each had a hand stamp showing an infection test. They were looking, I was looking, and it didn't take long to convince them I was interested, and of course I was fine with both of them. I was pretty sure it would be tag team, not sandwich.

I was close. Two hours later I was on tight all fours with my mouth and my cooze full, and then very full. Hands ran over my back, belly and breasts, and I rode the waves as they shuddered and throbbed, and I was still just sparkled enough to feel like I was tumbling. Orgasm and euphoric is an amazing combo, if you get the dose right.

I was glad I had the large room.

Dale had come in my mouth. He wanted to fuck me, so I rolled back and pulled him on top while Jacques took some time to recover. An hour later, I got them both off again, in a sort of reversal.

I was stiff when I woke up the next morning, but I felt great. A little naughty hedonism is great for my mood.

There were a lot of troops around the station, mostly in small groups. I wondered what was going on. It was the War, of course.

There'd been talk of a UN mission to the Freehold. What we found out was that it had been an actual attack. They'd gone in with ten drop landers, and pretty much lost a chunk to Orbital Defense. Then the rest had been captured and held for repatriation.

The troops here were because the UN had planned on a larger mission, with these guys staged to be support.

I'd invited what were basically two enemy soldiers into my bed last night.

That took some of the buzz off.

I saw troops everywhere. Doc, clubs, shopping. I think they were billeted in pods in a load bay.

I wasn't able to catch back up with that amazing couple. I was at Ice Palace all three nights, and nothing.

But I still had most of my funds in my pocket when we boosted out, and I'd been very well spread. I'd look in the same club if I legged back soon.

I didn't see any troops in Caledonia, and two days after docking, I pulled out doing intra-gate work from their JP2 to JP4 to get around the bottleneck going through the Freehold, on a volatiles hauler, the *Wheezer*. Instead of attached pods and a towed train, they had a fixed tanker frame. I had to monitor Temps and Press, and keep the crew fed around the clock. It was twelve days transit, with lots of routine and nothing else.

That put me close to Ramadan, of course, and I had to juggle to avoid Arabish ships. Some of them are really pushy and abusive of female crew, and you won't find a court to help. There's no clubs, either. Or, there is, but the dress code makes dancing pointless.

There were troops there. I took a count. They'd arrived just after the ones at NovRos, which made sense, given transit time.

It matched up with that botched assault.

Three jumps and a month later, I was back in Caledonia. No troops there. They were pretty close to independent, and I thought that mattered.

Interesting.

It was then that the real attack took place. The UN used kinetic weapons to smash our ground bases, which was odd. Space assets are a lot more important. I had no idea why they'd chosen that approach. I never studied tactical or strategic calculus. I couldn't figure it out then, and I can't now. I've had people tell me it's an institutional mindset that can't adapt, but it's so ridiculous I can't see it even with that.

They landed and started moving in, and then spread back to some of the habitats. I didn't know that then, though. Just that they'd landed and occupied and called our government a "junta." I had to look that word up. They lied outrageously that our government was a military government, and they claimed to be liberating our residents.

People believed it, even in Caledonia. Apparently, on Earth they ate it up. It was complete vent waste, but people would believe it for years or ever.

The biggest thing I noticed about the War was shipping stopped dead for a week.

The news from the Freehold was limited. At the time, I could tell the UN had moved in and had control of media, but all that means is they controlled the Jump Points, or at least some Jump Points, since news has to go through shipboard and be recast on the far side.

I was glad I had Caledonian ID. I might not be going home for a while. I sat around the station, and there were ships to Earth, a few back to Govannon, some going through-system for Novaja Rossia. Nothing was going to Grainne.

Then flights resumed, with stringent examinations.

The good news there was that the backed-up ships had lost some crew to other transits or routes, and wanted to unload in a hurry when they got there. There were support materials for the war they wanted to haul.

I got on a large tramp—the *Ronson*, 500K tonnes, with a crew of fifty. We loaded in a hurry, then spent the trip tetrising stuff around in the holds, so it could be unloaded in proper order. That saved time on loading, would save time on unloading, and kept us busy meantime. It meant they were short on mass, but I guess the time saved made it worthwhile. That's a purser problem, not a cargo-handler problem. I got paid Freehold Cr5000 for the trip, and damn, I earned it.

CHAPTER 3

Station Ceileidh looked nothing like I remembered. Things change constantly, but this wasn't even home. There were UN troops watching the dock as we unloaded. We were required to wear ship badges while doing so. I got checked out twice to make sure it was real.

Luckily, they don't know accents from spit because I don't sound Caledonian.

Then I was free to move about the station. Sort of.

As I headed out of the dock, there was a checkpoint, and it was backed up.

"What's the thing?" I asked the guy ahead of me.

A guy ahead of him said, "Mandatory ID chip. Necklace for now, but they're talking implants later, like on Earth."

I wondered why anyone was putting up with that. Then I realized most of them either weren't local, or didn't spend a lot of time slumming. There are several discreet ways out of the dock.

"Oh, damn, I forgot . . ." I muttered, and headed back toward the ship. A couple of people watched me for a moment, probably for my ass, since I was female, but no one followed me.

Then I went past the lock, past the dock, down into the maintenance area. It has the controls, seals and power for the locks. There weren't any troops here. A couple of maintenance people did look at me funny.

"Which way to Seventeen?" I asked, and pointed both ways.

"That way," one said. "Five slots. Watch for the pressure bulkhead, it's just beyond that."

"Ah, great, thanks."

I knew where 17 was and actually planned to stop at 15.

Number 15 had a tunnel that dropped down and ran parallel to that pressure bulkhead. It carried main power from the plant. I may have gotten laid there once. I also may have helped a friend who was lit up, come down there.

I had to duck and hold my backpack in front after I loosened the straps, and slung my rolly bag low behind me. The passage went in-station, and would come out in the plant proper, but there was a hatch before that.

That hatch was alarmed. I didn't want to open it, so I had to decide if I could find another, or risk the powerplant, which was probably guarded. Unless they were trusting local guards. Power out in a station was a catastrophe that could kill everyone.

I found another hatch that went somewhere else and was bolted. I dug into my tool pouch and managed to get a multispanner to fit it. I leaned and strained and it moved a fraction, then stopped. I forced it back up, then leaned in again, and got it to move.

It opened easily once I unbolted it. As long as it didn't go back to the dock. This had to be on some blueprint, but did anyone know it was big enough to get through?

It almost wasn't. I shoved my luggage through and followed it, twisting my shoulders and ass as I went. I had some dust and stains now, and could probably pass as maintenance if I needed to.

I was annoyed, and a bit hungry. I'd been waiting to get dinner, because the best fishballs and noodles in space were in a little hole in the wall just past the ID check. I'm told you can get better in the Southeast Asian Federation, but I'd never get there. I had energy bars in my pack if I needed them, but I could last a few hours.

That passage came to a dead end at another hatch. It was set to hold pressure on the other side, so I was safe— it wouldn't open if there was an imbalance. I tried to calculate angle and distance, and estimate gee. I shouldn't be anywhere near the docks, but I wasn't sure where I was. The hatch wasn't coded, but was secured. I took a listen and heard generic mechanical noise, and decided to risk it.

I undogged the catch, leaned onto it, opened it and stepped out.

It was a secondary environmental control. There were two guys moving around machines at one end, that looked like supersize versions of shipboard air plants.

There was nothing to do but close the hatch, grab my gear, and start walking, carrying them like tools. The two of them heard me, glanced over, and one of them made a pointing gesture in line with his body. I saw where he pointed. There was a gap behind two tool lockers. I walked over, backed in with the bags and left them stacked in front of me.

Okay, so he had some reason for me to hide, and seemed to be on my side. I caught my breath and waited. I could see out through a slit of gap between my duffel and the locker.

A couple of segs later, I saw a UN uniform walk into view, check the hatch with a glance, check one of the consoles and a catwalk overhead, and walk back out of view.

Trif. How long would I have to lurk here? Could I get out without one of their chips? Should I retrace my steps and accept it?

My legs were aching by the time one of the maintenance crew came over and leaned against the wall.

He muttered to himself, "Goddess, I can't wait for that nosy fucker to take a break. He keeps butting into my overhaul. Maybe I can get something actually done when he takes lunch. Yup, there he goes, to the back corner, where I don't have to look at him."

He glanced over at me and flicked his eyes toward the main hatch. Then he stood up and walked back to his job.

I took the hint, slid out, walked to the hatch and through.

There was another UN uniform on guard there. She looked me up and down as I carried the bags, so I said, "See you in two divs if you're here." I figure our clock would confuse her, and added, "About seven hours."

She started to say, "Nah, I'll be . . ." then realized it was none of my business what her schedule was, and shut up, hoping she wasn't getting herself in trouble.

I don't know if she thought about it anymore, but I was around the corner and out of her sight by then.

Fuck. They'd moved in and held the stations at least. I didn't want to be dirtside, but that might be safest if I could get a flight in. I just barely had enough funds for that.

I hit a bar and watched some newsloads while eating a codfish sandwich. I caught up on the local codes on the station. It was a spacer and engineer bar, with lots of screens and chairs with small tables, and no music.

I'd be able to walk around without being scanned, apparently, in the "interim." I'd need the chip to rent lodging, arrive or depart, or take a job beyond day labor.

That was a pain in the ass. I understood why day labor was exempt. A lot of transients arrive here, run out of funds, and our government won't pay to send you anywhere. You can work or starve. Periodically, there's an emergency appropriation to deport a couple of hundred of them to Sol system and throw them on the dole there. In between, they'll do anything from hauling trash to sucking cock to publicly humiliating themselves for a cred or a mark.

It's not all that bad. But there's a lot of them, they're paid cash, and tracking them would be almost impossible. Some of them couldn't even read and wouldn't be anywhere near polite company for weeks. Some were sex slaves. Those poor people would actually benefit from this.

I'd get screwed, and not the fun way.

I had spendable funds in discreet cards, and I could tap my account here with a day's notice, but I'd rather not. So I needed a place to stay.

I had a couple of friends I could call, if they were still here. I wondered if it was safe to call, or if I should just show up in person. No one knew who I was, or even that I was here really. I hadn't reached customs. I didn't know how far they'd gone on surveying the resident population, or whatever it's called.

I called, voice only.

"This is Lee," he said as he answered. Lee runs a small repair shop that stays busy making components for trampers and station businesses. His wife programs nav systems and sometimes has to go aboard to tune and zero them. And that's as much as I know about astrogation.

"Lee, it's Angie. I'm insystem."

"Oh, hi! How are you?"

"Broke, I'm afraid. Can you put me up for a night or two? I don't mind sharing." I really didn't. He was quite good.

"Damn, you always call when my wife is outsystem," he said. "When am I going to get you both together?"

"When does she get back?" I'd met her twice for a div or so. She was okay, he was hot; I wanted to try the combination, but we all had to coincide for that to happen.

He said, "At this point, who knows?" So it still wasn't happening.

I turned it back to business. "Yeah. Well, got room?"

"Sure, come on over."

I had no trouble finding his place, and didn't see any

UN goons. I guess they were at the docks and critical facilities.

I knocked, the door slid open, and he gave me an inquiring look. I stepped forward and planted a kiss on him, and let him have it as long as he wanted. Damn, he's got good breath control. Strong hands, too.

"Good to see you!" I said with a smile. I knew where this was going.

"And you," he said. "Just arrived?"

"By a roundabout way from Caledonia." He pointed to the couch and I sprawled. He took his lazy chair and tapped for drinks. Ginger lime ice showed up. I needed that.

"Yeah, it's not a good time here," he said.

"Oh? Fill me in." Yes, hydration, and maybe food. I finished the glass and he sent another.

"Well, you got tagged by the Aardvarks, right?" he asked.

"Aardvarks?"

"Earth pigs."

"Oh, that, yes," I lied. I trusted him but he didn't need to know. How fast had that nickname come up?

"Yeah, they've got a fight on the surface. It's bad. But we don't have a lot of choice here if we don't want to breathe vacuum."

That was what I expected, but not what I needed to hear. "Crap. Should I cadge a flight back out?"

"You might wanna," he said.

I made note, and shrugged. "Well, for now I have enough for food, not lodging."

"You're fine here," he said. "No worries."

"Thank you, I appreciate it," I said. "So . . . wanna fill me in?"

"However you like," he said, grinning and grabbing for me.

We went straight to the shower. I guess I have a fetish for hot running water, hot male, and sex toys. I was limp against the wall in a minute, feeling delicious sensations inside and out while getting clean. His shower has a setting to blow air near your face to keep it dry, while misting the rest of you all over and draining down.

I suppose someday I'll find an actual family, but I'm too much a hedonist. And flaky. As long as I have a roof and few creds, I don't need more, really.

We got out and he made me some tuna and rice for dinner. He had chicken, and didn't mix the dishes. It was good stuff. He knows to use enough spice without killing the flavor.

Afterward, I tapped into his access and got the news.

Yeah, it wasn't good here at home. But, it looked as if I could find a sleep cheap in the day-labor area. If I could book back out to Caledonia, I'd be fine. I was even considering NovRos. It's harder to work there without connections, and the connection they'd want from me could involve things I do for pleasure that I don't want to do for work. But I might have to.

Here was fine for a couple of nights, but I needed to work or move, money or distance.

I did more looking, but I was going to have to do footwork to get anything. In the morning, I went out and took a back service route down to the levels where most of the transients hung out.

I wasn't interested in the grunt labor they were paying a few creds a div for. I wasn't qualified for any of the really technical stuff. I didn't want to cook in the one place that was hiring. I know ground rat meat when I smell it, and cat never tastes or smells like chicken. My options were limited.

I made it back to Lee's place in time for dinner.

"No luck yet," I said. "I'm definitely going to try to fly back out."

"I don't know what's going to happen," he said. "There's almost no news from groundside, but there's a lot of ships coming in, and not many going out. We may have declared independence too soon."

"I don't know the politics," I said. "Caledonia, NovRos and Meiji haven't had problems."

"We have a lot more resources and national capital," he said. "GDP high enough to embarrass them, and increasing mobility and transportation infrastructure. We're not beholden."

"I know it's always easier to get ships here," I said. "Or it was."

"Exactly."

I appreciated his hospitality. That evening I painted my lips up and gave him the best mouthjob I could. I love the texture of skin against my lips. And he was warm to snuggle with. I can't have pets with my lifestyle. I miss snuggling.

CHAPTER 4

The next morning I decided to risk the better areas. It was entirely possible I could talk my way into a position and not have to be scanned. I was getting the impression no one was cooperating if they didn't have to, and unless they had detailed employee records, who would know? The big corps would be doing that. The private businesses, not so much. The Freehold of Grainne is an entire system of small businesses.

I followed Lee to his shop. There are several of those, metal and plastic suppliers, food provisioners of hydroponics and ground-based products. The usual luxury goods. I'm not bad at sales, actually. I could work for a hotelier directly. There are stowage companies.

I was hindered by being physical, not intellectual. Groundside or in the inner Halo, I'd actually consider stripping or sex work. It would be safe and clean, and you get paid depending on the clientele you choose. Here, there wasn't much. The ones catering to the hotels were a closed shop and very expensive. The good ones dockside were a closed shop, and I knew several of them. One of them taught me my eye-crossing tongue action. I wouldn't cut into their work even if I could, and theirs was down. That left the cheap ones. There was no advantage and I wasn't interested. I was better off just fucking Lee and lodging with him honestly. I wasn't obligated, either.

Luxury retail wasn't hiring, and leather was effectively shut down with UN regs on animal products. Govannon didn't have that problem. They grew their own insystem, and the Prescots have more money than most of the nations on Earth. No one dared screw with them. They'd once bought someone out to the point where he starved to death. They paid for every departing ship, every cargo, every supply, and left him in his flat with nothing. He had it coming, but that was a lesson that was remembered fifty years later.

We're a rich system, but not that rich, and we had occupying troops.

I didn't want to panic. I could stay with Lee. I might even get to meet his wife at last. Intimately, I mean. We all agreed it was an idea, but we hadn't got there.

But if I stayed here, I wasn't leaving again for a while. I'd passed through Sol system twice. They have those tags, and so many rules, regulations and bureaus you can't actually do anything. I'd had to petition for exemptions from their rules, and could only fly on Freehold-flagged ships. That's when I'd started Adminwork for Caledonia. Sol had fixed wages that made it hard to find cheap transport. I'd been there months the first time, and got out by bribery the second time. It took half my savings and a fine piece of East Sea spectrashell.

I was running out of options.

Well, there were service jobs, and those did pay. Not many. The really rich had private nurses, the poor made do with automated monitors and on-call response. In between, there was one hospice. There was child care for any number of transients and locals, but the locals often found ados to watch the small kids.

I was actually thinking of that as I passed a daycare not far from the docs.

I sat down and ate lunch, and watched the passersby. They were few.

Overhead, I could see the tramway looping around the far side. A planetoid inflated like a bubble looked cruder than a station built from polyfiber and steel, but it worked just as well. I had two kilometers of diameter by ten kilometers length to use to hide, and I knew a lot of alleys and crawlways, if only I had money.

Right then the lights went out.

There were screams of panic.

The lights came back on, on the emergency circuit, at about forty-percent brightness.

Then there was a loud crack and a slam of air, and pressure dropped. Only a little, but in a habitat that makes people panic, and should. Alarms started wailing. Three warbles and a steady. Pressure malfunction.

I couldn't remember if Lee had emergency O2 at his apartment. I knew his shop was at Radius 73, but that was a long way from here.

It wasn't obvious, but I felt the temperature dropping, too. That leak was still going.

Would someone actually sabotage the station? There

were thousands of people here. But if they thought that would stop the UN, they might, if they didn't care about us. Ground dwellers might.

We needed the station too, and it wouldn't stop arrivals. They'd set up some emergency control from a command ship.

I had no local paid-for shelter or oxy, so I needed to find a ship, even if it meant getting tagged by the UN.

Then I wondered if that was it. It would take a long time to depressurize the entire station. If they could cause panic, everyone would rush for the docks and could be tagged.

Or was it our side doing it just to create panic so we'd swarm them?

I had no way to know. I did know I needed to reach a ship. They probably didn't have room for everyone. I wanted to get aboard early.

The train was working, but was packed like a cargotainer and had people hanging on the outside who were going to get smashed off through the terminal tunnels. This was getting bad fast.

I hoofed it. I had my backpack. My other bag was at Lee's, but I trusted him with it. It was mostly more clothes and boots. This had my work clothes, cash, ID and a couple of personal items and tools.

I got to a fair jog, but I was never a good runner even in service, and spacers don't run. We get flexible and strong, but not fast.

Then I started hearing PA announcements. They were fuzzy and hard to hear, but it sounded important, and people started to flip.

Then my phone alerted. A trembling female spoke.

"Station integrity compromised. All occupants should seek immediate shelter in place, or go to the dock level for rescue. Station integrity is compromised . . ."

It repeated, and she was live, not recorded. That was bad.

I was definitely better on foot than train. I was running across the panic, as people ran from shops and offices to the train, shoving in front and behind me. I elbowed one asshole who tried to push me with him, and had to slap another who thought he was helping me.

I was panting very quickly. I thought about dumping the bag, but without it, I had no clothes or gear. I wanted my lock pin in hand to bash people with, but I'd have to stop and open the pack to get it.

I just kept shoving and jogging.

I took ramp after ramp, following the signs for each level. I wasn't spiraling, but I was doglegging. At least G was dropping as I got closer to the axis. That meant the mass felt lighter, but it also meant I felt more inertia. I had to dig in, lean back and shove to slow myself before direction changes. The dim light didn't help.

It was definitely chill, and the air felt thinner, more like NovRos than Freehold. That meant the leak was huge. I couldn't really guess, I didn't have the geometry memorized. I worked it out afterward and figured the hole was several meters across and it had to be in the main pressure or it would have been sealed already. Spacewatch should have caught any debris, and there shouldn't be many rocks moving anywhere fast enough. So it was attack or sabotage, by all my thinking.

Then I was at the axis level and the mass of people suddenly enveloped me.

At the gate to the docks, the guards were overwhelmed. Hundreds of people were shoving past them, batting their batons away. If pressure dropped, you went anywhere that could hold it, fast. That was a few facilities, and any ship.

Ahead of me, the crowd shifted to the right. I came to what looked like an edge, and found myself facing a bunch of caretakers with kids.

The adults were trying to keep scared kids corralled while scared adults shoved past them.

This really wasn't good. I wondered if the ships would run out of space soon and have to button up. There are gas dealers with oxy, and a number of short-duration emergency bottles at any dock, then some machine shops have gas. They couldn't handle everyone, though.

The guards had apparently given up trying to tag anyone. They were being swarmed. One was missing his helmet and had a bloody nose. Another was welting up around his cheek and forehead. I guess people didn't like being told they had to wait for permission to breathe.

I hoisted my pack onto my shoulder and scrambled through the crowd, then through the turngate. My strap caught on a gate rod and I had to twist around as three people went under my arms.

"Move it, slunt," some guy said and jabbed me hard with his elbow.

I said, "Fuck off, dickless," and kept pulling the strap.

Then someone else shoved through and it tangled even worse and jammed the gate. I managed to reach the strap lock, pop it, and pulled the strap through. I'd have to get replacement hardware out when I had a chance.

I slung the bag over one shoulder and shoved through.

Then I bumped something and came to a complete stop.

It was a little girl, maybe from that crowd of them. She was tall enough to bump my hip.

I didn't want her getting trampled, so I scooped her up in my left arm and carried her.

"You're in the way, sweetie, we don't want you to get hurt."

I shouted, "*Does anyone belong to this child?*"

Several people looked, but none answered.

She had a bag in her hand, and I realized there was a leash dragging behind her. I managed to flip that up and catch it, then shoved it through the bag handles while using my elbows to stop people from crushing us.

I didn't want to abandon a kid, and I did want to help get her safe. There's positives and negatives to having a kid with you. You get a certain amount of leeway, but you can't leave them and run. They also stand out some places.

Only, I wasn't heading for a ship. I was planning to find a station safe cell and shelter there, with crew and labor. They wouldn't turn me away with a kid, no. But she'd make me distinctive.

And she was screaming.

"Hey, hey! It's okay!" I said. It was a rhyme. I went with it. "Can you clap your hands?"

This was bad. The only training I had for child care was watching friends and memories of growing up. I was faking it as I went.

Then I saw a skirmish line of UN police moving toward us. That's why the crowd was so thick. The goons were still trying to scan their fucking IDs while we were trying to get air to breathe.

I didn't have one, and didn't want to be questioned about why not.

I saw a restroom and pushed sideways and backwards, like I was swimming across a river current, which I hadn't done in ten years.

Once there, it got easy. No one was stopping to pee. But the girl was hopping around and ran straight for a stall.

Then I heard shouting outside and ran in with her.

I heard the door open and a rough female voice shouted, "Who's in here? You better have an ident when you come out. Anyone? Last call."

Then the noise faded as the door closed.

Well, shit.

The girl looked scared at all the yelling.

"It's okay," I said. "Let's wash our hands, okay?" I wasn't sure that was safe, but I wanted to keep her quiet and be a responsible adult. The delay was safer than the screaming.

She nodded and followed me, pulling at her pants as she came.

I helped her clean up and wash her hands, and she said, "Tank you."

"You're welcome," I said.

"Where's Mom?" she asked.

Any question but that, please, kid. "What's your name?" I asked.

"I'm Juwetta," she replied, grinning broadly.

"I'm Angie," I told her. "How old are you?"

"Where's Mom?" she asked.

Sigh. "Mom's not here."

"Find her," Juliet, or Juletta, or whatever her name was said. She strode determinedly toward the door.

"Wait here," I said, and held her arm.

That was a mistake. She turned and grabbed me, and yelled, "YOU STOP DAT!"

I let go quickly, but dropped down to one knee to negotiate. She had to be quiet. There were still troops pouring through the station, and they'd drag us off. Whether or not they were taking prisoners, keeping them together, or doing anything besides shooting them or stuffing them out the airlocks, I didn't know. But I wasn't going to be found. I also knew I couldn't leave this kid alone. This was worse than a stray kitten.

"Listen," I said, "Mom had to go away, but we can find her, okay?"

"Yes!" she said brightly, with a big grin.

"Okay, but we need to go quietly, okay? There's bad people out there."

"Scaiwy people?" she asked.

"Yes, scary people. Can you be very quiet?"

"Okay," she agreed, and reached for my hand. It was a start.

I just hoped she was as reasonable if Mom never showed up. I had no idea if she'd been in day care, with a family, or what.

"You call me Angie, okay?" I said.

"Anzhee," she replied.

"Yes. How old are you, Juletta?" I asked again.

But she wasn't old enough to tell me. Less than three local years I was sure, even as tall as she was. Older than two almost certainly.

If I remembered right, there should be a rear access for cleaning. They didn't like dragging carts or bots through the public passages even at night. I led Juletta back to the blocked staff door, then reached into my pack for my lock pin.

I stuck the point into the door, right above the latch, and threw my mass against it. Even in low G, it caused the sheet polymer to bend and deform. Then I put feet against the sink shelf and pushed. The latch pulled free and the door swung.

I closed it behind us, even though it was obviously wrecked. Juletta stared at me with large eyes.

"It's okay," I said. "We have to get around the crowd."

"You broke it."

"I'll pay for it later," I told her.

"Okay."

Access to the rear passage was easier. I opened the door, and it blew wider, with a warmer, brisk breeze coming through. I realized I could probably trace down the puncture, if I wanted to. I didn't want to. I wanted to get to secure pressure.

I didn't see anyone at first, so I grabbed the girl's hand gently and guided her toward the dock access. If I recalled, we had two pressure hatches and one locked screen between us and there.

"This way," I said.

There were a few people, but not many, and all either

had masks on their gear or badges that would let them into controlled space. A few of them glanced at me, but no one tried to stop me.

I knew they'd take some people into their areas, but they couldn't take many, and trying to push it would get you spaced. It wasn't that they were cruel. There just wouldn't be enough air. Especially if the life-support plant got damaged and they couldn't split or grow more. They had a combination of extracted O2 from water vapor, and stuff from hydroponic tanks. But if the tanks died, then they'd be down by half, then down by whatever leaked.

It wasn't going to be pretty. If people were scared now, they were going to get violent when the emergency bottles ran low. The station was effectively out of commission. They'd need weeks of major repair to get it back.

Juletta hung onto my hand now. She seemed to realize it was bad and she was lost.

We definitely needed to get off the station. There wasn't time to try to find her family. That would have to wait.

We passed one of the pressure hatches, and the access was unlocked due to emergency. Perfect. It was working the way it should, which was also in my favor.

Tucking her up on my shoulder again, I used the service passage to get to the outside Radius 30 of the outer dock. It was easier to walk with increasing G, but harder to carry the girl.

At the dock, I just pushed the exit lever and walked through. That was a mistake. The UN had had enough brains to post guards, even if they didn't have enough brains to bypass ID for emergencies.

There was a single guard, but he was bigger than me and armored.

"Stop, you. What the hell do you think you're doing bypassing the corridor? And where—"

I threw my hand up and slammed the lock pin under his chin. His teeth clacked hard and his eyes rolled up as he went down. I bounced in the low G, but I'd managed to transfer most of the energy into his jaw.

I was no longer in a mood to be fucked with.

I looked at Juletta, who just stared at me.

"Bad man?" she asked.

"Yes," I said.

"Safey is good man."

"He wasn't a real safety officer."

"Oh," she said. She seemed to trust me on all this. I wasn't sure if that was good for her, but it worked for us for the time being.

The crowd wasn't as bad up here. In fact, it was light. I'd managed to bypass the mass, and they were all trying to cram into the nearest ships first.

CHAPTER 5

The nearest ship to me was a decent-sized freighter with passenger modules already locked in place. I took a deep breath and headed for it, Juletta still clinging to me. In fact, her nails were cutting into my neck.

"Not so tight, sweetie," I said. "We're almost to the ship."

"Mom and Dad?"

"Ship first. Have you ever been on a ship?"

"No. Not without Mom and Dad!"

"We have to find them, Juletta."

I wasn't sure how long I could keep her from a tantrum.

I reached the lock ramp and the crew were armed with stunners, standing behind clear shields they'd either had on hand or fabbed fast.

The guy in front of me was huge, mostly muscle with a bit of padding, bearded and bald with a mean stare.

I walked right up, slowed enough to avoid a fight, stopped three meters short and introduced myself.

"Hi. Angie Kaneshiro, Able Spacer, certs for medical, internal and external cargo, galley and services. Distressed Spacer Rule. I need transport but can work my fare."

He shrugged and nodded.

"Better than the shallow bitches following, I guess." He turned his head, "Phil, got an actual spacer. Sending her up."

He turned back and waved his thumb over his shoulder.

"We're bound for Caledonia. If that's not where you want to go, too bad."

"That's where I'm from. Perfect."

"Yeah. Good luck with the girl. We don't have much for kids."

"We'll be fine. Thank you very much for your help."

Behind me, a crowd was gathering. I'd beat the rush by about thirty seconds.

At the top of the ramp, a woman said, "Aft twenty, Portside up . . . no, let's make it level," she said, looking at Juletta. "Double for the two of you, but we may have to put someone else in as well."

"I'm sure you will. Thank you."

I found the stateroom. It was minimal crew quarters, but workable. I dropped my bag, slapped my phone against the terminal to access it, and punched in a hatch code.

I turned right around.

"Come with me, Juletta. We need to go see the captain."

"Ship captain?"

"Yes, he is."

Actually, any officer would do, but I wanted to explain things to someone.

I secured my hatch, went forward and hoped things would keep working.

I made it through two hatches before I did run into the captain. They had a roomy lounge behind the C-deck, and he had a polo with four stripes on his shoulders. He wore a headset with glasses and was talking to someone. I waited until he was done giving orders, which seemed to be about how many people they could stuff aboard.

"Sir, Angie Kaneshiro. Able Spacer, medic, cargo, cook, clean. Thank you for your hospitality. Your crew let me aboard. I can work while I'm here. What do you want me to do?"

He grinned and said, "Well, we're tossing our ID chips. Want to join the party?"

Behind him, someone was running a chip through an arc demagnetizer.

"I, uh, already ditched mine," I said.

"Hah. Most trif." He looked impressed. He spoke my dialect. That felt so good.

"Yeah. Thanks for the lift. It's getting ugly there, fast."

"It is. I wish we could pay you, but given the loading and all . . ."

"Yeah, I know," I said. His margin wouldn't support paying deadheads, even if they stretched out the workload. "It's fine." I pointed at the girl. "Juletta isn't mine but she's traveling with me for now. You're flying, I'm working. Tell me what you need."

He said, "I put all the women with children in Port

Mod Two. I'm keeping the men back in Starboard Three. Can you take charge of those habitat bitches and show them how to survive aboard ship?"

Yeah, he'd need that. His crew didn't like station women, I gathered. They seemed to like having me to help, at least.

I said, "I'll do my best."

He actually smiled. "Good. Be all MI on them."

"Got it." I'd try.

I wasn't sure what I was going to do in Caledonia with a stray child. I wasn't sure what I was going to do with her here.

Juletta went with me, clinging on my arm and neck. I closed locks on the way. They'd all been left undogged, which was really stupid after a pressure failure.

"Mom?" she asked.

"We have to keep looking," I said as I monkeyed back, walking and grabbing stanchions. "There are too many people here. We're going to a meeting place. You know, like school has a meeting place for fire or air incidents?"

"Yeah."

"This is a stationwide air incident. We all have to get off the station, then meet up. Mom and Dad should be there."

"Cap'n will help?"

"Yes, he'll take us somewhere safe."

"Okay," she agreed, as we reached the passenger space.

The pod was full, with kids in a mostly happy swarm and the women chattering away, but some were arguing,

two of them face to face. There were four men with kids.
Kids adapt fast. It's always amazed me.

Why does everyone think their kids look cute? Some
were. Some were little trolls. One was shoving another
and shouting, "Bitch!"

Several of the adults looked at me. Some were
hopeful, some looked like they wanted a fight, most just
curious.

"Listen up, please," I said. The rest turned my way and
the volume dropped. Some kept whispering.

"I need all your attention for a few segs or you might
die in space."

A chick who looked about eighteen G-years, dressed
like somebody's trophy wife or escort said, "We've lived
in space most of our lives." She was leaning across a bunk,
careful not to mess her hair, but still taking two people's
seating spaces.

I looked back at her and asked, "On a ship? Or just
one of those artificial island hotel thingies?" I waved.

She wanted to argue. "Pressure, water, bulkheads,
clock cycle. Got it."

I was learning quickly how a military instructor felt.

"Where's your nearest egress? What is your evacuation
drill? What is your hull breach drill?"

She looked at me and started to open her mouth again.
It looked out of proportion. She didn't know how to do
lipstick.

I cut her off with, "Shut the hell up and listen."

She still came back with, "Yeah? Who the hell put you
in charge?"

I didn't raise my voice. I did lean forward slightly and

focus on her. "The captain. If you have a problem I'll give you a chit to see him. He might just leave you here. There are plenty of others who won't cause trouble."

That got her attention, but I wanted to drive it home.

"So, can I be in charge now, Miss Gio Pants Ensemble with Diamond Accents? All I have is a shipsuit with two thousand light-years of wear on it. Will that satisfy you?"

"Uh . . . yeah, go ahead." She tried to shrug me off and sat back, trying to look casual.

Oh, hell no. "You can address me as 'spacer,' 'crewwoman' or 'lady.'"

There was a pause that started getting embarrassing, with people staring at me, but mostly at her.

An older lady said, "She means it. I know a vet when I hear one."

The woman finally said, "Yes, Spacer." She wasn't going to call me "Lady."

The matron said, "I'm a vet. Groundside only, but I can take and give orders. I'll help."

Oh, good. That would help a lot, and I was glad the faceoff was over.

"Thanks. What's your name?"

"Claire Copley."

"Thanks, Claire."

I looked them all over. "I'm Angie Kaneshiro, medic, stevedore, cargomistress, Able Spacer. This is what I do for a living the last seven years. These pods are really tight for space at the best of times, and this one is basically a bunkroom for laborers. Now, you each have a rack, and either the kids share with you, or we'll improvise some bedding for them. You need to hold onto them, with webbing, during Jump Point transit. They may feel nauseous; I'll tell you what to eat before we go. One person sleeps per bunk. This pod is women only. Men are diagonally across and aft. If you want to bump or spread you can use the shower in the head together. We're going to appoint people to cover stray kids while we work. You'll be keeping this clean, getting your own meals, and staying out of the crew's way . . ."

They listened to me, and didn't argue much.

In five segs they had a summary I knew they'd forget, but they knew I was in charge. I hoped.

Intercom sounded, "All hands, secure for space. Departure imminent." I felt the outer lock seal.

The next announcement was, "Umbilicals separated, vessel secure. Undogged and moving." I could feel it. That wasn't just a ram. There were maneuvering engines at work. That probably wouldn't hurt the station regolith, but it might melt hatch equipment.

Then, "We are in space. Duty rotation to commence. Passengers stand by and await instructions."

That was the most abbreviated pullout I'd ever experienced. With a ship, I mean.

I wasn't a passenger, or was I? And I had Juletta.

She looked up at me with big eyes. I figured she wasn't sure what I had been doing, but I'd been telling adults off. She was probably either scared or impressed.

I gathered her up and stepped through the hatch. As I dogged it, she said, "You strong, Anzhie."

"I am when I need to be," I said.

"Are we friends?"

"Yes, Juletta. We're friends." I fastened her hands

around my neck and started dragging myself along grips, glad I was only in the passage, not in the long umbilical to towed pods.

"Where's Mom and Dad?"

"We're still trying to find them. There's an air leak in the station, so we have to go to another."

I hoped we'd meet them in Caledonia. If not, they'd still be in this volume of space. Assuming they weren't dead, but with what info I had, I didn't think many, if any, were.

"Find a safety ofser?"

"They can't help with that, sweetie. We need the ship for that. Have you ever been on one?"

"No."

"Well, it might be a few days, but we'll be safe."

"You make me safe."

I'm going to try. "I'll do my best."

How did I get into this crate?

I got into the stateroom as engines started thrusting. I lunged for the bunk, grabbed her with me, and said, "Hang on, we're moving."

"Rockets?"

I didn't even know if this one was string drive or forceline propulsion.

"Yes," I agreed.

CHAPTER 6

I heard all kinds of stories about the "Spacelift" as it got called. There wasn't any official request or SOS that I know of. The haulers and trampers just decided that people needed help and moved to evacuate everyone who showed up. Some had access to long-duration O2 supplies, but even most of them pulled out. No one knew if there would be any resupply, or what the damage was.

I got a tx from Lee that said he was riding down insystem to a habitat around Dagda for now. I wished him luck back.

My phone told me we were queued for a jump and our number was three divs down. That was going to be well into third shift, and I'd have to stay up to coddle the stationers.

What would I do with the girl?

I expected I'd have a bunkmate, but I didn't. It might mean I'd get one after we shuffled other refugees around. On the other hand, I wasn't going to offer if it wasn't necessary, and I'd wait for the crew to make the call. I didn't want to ask the crew to do anything they didn't have to. With this kind of crowd, they were going to be holding things together by hand until we docked.

"Juletta," I said, as I sat her on the bunk. "I have to go help people some more. Can you stay here?"

The expression on her face said I couldn't. She looked like a puppy about to be abandoned.

"Okay, you come with me," I said quickly. "But you have to be quiet, and wait patiently. No fussing, okay?"

"No playing with kids?"

"Not now. Maybe later."

"Hungry," she said.

"Yeah, let's find the galley."

How much food was aboard? This was going to be a four-to-five-day trip at least, if we could transfer direct to Shetland Station. I figured that wouldn't be likely.

Galley was forward, inboard and down one gangtube, which wasn't easy. I finally had her sit on my shoulders and hold my head. She managed to pull hair and cover my eyes, but we got down.

One of the regular crew was in the galley. It was small. I mean, the right size for this crew, not enough for the passenger load.

"Hey, who are you?" he asked. He looked ready to order me back wherever I came from.

"Kaneshiro, Distressed Spacer. The captain put me in charge of the inboard refugees."

He nodded and asked, "What do you need?"

"Food for the girl, then for me if you can. Can we do anything for the others?"

"Food isn't a problem for a few days. We stock in bulk," he said. He looked at Juletta. "Would you like a peanut butter wrap, honey?"

"Yes!" she said, very seriously. "Thank you."

He slapped one together, rolled it up and handed it over. She grabbed it, started munching on it, and smeared some on my right leg.

"Whatever's handy," I said. There was no time to be picky. "I just need protein."

He passed me a package of tuna. I ripped the top and started munching it straight.

"Thanks. Can I get a spare for later?"

"Sure." He tossed one and a pack of Cheesy Cracks at me. He then said, "Food worries me less than recycling capacity. We're rated for fifty inboard. We have probably double that. The towed pods are rated for a hundred. They're probably at double *that*. So we're going to have a lot of water, some solids, and exceed filter capacity."

"Right," I said. They'd hate to dump water or solids. Those were sellable commodities in space. If they had to, though, they would. But once the filters were exceeded, they'd have to dump, then pump all the waste into the primary tanks, which meant cleaning the entire recycler, and limiting fresh water.

We wouldn't run out of drinking water, or shouldn't, if they managed it well. But we would probably stink.

"I won't tell them yet," I said. "But I will if we get to that. I see we're on sked for jump. I'll go instruct them."

"Roger. I'll report that for you. Kaneshiro?"

"Angie," I said.

"Travis. Second Officer and Second Engineer."

"Pleased to meet you. Juletta, we're going back up. Are you ready?"

"Okay," she said, and clung to my hair.

"Ouch! Careful," I said.

"Not yours?" Travis guessed.

"Refugee," I explained. "I don't know where her parents are. I'm hoping they make it through."

He nodded. There wasn't anything to say, really.

The kid hung on as I climbed back up, and let me carry her back. I reached the cabin, opened the hatch, and looked around.

They hadn't trashed the place, but they weren't very organized.

"Okay, we're queued for jump to Caledonia," I said. "It's going to be a couple more divs, and the actual time marked on the console there can change rapidly. They're probably going to shove us through as fast as the gate resets."

They looked at me as I said, "That means you need to be ready any time in about a div, so starting now. There should be mesh over your bunk. I'm serious about one adult and one child per bunk, or two small teens. You lie back, pull the mesh down. You," I pointed at the woman from earlier. "I'll demonstrate. Lie back."

She hesitated but complied, and I showed where the harness attached.

"It's just in case of a displacement shock, but you don't want to be slammed into anything."

I unfastened her and helped her up, to show I wasn't holding a grudge, even though I was.

"If we're here long enough to shower, you get two segs. Rinse, water off, soap, rinse."

Claire asked, "I thought water wasn't a problem aboard ship?"

"It is at double capacity inboard and double capacity in the pods. But we should be through in a few days max." I hoped.

They seemed a bit bothered.

"This is a rescue run," I said. "We weren't counting passengers, just filling space."

I ran through the rest of the predeparture brief, adapted for stationers and with not enough resources, then excused myself to go to the male bay.

I actually got fewer arguments from them.

Naturally, when I opened the hatch, I had the attention of every man and boy over the age of ten Earth years in about five seconds.

But I was able to abbreviate the speech.

"Angie Kaneshiro. I work cargo, services and medic. The regular crew is flying this tub, I'm in charge of passengers. One person per bunk if you can. Small guys and kids double up if you need to." I pointed to a guy about fifteen for my demo. "You, lie down and I'll demonstrate the safety mesh . . ."

I covered signals, showed them the commo and reporting gear, explained protocols. Luckily, there were five men who'd done a tour either commercial or on a warship, and said they'd keep everyone else in line.

I took count and had them ping ID by phone, including onboard NoK. I had to put together a manifest. I'd have to do that for the females, too.

Then I dragged myself back to my bunk again.

I was getting a serious workout doing all these meters by hand, combined with the running earlier.

"Okay, Juletta, we're going to cuddle up on the bunk, and wrap under the net like I showed them. Then we have to wait for the ship to jump to the next station, okay?"

"But . . . I need Mom and Dad," she said again. She looked a combination of fatigued, abandoned and scared.

She had been amazingly well-behaved. I like kids a bit, but I don't do anything with them.

"Sweetie, everyone had to leave the station because of an air leak. We're all going to Caledonia, just a few divs away, okay? Then we should be able to find them. Or else we'll come back here and look here, okay?"

She shrugged.

I asked, "Do you live on the station?"

"No. We live in Tani."

They were groundsiders. I had no idea why they were at Ceileidh, unless they were already skipping out.

"Okay, well, they should be at the station we're going to, and if not, we can go back eventually, okay? It won't be safety, it will probably be soldiers who take us."

"Is there a war?" she asked.

"I don't know, sweetie. There's been some fighting."

She said, "I thought you didn't like the soldiers."

"Those aren't our soldiers."

"Are they bad?"

That was tough.

"No, most of them aren't bad, but they've been told to take over the station, and we don't want them to."

"Why?"

"Because they run things differently. It works for them, but it wouldn't work for us, and they don't understand that."

"Did you tell them?"

"Other people did. It's something adults don't understand."

"Like when I tell Ritchie and he won't listen?"

"Exactly like that. Who's Ritchie?"

"My big brother."

"Yes, it's exactly like that. We need to rest now, okay?"

"Okay, but kids don't rest with adults."

Good training. Luckily, I was able to work with that.

"I understand," I said. "So you will be in that blanket, and I'll be in this blanket so we're apart. You can have the fleecy one, okay?"

"Okay," she said, looking unsure.

"Lights ten," I said, and the illumination dimmed from daylight shift to steady low glow. "In ten segs, go to lights five."

I wasn't sure when we'd jump, so I set the alarm for a div, and fastened the mesh over us anyway, just in case.

I can't drive a ship, but I can do arithmetic. There weren't nearly enough ships to evacuate the habitat. Unless someone came along with something big, or patched that hole fast, there were going to be casualties. The emergency O2 would probably cover everyone for a week, and by then they'd be hungry, thirsty, filthy and bugnuts. After that, it would get very ugly.

I didn't sleep well.

⊕ ⊕ ⊕

I woke, warm and damp and itching, and thought at first I was just hot. Then I realized Juletta had wet herself. Apparently she was still toilet training, and didn't have control at night. That was annoying. I'd have to change her outfits more often, then, as there was no way I could get absorbent pants for her; whatever they call those things they use after diapers.

She'd leaked all over my right side, from breast down below my waistband. That was bad, too. I was wearing this coverall because the other one in my bag was filthy. Damn! I'd have to get them into vac wash or water ASAP.

"Wake up, sweetie," I said. She mumbled and rubbed her eyes and didn't. So I worked around her. I skinned down, wiped with an alky wipe, and swapped for a clean bodybrief, which is what I wear shipside. I peeled her pants off, but I didn't have a change for her, so I wrapped her in a towel. I laid another towel over the puddle under us and tried to get back to rest.

Then the klaxon sounded and my phone said, "All hands and passengers stand by for jump. Crew check passengers. Ten segs."

I wiggled out past her, got feet on deckplates, and figured slacks and a tunic would work for right now. I dressed fast, checked she was still asleep, then unlatched the hatch and dragged myself back to the bays.

The men were further back by one bulkhead, so I checked them first. They were all down and ready, meshed in and talking to their kids.

The women were mostly good, including Miss Gio Pantsuit. There were a couple lagging and jawing.

"That warning means you, too. I'm the medic, so it'll

be me fixing your broken bones or dislocated knees if you slam against a bulkhead. Get secured."

I turned and dogged the hatch before they could argue.

I just got settled when the One Seg warning sounded. I wrapped an arm over Juletta's shoulder, and waited through the count.

I'm always tense, because it's disorienting. I wasn't sure how the little girl would do.

The ten-second count came along, and I tried hard not to tighten up. I took deep breaths, and tried to focus on the bulkhead.

It only hits me for a moment, but that moment is nausea, headache, stinging pain and that feeling of dizziness like when you're rolling drunk. Then lateral G hit because space is a different orientation there. I don't know how that works, but it's something astrogators account for.

Juletta clutched at me and cried out, and woke up fully.

"I'm wet," she said.

"It's okay, sweetie. We can fix it in a bit."

"I hurt."

"We just shifted through space. Now we have to find a place to dock." That was going to take a while, if every ship from Freehold side had jumped to this side, full of refugees. Then, because of the amount of rubble in the Loop (their outer Halo), the station was a good three to four days from the Jump Point.

Juletta had one change of clothes in her backpack. She had jeans and a shirt with chocolate monkeys on it. We'd have to wash her other clothes fast, but she was dressed for now. She couldn't change by herself, but did cooperate with me. I brushed her hair out. It was straight, but fine enough to have long curls at the ends.

The all clear sounded, and I took her with me to check the passengers. A couple had puked, but everyone seemed okay.

"It may be a couple of days or more before they can even slot us," I warned. "I don't know how many ships came through, or how many people. Some went insystem, but most came out." Though really either Grainne surface or Caledonia was closer to the UN, just that Caledonia had colonial sovereignty as long as the Earth didn't decide they wanted the hassle of administrating at a distance.

I got Juletta washed off in the head, before the rush to clean up hit everyone. I soaped and rinsed her clothes and mine and dried them in the vacuum dryer. They came out cold, but dry and clean. Then I went for food.

The crew galley was steady with two to three people at a time grabbing grub. I blew a pot clean, punched a button for fresh chocolate, wiped down the table and refilled a couple of dispensers to show I was useful. They were going through pre-packs instead of trying to cook.

Some guy I didn't recognize asked, "Do you space with the kid?"

"Refugee, not mine," I said. "But she's a good girl. Better than the bitches back in the pod."

"Seems like it. I'm Astrogator Jones." He was young but seemed comfortable with the situation. I guess if he could steer this thing, anything else was boringly mundane.

"Angie Kaneshiro, lugging along and I can help with Galley and Med."

"I heard. Main thing's to keep those habitots in line. Is that going?"

"Yeah, they're mostly under control."

He nodded around a sandwich. "Good. We're glad to help them, and we do appreciate your help. It lets us deal with this bucket of scrap."

"I've crewed in older and worse."

"Oh, it's not a bad ship at all. But they all have quirks."

"Yup."

I fed Juletta a bowl of chicken stew that was surprisingly tasty. I wanted to find the recipe. It was savory, rich and filling. She sat at the table and slurped. She spilled a little, but not much, and watched us talk as she ate.

It was four more days of boredom and periodic checks before we docked. The kids in transit were increasingly frustrated and got cabin fever. I let Juletta play with a couple while I sat and watched from the bulkhead and listened to Renmin and Pass Ghoul on my phone. I didn't want to talk to any of those women. We had nothing in common and never would. I got them onto a shift to feed themselves, made sure the kids got fed and the adults didn't take too much. It was work. The crew set the showers to do a thirty-second soak, a seg pause, and a seg rinse. The air got strong even with that, because we were way past capacity.

The good news from Ceileidh was that an emergency seal from the inside slowed the loss enough they could build a larger plate to reduce it to a leak rather than a blast. They'd even managed to seal off the zoo and save the animals. There were still hundreds of casualties in the area around the rupture, but that was better than thousands or more.

Then we docked, sort of, on a tether with a long gangtube set up by military engineers. We were five hundred meters out, and I was glad I hadn't seen the docking from outside, assembled by tug and cable.

I let everyone pull through the tube ahead of me. It took them a long time, being unfamiliar with emgee. Two of the crew went ahead and stationed themselves.

After they were all queued, I checked both pods, and scrolled through as their phones logged them off-board. A couple had theirs turned off, but I was able to get them from memory.

Astrogator Jones was on duty at the lock. He had his own small daughter with him. I wondered. A lot of ships are family businesses, and I could guess why they wouldn't risk their kids running around the refugees.

"Hi!" I said to her. To him, I said, "Sir, that's everyone as far as I can tell. You're clear."

"Thanks, Spacer," he said officially. "We can't pay for Distressed passage, and we're short fuel and op cost for this anyway. If we could we would, but . . ." He paused and I nodded. Then he said, "We appreciate it, Angie. You took a lot of the load off. Safe space to you, and good luck with Juletta's family."

"Thank you. And same." I reached into the tube. "Hang on, Juletta, it's time for that ride."

I hate long tubes, but I went hand over hand and built up a good clip.

Juletta went, "Wheeeeee!" and seemed to enjoy it a lot.

Then I ran up against the rear of the habitots. That term so often fits them. I slowed to a crawl as they figured out how to get out of the tube and into the station. The tube swayed and shifted and felt entirely unsafe, even though I knew it was. An entire ship can move and I'm fine. This was a shifting deck. The floor is supposed to be solid.

Once in-station we had to go up from the cargo level to the docking level proper, then through another field lock, and finally into the dock itself.

Which had about a million people in it.

"Hold my hand and don't let go," I told her. She could get lost here and never find anyone, including me. I took a few moments to unpack her leash.

There were station crew around with floating banners that said, "LOCATOR."

I found the nearest, then looked for one further away. I hoisted Juletta up under my arm, with my bag swinging around me, and pushed through the crowd, never letting up, and moving forward inch by inch.

Once I reached that one, I had to wait for several others to finish asking about their families. The crowd was a loud, shouting, crying mess, and there was no line.

But he saw Juletta, and that she didn't look much like me—she was pretty much Anglo all through.

"Name?"

"Juletta. She's not good with her last name."

Juletta said, "Pkason." I was surprised. I didn't know she knew it at all. I guess she was being private and safe, even with me.

"There's a Parkerson," he said.

"Yes!" she said.

"That way, third alcove." He pointed along the pax terminal.

It wasn't a terrible shove to get through, through, but gods, my arm was tired from carrying an eighteen-kilo kid, even in reduced G. I made it to that alcove, and there were actually gaps between clumps of people. That was as organized as it was, though. I joined the milling about, listening to shouts as people were reunited.

Then suddenly—

"DAAADDY!" Juletta screamed, yanked loose and ran across the bay, dodging and shoving past legs. I followed as best I could, bumping people with my pack.

A man stopped and turned, stunned. The woman next to him came around to see what was going on. As soon as she was visible, Juletta yelled, "MOOOOM!" and quickened her pace to a sprint across a small clearing. I was running to keep up, trying not to batter through people.

They both looked thoroughly in shock, and he dropped to his knees. Juletta launched herself from three meters back, and landed like a cat, all four limbs wrapped around his neck and torso. "DAD! I'M GLAD TO SEE YOU!" she shouted.

Her mother threw herself around the side, and there was a veritable river of tears. "Oh, I love you, little girl!" he said. Her mother couldn't speak. I just stood back for now. This was going to be awkward.

"Lovey too!" she said, a bit calmer. They stayed like

that for a long time, and I didn't interfere. I actually looked around to see if I could sneak out, but I wasn't sure if I needed to sign anything.

As they regained a tad of composure, she noticed something that had obviously changed. "Baby's walking," she said.

"Yes, he is," her father said, still very cautious. He was looking at me, trying to gauge how I fit in.

"Hi, Ritchie," she said to a boy who was a year or two older. He kept wrinkling his brow at her and then at me. He wasn't sure about this whole thing.

Then she threw her arms around him, too.

I was about to make introductions when she came running over and said, "Come here!" She snatched my hand, turned and began stomping back toward them, dragging me.

I let her lead me, and she said, "Anzhee." Then she held my arm out toward her parents and said, "Mom's name, Ruth. Dad's name, Mawhk."

"Hello," I said.

Ruth said, "Thank you. Angie?"

"Yes, lady. Angie Kaneshiro."

"How did you . . . ?"

"I was passing by the school when pressure failed."

Mark asked, "But why so late?"

"I had to take a detour. The crowd was bad, so I went straight for an empty ship, not the nearest." I really didn't want to tell them I'd been passlegging. "I got here as quick as we could."

Mark said, "Please, come eat with us."

"Uh, okay."

Money didn't seem to be a problem for them. We went to a place I'd walked past and never had the creds to go in. Even now, there wasn't a huge line. We got seated, and served fast.

Juletta babbled, and they sat on either side, hugging her constantly, while the big brother sat next to me, right across from her. I just paid attention to my deep fried chicken, which was really good stuff. Juletta munched french fries and bacon sticks.

They had much neater table manners than I did, too. But they didn't mention it.

"Can we offer you a reward?" Ruth asked.

I could always use money, but, "Uh, you can offer, but I didn't do it for a reward, and I had to evacuate, too. I'd have taken others if I could."

"What do you do for work?" Mark asked.

"I'm contract on cargo ships." I finished my chicken and washed down the rest of my limeade.

"On contract now?"

"Not after that, but as soon as I can find one I should be." I wasn't sure that was true at all.

"At least take a token," he said. "You saved our little girl." They all grinned at each other again. She really was a cute thing.

"Sure," I agreed. "And thank you. Though I would do it again either way."

He slid his hand across the table with five one-hundred-mark notes. Not as good as Credits, but they'd last me a couple of weeks if I was frugal.

"Thank you very much," I said.

"I don't know how things will play out back home, but

here's my card in case we can meet again. Our address is global and portable."

I looked at it. He was some sort of investment adviser.

"Okay. I'll ping if I can. It would be neat to see the little weasel again," I said. Hell, I'd been grinning, too. I'd done a good thing.

I slipped off my stool, walked around, and bowed to both. Then I gave Juletta a big hug. She was warm and cuddly still.

"Good luck, little girl. You be good."

"I will! See you soon, Anzhee!"

Yeah, I wasn't going to explain how that was unlikely. She should have fond memories.

I shouldered my bag and walked away. I wanted to look back, but didn't.

CHAPTER 7

I spent a few hours in a waiting room off one of the alcoves. I didn't sleep well, but it was free. The chair didn't recline and had no headrest, so I leaned across my bag. I wasn't going to waste cash on a room for the time I had, even a bunkie. I just wanted to get onto second shift to try to find a job. I figured there'd be less traffic for midwatch.

Pretty much everything was full, or not moving. Nothing was going in-Freehold, little in-Earth. Lots of ships were parked in orbit waiting for something, and eating assets while they did. I considered a bunkie but they were all full, some of them double. I settled for a dock shower for ten marks and got clean, washed both suits and aired them dry, and even caught a nap in the heat dry nook that helped a bit. I'd need real berthing tonight, though. There weren't going to be many hangouts. Everything was full with transients, and the cheapest all booked. Well, not the very cheapest, but ugh.

There weren't any openings stationside, either. I was glad for that M500. It was down to M450 and once that was gone I was down to my savings and previous pay.

I went back to that nice restaurant, ordered their M10 hot chocolate, told the server I'd be right back, and went to their bathroom.

Damn, it was nice. I cleaned up some more, brushed on some eyes, painted my lips and swapped out for my third outfit, a ziptop, diagonal zipped skirt, and stockings. I left M13 with the server, chugged the chocolate, which was good, but damn, that was a lot of money, then headed back to the dock.

It was quieter, though still busy. I found the locker I keep there in Spaceman Spiffy's Storage, shoved my bags in and pulled out a mini-pack. It was a bit musty, so I spritzed it with lemon sanitizer, shoved in money, batteries, my lock pin and some makeup, and closed back up. I chewed my lip for a moment, being careful of the lipstick, and decided to drop M25 on another three months' locker rent now, against trouble later.

Then I took ramps and slides to the Orbit Room.

At the door, I heaved my cleave, glinted at the door dude, and he let me slide. I was dressed upscale enough, and was obviously going to milk customers for business. He understood I was freelance, not a pro, and there wouldn't be any trouble.

I was dizzy-tired, so I bought a stim and chugged it. In a few moments, I was dizzy-tired and wired awake at the same time. I knew I was going to be a bit off.

The guys in the place saw skirt and cleave. I knew what they wanted, they knew what I was offering. I waited for the music to shift to something I liked, and slid onto the floor.

At .8G and in those lights, the ziptop bounced with my chest and flickered colors. That was exactly what I wanted.

In half an hour Caledonia clock, I had four men watching me very closely. None of them were hideous, but one of them would have to be very nice and loaded to be worth it, or have a Dick of Death.

One of the others was probably married, if I guessed right. I wasn't going to help with his drama.

One was young. He was very nicely built on the slim side, and a charmer. One was right in my favorite zone, about thirty-five Earth years, confident and probably had decent money.

I waggled a finger and he came out onto the floor. He wasn't much of a dancer, but he could move and kept a nice touch on my shoulders, then my hips, without trying to grope. Oh, but he wanted to.

I turned and rubbed close, then stepped back, and kept dancing. I let three songs go by, then stopped, and took his hand back to his table.

"I'm Angie," I said.

"I'm Byron," he said. He held my chair. That doesn't happen often.

"Thank you, and glad to meet you."

I like dancing. I like the lights, the movement, the shifting sensation, and that can be better on a station. I'd have stayed all night and skipped sleeping. But I really needed sleep, and a place to sleep.

"What are you up to?" he asked.

"I was on station in Grainne when they had that atmo leak. You heard?"

"Yeah! What was that like?"

"Scary. I hopped a ship and came here. I'm trying to get back onto another freighter, but it's going to take me a couple of days. I haven't been here since April, I think. I figured I'd stop in and dance."

The place was suddenly very full, all the chairs, all the floor. I'd been raising my voice to compensate.

"How bad was the leak?"

"Big enough I felt it," I said. We talked on that for a bit, at a shout. He ordered a beer and got me a lime cooler. I wanted my breath fresh.

We went back out to dance, tagging the seats so we wouldn't lose them. This time we were closer, though we wouldn't have had a choice. This time his hands were on my waist and along my sides.

I was loopy from fatigue, stim and a little booze, and I wanted to get to sleep, but I didn't want to come across as a quickie or a pro.

We didn't talk much when dancing. He did have good feedback senses, though, even if he couldn't dance well.

But, an hour later, he asked that important question.

"How long are you staying tonight?"

"I'll let you decide that," I said. "I could dance all night, but I am tired, and if you've got something in mind, tell away."

"Is my place out of the question?"

"That depends. Is it nearby and nice?"

"Yes and very."

"Then it's in the question." I smiled.

He waved his chip and we got up to go.

I talked him into a chicken burger. I tried to eat neatly, because I eat like a pig. I went from modern hippie living to the Forces to ship crew. I just sort of stuff it in my face, but I've learned from watching what neat looks like.

While we ate, he rubbed my thigh and I wiggled and grinned.

Slideway took us to .5G, and around radius. That was Posh Side, as they call it, and I figured I'd done okay that way. He seemed decent. Whether he was like that in private, and if he was any good, I'd find out. But guys in those quarters don't tend to be thieves and he didn't look like a smuggler or narco—using or selling drugs that are restricted by law.

We walked into the Windsor Arms, and I was impressed. I'd seen the place. Going inside was exciting. They had a lot of cube in the lobby, which cost them money. His room was on the radius flat, not up or down. It wasn't a suite, but it was still a nice room.

He waved the door open and I walked in.

Damn. Nice room.

UltraRez screen window. Fleece and cotton bedding over memory cushions. Panto chairs. The bathroom had all the fixtures including rain and six-way shower and hot soak.

"I'd like to shower before anything else, if you don't mind," I said. "It's been a long couple of days."

"Surely. Can I help you wash your hair?"

Oh, my.

"After, you can definitely wash my hair. Right now I just want to get clean. I won't take long. Fix a drink?"

"I will," he said with a smile.

I grabbed him and got a liplock on him. He could kiss. That was very promising.

I skipped into the bathroom and closed it.

I did shower fast, getting soaped, scrubbing skin, and moisturizing with a blow dry. The shower did all that for me with jets of water, air and subsonic tickles. It even had an option for sensual massage, but I was going to let him do that first.

I got out, dressed again, and stepped through.

"That was fast," he said.

"I'm girly, but I'm also crew. You can't waste time aboard ship."

"Gotcha," he said. "Solid state materials analysis isn't as tight."

"You're good at engineering?" I asked.

"Good enough," he agreed. "Why?"

"This outfit has two zippers. One pulls down. One pulls diagonally up."

He came out of the seat, right up to me, grabbed both, and pulled perfectly.

I sank to my knees. His pants were more complicated, but I managed.

I woke up. I blinked, felt around, and he was next to me. Right. Byron. The lights were about five percent.

I honestly couldn't remember what we'd done. I'd been that tired. I glanced for time, and I'd been out for three hours solid.

I wasn't sure about etiquette here because I wasn't sure what his schedule was. I figured it couldn't hurt to gently try, though.

I kissed down his side, over his hip, and got my mouth on him, and he woke up.

"Mmm!" he muttered.

"Mmmhmm," I agreed. He was shapely and tasty and this was going to be fun, now that I could remember it. I had no idea what we'd done earlier.

I did this time. And again three hours after that, which included bacon (turkey for me), eggs, rice pudding and fresh melon. Gods, that was good. I sat there in a robe making sure he had glimpses of my cooze and cleave and smiling whenever he looked at me.

"When do you need to leave?" he asked. "Waiting ship?"

He didn't remember what I'd said. Otoh, I didn't remember a lot of what he said. That wasn't why we were here.

"Variable," I said. "I can leave whenever you're ready. If I don't find a ship at once I can lodge."

"I can spot you another day if you need," he said. "I have to leave here in an hour, but I'll be back at nineteen hundred clock. Tomorrow I go groundside again."

"I accept your hospitality," I said. "And you said something about washing hair."

"If you like."

"I do."

He washed good hair. I was clean and my scalp massaged, and ready to melt.

I went to my locker, being stared at dressed in that

outfit. There were a lot more crew moving around. I drew a shipsuit and changed in a bank's restroom, pulling it up, zipping off the skirt, and repeating for the top. Then I wove a bodysuit in, and reached in and out to fasten it around and under, inside the suit.

Byron had even helped me pin and tie my hair. I looked professional and was ready to shill.

There were no ships.

Nothing was going back to the Freehold. Traffic with Earth was slow. Stuff was coming out, but nothing was going in for the time being. I checked Novaja Rossia and Alsace. All the ships not on the other legs had diverted, and were full. I passed out some cards, inquired at offices who knew me on sight. Nothing.

I held off on replacing my V-suit. I did get another rolly, some makeup and extra clothes with a spare, slightly used, shipsuit. More funds I couldn't spare.

I was back in the lobby, still wearing my work clothes, a bit before 1900, hoping Byron had been honest and wasn't delayed.

He showed up about five after. He looked mentally wiped out, but cheered up when he saw me.

"You're still here."

"Yeah, ships are still diverting."

"Sorry to hear that, but I'm glad to see you."

"You too," I said.

"Can I take you out for steak?"

"Make it salmon or hake and I'm in."

"They will have it. Want to change?"

I took the hint. We went to the room and he swapped jackets. I had a small bag with me, and put on a basic dress. My hair was still up, so I did a quick paint on my outer lips, since I was going to be eating, and highlighted my eyes.

The Conway was higher end than any restaurant I'd been in.

We walked in, and they had an actual maitre d' whatever.

"Good evening, Mister Vyas. Two this evening?"

"Please," he said. "Quiet, if possible."

"It's always possible, sir. This way, please."

So, they knew who he was.

In fact, as soon as we sat down, they slid a gin and tonic with lime in front of him.

"For you, miss?"

"I'll try one," I said.

The barman was mixing it manually as soon as I said so. It was there in thirty seconds.

Gin and tonics are tart, slightly sweet, and have a . . . bitter taste, I guess. I prefer beer or fruity wines, but they're drinkable.

"Client is paying for this," he said. "But I don't want to soak them too much. They were good people."

"I got it," I said. They had an itemized menu, so I picked the smoked private vat salmon, tunnel mushrooms and broccoli. He ordered a ribeye steak.

They delivered seared tuna on cabbage with horseradish shavings, and sparkling water.

"This is good!" I said, and reminded myself to eat politely.

"Yeah, I can't afford them often, but on contract I make a point of concluding with a good meal."

"Definitely," I agreed.

Anything we needed was there without asking. Refills on drinks, a spare napkin when I had to wipe up a sauce spill, and a dessert menu.

"Oh, damn," I said. Cheesecake with black raspberry ice cream and chocolate chunks.

"Yeah, I love that stuff," he said. "It's hard to avoid eating too much here."

They brought it out and it was amazing. I wasn't sure I could bend enough for good sex.

I asked for hot chocolate while he had tea. "Bittersweet," I said.

"Alcoholic?"

"Well, sure."

Almost at once, the server slid it in front of me. The real crystal mug was a work of art and the drink in it had layers of color and cream.

I tasted it, and about had an orgasm.

"What's in it?"

The drink server said, "Milk and dark chocolate, heavy cream, Irish cream, Chambord and dark sweet rum. It should complement your dessert."

"If I hadn't finished it, I'm sure it would." I wanted to write that down.

"I'll get another if you like."

"No, no, I'm stuffed. Thank you so much."

Back at his room, we kissed deeply, and I groped him back.

"I'm still stuffed," I said. "But if I lie on the bed and bend back, my throat's pretty flexible."

His expression was amazing. I laughed.

I stripped the dress and hung it, flopped across the bed, bent my head back, and slid a hand into myself. He got in position and I put my other hand on his ass. He grabbed both breasts, and I felt decently used. I kept control of my muscles and felt that otherworldly glide instead of a gag.

After that I pulled him down and straddled him. It kept weight off my stuffed belly, and let me find a nice angle for an inside belly rub. I felt my brain disconnect.

The next morning we had to leave. I took his card, and made notes. It wasn't likely we'd meet up, but things happen.

CHAPTER 8

I went back to the docks, stiff in the thighs, worn in my cooze, tight in my jaw and stretched in my ass. I was sure I looked as thoroughly fucked as I was, but I put on my professional mask and went to work.

Nothing. But, I did find an open bunkie at barely over base rate. It was worth it for a shower and a rack, but if nothing moved soon, I was going to slip into the underdecks and sleep for free.

I lucked out the next day.

A lot of cargo routes go through Grainne on their way to Alsace and Meiji. With the UN occupying, everything slowed, so quite a few detoured around through Caledonia and NovRos. If they could drop cargo en route, they could actually squeeze more money out. So the tramps were running packed to capacity and some over.

There were several possibilities. I nixed a couple who I figured were running over mass capacity, straining their drives to get a few extra credits.

There was a lot of stuff through NovRos. I was not thrilled. Discretion is good, but there's so much clandestine activity it's like they have three governments. There's the official one, the mob, and the practical one that works between them, nodding at the law while turning its back on the crooks. I'm pretty cool with what most places call smuggling. Most spacers are, and I'm a Freeholder with rebel parents. But the Ros will commit murder to keep deals quiet. It doesn't happen often, but it has to be a calculation, like all-male ships when you're female.

I found a berth. They needed a second cook and would take hands for cargo. The head cook, Mrs. Ponte, had me scrubbing filters and tables, stacking trays and heating pre-pops, and delivering them to crew on shift. It was scut work, but it paid okay, and she was apologetic.

"These boys and girls eat like pigs. It must be a youth thing. I have no idea how they pack away so much."

They did eat a lot, and didn't even have the high-G excuse Freeholders or Meijaps have.

We transited, and I helped sling pods at the catchers, and move containers through the lock. I took my pay and went to find my friends.

Bob and Ray were home this time. They have nice quarters and are happy to host me. They're an odd couple. They're married, but they're straight. Yes, that's what I said.

They hang out together, joke, hug, cook, share house, even sleep together. Sleep. They're not sexual with each other, though they'll do interactive vid at the same time while plugging off. They're definitely a couple, but they don't do anything sexual together alone.

If they find a compatible woman to share, though, it's all on.

I pinged Bob's code and left my note. It was scroll and vocal, because I didn't know if he'd be free. "Hey, goz, Angie's on station! Hoping you guys are free. Buzz me."

I got a scroll back almost at once that said, "Come on over!"

Just because I could, I went to the service-escape passage and down the ladder. It was easy from ten-percent G, but was a real workout even at fifty-percent, because I'd been climbing down for fifteen minutes. No one questioned me. Who'd make that climb who didn't have a reason?

I just like climbing sometimes. I probably miss trees.

At the bottom I took the passage, followed it around and through C zones to R zones. They have a small water garden outside their door. I grabbed a tiny pear from the bonsai and rang.

Ray opened the door with a big smile under his blond buzz. He was wearing cargo slacks and shlippers.

"Angie!"

He waited about a second to be sure I was available, then kissed me hard. His arms flexed, his shoulders bulged, and I gripped him back.

Bob was right behind, and he dragged me over for a kiss with a hand brushing down to my hip. Very nice.

"Hi, gozi!" I said. "Mind if I come in?"

Ray said, "Sure! You're already in."

Bob asked. "Staying long?"

"A couple of days, probably."

"Want to stay with us?"

"Definitely," I said.

They have a mammock. That's a mammoth hammock. It was slung across half the common room, and you can either cuddle up or move to separate hollows in it. I took the middle, stretched out and grabbed a pillow to prop my head up, and had awesome guys on each side. Much better than a bunkie.

Across from me was their huge main vid tank. It was the kind of system wealthy engineers would write off for research purposes. I actually got up to date on the news.

Ceileidh had been ruptured by a large chunk of planetoid. However, there were questions about whether it had been a natural event, especially as there is an impact watch with force beams and missiles, or if it had been sabotage. The trajectory was inconsistent with normal orbits, but not impossible. And of course, no one had IDed it before it hit. The video was blurry, but the hole was sizeable. It wasn't going to be an easy fix.

A large volume of the station was closed because of structural concerns, and they were planning to glaze a patch over it, with struts and thickeners. That was going to take a while, because with the UN in charge, there was a lot of Adminwork.

Ray said, "I've worked with some of those issues. So, they're going to have to get approval on structure, then approval on materials and effect on the environment."

"Vapor inside is an issue," I agreed.

Bob got up to check on food in the kitchen nook. He chuckled as he walked over. I guessed he'd heard this already.

"Oh, no," Ray said, leaning forward onto an elbow to

face me better. "Well, you're right, but this concern is about the outside native environment."

"Huh? It's an inflated planetoid with some outgassing from the ports and locks. There's probably a few wrenches and screws in orbit."

"Yes, but these forms date from when they were planetbound. You have to have a study of what will happen to the native environment."

That was ridiculous, but I believed him.

"Fuck."

"Then there's labor and hiring issues—who is poor enough to bid on it."

"Poor enough?" I didn't get it.

"The number of jobs involved is relevant to UN metrics. Small companies get preference."

I know a bit about that. "Anyone fixing it is going to have to borrow cap-habitat gear from Lola or Bizen or Mandrake. They all use stuff license-built from Prescot."

"But the point is, small businesses have to have a chance to make money."

"By subletting gear and upcharging?"

"Exactly. Then there's discussions over what will be reconstructed. If there's enough left, you can do a one hundred percent buildout. If there isn't enough left, you have to get permissions, or it gets assigned to a committee to decide what type of construction and zoning should be there."

I shook my head. "You're really not joking."

"No. That's why nothing gets built in UN space anymore, and most of the transfers are on this side of the Points."

Bob had steak for both of them and salmon for me. He came through, put a plate down for me on the table in front of the mammock. He hugged me, then hugged Ray close and put his plate down, then got his own.

"I love you, Big Guy," he said.

"And you, Dude," Ray agreed. "Oh, man, this is good steak."

I said, "I'll try one small bite. Just to be polite."

Bob said, "Okay. I know you don't eat mammals."

I took a bite off his fork, carefully.

Damn, that was tender and sweet. I almost converted.

"You did great," I said. "The salmon's amazing. Lemon grass?"

"And hickory salt, sage, rosemary and garlic."

"Damn. I'll have to try that. Thank you."

We ate and had beer. They have a dark wheaty ale that's got an almost nutty aftertaste.

Ray continued, "So anyway, it won't be fixed any time soon. Because before all that, the UN has to organize a bunch of Freeholders. Habitat Freeholders."

"Yeah," I agreed. That wasn't going to happen.

"What about you, Bob?" I asked.

"Oh, things are decent. We're bringing up a new vatory here, so there's a lot of water chemistry and mesh layout. They're doing some new work with a salmon tank, too, to increase productivity. They're getting big. That's why I was away last time you were through. I was actually dirtside looking at materials before they lifted them."

Food production up was good. Due to population, I asked.

"Some. And shipping's been on the increase even before this workaround, so there's plenty of market. I also have reservations about possible Jump Point issues, either from station damage or from astrophysical damage. I'm going to be stocking extra in our freezer."

"Yeah." There's only so much you can do in space, but large habitats are mostly survivable, more than ships.

There was cheesecake for dessert. It wasn't as amazing as the stuff I'd had at Conway, but still, it was cheesecake. I sprawled across their laps on the couch next to the mammock, getting my legs, ass and shoulders massaged while stealing bites from them. They grinned at each other. We were theoretically watching a zero-G dance and athletic show, but they were paying attention to me.

Sometimes they have me in turns. I figured tonight I was getting sandwiched one way or another.

It was right on the couch. One moment Ray was massaging my hips, then he was opening the gussets on my suit and touching my flesh. Bob bent down to kiss me, and it just went from there. I got naked, they got naked, and I turned face down and turned around.

Two days sleeping between them, warmth on both sides, and letting them catch up on their need for female flesh alone and together, was a lot of fun. I didn't spend a cent. They covered it all. And me.

They're strange, but so sweet, and I love hanging out with them.

During the day I took care of everyone's laundry and general cleaning, and caught more news about UN troops moving "through" the system.

Even if they were going through, they were going to

be present. There were better places for me to be. I started watching the manifests for a slot out.

Three days and plenty of double man fun later, I had passage to Alsace. I kissed them both, promised to be back again soon, and grabbed space.

The ship was a standard frame from the Martin co-op. They looked at overall requirements, designed a standard frame to fit most of the needs, produced it cheap on pre-order, and sold them all. They're reliable general craft, but no good for specialty hauling. I counted mass on loading, then cooked and managed waste en route.

On arrival, I saw Alsace had a detachment of UN troops on station. Their uniforms were mostly administration, but I saw a couple of Battlespace Management insignia. There weren't any warships here, but there could be.

Then I heard news of construction across from the civilian station, of a dedicated military terminal that could take a squadron of ships and support functions. About that time, space engineer badges started showing up on uniforms.

I was earning enough to keep going, but I wasn't able to save any. Bunkies cost money, and in Alsace they were all filled. I wound up in a fleabag sotel, and was afraid I was going to have to resort to crash holes and back passages. I didn't have any established chew toys on this side of the system.

What I noted was that the UN was putting troops and facilities everywhere in colonial space, and even in NovRos, which was theoretically independent.

I thought everyone knew that as systems reached a

certain point, they'd become nations, then member nations. Some of them were working on secondary colonies, mostly still habitats so far, but eventually, they'd join the Colonial Alliance, and people would keep expanding through space.

But now the UN was moving in, and pushing for stronger ID and chips. I guessed they wanted to tax all that lovely money people were making.

They'd want it all eventually.

I ran into some troops at Lune Grotto. They were in okay shape, but definitely not the buff guys I'd met in NovRos. Those were engineers or combat troops. These were support. There were two chicks. Their hair was far too long for space, and too dressed up. Eight guys were paying all their attention to them, and so were some locals who had a fet for uniformed chicks. Well, I like uniformed guys, so why not?

I sat down nearby and smiled. We were well off the dance floor, with sound paneling so we could talk. It's not dark, but the dark crete makes it look that way. It's just far enough off the axis to have .5G, and against the hull so the "rock" is actually based off the outer regolith. There's a maintenance hatch in their storage cube that goes to the gap between deck and hull, but I've never been down there.

"Hey. Want to help me with a pitcher of Alibis?"

"Hey! Sure!" one of them said. She was bubbly. I hate bubbly.

The other shrugged. "I can help a little, I guess."

They weren't going to take drinks from men, but they figured I was safer.

One of the guys asked, "Do you mind if I chip in?"

"Go ahead," I said. I coded the order and waited for the serverbot.

They all liked to talk, so I sat back and let them.

When they drank, they talked even more.

They had admin and process problems. That's nothing unusual in the military.

But theirs seemed more fucked up than ours. The whole group got in with stories about it, including about Mtali. I'd missed Mtali. It was mostly Third Legion, and I'd been Second. I knew it had wrecked some troops emotionally, even if casualties hadn't been that bad. I'd heard rumors of all kinds of meddling.

They had, too.

". . . I mean, I saw cargotainers of stuff go into Logistics, but we'd go in to get stuff issued and they were out of stock, or awaiting delivery, or awaiting process. Every freaking time."

His tall buddy said, "We're in a bar, Shaddy, you can say, 'fucking.'"

"Yeah, but I might slip and say it in front of the captain."

"Yeah. He'd . . . never mind, I shouldn't say it." Buddy shrugged.

"Cargotainers?" I asked.

He turned to me, "Mate, everything went in, nothing came out. Packs, body shields, optics, weapons. Everyone was begging for gear, and we saw landers, and trucks, but there was never enough when we went for it."

The tall girl said, "And then we hear that most of Log was selling stuff to three different local factions."

"Yeah, that. It must be nice to be in Log."

Buddy asked, "Are we getting our materials here?"

The other chick was an engineer. She said, "Mostly. Just occasional shortages on fasteners and welding wire. Especially since the fusion welders need very specific wire. I hate those Allah-blessed things. The old style wire feeds can take almost anything in an emergency, even strapping wire. These things, one gauge, specific heat and freq for each alloy, no mixing because of vapor danger, even in a freaking vacuum. The safety guys are as bad as Log."

The first girl said, "Just remember when you want to bash Admin, we're right here."

"No, I like you guys. You make sure I get paid."

"Damn straight. A lot of boots don't appreciate that."

They all paused for a moment, and I wanted to offer just a little to be friendly.

I said, "I wasn't there at the time, but we get light cargotainers on trampers sometimes. You know from the bill of lading it's got to be a twenty K unit, but it masses in at sixteen K. The stuff never got in there. They're sealed, so we can't screw with them."

"Yeah, but this stuff was definitely being sold in-system. They made a bunch of arrests and there were troopies running for holes. I have to wonder how many were actually guilty. It wouldn't take many if they were on the right shift. Most of them are probably just boots who got hosed by the Justies."

"I believe you," I said.

"Still," he said with his eyes staring at nothing, "stuff could go missing en route as well. We'd never know."

I asked, "When's the terminal going to be functional?"

The woman engineer said, "It's functional now, for combat use, which doesn't apply, even in combat with the way the safety managers are. It will be safe in a few weeks. It'll be signed off some time after that. Then they'll start cramming so much unauthed crap in there it'll overload life-support and gen, and we'll get blamed for not anticipating, even though we're not allowed to. Jackbags."

I learned quite a bit I thought would be useful for planning my routes.

I figured it wouldn't be safe to spread with any of them, in case some UN cop thought I was trying to spy for someone, especially since I'd just come from NovRos. So I finished my glass, and stood.

"I have schedule to manage, but keep the rest and be safe. Good luck."

"Hey, and you, spacer. Thanks very much."

"Thanks, definitely."

I said, "You're welcome. Safe flight."

I went back to my room. Since I had plenty of space and a wide bed, I plugged in my Body Buzz and ran a program. Tactile pads all over my neck and torso, 3D vid and two vibes and fingers on my lips wasn't as good as real sex, but sometimes I like just how much overload it can offer all at once. I came hard enough for green sparkles behind my eyelids. I knew I'd hit a good release. I managed purple sparkles once. Green is really good.

CHAPTER 9

I managed to book on a mid-size slow tug that was going through Meiji and around, to Earth and around, and back to Caledonia. They hired me for the duration up front.

The slow tugs take more work and carry more sensitive cargo, but the flights are longer. The per-day rate wasn't quite as high and meant a little more work, but I'd have a nice chunk at the end.

There are people rich enough to ship exotic wood between systems.

There are people rich enough to ship finished furniture between systems.

The stuff was packed in hermetic wrap, inside aerogel, inside custom cases, inside crush foam, inside crates, inside spring padding, inside cargotainers, inside pods. It had to be bonded through Earth, because they consider it some sort of environmental sin. So those pods had to be separated, and cargo had to be planned around it because we legally couldn't open those pods in Earth space.

In Meiji we dropped cargo and picked up handmade artifacts in precious alloys. I saw attached images. The stuff was gorgeous. We also picked up high-nitrogen gas in containers, and fairly heavy elements from their outer cloud, which they call Sutā Ringu.

I don't do much socializing. Meijaps left Japan because they thought it was too open. They don't like halfbreeds. I'm a quarter. Then I have that red-gold hair over my eyes. They think I'm hideous, and some sort of freak. If I leave the docks, I put my hair up, wear a hat or hood, and don't try to speak Nihongo. I did that once and they were very, very offended.

There wasn't anything I needed, so I stayed aboard ship for the short layover.

Next we were through to Earth, where we dropped some of everything, and picked up more stuff.

It was wine again, and exotic liquor. To me, liquor is something you drink or mix with a drink to get drunk. Some people insist on weird stuff. In Earth system, we picked up some Penderyn au Cymru whiskey from one small part of Britain, that was aged in honey-sweetened charred oak barrels for twenty-seven years and packaged with a small bottle of spring water from a particular spring, that you were supposed to mix in, I'm told, three mllliliters per serving of 44.36 mllliliters of the whiskey.

I suppose if that's what works for you and you can afford damned near Cr1000 a bottle at our end, and similar prices elsewhere, enjoy.

We drove around Earth's Oort cloud instead of going through-system. Traffic is too heavy, as are the transit charges. Then there's all the rules and policies that they have in-system and would have outer if they could get away with it.

Still, the ship had a decent vid library. I caught a couple of comedies and a ground chase action flick. They had good audio. I took in some classics I'd always meant to hear. Eh. They were okay, mostly. I guess I'm not suited for The Arts.

I took care of second shift food, which was all of three people plus myself, mostly warming what first shift had cooked, but I did electrosmoke some salmon and grill ribs for the meat eaters.

Almost a month later we jumped back into Caledonia, at which point I had to help dump waste tanks, refresh atmo and water, clean cyclers—all the sweaty, grubby maintenance you never see in vids. It's not glamorous. It's work.

Twenty-seven days in cross-space is draining. I was going to have to do that again, too, because I needed to get to the other side of this system.

I have intra-system experience (which is different from an intra-system annotation for deep space, which I obviously have, too). But, it's a different community. Those legs are longer because of how the Jump Points speed everything up.

Then there's the new phase drive that the Freehold is starting to use on warships, and a handful of civilian craft. It's a billion credits or more to equip a ship right now, or rather, was when I wrote this. It's slowly getting cheaper, but that will change everything around again when it's more common. I'd never been on one in use.

But, I was either going to have to cross to the other

side and try for an intra-leg, or go around the long way again. Traffic was flowing to the Freehold again, with lots of inspections and tags that were a pain in everyone's ass. Still, it was something.

I knew this station, but had only been here twice. It's gorgeous. New Liverpool isn't very original for a name, but the structure is amazing. It's six rows of spokes with a long outer ring over all of them. One end is enclosed and has emgee zones for lab and recreation. Three of the spokes have trees and vines climbing up inside, and one has a waterfall. It starts at barely .1G but is at a full G at the bottom, which means it looks like the water is racing, and the Coriolis force pulls it into a spray on the far side, so there's a clear garden under a falling wave.

It has every ship-fitting function imaginable available on call with tug and sled response if you need it. Ships can dock attached, by umbilicus, by tether or in slow orbit. There are huge floodlights and reflectors for work zones. And there are clubs, hotels and bunkies, most of them upscale but reasonably priced.

It was government built, and they're still paying off the cost, so we'd never have anything like it. But damn, it's neat.

I was actually able to find a maintenance shed in the garden, hidden under a fake rock outcropping. I wedged the door closed and slept wonderfully in G, with the hissing roar of the cascade overhead. Okay, I may have mouthed an engineer I know for the info and the "romance" of sleeping there. Totally worth it. I wasn't going to abuse the access code. I moved to a bunkie the next night.

But I specifically needed to find either a cross-system

leg or one that was guaranteed through Sol back to somewhere else.

A seven-day week later, I had one that took me all the way to Caledonia's L5 point where I could actually see a planet again for the first time in months. Very pretty, but I just feel right in space. We dropped cargo, stowed more, and boosted for their JP2 to the Freehold.

So I was back in one of my homes, in my regular work environment, and the routes were all screwed up because the UN bureaucrats were trying to put rules on top of the existing rules, on top of the established way of doing things, on top of the ornery spacer way of life, on top of the anarchic Freehold streak, on top of the Freehold spacer lifestyle of "fuck everything except real world safety."

They weren't having much luck, but they were still keeping things slow.

It's impossible to explain how it works. It's a culture. There are habitat people, deep spacers, intras in a different loop. Techs, sales, astro. Each system has its own influence, stations aren't like ground, spacers aren't like habitots. If you haven't worked in it for at least several months, it's just a bunch of people moving about.

Apparently, the people in charge of "space occupant movement management" were all from Earth proper. As in, dirtside. They were completely without grasp. They didn't manage to organize anything, just piss people off, get in the way, slow travel. That pissed off habitats, grounders, businesses who needed those metals, gear and gas.

Everyone saw them as outsiders. They had no friends.

They still got in the way. Even though they weren't touching intra-system traffic, it depended on out-system loads.

Every bunkie was booked, and I couldn't afford the sotels that were available, never mind the actual inns. I was going to have to doss creatively.

I didn't have any playbuddies in that station. I didn't want to take short naps in waiting rooms and lobbies. Sitting up to sleep is rough, even in low G. Short sleep isn't productive for very long. I also didn't want to annoy the locals or be seen doing that while trying to cadge a berth.

But I needed somewhere clean.

I walked around looking as if I was going somewhere, keeping my eyes open for signs.

I found a bay used for automated dollies, where they plugged in to charge. Back behind there would be okay, even if it would be a bit loud. But there were already a couple of whole crews back there. I figured they'd gotten permission, and I shouldn't get into their space.

There was a gated supply area with spare cable, bearing and mounts. It had space and wasn't likely to be entered, but it was officially locked. I could hop the fence, but I'd be trespassing.

The rest of the dock was like that. Workable spaces taken, others not available.

Down the hub were the usual machine shops and outfitters. I could find a place in the back passages, but they were dusty, with lubricants, goo and polymer gels making it messy and occasionally toxic, no matter what the air laws said.

Past that were bars. Absolute worst case, I could try

to sling hash or drinks, or strip, and sleep in the dressing or storage room. That would make getting hired even harder, though.

I grabbed a tuna sandwich and kept looking.

I found what I needed in the oxy hub.

The oxy hub has full and empty bottles for suits, scooters, runabouts and emergency supplies. There were three dealers, all around one power bus for their compressors. The bottles were cordoned off for safety, non-sparking gear was mandatory, and it was secure and patrolled.

A lot are stored and filled outside, but some are inside for station use and easy carry by crew. The empties were stacked on the deck around the bay as a buffer in case someone tried to damage the full ones. I guess some deranged loon tried it once, but it's exotic suicide. Spark in an O2 environment and you just become a flambé on the spot.

The empties were in cages, racks, stacks, pallets, skids and had gaps. They also weren't well-lit. Usage was down with the traffic reduced. All I needed was a chance to get into a gap.

I found one I liked, slowed my walk and pretended to fumble in my pack, and waited until the roving rentacop and his drone turned laterally.

It took three seconds to slip into shadow, and a few more to carefully crawl into a space under a rack. I was covered by large tanks on each side, and clutter and the depth of the rack. There was no reason for anyone to look for me or see me. I shoved my ruck in first, with some trash ahead of it, so it shielded me from that side.

I had a rolled sweatshirt as a pillow, and a cloak to wrap in. The deck was cool, but at .3G, I didn't need a mattress.

It took a while to zone down for sleep. I had to learn to ignore local noises from passing vehicles and personnel.

I got a couple of divs' sleep, some of it solid, some restless, but it was enough to function. I rolled my gear, packed it and managed to get back into traffic unnoticed.

Back in the dock lounge, intra-system was paying dirt wages. They had a lot of people trying to cross, some with quals and some without, and not many slots. The ships were taking advantage of that, but then, their transport was down, too.

I had to decide if I wanted to break bottom scale and help lower everyone else's wages, too. It could also hurt me later if the crew prices here dropped too much. But I wanted to get across.

I found a small specialized transport that took processed chemical tanks between the Jump Point stations, just providing materials faster than they could be produced locally. They had a tiny crew.

When I laid down my certs, the captain-owner said, "You can do cargo, cook, medical and Class 2 maintenance? I'll take you. But I can't pay above minimum scale."

"That's fine," I agreed.

I was a bit nervous because it was an all-male crew. However, it turned out he had a wife at the other end, and two of the four were otherwise in partnerships. The astrogator stared at me every chance he got, but only for short glimpses and he never made a move.

Two weeks later I was where I wanted to be.

CHAPTER 10

I was able to find a bunkie in Shetland habitat. I was able to access my backup account, and I actually had funds to deposit. I swapped out some outfits and personal stuff from my locker, and planned to hit Lunacy Bar after I got cleaned up.

But things changed when I went to the Lift Lounge and listened for routes and such.

The whole system was like it had been at the other side.

Apparently, the UN had warships and construction here, too. They were putting a facility at every Jump Point. They'd only restricted some traffic so far, but we all felt it.

"Goddam Unos want to strangle commerce," I heard one captain bitch over his beer. "It's like they're afraid of money."

Someone else said, "Blame that so-called 'Freehold' for opting out of everything. They've always been cheap fucks and trying to screw people for a buck."

"Eh, they sell exactly what they say they do."

"Yeah, but there are standards that we all developed, and not pissing off the UN was one of them. They enjoy doing it, and this is what they got. We're paying for their fuckup. Fuck them."

"It's not their warships and troops who are slowing us down."

"No, they just caused it. Like bacteria."

I really wasn't going to get into that argument. It never turned into a fight, but it got rude.

I pretended to drink, while the drinkers did drink and taunted the two.

I realized something, though. The UN was planning to control commerce, and we were the reason. We'd taken control away from them in our system and others. They wanted that back, and the rest.

That was when my conclusion led to a decision.

I was going to have to go home and do some things.

I kept an ear out for anything going into the Freehold. There really wasn't much, and none of them had slots. I also did some anonymous core searching on where I could check in when I got there. I didn't find much. I'm definitely not an intel type, even now.

A week later, a Freehold cruiser came through. It was the *Jack Churchill*. I'd never been on it, but I remembered the schematic from recruit training. Caledonia was a neutral party, so the UN couldn't harass or attack the ship while in local space, but they had only minimal time to provision or fuel and depart.

Could they take on crew?

And did I want to go back to the war zone I'd just

escaped from? I was a papered resident here. I should
be safe. But part of me was afraid they'd finish with the
system then come out looking for any of us who had
residence status. Did I want to try to totally deny my
home system? All I'd have to do is shred my passport. I
hadn't paid a residence fee since I left. I had no reason
to. There shouldn't be any records except biometrics on
file with the Freehold military. They'd already nailed a
few people that way, who weren't even combatants. I'd
also have to hope they never asked for my birth
certificate.

The decision I'd come to was because I realized even
if I avoided that, they might not stop. If they could drag
us down, then they'd go after other systems, too. If
everywhere got like Earth and Sol, I'd have nowhere to
travel.

It also seemed pretty crappy, being a veteran, to run
away from my system. I guess I owed them my service. If
they'd take me.

I also realized just walking up to the dock might mark
me.

How full was *Churchill*? Did they even have berths?

If I was going to do this, I was going to do this.
Technically they had to take me space-A, but that
assumed they had room. I hit my locker and grabbed the
rest of my possessions. I wasn't likely to come back here
before the war ended. I grabbed my big pack, my garment
bag, and started stuffing. That rolled bundle was my rifle
with my kataghan alongside. That case was my pistol. I
took it all, figuring they could tell me to dump stuff if they
didn't have room.

Technically I could only take the weapons directly to a ship I had passage on. I could be considered a combatant now, and the station at least was neutral.

One gate of the dock had a squad of Royal Caledonian Marines, though one was a naval petty officer. I walked up to them and had my ID in hand.

"Aonghaelaice Kaneshiro, veteran, Freehold Forces. I need access for boarding."

The Marine sergeant looked at my ID and then at me. He didn't seem sure. I knew my training was supposed to be better than his, but I was a medic, not combat arms, and I was out of practice and wasn't going to fight. I didn't like his smug look, though.

The PO said, "I'll have to check. We're neutral, so they can fuel and depart, and do repairs. I'm not sure about taking on crew, you understand."

"Sure," I said, and wondered if I should have checked Underdeck for a way past this. That would be illegal, too, but probably less obvious.

I put my ruck down and sat on it. It was going to be a while.

Several minutes later, he came back and said, "Okay, you can pass."

"Thank you, Petty Officer, Sergeant," I said, as I shouldered everything. It was a strain, but I wanted the smug jerk to realize I'd just shouldered his mass and walked with it.

Jack Churchill wasn't docked directly. She was tethered at the axis and had a gimbaled access tube with a pressure elevator. Dockside, they had a small terminal with three seats. Sitting there, or rather, strapped onto the chairs in near emgee, was a lieutenant and a sergeant. I pulled myself along the ladder and drifted across the compartment. They saw me approach and watched as I dragged to a stop with a foot against the deck bulkhead, and caught the railing at the desk.

"Good morning," I said.

The lieutenant, nametag Broud, said, "Good morning, lady. How can I help you?"

He called me "lady." Not "Miss," "Ms.," "Ma'am." I only ever got that insystem. It probably doesn't mean much to you.

"I'm a veteran. Clinical Specialist Kaneshiro. Rating Four. Discharged seven years ago. I'm volunteering for duty."

They looked at each other.

Lieutenant Broud said, "That's generous and patriotic of you. I'd really like to take anybody we can get, but we're already overmanned. We took some of the crew of another vessel that got seized, and some transients on leave. It's ass to nose aboard now."

I decided to improve the odds. "I have other shipboard skills," I told the lieutenant.

"What can you do?" he asked.

"I have civilian certs as cook, shipboard maintenance, cargo management, and I can manage as a social companion." I'd have to work at that, but I could do it. I knew our people were clean.

"You realize we may be in combat as soon as we hit the Jump Point? We don't have a fleet carrier, so there's no phase drive. We go where the Points dictate. They're probably waiting."

"Sure. But I don't want to stay here and wait to be pulled by the UN. I just want to get to the Freehold."

The sergeant grabbed his phone and called aboard. "Can we ID a vet from seven years ago?"

It turns out I was actually safe in that regard. Any records there might have been were at HQ and probably scrambled already. The ship's archive didn't have anything. So the UN would probably have never IDed me that way.

It got uncomfortable. They didn't want to take a possible spy or wannabe. I didn't have much to offer. I had my old ID, but that could be faked.

"Weapon in my bag," I said. "Can you date the issue number?"

"Probably," the sergeant, Bandan, said.

"Five seven niner six five four one. M Five with the Second-Gen upgrade. My training company was . . ."

Someone on the phone said, "Yeah, that's her. Screwy spelling on her name."

I didn't recognize them, but once I was in view he said, "I was in Fourth Regiment Personnel Section. I remember seeing you, and your name is unique."

"Thanks," I said, sounding stupid. What else should I say?

Lieutenant Broud said, "Welcome aboard, Medic."

I was on the next lift over.

The 'vator rattled through the gangway. It sounded a bit rough, and was rather dark. I wondered about maintenance. But, as long as it lasted until I reached the airlock, it wasn't my problem.

Once aboard it was almost like training again. They

towed me to a bunk room and assigned me a rack. I had to share it with another specialist on the opposite shift. I had just enough room to stow both bags and my weapon. I got one shirt to wear over my T-shirt, that had a generic rank and no qual badge. I was assigned to two sections—Galley and Infirmary.

The galley chief was a sweet old lady. Warrant Officer Haskins looked about forty F-years, but could be older.

"Good to meet you, Specialist Kaneshiro. Have you worked Galley before?"

"I've spaced most of the last seven years. I've done my share."

"Oh, good. I'm a stickler on sanitation, and on keeping food prep clean and ingredients refrigerated. Spacers need to be healthy to fight."

"Yes, Warrant, I agree."

"Then I'll have you help out with support and cleaning. There isn't enough of that. We're so busy slinging hash we can't stay on it."

It wasn't glamorous, but it was necessary. I said, "I can wash dishes and scrub decks."

"Excellent. Never let anyone tell you that's not a critical war skill."

I knew it was. It wouldn't be a tasking aboard ship if it wasn't necessary.

We pulled out of station a couple of divs later, and they ripped serious G heading for the Jump Point. After ten segs, I wondered if they were going to boost the whole way, but then they dropped to emgee, then resumed Grainne standard, G, more or less. It varied a little. I wasn't sure that was of any use for evasion, but maybe it would help mask their transfer time. Or maybe they were trying to cut through before any Sol ship could let them know we were coming.

It was entirely possible we'd break through, get nuked, and be a cloud of vapor. This was a warship, we were at war, and I was now a combatant. It was too late to consider if I'd made the right choice, but unless I wanted to be a lone assassin, there wasn't much else I could do. I had no training for that and wouldn't know where to start.

They did have sufficient cooks, but there was a lot of cleaning to be done. They'd been shorthanded on galley and services help when they departed, and full battle crewing plus overmanning had hurt them. I scrubbed grease and dust from filters and ducts, assisted in linen and laundry, and cleaned parts in the maintenance racks in the boat bays. They were using equipment that fast.

At the end of the shift, I reported directly to Infirmary, after I found it.

"Kaneshiro?" the section chief, Lieutenant Doctor Udal asked.

"Yes, Doctor," I said.

"Okay, I've got you as medic and recspec. What is your identifier?"

"M Four Infirmary Medic, Specialist, Rate Four. I have current civilian certs for CPR, Airway, Trauma and Vacuum."

"I'm very glad to hear that, and I hope we don't need you. We do training every shift, just in case, and we get a lot of minor dings with this many people and running all out."

"Yes, sir."

"RecSpec?" he asked.

"Freelance, but I can do it. I volunteered."

"Okay. That's still a skill, you realize."

"Yup . . . sir," I said. I didn't want to discuss my sexual techniques with him, but that wasn't his concern.

"The summary: Listen for any emotional issues that might need followup, or any tendencies to violence, as opposed to fantasy ideals. You're not required to serve anyone you don't want to."

"That makes sense," I said. "I take it you need me?"

"Yes. The crew are young, stressed and facing combat in less than a week. It's sex or drugs or fistfights. We'd prefer they were having sex."

"I'll do what I can, sir," I assured him.

When I was done with my shift of scrubbing the next day, I checked in at the infirmary and demonstrated some techniques for training and got quizzed, to convince them I was capable in an emergency.

Warrant leader Dunstan, second in charge, asked me, "A spacer is brought in from explosive decompression with vacuum trauma. He is not wearing a mask or V-suit. His eyes are bloodshot and puffy with swollen lids. He clutches at his ears and gurgles when he tries to talk. There is no pressure containment module available."

"I listen to his lungs for any bubbling sounds. If they're bubbling, I grab an emergency oxidizer, and use the lowest vein and artery on his left hand—"

"Why lowest?"

"Because if there's trauma I can always move higher up the limb. I don't want to damage IV sites he might need later."

"Hmm. Good point. Go on."

"I check the monitor to get at least seventy-percent saturation. If he's conscious, I have him work his jaw and use sinus compression to relieve pressure imbalance on his tympani. I apply gauze bandages with an optical saline soak to his closed eyes, bandage loosely, and offer non-narcotic analgesic. I log for the pulmonary surgeon to be ready for reconstruction."

It took two divs of hard questions, but they agreed I was trained and signed me off.

Then I cleaned up and pulled the rest of my shift as a social companion, before I was going to try for two divs' rest then back to the galley.

I'm told RecSpec work often involves massage, chat, and other things nonsexual as well. With seven times as many men as women in the Forces, a lot of males wanted a girl to hang with as much as sex. That didn't happen on my rotation.

Combat had the crew stressed, and they really needed to release tension. They had three women and one man already in the department, and they were tired, the crew backed up, and I was a welcome addition. I got more response from the gay women, actually.

The men were easy; they aren't nearly as picky regarding sex, I'm comfortable with it, and these were soldiers. They were all clean, healthy, and in good shape. It was bit tiring physically, but not a chore. Naturally, they wanted mouthjobs. Whether straight or gay, men want mouthjobs. I kept a drink handy to wash the taste out. I love giving head, but you can have too much of a good thing in a hurry.

The first one came in, and seemed relieved to actually find a person, not a simulant. He visibly relaxed, and I did in fact massage his shoulders.

"Oh, thank you," he said.

"You're tense. Long shift?"

"Hard shift," he said.

I helped him peel out of his shipsuit and he was already stiff.

"I get the idea," I said, as I took him in hand. He arched and stretched and I went to work. I made sure not to rush, so he got some emotional release as well as physical. His hands were in my hair and on my back, and I hoped a few of them would want to fuck. I was going to need some stress relief myself.

He came so hard his heels drummed on the couch. I grinned at that. I knew I was good, but that was high praise.

I managed five of them in a row the third day. I was proud of myself. One of the other women handled nine. I have no idea how. My jaw would be cramped by then.

I worked out a routine of some massage, small talk, a big show of putting on my lips or peeling out of brief, and running them hard. I got enough for myself, and I managed to help them with the strain.

I hadn't done much with women since I was an ado. The mechanics weren't hard—I can rub and lick and work on the feedback I receive, but I can't read them the way I can read men. It was serious work. I apparently did a good job, because even some of the women who didn't swing gave me a whirl at the growing suggestion of their friends. The one man just couldn't keep up with fifty women. We had to take up some of the slack.

Apparently, quite a few women are gay for the flight. They'd rather sit down and chat with another woman than a man, and as long as they have good toys and company, they're more comfortable with a female. They might have husbands or manfriends at home, but aboard ship, they wanted girltalk and release.

One came in with three toys, had me plug her in, wrap her in an embrace, and just nuzzle her neck with my nipples rubbing against her shoulders. She wanted human touch. The machines were industrial. I could feel them myself. I gripped her breasts and muttered and breathed on her neck and she rode herself into oblivion.

The next one was barely adult, only a Spacer 2. She still had a bobbed haircut from RT, looked really slender and awkward. Her hair was glossy black, her eyes dark blue and very wide. She insisted on sharing fingers and lots of eye contact. That was intense and a bit too personal. I could see her reactions in her pupils. I squinted now and then, and did my best to let her see my eyes in between, but it felt a lot more intimate than just release. She was pretty good with her fingers, too, and kept licking them for spit, and apparently liked how I taste. It would have been okay, except I didn't get her name and knew nothing about her. It was too intimate for work. But I did orgasm, tight around her slim hand and leaning on her shoulder.

There was a fringe benefit. They tipped me. It wasn't as if most of them would be able to spend the money, but I might. I accepted politely and stowed it deep in my bag.

CHAPTER 11

It was a long six days to the Jump Point, even with a split-shift and lots of work. Offshift, I had to log in with Finance and Personnel, so I might eventually get paid for this, if we survived and the war resolved.

Yes, six days. They apparently took a bit of a detour to confuse things. I guess it could work either way. Rush through, hope to beat their response. Take your time, wait for them to get bored and not know the exact schedule.

The closer we got to Jump, the tenser everyone got. We'd certainly make it through. It was almost impossible anything would hit us right away. Speed of light lag and safe arming distance would ensure that. We'd have at least ninety seconds after transit. After that . . .

I wasn't sure if I wished I knew more about fire control, or was glad I didn't. The entire helm, astro, fire control and command crew was in the hole as we neared Jump. They were ready to toss radiant death at anything on the home side. We might at least take a ship with us.

If so, it would be a good trade. I hoped there was nothing there, but I realized we had to kill people to win.

Churchill was named after an old military hero, and he and we had the nickname *Mad Jack*. I figured we were going to earn that name.

"All hands! All hands! Secure for jump transit," came through the intercom and my phone. I got to the bunk. I was going to be sharing it. We hot bunked between shifts, but we all needed support for the Jump.

My bunkmate, whom I almost never saw, was an electronics tech first class. Cally Birtek. She was already strapped in.

"Hey," I said as I climbed up.

"Hey."

"Can you scoot another fifteen centimeters?"

"Yeah." She wiggled over, loosened her harness, and I got onto the bunk except for one shoulder that hung off. I had bungee cords for my legs, attached to her harness and the bunk frame, from my belt to the harness and frame, and around my shoulders and to harness and frame. I hoped they were strong. I hoped they weren't needed.

"Scared?" she asked quietly. I think she was eleven G-years, twelve tops.

"Yes," I said. "Jump always sucks. This is worse."

I felt her fingers near mine, clutching, and we gripped hands and held on.

There was a countdown on the system screen above us, in the bottom of the third bunk in the stack. It was a good thing I was used to living in bunkies. This had even less space.

I wished for some Sparkle, some red wine, and a buzz

patch. I thought we were evasive maneuvering, but it was just my head spinning in panic.

Command announced, "Transit in three zero seconds . . . two zero seconds . . . one zero seconds . . . five, four, three . . ."

I closed my eyes even though there was nothing to see.

The universe turned inside out and we were in Freehold space.

Then I was crushed into the couch. We were at full thrust, pulling possibly six G. I was thrown into Birtek, then she into me and I rolled halfway out, hanging by the bungees as they cut into my flesh. They held, but then I was thrown up and bounced off the rack above back onto the bunk. I had a welt over my right eye. I threw my other arm over her in a hug just so I could stay in place.

Then the Gs went up even more.

The frame rumbled from that level of boost, and I wondered how hard we were driving. I was gasping for breath and had a throbbing headache from the acceleration.

Then something punched me all over. Everything shook and there was a loud bang, lots of creaks and whining buzzes, then nothing.

Emgee, and floating, then thrust resumed.

"All hands, all hands. Secure from G couches. Alarm red, we are in combat. Battle stations, battle stations, stand ready to secure at duty section."

She clutched at her releases with shaking hands. I managed to unloop the bungees and then helped her with her leg restraints. That done, I rolled out to the deck, and almost got boots in the head from the large chick above us.

I was a ground medic. I was a civilian spacer. Crew response in a combat ship is nothing like a cargo hauler. The passages were packed, all the airlock doors open. If we got hit now we were all dead.

I made it through crowds and up the powered ladder to the infirmary.

We had casualties.

Lieutenant Udal said, "Kaneshiro, triage."

"Yes, sir."

I'd served mostly peacetime, then went to space. I'd dealt with injuries from loaders, slammed hatches, a couple of fistfights and some industrial accidents, and one negligent gunshot wound. This wasn't like that.

It was bad. The nearest guy was supported by a buddy, and coughed in a horrid rasp. His face was flushed and bruised, and I knew he'd hit hard vacuum. We could treat that, but it would have to be soon. He wouldn't be on duty for some time. He sounded ugly, and I didn't want to listen to that awful sound. It was creepy.

"Specialty?" I asked his buddy.

"He's reactor and fuel management."

I read my phone, that told me there were four of those. Unless the others were in here, he wasn't yet critical.

Thrust tapered off and we were in free flight. That made it different to work. Not necessarily harder, but it required free flight maneuvering.

"Vacuum trauma. Lungs. Number three." I tagged him and turned to the next, hoping I hadn't sentenced him to die.

There's four considerations on the scale. How critical

is this person's specialty and can they be replaced? How many resources will be required to save them? What are their odds of recovery? How soon do they need treatment for it to matter? Someone who can't be saved is low, but someone with only superficial wounds is lower. Someone in a critical specialty with minor trauma gets treated ahead of someone with severe injuries who isn't.

The next one was a mass of bruises and contusions. He'd been slammed into a bulkhead.

"What's your specialty?" I asked.

"Engines."

There were two others in his specialty, but he was certainly savable. I tagged him as a Four. He wasn't going to die.

The third had the same buddy as the first one. She was convulsing. That was so grotesque I looked away.

I looked at the buddy.

He said, "I think she took a radiation hit. She was farthest stern."

I marked her a five. We probably couldn't do anything.

We had thirty-seven casualties. All of mine got bumped up a level, and I was glad. They were some of the worst, but the better ones were easier to address.

Once that was done, Warrant Dunstan said, "Kaneshiro, deal with the superficials, please."

"Will do."

I grabbed spray, bandages, topical and injectable analgesic and got to work. First I dosed the bump on my own eyebrow. The sting had turned to a throb that distracted me.

My first patient needed sutures in a pressure cut. One

did fine with staples. Several just needed bandages and spray. Well, not "just." One guy had a bruise across the entire back of his scalp. I was amazed he didn't have a concussion, but he seemed fine.

I told him, "Have them check your skull later. Report any tingles, or any functional problems at all. You're good to return to duty, conditionally."

"Thanks, Specialist," he said.

I recognized him. The first guy I'd sucked off last week. He was a lot less tense now. He was wobbly. I wasn't sure he recognized me back.

I didn't go in for any galley work. I stayed and dealt with minor injuries, massive contusions and lots of pain. I sprayed and injected and handed over pill scrips as fast as I could, while clinging to a saddle with my knees.

The guy with the lung damage was stabilized into a respiratory support unit. The girl with radiation burns wasn't going to make it. They doped her up so she wouldn't feel anything, and gave her a bed. I felt ill myself. She'd been cute, and young, and now she was half cooked.

They posted a report on the battle. Actually, they'd posted it a half div before, but I'd been too busy to read it. We'd come through, and there were two UN ships waiting, one capital, one chaser. But we'd come through at velocity, then nailed it again. There was no way they'd intercept. They did have time for one volley of a lot of torpedoes. We'd caught a near miss with one. That wave front overloaded the reactor. I guess radiation adds to the existing radiation if it gets through the shield, sort of like throwing fuel on a fire. Or I may be completely wrong. I don't know nuke stuff. From that we had the one casualty who was dying, and four others, not as severe.

We'd gotten off a volley back, and probably hit one of theirs, but we didn't know if we'd hurt them yet.

Once in free flight, we were much harder to track, but not impossible. The energy needed to move ships around is "lots." I wish I could be more specific, but it's like entire city-levels of power production, and continental levels for star drive. That's why transport costs so much. Even with fusion or A-matter power generation, you need a lot. That much energy is easy to find, relatively.

Once in free flight, we dialed the engines back until they just powered the life-support and onboard operations. That's as much power as a small village. Most of it was contained inside the hull. Some was used for particle shielding, but even that was contained within its own radius. Finding something that small at a distance is doable, if you know where to look, and if you have enough time. It doesn't take much maneuvering thrust to throw you off the original trajectory. They have to search an expanding cone.

But we were still at risk and massively outnumbered.

Believe it or not, quite a few guys didn't want sex the first couple of days. They wanted to be cuddled. I had one guy come in, just barely beyond recruit training, who started blubbering and threw his arms around me. I turned him so I was against his back, wrapped around him and held him for twenty segs. He gripped my arms and rocked slightly. He'd shiver occasionally and sigh. I gather he'd have taken me to his bunk to snuggle if he could.

I had no idea where we were going, until they announced to prepare for docking. Given the time, it could be our moon Gealach, or somewhere in planetary orbit, but I didn't know.

The chief of the ship came on intercom.

"Soldiers and Spacers, attention please. We have docked at a clandestine location in the outer Halo. We will be refueling, rearming, and receiving orders and intel, before resuming flight. There will be limited passes, but will include recreation and shopping, although only military necessities are available and not many of those. Communications are strictly controlled. There is no way to send signals groundside or outsystem."

"Additionally, we expect to reassign personnel as needed, to any vessel we encounter. This may include anything from gunboats or other J Frame craft, all the way up to a Fleet Carrier. This especially applies to those we've picked up en route from other ships.

"On behalf of myself and the captain, you are all to be commended for your courage, determination, and tireless efforts. Thank you all. Chief out."

That all made sense. I was shipboard somewhere for the duration. However, he'd said something that made me want to change that. I was limited in what I could do here. There were better ways I could serve.

I assumed I was a medic first, cook second, since I'm rated medical. I went to Doctor Udal and said, "Sir, I request permission to take care of professional business aboard the station, with a military office."

"Something you can't do aboard?"

"Yes, sir."

"May I ask?"

"I'd rather not say, sir. It's relevant to our operation."

"I'll have to ask Command, but I'll put it on the discussion."

CHAPTER 12

The Captain said no.

I'd been afraid of that. Now she needed bodies. There are no non-necessary slots aboard ship; you only take what you need. I was filling one slot and half of two others, and we expected more casualties. I doubt she'd transfer me off, given the choice, unless it was to a small in-system craft who needed all three slots filled.

What I did next was a disciplinary violation, but I needed to. And what could they do to punish me? Put me on a warship in combat, outnumbered and overtasked?

I would have to leave everything here and replace it later, or recover it, circumstances permitting.

Of course, I didn't even know where I was, precisely, other than inside the Grainne system.

I made several passes of the docking umbilicus, and determined the schedule. I'd have about three segs after my first shift to get on it. I'd be reportably late by the time it arrived at the station. I'd be AWOL as soon as they figured it out. Since I'd asked about leaving, that wouldn't take long. Once again, I should have kept my mouth shut.

But I did it. I pulled sutures from the same engine tech I'd put them into, checked a couple of others, scanned in my notes, and excused myself. I hurried through passages, and found a small box of something on the way. It was a crate, it had labels, it would give me cover.

With it in hand, I jogged for the lift. Just around the radius from it, I left the box inside a lock, then sprinted.

"Hold, please," I called, as they were about to button up.

I was already late for my shift, and hadn't been in the twelve days I'd been aboard.

No one in the tube said anything to me. There were ten of us, three carrying boxes, two with terminals I recognized as Logistics scanners. The rest hung onto stanchions and waited quietly.

Someone said, "I wish I knew where this was. But as long as they have uniforms, I can at least get some of my section taken care of."

"Good luck. Though I'd deal with civvies if we could get another ship for joint ops."

A Drive officer said, "Or a phase drive unit."

"Yeah, good luck. I'm sure Brandt's offices are locked up tight."

One of them glanced my way, and I recognized him. He recognized me.

"Hey, RecSpec," he said. That was rude. RecSpecs aren't mentioned in public except by rank or except as part of Emotional Health.

I nodded marginally and hoped he'd stop talking. The warrant leader next to me gave him that "are you that stupid?" look. He seemed to take the hint.

Through the tiny port, I saw the station approach. It was a black something against the background of stars. It was some kind of planetoid, not inflated, and about as invisible as it could get.

We disappeared into the receiving lock, thumped into place, and the plenum connected.

The lock opened and I tried not to cut past the others.

I was third out, and since I wasn't carrying anything, the Mobile Assault troop on security duty just waved me past. He did make a point of checking all incoming containers with a scanner and by eye. I signed the station log roster and it spat a badge at me. I'd been afraid it would ask for clearance back from *Mad Jack*, but it seemed happy just to log me. Likely because we still didn't have everyone accounted for.

I got down the passage fast without looking as if I was fleeing. Behind me, someone shouted, "Hey, Kaneshiro!"

Then I ran. Or rather, bounded and skidded at .12G. I realized they were rotating the rock to even get that much G.

I got around a corner, around another, and slowed.

I found a sergeant, and asked quickly.

"Hey, Sergeant, I may be lost halfway around the station. Where's Intel?"

"Nah, you're not far off. Two down, one left, three forward."

"Got it. Thanks."

I was near a ramp, and took it down, then headed

across to get the left out of the way. Down again, and forward wasn't hard. Nor were there that many people. I used hands on railings and stanchions and barely touched the stone deck. The railings were just bolted to regolith.

I got to the intel office and buzzed for entrance.

"Identity, please."

"I have movement intel on UN craft I need to give you," I said. It wasn't entirely false. "I need to be discreet."

I was buzzed in.

There was an orderly at a window that was obviously well-shielded, as well as being thick ballistic polymer.

"ID, please."

I slid over my passports, both Grainne and Caledonia.

"Kaneshiro. You were just reported AWOL from the *Jack Churchill*."

"I felt it was important enough to get here to tell you. I didn't want to tell them."

"You didn't want to tell your commander about ship movements?"

"I would like to speak to an agent or investigator. I've got more than that."

"Stand by."

He turned and talked into a hush veil, for about three segs. I stood and waited. I was used to waiting. It's part of spacing.

Eventually he turned around.

"Door on your left."

"Thank you."

It was almost a lock, since it had a gasket seal. I waved it open and went in. The space inside was cut from the rock and had sealant over what were probably fissures.

The desk was a slab of extruded poly with four tubular legs, and the chairs were fabbed folding slat backs.

I assumed the woman at the desk was the investigator. She displayed ID that glowed with airmark.

"I am Special Agent Jeanette Garweil, Freehold Military Intelligence."

I examined her ID briefly. I had no reason not to believe it.

"Yes, ma'am," I said.

"Ms. Kaneshiro. Angloyce?" she guessed, reading from her tablet as he offered a hand.

"Angelica," I corrected, and shook hers with a bow.

"That's an interesting spelling."

"My parents were alt-agers. That's not important right now."

"Agreed," she said, with a return bow that was mostly nod. I got it. She was busy.

"You need intelligence," I said.

"Lots of it. I gather you have some."

"Yes. I saw a lot of UN uniforms in Jump Point stations recently."

"That's not news. Unless you know the units?"

"Some. I managed a few images, too. I also danced with a few in clubs in NovRos and Caledonia."

"That's more interesting. What did you find out?"

"Some contact addys and names. I didn't know what to ask. But I can ask if you tell me what you need."

"Ah. I see. We do have intelligence specialists for that. You're a medic, yes?"

I wanted her to figure it out, not to blurt out a story that would sound boastful.

"Sure. Do your intelligence specialists have friends and lodging pre-staged in NovRos, Caledonia, Earth, Govannon and Alsace? I have accounts, lockers, regular bunkies and clubs, contacts, and I know all the main passages and a lot of the clandestine and service passages."

"You mean to tell me you're familiar with every Jump Point station in the galaxy?" she asked incredulously.

"Well, not all," I said. "Only about fifteen."

"You have lodging and possessions, established presence, and know the club staff?"

"That's what I said," I replied. "Also make-out cubbies, rental racks, access passages and cargo bays."

She almost quivered. She was obviously thrilled.

"Yes, then thank you for not mentioning it aboard ship. Things like this are much better kept close."

"That's what I figured."

"Are you offering this information? Maps, charts, whatever you have?"

"It's all in my head," I said. "If you have charts, I can give you what I know, and you're welcome to use my accounts and any gear. I can give intro letters to my friends. I figure there's people you need to extract and information you want to find."

She said, "We do have all their schematics and maps. They're complete."

I said, "No, they're not, especially on older stations. Stuff gets rebuilt, shifted, covered over. Volume gets adapted for use. If people are lazy or crooked, the updates don't get logged. Each mapping is only complete within itself, and often doesn't show bends or shifts as long as the terminal ends are correctly placed. That's assuming your copies are up-to-date, and no one notices you trying to hack in for updates."

"That's valid," she agreed.

She sat and thought.

"Specialist, that's a very generous offer, but it won't really help."

"Oh," I said. "I'm sorry, then. Can I request you excuse me back to *Churchill*?" I felt embarrassed. I was all ready to be a useful asset, a low-level hero, and it was all pointless.

She replied, "I can, but I need to elaborate. There's no way to relay that intel quickly, or answer questions on location. You'd know what you were looking at, any assets wouldn't really. If you were already trained as an intel operator, it might be workable, but even if we ask the right questions, you don't know how to phrase the answers."

Damn. "That makes sense. I'm sorry."

"Don't be. It might still be useful. Could you redeploy to those locations and provide real-time intel to any assets we had on station?"

"Yes," I said. "The problem is I don't have any way to justify that kind of money for jumping around, and getting work passage takes time. I'd have to have weeks to get into position."

"I can arrange to get you into position. There are two problems. The first is that you're neither trained for intel, nor properly vetted for clandestine warfare. I can't read you into the things you'd need, and if anything happens, it could be a huge war crimes issue if you don't. The second is that it's incredibly dangerous."

I said, "In the last month, I've avoided being tagged

by the UN, hopped systems twice, made it out of the blowout, saved a little girl and was on *Mad Jack* when she got hit. Before that I spent seven years floating around tramp freighters and station docks. I know what all this means."

"Then I will transfer you to our branch. I will call your ship," she said.

"Thank you." That was good at least.

"We have our own lodging in this space. You will be locked in. We all are. You can leave with notice, but we don't want a mole doing what you just did to your ship," she said, with an almost-smile.

"I understand," I said.

A div later all my personal gear was delivered to their outer door. A note attached indicated I was transferred from FMS *Jack Churchill* to *Station* [Redacted]. I still don't know the name or location of the rock they used. I never actually got to say goodbye to anyone.

I felt like crap about that.

CHAPTER 13

The lodging was more than adequate. Much better than a bunkie or a ship rack. I had a king bed I could sprawl in, vidcom, fridge and stove, a separate desk, and a bathroom with a shower big enough to play in, with multiple jets. It was even better than Lee's. At .12G I slept and showered great. It was still only about three meters square, but I could stand and walk.

I spent two days summarizing the stations I knew, club names, everything I knew about staff and the dates I knew it, cubbies, ships I'd crewed on, even shop names. They didn't ask for details, but listed my contacts as "professional," "personal" or "intimate."

Garweil had the report up on her desk when I saw her next. While she read, I looked at the stone behind her. It had interesting bubble texture, unchanged by gravity. I'd never been on an unblown rock.

"That's a lot of personal and intimate contacts," she commented. She didn't sound like she was insulting me.

She sounded impressed. I don't know if being impressed was strictly professional, or also personal.

"Yeah, I know a lot of people." I was young and uncommitted. When I wasn't spacing, I was having fun. I had lots of space to play in.

She said, "That can be helpful, but also a hindrance if they recognize you."

I said, "They're almost all people who'd keep their mouth shut. It's a transient thing. Also, I'm pretty good at not being IDed, when in civvies."

"I see," she said. "Well, I'd like to introduce you to an element you'll be working with. I'm convinced it's worth the risk. Do you understand the risks?"

"I think so," I said. "We might be killed in battle. We might die in space. We might get hurt doing something we shouldn't be doing but will anyway. We might get captured. We might even intercept a load from our own people if they don't know we're there."

"That's succinct," she said. "So why are you willing to do it?"

"Because I like my freedom and won't have any if they tag us all. I don't like the delays in getting through their system. I'd rather just travel when I need to. Their way is about like living in a prison anyway. They're also willing to hurt people to accomplish it. So I'm willing to hurt them to avoid it."

We'd talked about this before, but I knew she wanted to be convinced that I was serious, and that I wasn't a mole.

"I expect to kill a lot of people," I told her. "Or help others do so."

"Exactly," she said. "You will be an attached contract asset, not military. That way we can deny you if there are certain repercussions."

"What happens then?" I asked.

She said, "Exactly that. We don't know you, and you'll be on your own. The element you're attached to are military, but they've been covered multiple ways to avoid IDing them. Even if we took you at rank, you'd still not really be on file anywhere except here."

"That's the part that has me worried," I said. I really was. I was nobody, and they could flush me.

"I understand," she said. "If it's too much, we can revert you to medic and find you a billet. But if you can do it, we really could use your help. It just has to be unofficial."

"Do I get paid at all? Or is this strictly volunteer?"

"Contractors get paid," she said. "I had in mind equivalent to a major, with bonuses."

"I don't think that's enough to be completely deniable. On the other hand, I want to make sure you don't have reason to lose me, so I expect a penalty clause that pays my family or an estate if I don't make it."

"That's fair," she said. "Of course, you're trusting us to keep it filed."

I said, "I trust you or I wouldn't be here, ma'am. I don't know who else to trust."

"You also don't know who'll win," she pointed out.

"That gives me incentive, then, doesn't it? I do expect to be well paid," I insisted.

That got a rise from her. "Aonghaelaice, the entire Freehold is at stake here," she said.

"I know, which is why I'm doing this," I said. "But afterwards, I expect a tidy chunk for betting my ass on your terms. I'm not a line soldier, and I'm risking my life here. You do need this info, no one else has it, and I have good odds of getting jailed or shot by the UN."

She looked a bit put upon now. "I thought my offer was generous."

I said, "I am a medic. You're asking for stuff outside my MTS. If I get caught, I won't be a Detained Combatant, I'll be executed as a spy."

She twisted her mouth and said, "That's outdated. They should still detain you."

"I may have spent more time around these systems than you, lady. They could just press me out a lock with a little extra air for delta V, and say they never heard of me. It would save them so many problems."

"True. What did you have in mind, then?"

"I want a good contract salary and lifetime Residency status paid. Start offering," I smiled.

She nodded, offered an adequate salary that I sneered at, then made a more reasonable offer. I held out until she cringed, then accepted.

I would never have to work again. I could travel where I wanted, work if and when I wanted, and be completely free.

If I survived.

The next morning I was taken to a literal hole in the wall space and introduced to nine people. They had folding seats with one for me. There was barely enough room for all of us.

Garweil said, "There are no real names here." I figured that was for my benefit.

"Troops, this is the facilitator you have been advised of. She has traveled extensively in civilian craft and through numerous stations. You will consult with her on travel and cultural climate, and take her advice accordingly on maintaining cover and concealment."

She looked at me. "A, you understand that they will choose their mission parameters and you will advise them how to accomplish them within the scope of your knowledge. They have ultimate say, but I expect they will defer to your judgment when possible."

"I understand," I said. "And none of this will be archived or recorded, of course."

"Correct. It's an entirely free form operation, and you're an attached, consulting, subject matter expert. You are not a combatant under their command, but may engage as one when necessary, reverting to rank for the duration."

"Just the duration of combat, right? Not permanently." I had an image of shooting back at someone and getting my pay slashed.

"Correct. During engagements, pay reversion if they happen to last more than half a day. And if they're logged on return. It's a legal matter, so you're a soldier during those times, not a mercenary."

"Understood," I agreed.

She said, "Then I'll leave you to get introduced." She stood and bounded out of the room. As the door closed, a faint hiss of jamming started.

There were nine of them. Two women, seven men. They were all young, fit, and could mostly pass for crew.

"Are you all space qualified?" I asked.

"Very," one said. "I'm the ranking member."

"I'm Hazel, I guess," I said. That was my grandmother's name.

He grinned. "It's fine if you use a real first name. Unless it's something really off the wall."

"No, call me Angie, then." That part was normal enough. "I assume you're all Blazers," I said.

"Most of us have been to the school," he said. "Among other skills. The technicians," he pointed at three, "have relevant support training. We're good in space, on the ground, on surface transport including ocean, and pretty good with accents and languages."

"Then where do you want me to take you and how do we get there?"

"Well, to start with, we have a transport, registered out of Alsace, and we can ID as crew."

"I've been to Alsace recently," I said. "They're pretty strict on documents."

"I'm told they were. The ship is real. We have these names for that purpose."

"Okay," I said. So, these were professional spies. This was something they'd been working on.

He said, "I'm Juan Sylvestre Gaspardeau." He extended hands, we shook. "I'll be acting captain." He looked about twenty-five our years, very fit. They were all very fit. Far too fit for lifetime ship crew. I mean, you can maintain that shape, but it takes a lot of work. I carry weights in G, and try to gym when I can, then go dancing. I'm in good shape, but not what I was when active duty. This guy was. Toned, tan, dark/dark hair and eyes, and a faint arch to his nose.

"Shannon Patrick," offered the guy next to him. He had ruddy-blond hair a shade lighter than mine, lighter skin, was quite tall, and lean to the point of being wiry. "First officer."

Sebastian Rujuwa was a rock. He was huge all over, not just fit. He looked like he could move cargo cubes by himself. He looked to be a mix of Zulu and Chamorro.

"I do engines," he said, and I wondered how he'd get into most access tubes.

Roger Chalfant was almost normal looking, just toned. He had a glint to his eyes that made me wish I'd met him socially. He was measuring me for dinner. He was the purser.

Dylan Rausch was an odd mix I couldn't place. "Maintenance," he said. "Of anything."

That group had one woman.

"Mira Chesney Zelimir," she said. She was my size, of very mixed ancestry, and looked like a gymnast, only too tall, taller than me. "Astrogation, life-support, and equipment."

Gaspardeau pointed at the others and said, "Our technical staff can provide pretty much anything we need. At first it was a challenge, now it's just hilarious."

"Jack Geranio," said the one. He was plenty fit, but not the obvious gym monsters the rest were.

Teresa Kusumo looked Indonesian and European, very common for Grainne, not that common anywhere else. She was also a bit mousy-looking. "I do equipment maintenance."

"Mohammed Larssen," the last one said. I could just see the Arabic under the Scandi, under the Grainne tan.

He was my height and didn't look as imposing, but that was because his torso was a tube. He wasn't fat, he just had a very straight build.

Gaspardeau said, "Call me Juan, Angie. Or 'captain' when we get into flight."

"Will do, Juan."

"We need to get you ID to go with ours. Then we have to load up. Teresa, get her going."

"Will do. Angie, I need to ask details."

She got all my vital stats, then faked things like my birthdate and place. A div later I had a new set of cards, chips and scans for my neck wallet. They all looked well-used and well-stamped. In fact, they covered most of the places I'd been professionally. It did say I'd been with this crew for a month, and they even gave me some velcro patches to show I was contract crew. My Alsacien ID said I was "Angelie Brigitte leBlanc." It sounded very pretty. I spent a few minutes getting the pronunciation right. I was half-Alsacien, quarter-Japanese from old Japan and a quarter Caledonian. I had no idea how well those IDs would hold up to detailed analysis, but I didn't think they were supposed to. They were just supposed to pass checkpoint scans. They looked good enough for that, and I had no idea about database interaction.

Then I told them everything I knew about what I'd seen recently, and they asked non-stop questions.

"Does this insignia look familiar?"

"How many space engineers? Either ratio or numbers?"

"Did you see any of their equipment?"

I was able to ID some units by insignia, and some of

the crated gear. I gave the numbers I could, locations, and we compared it to the lodging capacities of the stations and my perceptions of available space.

Garweil was present for some of this, and had a tablet with notes. I sat with her and noticed the screen listed "Facilitator Angeleyes."

"Isn't that a little dangerous?" I asked.

"No one knows your name except me. It's in a sealed file not attached to any net. There will eventually be another encrypted log sent to HQ. It's a reference only used in this context so I can find the file."

"That's good," I admitted. "What happens if you die or the station gets melted before that gets sent?"

"Then you never existed and you don't get paid."

"Uh huh," I said in disgust.

She shrugged. "If it comes down to that, none of us are likely to survive anyway. I was completely serious about this being war to the knife."

"Yeah," I agreed.

I was a spy. I had no idea how to be one. I should probably get some loads on the subject when I could.

I was pretty sure spies didn't live long.

I wondered if I'd figure out how to bail if I needed to.

The rock had a long portable docking assembly, something the engineers had put together from either spare parts or some made-for-wartime kit. It swayed in odd bounces from the harmonics of people and loaders moving through it.

I saw *Mad Jack* at the end. Before that were three smaller boats, two supply tugs, and two others that looked like old civilian or conversion craft. The first one was my destination.

It didn't have a name on the lockway. I knew it was named *NCA Henri Pieper*. The hull design looked fifty Earth-years old, which wasn't great, but I knew of older ones.

I swam aboard and realized this was already starting out hazardous. *Pieper* was not in great shape.

Juan was waiting, and said, "Yes, she's rough. We had to take what we could get, cheap."

"I understand," I said, as I brushed some peeling laminate off the lock controls. That would have to come off before it clogged vents or got into someone's eyes.

The galley was old. The infirmary had adequate civilian gear, but nothing for serious battle trauma. Many of the meds were within months of expiration. That's not as critical with modern storage and the ability to reprocess, but it's still less than ideal.

I was glad I didn't know anything about engines. I wasn't sure I wanted to know what they were like. I did recognize the controls. I've been on ships fifty E-years old. I changed my guess to seventy. I had no idea where they got spare boards. Then I realized some of them were newer boards mounted in cases fastened to the existing cases. The air plant was old, with lots of brazed and epoxied repairs, but it seemed sound. I assumed the tech crew trusted it. They'd be as dead as the rest of us if it failed.

I stowed my gear in the locker under my bunk. All three females were in a bunkbay made for four, the men in another, with Juan and Shannon in officer staterooms.

There was little privacy, but at least they had a good shower, with jet sprays all around.

They had a hold full of cargo. I figured out a lot of it was supplies for them to use—vacsuits, tools, refined metals for electronic supply. Chemicals for explosives. You'd have to know what you were doing, and it was all tagged for delivery. But I found out by accident later that all the masses were slightly off. They could make stuff disappear and still be on manifest for payload.

I wondered when and where it was going to go, and how they'd keep it hidden. I assumed they had a plan, and there are a number of places you can stow stuff on a ship so it can't be found without a plate by plate sonar or mmw scan. No, I'm not going to tell you. It varies by ship and I might need to do it again.

There were a handful of small arms aboard, but nothing bigger than a standard rifle. Some were hunting rifles or shotguns, some appeared to have been acquired from terry gangs, and they had stuff from several generations and militaries. I could swear a couple of them were a century and a half old. There was even a revolver, if you've ever seen one of those on a history load.

A couple of the rifles were gorgeous. Carved stocks inlaid with engraved metal work. They were high-end hunting pieces. Except, I took a closer look at one, and the engraving wasn't hand done. They were clones. Still, they were tagged from a supplier, to a receiver, which meant they weren't really our business, except as cargo. I hoped that would work, and I wondered what they planned to do with them. Or perhaps they were actual cargo. There was so much in cubes, TEUs, pallets, cages and nets I wasn't sure which was which.

I helped make sure it was all pinned and tied, and went EVA with Roger and Dylan to attach a short cargo train. It wasn't much, but if we were a tramper, we needed to look like one at least.

"Roger," I asked.

"Yes, Angie?"

"I assume you have some sort of track of all this."

"Yup."

"It's all bound for destinations?"

"Yes, everything is itemized and billed."

"Except the bits that are overmass."

He raised an eyebrow and smiled. "Well, occasional errors do happen. Better to estimate slightly over for mass ratio balancing."

"Natch," I agreed.

I didn't want to know more. They'd already started something.

CHAPTER 14

I still don't know where that rock was. I think there were at least three, because I talked to other people who'd gone from them to the Jump Points, and unless some megafast drive was involved, they were all within a few days flight of a Jump Point. Since they were in the outer Halo, not in-system, that meant there had to be multiples.

Mira and Juan dialed up the drive until we were above Grainne G, probably at one hundred thirty-five percent of Earth G. I had to guess, because I'd never experienced natural E-g, and it had been years since I'd felt G-g. Whatever, we moved at a good clip, and five days later we were in pattern for Jump Point 2 back to Caledonia.

I had a flashback to *Churchill*. I'd crewed on her for two weeks, and served in combat, and I felt crappy for running out on them. Part of it was I knew I was less likely to die here, though more likely to be captured. If I did die, it would be quick. But I wanted to live, and I guess that colored my departure. I wished *Churchill* well.

I had no idea at the time what their mission or combat status was.

That was how most of the war was for me, honestly. I wasn't sure where we were a lot of the time. I didn't know who the targets specifically were, or what, until after an explosion. We did a lot of running for our lives.

The food was decent enough. Much of it was pre-prep, but Roger and Teresa were both good cooks and switched off with me. I'd figured to be bored in my cubby, but Juan was captain and insisted we run through all the drills—Reactor Overload, Puncture, Dutchman, CO_2 Overage, everything. I was brisk enough, but they were very rusty. So we ran through again, and they were spot on. I remember the klaxon sounding for Puncture, and running for the nearest kit. I had the mask on in under eight seconds, per the manual, snugged to my head, and had my hand wrapped through the harness as I snapped that to a stanchion. That helps keep you inboard if an entire plate fails. I turned as I shimmied into the harness properly, and saw the rest were already in four points, adjusting the tension.

After two days of drills and inspection, we fell to and scraped paint, laminate, oxide, checked fasteners and covers, ran resistance tests and photon leak tests on all the cabling, and generally checked her over. Teresa, Jack and Sebastian fixed a few things that were shaky. I felt a lot better when that was done.

After that, Juan wanted unarmed combat and boarding practice. It seemed to make sense. We were combatants, and this was a military transport, though I wasn't sure what ten of us could do against a real warship.

Still, exercise is good. Or rather, I hate it, but I hate not exercising more. So we pulled tensioners in the hold, under G and under emgee, and Juan had us pair off for unarmed combat.

I was a bit bigger than Teresa, and she was squirmy, but I was stronger. Actually, she was fun to wrestle. I'm not much into women, but she had nice form, and feeling her strain out of my clutch was fun. She got my arm against my neck the next round, and I had to try to scissor her. She was so lithe I got my knees together and it didn't bother her at all.

After ten minutes of struggling, I had about three points on her. I wanted more practice.

Mohammed, who went by Mo, and Sebastian—Bast—paired off, and I thought they were going to break things. They were big, tough and bounded around the compartment, sort of a 3D sumo or Icelandic wrestle. I was sure some of those impacts hurt, but they only grunted from time to time. After a couple of minutes, Sebastian bent Mo in half over his knee, and Mo tapped out.

After Juan and Roger, I matched up with Mira. She was my size, close enough, though she was a bit taller and I thought I was sturdier and a bit better padded.

She came at me, grabbed, twisted, and she had her arm across my throat while my shoulder was bent in a way it shouldn't. She leaned in slowly, and when the nerves started firing, I tapped.

That was frightening. It had taken three seconds from contact to disable.

What was terrifying was when she and Shannon paired

off and he bent her into a pretzel in under five seconds, her hands out between her thighs and a foot behind her head with his knee across her throat. I'm sure there's money for that, naked. I just hoped they never got drunk and wanted to slapfight with me. They were insanely strong.

Had I been that out of practice and out of G? Or were they complete unarmed combat bamfs as well as everything else?

I decided I'd get into the gym and work on some muscle groups.

We didn't have much for repelling boarders. There were plenty of tools to use as melee weapons, and Juan had one stunner. The real guns couldn't come out except under extreme circumstances. Mostly we practiced depressurizing spaces and pressure-locking hatches. And really, boarder repel is a tradition, but not something that's ever going to be needed in the real world.

A lot of this was to keep us busy. Commercial ships can be lazy in between. The pay per functional work time is ridiculous, because there's little to do in between, but people need enough money to take the job. That's also why most ships have pretty damned good cooks, VR kits, and yattobytes of porn, with either simulacra or paid companions.

This was a poor tramper. We had neither of the last two. I thought about offering services, but it was too small a crew to keep any sort of emotional distance.

The next day, we apparently sent a signal to Jump Point control that we were outbound with cargo. Juan looked really tense in case. I figured the cover story was limited. What had this ship been doing previously? Was there a real crew who might be known? Had they been paid off or killed?

It occurred to me I had no idea at all who these people were, other than "military." There were rumors of Blazer teams trained for all kinds of barely legal viciousness, and someone on Mtali had wiped out an entire district. That was groundside, though, and these were spacers. Did Space Force have their own Blazers?

Still, I was on their side, and for now, it was a paid job hauling cargo.

Whatever info he'd sent checked out. We queued up, jumped into Caledonia, and took a berthing number to dock and unload cargo.

Five days later we grappled in and started undogging pods and tainers.

Roger said, "If anything odd happens, just ignore it. If you really think something's out of line, call me first, just a, 'Hey, Roger!' Got it?"

"Sure. I'll be discreet."

He clapped my shoulder and I got to work.

I lit up my loader, annoyed that it was a -4. Otoh, the others were -2s, way out of date. Mine had a plate from another ship on it, stamped out, with a riveted overplate. I was just happy they were Hevi-6s, not Isorus. Those things are horribly uncomfortable and rough to handle. I pulled the first pallet of chemical pellets and rolled down the ramp.

As I passed through the hatch, someone in gray coveralls and cap jumped up, snagged one of the boxes and pulled. The banding wasn't as tight as it could be, and it wiggled loose. Then they disappeared back underneath. I looked back at Roger, and he just nodded.

And that's how someone got hold of some chemicals for explosives. I think.

I'm sure, I know, other stuff went missing. Any time we had an overestimate, either we pulled stuff off, or someone else showed up to sign for it, or just filched it. I don't think we ever made a delivery where all the numbers matched.

When we were done, Juan asked, "Can you take us somewhere to eat? Anywhere a crew might go after finishing a load and awaiting a new one."

"Sure, how many?"

"All of us. I've contracted with Hallog to patrol the *Pieper*."

I thought about that. I guess it would help argue against us being criminal, if we'd all leave and let an outside party do that.

"Sure. I guess you want someplace where no one will know you're not Alsacien?"

He shrugged and said, "*Ça fait rien, Angie, ils ne savent pas quand même.*" I guessed what he meant, and his accent was perfect. Damn.

"Fish dinner?" I asked. "There's a great salmon and shrimp place a couple of ramps out."

"Perfect."

The guard showed up and checked in at the bottom of the ramp, Roger and Mo ran a mesh across the open hatch, Juan locked the pax hatch, and we bounded along the hub. The lead six chattered in French, and I was sure it was real, but that made me more nervous. I knew it was an act, so they were doing something, and it was probably illegal, possibly a war crime, and might get us captured or killed.

There were UN guards at the gate between dock and station. They weren't tagging people, but they were checking ID. I had the one I'd been handed, and hoped it worked. I assumed so, but I didn't know. I handed it over and looked bored.

"You're native here, Ms. leBlanc?" the goon asked. They'd gone with my existing docs and basically cloned them.

"Yes, I am."

He said, "Your accent's funny." He wasn't even really looking at me when he said it.

"I get it from my mother."

He looked up. "What, your citizenship or your accent?"

I rolled my eyes and acted as if it was a come on. "Both."

"So what's that in your pack?" he said, looking at the screen next to him.

"A lock wrench."

"What does it lock?"

Damn, this jerkweed was a grounder.

"Airlocks."

"Okay. It's just that it's shaped and massive enough to be a weapon."

"Yeah, but that would be illegal," I said. I tried to look clueless.

He seemed completely serious as he said, "That's why I asked."

They definitely weren't sending their better troops. I wondered if he knew his general orders, or if they even had any. I still remembered mine.

Teresa was behind me. The others had split up. We all regrouped and made small talk about "Here she comes" to avoid comments that would piss off the idiots at the gate.

We bounced down three ramps, G increasing slightly as we went. The first level is all urgent stuff for spacers— transcoms, oxy, power sources, customs agents, stuff like that. The next is really cheap stuff, the third is much better.

The Silvery Catch was at the high end of my budget, just where a lot of crews went to relax after a haul, especially if they had a day or two layover. They had a huge holo of a swordfish over the entrance. It covered an emergency pressure curtain that could deploy down. Most stuff this close to the docks had reinforcement in case of a crash causing a leak.

The server was cute, and I wondered how she got here, because her physique was groundsider, even more than mine. She had a wedge do with blond highlights and was cheerful without being icky.

I do like salmon. I had mine with a teriyaki lime glaze and mushrooms on a bed of rice noodles with broccoli. It was moist, flaky and delicious. I've been told that describes me, too. The others chose anything from whiting to buffalo shrimp. Juan and Sebastian ordered chicken. It was good, and we had a couple of drinks each, while Juan, Roger and Dylan swapped jokes in French, and the rest of us spoke English. Mira's French was pretty good. I understood one word in five when they spoke slowly.

We loped back up to low G, the booze making us even dizzier. Or at least it made me dizzier. Juan glanced over his locks, signed off on the rentacop's phone, and we boarded for the night. We had another day and a half before our scheduled slot out, and about empty masscube to fill if we could find contracts. We were actually working as a freighter so far.

In case you're just a groundsider—the primary things shipped between planets are people and luxury goods like gems, foodstuffs that grow in specific environments and original artwork. Most other stuff is cheaper to do with fabricators and transferred files, since you only have to pay for the data once. But if a ship is jumping through, they're going to charge for data. That market isn't very expensive, but it depends on how critical the info is and on how fast it must be transferred, so there's some variance in price, and all ships that can take in data right up to Jump, and resend on arrival. Then, some are bonded and Space Material and Data Transfer Accord rated for secrecy.

However, between habitats, all kinds of stuff xfers. There's a lot less energy involved in near-space transit and through the Jump Points. So the stations near them are huge with populations in the hundreds of thousands, and the ones in Sol system actually can have millions, though they're scattered through linked habitats. The outer systems just run shuttles. Most systems have transfer stations, too, partway between the industry and the point habs.

Once stuff is in space, it tends to stay there, swapped around as needed. Organics, metals from Govannon (everyone deals with Prescot Deep Space), repair parts, tools, and even medicine if it's faster to ship a nano then get the data and build it yourself.

So right up to the last div or even hour, someone might have a package or shipment they need sent, and pay for it if you have mass-cube left. Then there's personal documents and digital data.

We had a day and a half. We'd try to max out on that mass-cube and data to make a bit more profit.

I had music, vid, sens and a mostly private berth. We'd dogged tarps up to screen it into cubbies. For very private time the head had a locking shower with interactive holo.

When I overheard Juan and Shannon talk about "Sol system," I got nervous.

"Is that safe?" I asked.

"Probably not," Juan said. "What do you know about their Jump Point Three?"

"They're pretty good at keeping everything patrolled. They tag everyone, even short transients. They also scan all cargo and try to inspect or check bills of lading."

"Heh," he said. "You think they scan all cargo."

"They do."

"They maintain that image. We've proven they don't."

"Oh?"

"You can figure it out," he said. He wasn't going to tell me. I assumed they'd done this before. So either there were regular smugglers, which was likely, or they'd planned ahead for this war. That was possible, but bothered me.

If we picked up anything special here, I wasn't aware of it. Cubes, cargotainers, vac-packs. We had a leisurely load to start with, and Roger had a load plan for the intended manifest. I put stuff where he said and let him worry about the thinking.

I expected we'd have a rush toward departure time. Lots of transshipments look for available craft, or get delayed, or travel space-A, or hope for a discount on an already full load. It's how trampers stay in business.

It was eight hours and a bit until departure when Shannon said, "Angie, can you come dockside with me? I'd like some info."

"Sure. What?"

"Can you show me a couple of emergency safehouses here? Do you have any?"

"Bypassing the gate, hiding out for a nap and some privacy, or being invisible?"

"Whatever you have."

They wanted proof I was bona. It made sense. Worst case, I was in Caledonia.

"Okay. Dark coveralls, and follow me."

I went to my cubby, found a maintenance cover, pulled it on and met him back at the cargo lock. He was dressed the same. He handed me a badge that would clear me out and back in through the dock.

I led with chatter, and hoped he'd catch on and play along.

"So we're off the ship," I said. I was quiet and conversational, but paranoidly assumed someone might listen. "You realize the captain will be a bit ticked if he finds out we're sweating together."

"He won't find out," he said, and gave me a grin that almost seemed real. But I knew he'd got the meaning.

There was the "AUTHORISED PERSONNEL ONLY" sign, and I said, "This way." I slipped past and into a door that led to a cleaning closet. That was smart because it gave distance to stuff they cared about. It was stupid because it was easy, unsecured cover. A few seconds later, he was in behind me.

"This is one," I said. "Good for a quick snog or a spread if you're adventurous."

"Are you?" he asked. It took me a moment to realize he meant that strictly professionally. He was asking if I had.

"I have been. Now and again and again."

"Go on," he said, and it took me a bit more to realize he meant about hideouts.

"Up there," I said. "The grill pulls off, and there's a large air plenum. That's used . . . not often, but it's not that uncommon . . . and laborers use it to get past gates when they miss a sched. They'd report anyone really suspicious and figure to get a slap and a bonus for stopping a smuggler or whatever."

"Got it," he said, looking up. I'd had to toe the shelf to get up. He could reach it unassisted. If he was fit enough, he could probably spring up and pull.

"This way," I said. I cracked the door, checked, stepped back out and around into the main passage again. He followed.

Down two ramps was an under-ramp stowage, that locked. We went around behind it and I pointed, then kept walking.

Once around again, I whispered, "That takes a

standard key all the maintenance use. All it has is cleaning carts, vacuums, things like that. If you wait until traffic dies down, it's a quiet place to rest or sleep. They change the key periodically, but I spread with one of them two years ago and he let me have the login. It updates me when I hit system."

"Do I get that, too?" he asked, leaning close as if we were flirting heavily.

"Of course," I said, and licked the tip of his nose. Damn, this was distracting. He was built, smart, had a lot of charisma and I hadn't been properly boned in weeks. Shipboard release was work, not play, and not the same. It was more like petting a cat than real sex.

"One more?" he asked. "Somewhere more private?"

I'd shown him two closets. He wanted something more serious, to prove I was.

"How long do we have?" I asked.

"A couple of hours at least."

"Just enough time," I said. "You can't rush these things."

I'd have to go in the back way from here. I hadn't done that before.

"It would be easier with blue coveralls for station staff, but these will work," I said. "Can we get a bit dirty?"

"Yes."

"Find some grease or dust as soon as we get into the service passage," I said.

Getting into the service passage wasn't too hard, but I did have to shim the latch. I carry a small tool that has a reflective surface that fools a non-locked latch into thinking it's been opened.

I had it out, he ran a hand down my wrist, glanced that way, and shifted his eyebrows to silently ask, "Want me to do it?"

I let the card go and he stretched up with both hands, touched the doorframe, waved it, and stepped slightly back as it opened.

Once inside, I glanced around, pointed low at a dumpster with some rags and other "clean" waste, and we walked over to it. I grabbed one, rubbed it between my hands and across my brow, then wiped it down the coveralls and across my ass. I was a well-worn laborer now, as far as anyone looking could tell.

Looking like that, I led the way down the length. It doesn't quite circle. It crosses another one that's polar rather than circumferential, and it stops before the next bay.

I spoke regularly, so it sounded normal. "We're needed down at Chinchy's in ten. This isn't really authorized, but as long as we go straight there, we should be okay."

We passed some guys unloading a flat behind a restaurant. It looked like new equipment. Two glanced up, and I said, "Sorry, can't help or would."

"Yeah, you better get back into transient passage," he said.

"Working on it," I replied, with a tone of *go screw*.

Past them, there were occasional others, but no one said anything, most didn't really notice, and those who did just sort of stared to make sure we kept walking. This was trespass, but mild.

Then I waved my thumb and ducked into a little side niche. This had a door that was almost a hatch.

"Watch this," I said, and punched the code I had from my phone. It clicked, I opened it, and he followed me through. Inside it was dark. This was a conduit for water and sewage, and it was hot, dank and almost pitch black. There were emergency lights every hundred meters or so. Actually, probably exactly one hundred meters.

He whispered, "Can we talk?"

"At a whisper, yes. There are camps out here from time to time. Refugees, homeless people, petty criminals, some of all that and more. If they're found, they get sent wherever home is or to ground."

"That's expensive."

"Yeah, they're very decent like that, though of course, a lot of us don't want to be on ground. But at least . . . I guess they're somewhere."

"How often do they sweep for them?"

"Every few weeks. The campers get good at moving around."

"Should we look messy?"

"Some do," I said. "Some are smugglers. Some scrape a living acting as go-betweens and shoppers. They look nicer. If someone can save, or has skills, they might find a slot on a near-derelict and relocate."

"I'm told there's a lot of these at Ceileidh and Breakout."

"Yes, and it's easier to make a living there, but harder to survive. Most of these can beg for assistance from the government and get it."

"Yeah. We actually do save some, though. We just can't save all."

"No one can."

"How do we get out of here?" he asked.

"Down this way about two hundred meters. There's five little alcoves along the way. A board or cloth hanging up," I pointed at the first one, "indicates it's taken. It's rude to shove in until at least a third of a day goes by. If you get snoopy, they might be armed and mean, or drugged, and the community of sorts will come after you as well."

He looked around as we walked, and I was pretty sure his shades were taking images.

"They'd leave us alone?"

"Mostly. If they thought we were doing what we are they'd turn us in themselves."

"Got it," he said.

The exit was behind a dumpster behind a restaurant. The dumpster wasn't supposed to block the access, but there wasn't anywhere else to put it. That passage was full. I gather they paid an occasional bribe of a meal to the safety inspector, and he mostly looked away.

"Straight back now," I said. "We're too dirty for this area."

"We should have brought spares."

He handed me a wash wipe, and I cleaned my face and hands at least.

In twenty segs we were back at the dock.

There was a note waiting, though. Shannon told us, "The UN has banned the use of V-suits by anyone not assigned to station personnel and authorized. They're worried about clandestine attacks. We can offload ours here for some credit in lieu. We'd rather not risk them on a search."

"Crap," I said. I'd paid good money for my suit, even if I'd been reimbursed for some of it. It was a professional tool.

I wanted to argue, but couldn't. I complied and handed the case over.

"Thanks," he said. "I'll confirm turnover and get a receipt, just in case."

In case of what? I'd never see it again, and I figured they'd offer five percent of actual value. I was wrong. I got fifteen percent.

In the meantime, loading started, and I joined in to help, with all the internal and racked 'tainers.

CHAPTER 15

✛

At the last minute, we had a passenger.

We weren't really set up for them, but Roger cleared out a compartment that was mostly pantry, and rolled in a folding rack. With that, comm access and agreed use of our shower and head, he settled in. He was slightly old, slightly gray, in really good shape, and quiet. He nodded all around, shook hands limply for his mass, and went to secure for launch.

We shoved out and immediately queued for transit across system, and then to Earth, which seemed like a dangerous thing to taunt. We were enemy combatants in disguise, and regardless of the bad publicity, could be executed at once. No one had done that in the colony battles, officially, but I'd heard rumors. I also knew some people got spaced from habitats, unofficially. I'd seen bodies twice.

I was curious as to why we'd taken him on. We didn't need a lot of money, and presumably had some clandestine backing. Yet here he was, going to Earth.

We actually went in-system and grav-slung around their gas giant, Titania, which I never remember without looking it up. It was pretty, in bands of bronze and red and amber.

It was four weeks, and the passenger only left his cabin to shower, and usually on third shift.

Four times he actually ate in the mess, but then, we mostly didn't either. He didn't talk much. No one else questioned him, so I didn't.

I mostly stuck on main shift, took care of meals, took care of cleaning. Roger handled cargo monitoring himself. Teresa pulled maintenance on controls and mechanicals as needed. Otherwise, we continued our workouts. Mira had third shift command, so we often didn't see her. She slept while we worked, and we tried to keep the noise down.

I helped Teresa strip and clean a shower head that got clogged. It was an easy job, but I was bored.

"How did you learn about all these places?" she asked.

"Clubbing, and hanging out with local drunks who want to be clever," I said. "It's just like the treehouse or cut through a field groundside."

"Only it's all artificial."

"Right," I agreed. "Most people have no idea how much maintenance space there is. Usually thirty percent of a station is support for the rest."

"It isn't even that secret," she said. "Hold right there and crank that down." She handed me one wrench and put another somewhere else.

"No," I said. "Just not something most people pay attention to."

"Do you have a favorite?" she asked.

I shrugged. "Depends what I'm doing. If I need sleep, Caledonia Three. If I want to dance and get spread, NovRos One, right across. The culture there, though." I shook my head.

"It's reported to be pretty rough."

"It's not if you avoid those elements, but it can be if you don't."

That was the most excitement we had on that leg. Which was good, I guess.

Once across on a far arc of the system, we ignored the station and instead went straight into queue to Jump. I wondered about that, because dead legs cost money, but it does happen. I really didn't know enough about what we carried to guess.

We jumped, and that put us only hours from Earth's JP3 station. But, there are so many craft going through that the wait for a slot can take longer than the flight. We were parked in a holding orbit far out from Haumea, which is some sort of dwarf planet. It was two and a half days before they called and slotted us.

I didn't realize then, but the private habitat Starhome across from the point was the original station during build, and was the first control center. When it got abandoned, the owners claimed it under salvage rights. There were a couple of those in Sol system. I have no idea how they survived.

During the wait, I saw our passenger pretty much at meals. He spent most of his time in his cabin and his head calls were short. Even so, his presence hindered us. We didn't exercise as much, and didn't do any combat practice. I spent a lot of time on vid and sim, and took long showers that took the edge off but weren't satisfying.

The station is so big that craft actually dock inside. Roger and I did nothing while the local crew detached the cargo train. They charge for that, of course, and you don't have any choice. It was supposed to "save money" and "level the playing field," but the big shippers don't lose anything, and the small shippers can't pay less wages for a leg, so they pay their crew to not work, while paying the station crew to work.

They weren't terribly slow, but an experienced ship crew could have done better.

Tiny one-crew rocket tugs came to meet us, and bumped us in a complicated game of tag. There was even a resonance to the bumps, increasingly fast and decreasingly noticeable, until we skidded down a long rail into the dock. It actually airlocked us in, vac-clamped the hull, pressurized and opened the inner hatch. Then huge motors chugged us into the bay proper.

Clamps secured us, with loud thumps, and that was scary, too. We were locked inside, strapped down, and couldn't leave without their say-so. We'd have scannable tags as soon as we debarked, and being found without one would get you harassed and questioned. A lot.

"Thanks, all," the passenger said. He had two large travelbags, shouldered one, dragged the other, and strode down the ramp.

"Take care, sir," Dylan said to his back.

I had to wonder a bit then, and more later. Given his build and silence, was he one of the infiltrators we sent to

Earth proper? Had I played a part in wiping out a large chunk of humanity?

But as fast as he debarked, we had Customs and Safety Inspectors approaching. Four of them.

"Good day, is the captain available?" one called up.

"I am Captain Gaspardeau," Juan said, with a bare touch of Alsacien accent. I couldn't tell it from a natural one. I wondered if they could.

"Permission to board for inspection," the team leader said. She wasn't really asking. It was a formality.

"Certainly," he agreed, with a smile that looked strained. It was the right level of strain for this. I wondered if he'd been here before.

They came up, and in a few minutes had logged in for the manifest and crew data.

One of them walked over to me. "Ms. leBlanc?" he asked.

"Yes. Cargo and cook."

"Here's your Personal Safety Tracking Unit. Have you been in Sol system before?" He handed over an ID dangly.

I had no idea what my cover background was, so I said, "Better tell me about it to make sure."

He rattled off the whole spiel from memory about "will respond in emergencies" and "enables easier access to support functions" because they wouldn't let you in without one and you better "report if lost or stolen, at once" or there would be "severe penalties for loss."

"Got it," I said.

The team leader looked up from her screen and said, "There are weapons listed here."

Roger took that. "Antiques, with licenses and EUCs, being shipped to collectors. They are secured and double sealed."

"I need to see the seals, please."

"Sure. Angie, can you pull C Five Two out?"

"I think that's double stacked, but I can if you give me a few."

"Take your time," she said. She didn't mean that of course. We also wouldn't get her name. They don't do that in Sol, claiming we have the inspection number, and they're chipped for scan, if there's a problem. It's less friendly, though.

I unplugged the loader, rolled back and pulled two cans, stacked them aside carefully in case they reported a safety violation, and got the one they wanted. Roger opened it, they walked in, and presumably the box within the box of the antique rifles was secure as it should be.

Eventually they left. They took some real Coca-Cola and some good chocolate with them, as a gift of hospitality, and if they got that from every ship, they were doing well.

That accomplished, we could start unloading the internals.

The dock is clear space and a controlled zone. We pulled the cans, unloaded partials, consolidated for next leg based on schedule tags, then went to eat, which meant going through security, showing ID, stating a ship, stating a "purpose" for being on the station, as if "transient cargo haulers" wasn't obvious. The food was bland and overprocessed, and cost too much.

While we were eating, I thought I saw our passenger

walk by. It wouldn't be that big a deal, and I might have been mistaken.

I shopped for some basics. I needed to replace three briefers that were wearing through, I was low on chocolate, and I wanted to pull loads of some new vids. I was also trying to avoid tackling the gauntlet back to the dock. Late night had less traffic. All those stores run three shifts, so I just grabbed it late.

To get back aboard, I had to do the whole procedure in reverse: ID check, listing of where I'd been, ship I was reporting to, they had to check with the dock side of security that I'd come through, then pass me in, and take back their dangly.

I did wonder how anyone we snuck in here was going to work around those tracking danglies, but I didn't want to ask.

That's why a lot of colonies and the Freehold don't want to deal with Earth, and why stuff is so pricey in their outer habitats. Delays mean you're not working. You are consuming mass and supplies. Then you have to be inspected by snoopy assholes, then carry a doggie tag. Doggie style I'm all about. Doggie tags, not so much.

As to doggies, back at the ship, Admiral Bertrand was waiting at the corner of the lock.

"Bert!" I said and knelt down. He trotted over and sniffed my hand. A moment later he started squirming.

"Your dog?" Roger asked from above.

"He's nobody's. Admiral Bertrand Russell is a rent-a-dog."

"Huh?" He looked confused.

"He shows up, waits for permission to come aboard,

and takes a leg. He'll get off at the next stop, and find another ship. He's been doing it for three years. There's about six others around, too. They're temporary mascots."

"So he wants us to take him aboard?"

"All you have to do is tell him he's welcome."

"You're kidding." He thought I was playing some prank.

"Is he welcome?" I asked.

Roger looked around and said, "I guess. He's handsome, and has sat there behaving himself. Jack Russell Terrier?"

"I think so." Bert was lean, brown and not much bigger than a large cat.

"So what do I say?"

"Just say, 'Welcome aboard, Bert.'" Bert looked up at me, then at Roger.

Shrugging, he said, "Welcome aboard, Bert."

Bert trotted up the ramp and bumped his head against Roger's knee.

"I don't fucking believe it."

"Just find him a blanket to curl up in and a chunk of carpet in a tray he can poop in. I'll take care of him."

I was glad to see Bert. I run into former crew and former buddies now and then, but hadn't really since we started this. Seeing him cheered me up.

I laddered up to the C-deck.

"You need to report the Admiral is aboard," I told Juan.

He frowned and said, "I'm not very comfortable drawing attention to it."

"It's tradition. You have to. You'll stand out if you don't. Even Earthie controllers have a sense of humor and know who he is."

He took my advice and said, "Ah . . . Then I guess we better."

I said, "News will get ahead. When we dock, there'll be people waiting for him. He gets snacks, toys, all kinds of stuff to fly as mascot."

"Why did he pick us, then?"

"I don't know. I've flown with him once. I know his story. Maybe someone here is really a dog person."

"I am," Jack said.

"See?"

Juan asked, "Is there a particular phrasing?"

"You just note manifest on file, sealed and checked, Admiral aboard and ready to depart."

He did, and Control replied, "Understood, *Pieper*. Our respects to the Admiral. We'll report his destination. Stand by for separation."

We shoved out, and met the train at their loading terminal. Their mechanical dock with their operators attached it. After they left, we inspected it ourselves, even though that was rude, if they saw us.

Roger grudgingly agreed it wasn't a bad job, but he tightened a couple of scaffoldavits.

Once hooked, we pulled out.

Bert was great. He knew Jack and I were friends. As soon as I was off shift, he followed me to my bunk, looked up at me until I pointed to the mattress, then hopped up. He waited for me to get comfy, and curled up against the back of my legs.

It was wonderful to have a sleeping partner to cuddle with. I had pressure and warmth all night, from ass to ankle. I'd rather have someone's arm around me, but that wasn't possible. Still, he was a friend and warm.

The leg across Sol system was longer, and we had a small robot escort that was basically a beacon to make sure everyone knew where we were, as if it wasn't obvious where the main routes were. Still, they get a lot of traffic, and even if an actual collision is almost impossible, trajectory diversions cost fuel, shake containers and sometimes require a rescue response. I wasn't going to call them out on it. It made me remember, though, that Sol system is packed. There's no privacy, no escape, even their habitats are megacities.

I made sure to have hot and cold breakfast and lunch available, hot dinner, and stuff in the crew fridge for late night. Mira tended to nibble in her G couch to stay awake, and drank coffee instead of chocolate. Other than that, I was second on maintenance and cargo and didn't have a lot to do. Not as far as ship duties.

With just ourselves, we managed to get in more drill on fighting. I'd qualified in recruit training, but that was a long time ago. I was older, had spent most of the time not working out except for dancing, and a lot of that was in low G. These people held Expert ratings or more. Jack built us a striking dummy to practice punches and kicks with, and we grappled every couple of days. I got better, but I was never going to match this bunch.

When we reached SolJP2, Lucashab, there was another remote scan of our manifests, and a query from Jump Control, then a "tax" on our overload based on our

approved capacity. I don't get it. It's not as if it takes any
more energy to open a Jump Point for a larger ship. Open,
closed. Those are your options.

CHAPTER 16

We jumped for NovRos and started in to their station. It's in orbit around a large dwarf.

The mesh loads updated, and news came through. Someone had just blown up one of the cargo linkers at SolJP3. Then they'd damaged one of the dockways. Station efficiency was down four percent.

"Was that our passenger?" I asked.

Mira said, "They don't have any suspects."

"Right, but I meant . . . never mind."

Either they didn't know or they weren't saying.

Four percent was a significant down, on top of the usual repairs that are always ongoing. If they had no suspects, there could be more.

And I may have given him places to hide out between attacks.

I actually felt pleased. I was pretty sure my conclusion was correct. We were starting to hurt them, even if only in small amounts. I wondered what was next.

We joined the queue and did routine maintenance and

management. Earth had managed to mis-tetris some of our tainers, so we'd have to undog, unload, reload and redog. We'd be doing extra work because of them, and no compensation. Roger and I worked out a plan for that.

They were all better at math than me. I can do cargo stuff. He came up with an algorithm for moving the tainers to minimize time and movement. Then he drew up a flowchart for it.

We pulled into orbit and Mira started the delicate process of sneaking up on a satellite. I know the rough problem is that faster takes you to higher orbit. So you slow to drop into a lower, faster orbit, then accelerate to match. It's a lot harder in low orbits. At a million kilometers it's not that interesting.

We moved in with little burps of engines and retros, chemically fueled. That gave her about sixty Earth-seconds of maneuver time. It's not a lot.

It was also disorienting in an old ship. I was dizzy and slightly uncomfortable, not quite nauseous when she got us to the davit and it snagged us.

Mira had IDed us moving in. Once docked, Juan took over, zipped down the manifest and reported to station control.

He concluded with, "Admiral Bertrand is aboard."

"Uh . . . understood, *Pieper*. We'll have a receiving party ready."

"'Receiving party?'" he asked me, looking confused.

"I don't know," I said. "I've never heard of that for him."

He asked back, "Traffic Control, what do you need from us for receiving?"

A different voice said, "*Pieper*, please disregard. New crew were unfamiliar with the Admiral. They know who he is now."

"Oh, good."

Really, it was. Actual honors would have been a problem. But we'd pranked a new guy without even trying. Funny.

Once we connected the tube, Bert was all ready to head off on his next adventure.

"Bye, Bert," I said. He rubbed his head against my knee and waited for scritches. He woofed once, did the same with Jack, almost bowed to Roger, then trotted down the tube for the lock to the station.

There were a lot of UN uniforms here. Several had engineer insignia.

"They are building that station you mentioned," Juan said. "It looks like they plan to have rapid response in every system."

"So they can do to others what they did to us?" I asked.

"I would assume so. Though the threat of it is likely to pre-empt the need."

We unloaded, ate, and waited for cargo. Roger had several contracted loads waiting. We apparently had dock time to spare, because Juan was in no hurry. I asked.

"I'm juggling dock fees against potential loadout," he said.

"How full are we?" I asked.

"Seventy-three percent."

"Right. I'm guessing with this frame you'd like to hit eighty." It was a wild-ass guess based on feel.

He said, "At least. Want to show us around?"

"I can. What are you looking for?"

"Surface access or crust."

I couldn't think of any positive reasons for that. But that was why we were there.

"I'll need to explore, but I have ideas." I'd been outside the hull of another station once before.

"How many?"

I understood his question.

"I can take two, I think."

"Jack and Mira." He waved.

"Okay."

They looked at me, and I said, "Basic coveralls, we'll hide our ship suits once we're away from the dock. What do we need to take?"

"Vid and notes," Jack said. "And I have a small probe."

"They track phones closely."

He nodded. "Yes, this one doesn't connect, it only has internal functions."

They both also had small backpacks with water and protein bars. The coverall they handed me was the exact leaf green color station staff wore. So this had been planned well ahead.

A few minutes later, after a head break and some water, we were ready.

The dock runs through the axis and they use centrifugal force for gravity, like most stations. Since it's an inflated rock, it's a long cylinder with irregular surface inside and out, so the inside has a pressure hull. There's a gap between that and the rock that's mostly sealed, but there are access hatches. At least, I was sure there were, but I'd never looked for one.

I went looking through zen, I guess. I didn't know where they were, but I knew where they might be. There's a large cargo lock actually through the surface from when construction was first done. It's mostly sealed, but they leave it in case they have to do a really major repair. It's at .2G, five hundred mils from the zero meridian.

There's a ring of reinforcement around it, and seals. I figured outside that ring would be some kind of access between the hulls.

The passages were a maze, twisty and all alike. They all led toward that huge lock, then turned down or past it. We went around, and up, and around again. I didn't want to do that too often. We'd get noticed. After the second pass we found a bathroom and slipped out of our shipsuits to the green coveralls.

On the next loop, I found it. There was a hatch back into station maintenance, with someone just coming out. Past him I could see where the outer hatch was. There was stuff piled against it, tools and scrap, so it wasn't used often.

Jack walked right in, and said, "Clear that stuff, and make a note for production control that it was blocked." He had a tablet with screen up, and made marks on it as we moved the junk. He grabbed a tool belt that was on a shelf and hung it over his shoulder. He grabbed two harnesses off the rack and gave one to Mira.

One guy walked by, saw the tablet, and kept moving. It's unbelievable how well that trick works.

Jack even had some real-looking safety tags, or they may have been real. He opened the latch and clipped one to the lock mechanism so it wouldn't close, and marked it with initials "URF, 1426 hours."

I followed him through, and Mira followed me. He opened the outer hatch and left it.

"You can stay inside if you want," he said. "If anyone asks, we're doing a hull survey and will be back soon."

"I can do that or come along and help."

"It's probably better if you stay here," he said. I took it as a strong suggestion.

So I stayed there, while they latched onto a channel rail and started bounding low-G ward between the hulls.

I waited, not diddling my phone, because it was turned off and unpowered for privacy. I had no idea what was going on or how long it was. Now and then I heard voices on the other side, and hoped we weren't going to get locked into deadspace.

And it was cold. The pressure was okay, but a bit low. But that rock was dull gray, painted with some sort of air and crack sealant, and directly in space. It had to be bright outside to be visible, in addition to having beacons, so it had a high albedo, which meant it didn't absorb even the light that was available.

There was frost on that outer wall, and I wished for more insulation. I was cold, and not moving made it worse.

It was a long time, with me shivering and bored and my ears, toes and fingers going numb, before I heard them coming back.

"You go first," Jack said. "Tell us if we're clear now, or need to wait."

I popped the lock, scanned around as I stepped

through, faced him and nodded. They slipped out behind me, and Mira started off ahead. Jack waited about twenty seconds and took the other catwalk. I hung around a few moments and then followed.

A local hour later, we were back aboard.

The crew were nervous. I doubt anyone outside noticed, but I'd been with them long enough to pick up the tingles. The other two had already cycled through a hot shower to warm up. I went in as Mira came out. A deluge of tub-hot water took the chill out of my bones and ears.

We loaded cargo, and Mira called for an early slot.

"We can still pack more in," I said.

Juan said, "We'll be fine."

That night, we detethered and queued for ram.

As we shoved out, there was a strong vibration, a massive bounce, and then alarms started howling.

"That's a bit close," Juan said, as an emergency flash ordered ALL OUTBOUND IN STAGE THREE CONTINUE UNDOCKING." There were other alarms, including, ATMOSPHERE LEAK, PRESSURE FAILURE, CONTROL FAILURE, HULL INTEGRITY FAILURE. RUPTURE OVER CONTROL CENTRAL. CASUALTIES. MEDICAL RESPONSE. ENGINEER EMERGENCY RESPONSE. MAN OVERBOARD. EMERGENCY SEALS ACTIVATED.

It just kept going.

I asked, "Did we plant a bomb over their space control?"

"They seem to have had a rupture right over the military management cell."

I was sure Jack and Mira had mined it.

"Casualties?" I asked.

"Oh, yes. There were sixty-seven people in that pressure, all of them management and control, and I doubt any had V-suits."

I'd helped kill them, and I felt worse than if I'd done it myself.

I reminded myself this was war, and those were military personnel.

We weren't in uniform, though.

There'd also probably been some maintenance personnel either in the hull like we had been, or near open locks.

We were bound for Alsace, and this was a major test, because it was our "native" space.

Juan and Mira spoke what sounded like flawless Alsacien French as we docked. It flowed like water.

Still, this ship had come from here, and it wasn't impossible we'd run into former crew.

They also didn't know their way around the station. They'd seen maps, but that's not the same as being aboard.

"We'll follow you, Angie," Juan said. "We'll gaggle around and you lead, just toss your head for directions. We'll be fine."

"I haven't been in Alsace from this direction in several years. I may be out of date."

"Understood. Do your best."

Alsace is a younger colony, and still growing. The station had originally been a hubbed ring. Now it was a double. The styles were slightly different due to improved construction methods, which probably irritates artistic types, but it meant newer tech, so I liked it.

A lot of business moved into the newer ring. Established outfits remained in the old one, anyone who could move to the new one easily, had. Both sides were only about half occupied, with large gaps not even built out, much less populated.

"I can't help much," I said, once I'd looked around. "I know where access hatches and such should be, and there's lots of empty cube I'm sure isn't occupied yet."

"That's fine. We don't have any business here yet. It's good to just be shipping."

True. If they struck a target at every station, they'd be IDed in three? four? And done.

What I did do was show them some of the businesses I knew. Mo and Roger took parts to several shops for "repair." That got them introduced and on file as clean. The repairs were basic, recurring maintenance that wouldn't draw attention.

Alsace can't afford to ship a lot in, but they try to ship out for the trade balance. They have exotic woods and a few mineral stones, local fish that's human compatible and apparently very tasty, and the outer planets have easily scoopable methane. Gas divers are yet another breed of spacer, though a lot of people don't think of them as spacing, since they stay so close to planets.

We did dinner, and I got to try flarefin, one of the fish. It was tasty, and I can't describe it. Nothing like any Earth fish. The flesh is more rubbery than flaky, but tears a bit like squid, with texture like clam, and the flavor is milder but . . . I don't know. It was good, but not better than good salmon, which is a lot cheaper.

We were loaded light mass wise, but full value wise, which is ideal.

But we were headed back for NovRos. That scared me.

CHAPTER 17

We queued, jumped back, and didn't get immediately tagged. They did have tight security with actual guards around every lock and access, though. Well, not all of them, but anything that I thought would go anywhere critical. The ones left open were okay for hiding and sleeping. I made a mental note just in case. Just keep in mind that it's not just the local gov and UN you have to worry about, but the vors and mafia.

We unloaded volatiles and some of the meats. Then Juan had us stop.

"It took a bribe, but I think we'll come out ahead. We're going to take it in-system ourselves."

"Okay." I wasn't sure why we'd do that, but I guess profit was a thing, to keep us in space.

We weren't using the spacewheel—it was a considerable way around the system, built for cargo from Caledonia. They'd probably build one eventually.

We had enough fuel, so Mira did a combination

maneuver that braked us in orbit so we'd drop straight in, and reoriented us to insert into orbit around Novaja Rossia itself.

It was a long, slow fall, and odd, as boost G started at once only barely present, then increased in odd plateaus, then tapered off the same way. The bulkheads shifted to decks and overheads and back, but nine days later we were in close proximity to their high orbital, which is in orbit around their poor excuse for a moon, a glorified captured asteroid that is barely massive enough to be spherical. It makes a good anchorage, though.

It is a grav anchorage, too. We took a parking orbit, and a lighter came up to meet us. Some of the heavier-built craft can actually land. It only pulls about .03G. But for orbiting, you move little and are easy to track.

The lighter made three trips, loping up to pull pods and haul them down on tether. They literally were that casual about the local mass. Then a cutter docked and had us sign for archaic eva-exos. An eva-exo is a pressure suit with an exoskeleton for EVA use. It doesn't have maneuver capability, but does have tethers, latches and grippies. You can stay linked easily enough. Just never forget to attach one before detaching the other. Roger and I donned them and transferred stuff from the inside hold.

We made a bit more money for this leg of the trip, though some of it had gone in bribes. We loaded up on raw mineral chunks that could be cut, polished, whatever. It's interesting how stuff is semi-precious on its home planet, and outrageously expensive in space or outsystem due to lifting cost. We declined a couple of passengers, and I didn't blame Juan. They looked mean.

But we pulled out almost empty. That's not a savings at all. I think we still came out slightly ahead even with fuel expenditure on the return, but then you add in wear and tear, spaceage and time. I don't think it was balance positive.

But, as I found out later, that wasn't the point.

We took a long, fuel-saving route toward JP6 for Earth. Most systems have JP1 with Earth, but NovRos was settled secondarily by contracting through Caledonia. Anyway, the numbers are just tags. They opened one with Earth a long time back, but it was number six at the time.

That station is also a considerable way from the point. They used an existing planetoid and just built domes, and use the same grav anchor system—parking orbits. I'm told the engineering is interesting, because the domes sit on a plain of frozen nitrogen, which would sublime to vapor if it got heated at all. They use insulated blocks for the foundations. I guess it's not any less safe than a ship, but the idea makes me twitch.

It was a fifteen-day coast with periodic course adjustments to gain shreds of economy from a couple of gravity wells, though we were distant enough from any planet I have no idea how that stuff is calculated.

I cooked, checked status on the hold—it was still there—and watched a lot of vid.

And showers. It was during a shower we had the excitement.

The shower was necessary for cleanliness in close quarters. It was a luxury, since we had few others, and a great chance to be alone. I had vibrations going and was quite filled, almost too filled behind, with hot water trickling all over. It was five segs a day when I could close my eyes and just ride my mind. I did wish we had a recspec on board, though. Some massage at least would make it even better.

I guess I'm what they call a hedonist.

Something happened, and it took me a moment to put it all together.

There'd been a loud, echoey clang. You don't get clangs in ships, unless they're metal hulled. We had modern composite molecule weave and boron shelling, with active rad shielding between. A clang wasn't possible. Then there were two more, one after the other.

Then over shipcom I heard Roger shout, "Hull breach! Hull breach! Hull breach! Seal and secure! All hands prepare for vacuum!"

Yes, echoes. Shockwaves down the passageways.

His voice got higher and quieter as he shouted, because we were losing air fast.

Klaxons sounded, lights flashed, locks shifted then slammed. We were still losing air, though.

I yanked out my toys, punched the water shutoff, and noticed the cube was steaming up but cold, as pressure dropped. I wiped my face with both hands, and headed straight for the nearest emergency O2 on the bulkhead, punched it, stretched the mask over my head, and had to do it a second time because I was shaking, and things were getting blurry. I panicked when nothing happened, then the emergency valve in it sensed the drop and popped, and oxy blew against my face. It was dizzying, sweet, buzzy. At the same time, the pressure drop made my guts ache, I farted and probably had some leakage, and my ears felt as if someone stabbed them. All in all I was about useless, but I was breathing. I could taste and smell soap and shampoo. I sucked in hard with my mouth closed, then opened it and yawned, and the stabbing pain in my ears eased off a notch or two.

"All hands to command deck." Juan's voice was tinny and high sounding.

I opened the hatch from the head, moved forward, and crap, it was even colder. There was frost in the air and condensing on surfaces.

Teresa, Mo and Jack came toward me and shoved past with patches and smoke dye. I watched it drift and swirl and suck, and she slapped a patch on an inner bulkhead. That was Shannon's stateroom. I hoped he was alive. Whatever had hit had come through the shell, the inner hull, and that bulkhead, and left scars on the passage side, too.

Teresa stared at me for a long moment, then shoved me into the lock ahead of her. With both of us in, it was tight, and our masks bumped. I was in a panic in case we dislodged them. Her skin was splotchy from pressure damage, and she seemed really nervous against naked me.

She punched to dump air in from the C-deck, and that hurt my ears the other way. It got us into pressure fast, though. The hatch popped, we shoved through, and she set it to cycle and pump so Mo and Jack could follow.

"We have pressure here," Dylan said. He was closest. "Stay masked, though. Need a coverall?"

I was still soap-smeared but dry and greasy. The water had boiled off me, and I was fucking freezing now.

"Yes," I said, as he lobbed one to me. I shimmied in

and zipped, and it helped a bit, but my toes, fingers and ears were still cold. Wrists. Ankles. It felt like I was outside in a blizzard, though it was warming up again in here.

Juan said, "Engineering is the problem. Bast says there's a punch through a control console. We're going to have to seal three breaches. Plus the one outside Shannon's cube."

I started to ask, "Is he—"

Juan said, "Yes, he's in engineering. His repair can wait."

Jack said, "I can EVA. We'll want to sandwich seal."

"Go."

"What can I do?" I asked.

Juan said, "Please understand I am very serious and will be very grateful if you can reach the galley and make some sandwiches. This is going to take hours and possibly even divs."

"I'm on it," I said. Yes, we needed to eat. I wanted to be clean, but that would have to wait for reliable pressure.

Most spaces were up now, except Shannon's stateroom, engineering and the utility hold next to it. We used the locks but only as safeties. There was no pressure diff. I cycled through, down the passage, into my cubby to take off the coverall and put on some worn, sweaty underwear and a polo, then the coverall back on top. I wiped off my feet, used dirty socks and got my spare shlippers on. I was sticky and nasty, but warm. And if you've ever tried to put on a polo over a mask, it doesn't work. I was about to stretch it up over my ass, when I realized I could unmask for the ten seconds it would take.

Dressed, I felt more functional, and warm. I went past

the head and grabbed my phone, ticked at forgetting it
earlier.

"Angie on open chat," I said. "I'll take sandwich orders
in a moment. Can you tell me what happened?"

Mira said, "We think it was a Volume Denial
Dispersed Mass Weapon. VDam. Tungsten pebbles."

I sort of knew what that was.

"Someone seeded the area?"

"Like jacks or four-sided dice meant for three-D
space," she said. "It's even slangly called 'jacking off.'"

Roger said, "Well, I'm guessing their logic was that
warships have heavier mass shields, and no civilian ship
should be in this space, and if anyone requested a variance
they'd be told 'no.'"

"So they're on to us," I said. I guessed we were in a
space we shouldn't be in, and ran into the space
equivalent of barbed wire.

Juan said, "They're on to something. But they're using
a lot of delta V and mass, not to mention operation time,
to do this. Unless it was a lucky leftover from something
else."

I didn't want to think about suffocating to death while
jilling off in the shower. Totally not my play. Would we
ever be found? And what would the recovery crew think,
finding me like that? What if they were serious thirty-
fours? Video for the mesh? Violate my frozen corpse?
What if one of the chunks hit me at flight velocity? I'd be
a crimson splash. And what about the engines?

Or was I just seriously fucking scared because I'd
almost died from enemy fire without even seeing them?
When would we eat a nuke?

"One at a time, tell me what you want for food," I said.

I couldn't even spread mustard or mayonnaise. I was shaking to shivers.

Jack came in and I fed him. Teresa went out to take over. A div later, Mo went out with Sebastian.

Jack went back out. It took that long to seal the hole outside, pull an access plate, seal it from inside as well, seal the two together, seal the inner hull, and then through the dead space behind the controls in engineering.

I spent the rest of the afternoon ruining baked trout. The butter cooked until it was sharp and they tasted like bad lobster, not good trout. No one complained.

Shannon said, "Next we need a clean, blended repair on each."

"Why?" I asked.

"Because if it looks like a patched hole, someone may ask. If there's more than one, they might guess."

"Oh, yeah." We'd been in a combat zone and had damage. That wasn't good for our cover.

"Then, three pods took damage. I don't know of a way to deal with the inside shell or the 'tainers in flight. We'll have to fix the outside as best we can and go from there."

"Will this affect our schedule?" I asked.

"No, because changing it would be noticeable. We'll continue through to Earth."

I went out with Bast to help with one of the pod repairs, handing him tools and acting as backup and company.

I do EVA to fasten cargo trains at times, and have done some routine maintenance. This was different. There was no one anywhere nearby to rescue us if anything went wrong, I understood if we came loose we'd stay in the same orbit as *Pieper*, since we weren't under boost. Still, hanging off the tether a kilometer back from the ship, which was pretty much invisible, was enough to make me clamp down and wish the tug had plumbing.

The hole we dealt with was a tear rather than a punch. It was long and oblique. Bast cut off the ripped poly, laid a patch over it and sealed it in place, and then buffed all the edges to blend it. He used vac paint very creatively to make it look old and worn.

"Doing okay, Angie?" he asked.

"Best I can," I said.

"Yeah, I hate it, too. Let's crank back up."

Cranking back up the line was straightforward. He ran the winch, we moved very slowly toward the ship. Watching the pods move past while we rotated was gut-clenching. We only had a pair of cables and strap harnesses, not a proper maintenance cage. *Pieper* had a small maintenance tug, but we didn't want exhaust wash over the pod, and those things are notional anyway. They barely hold one person, two if they're friendly, and can let you adjust a stinger or remove jammed matter from a lock.

I was very, very glad to get inside, and take another hot shower to warm up from radiating all my heat away.

We coursed back toward the Jump Point and queued up, as if we'd done a legitimate delivery on a slow orbit. I knew they didn't cross-reference schedules unless they had a reason to, but eventually, we'd give them a reason to.

CHAPTER 18

I've never liked Earth, and this was a station I'd hadn't been through since I was new to space. The station was another blown planetoid. Earth doesn't allow that anymore, but this one was old. We unloaded the rocks and other stuff, straight into quarantine, in case vacuum-transported rock contained something harmful to the environment of a station fifteen light-hours from Earth.

Still, our job was done. After that, we did dinner.

I really wasn't impressed. This was Earth, or at least Sol system, where salmon come from. It was bland and mushy. I had a seared tuna appetizer, and that was uninteresting as well.

The server said, "It's never as good up here. They need gravity to grow right. Down on Earth they're fantastic."

Possibly. Other systems raise them in emgee with no trouble.

Roger was definitely looking me over. I guess seeing

me naked and soapy had interested him more than before. I was sure he'd be great, too, but there were so many reasons not to cross that line.

He and Juan were in charge of contracting cargo. I ran bots to clean the hold, including moving some of the inboard cans to dust behind them. They get filthy after a few legs, even sealed and enclosed.

One of the other things about Earth is they don't enforce "petty" crimes against individuals. Robbery, theft, vandalism, assault and even occasional rape don't register. Misfile your docs and short them on your docking tariff, though, and you'll be facing a tactical team.

We registered as Potterite Sikhs and carried "Wands" as religious artifacts. Our wands all had one-shot stun capacitors in them, that could be yanked out the back and dumped in an emergency, such as if one had just stunned some yunk who wanted a grope inside the suit. Not me, but Mira came back one night and recharged hers. She summarized the story and let it drop.

From the news load, I guessed those capacitors carried enough juice to stun a Jump Point. The guy had contact burns, amnesia and cardiac arrhythmia. He wasn't out of the clinic for three days.

I managed to avoid using mine.

But that was the next day. The first day, after unloading and dinner, and while looking for our contracts and open lifts, was socializing.

Juan and Teresa came to me.

"You're not familiar with this station, but can you go clubbing?"

I wasn't quite sure what he meant. "As cover or for

intel? I usually do if we're not doing an immediate turnaround."

"Some of each."

I wouldn't mind dancing, but it was going to be work this time.

After thinking, I said, "I can. Tell me what you need or where to find the person."

Teresa told me, "We're trying to get ID and access strips for any of the mil and gov side facilities."

I said, "Yeah, they mostly use their implanted ID chips."

She nodded and held up a small stick. "We can mirror those, given a few minutes, but we need those few minutes in private."

"Okay. Just anyone mil or gov? Or do you have specific people in mind?"

Juan said, "Definitely the former, and if we see anyone we do have made, I can point them out. Can you link up and get them in private?"

I said, "Depends on if I like them or not."

"Of course. And you don't actually have to seduce anyone. We just need them in private for a few moments."

"Would it help if I did, though?" On the one hand, I didn't want to be a tease, on the other, I didn't want to spread for someone just to get intel. I suddenly had all kinds of moral quandaries.

"Absolutely," he said.

I shrugged. "Then I will if I can."

I was going to get paid a lot if I survived, and I'd promised to help them get all the intel they needed. I also might get spread and stretched in the process. I decided my moral issues about taking advantage of a fuck that way had to take a pass for strategy and survival.

I had to find clubs I'd like. One called Rockjam appeared to be all live music. I could handle that, but it wasn't really my type of music listed.

The Depths, though, had lots of trancy. That I could get into.

Juan said, "They're also near two other clubs we might get hits from."

"We'll start there, then."

Roger was going with me, and he was already dressed with his hair staticked up, wearing a black and silver thoracier and black kilt with edge piping. Damn, he looked smoky. With a jacket draped over his shoulders, he could distract half the ladies in whatever place we went to.

I knew some of the others came along to either overwatch or recon. Juan gave me a very simple code to find people he was interested in, which basically came down to, "Left, right, wearing this, that one." He was sure we could get away with that without triggering alarms. It made sense. People msged like that all the time while cruising.

I went for skintight purple with micropanties and a gelmesh bra. I wore "tumbler" earrings—gimballed stones inside three small hoops held in place with magnets. I left my hair natural but coiled it up and back.

The Depths was near the center of the planetoid, and there was even a large chunk of leftover regolith there. They'd built the club with it in the high overhead. G in the place wasn't above .2, just enough to keep food and drink down, and let people dance all out. I thought I'd like it.

I moved in, found a table facing the door and looking across the rear exit through the service passageway. I tagged it as occupied and punched for a drink. I took hard lemonade. Roger sat down with me, and I got oriented with the place.

It had a lot of potential, with the rock and the hub struts nearby, but they'd just stuck in some lights and booths around a basic tesselighted dance floor.

They had heavy traffic because the population was high. They had a good location and didn't waste much effort on making it special. Having seen it, I didn't like it much.

The music was good, but too mainstream. I recognized every mix, and all the squirming. It was like fifty other clubs I'd walked past to get to better ones.

Roger sat across from me, distant enough to make me available. We looked around and he nodded.

"That one."

I saw the guy he meant. He was part of a group of eight males and two females. He wasn't bad looking, just not great looking. I was distracted by the guy behind him, with a killer dreadhawk and demicup.

Back to work.

I said, "I can try to dance with him at least."

I moved to the edge of the floor and started stomping, bending, waving, and moving in. You have to stomp lightly at .2G or you hit the overhead. It was padded, because drunk dancers, especially if from ground or lux G levels, forget about the G curve.

It didn't take long to get to their group, and shimmy into the circle.

Then I made a point of not making eye contact, just keeping the rhythm going. I brushed shoulders with a couple, touched hips with one, and I didn't even check if they were male or female.

When I looked up, I was between him and another guy. That one was better looking, but didn't have as much character. He was all superficial. Still, I grinned and shimmied, letting cleave spill, then turned to our target, then back. I kept the two going through two long songs, and started keeping more attention on our mark.

Once I had his attention, I motioned him to the booth, and got another drink. Lemonade, plain, sour.

"I'm Betty," I said, not wanting to use anything real here.

"Carson. You move great!" he said.

"Thanks. I just sort of get into it, you know? Feel the music, pick up the waves, zone on the people."

He was good, and didn't roll his eyes, but obviously figured me for as much flake as I pretended.

"Yeah, I've heard of that," he said. "I just dance."

That was when Roger came back.

"Oh, hey!" he said, swishing just enough to not be any kind of a threat to Carson. "I'm Leslie."

"Carson. The lady here was dancing with me," he said, indicating me and wondering if there was trouble.

"Good to meet you. She always finds fascinating people, jig?" He knew Earth slang, even if it was more ground than hab. Still, it made him seem more local.

"Yeah," Carson agreed.

"So what do you do, Carson?" I asked, and his attention was back on me.

"I, uh, work for logistics on the gov side."

"Oh, cool!" I said. "I'm a loader driver. Prob'ly seen a lot of your stuff."

While we talked, Roger slid his cupped hand near Carson's right. Whatever device he had was in there, and he shortly slid it away again. He nodded and I saw a thumb's up under the table. He had what he needed.

Another song started. *Blow Me Like a Whistle*.

"I love the beat!" I said loudly. "Come on!" and grabbed Carson's hand.

I danced another ten minutes or so, then drifted around and out of their circle. I let a bald chick pick me up, back to the booth, and had an iced green tea. I let on that I liked women at times, and I do, but she wasn't anything like my type. I chatted a bit, Roger scanned her, and I don't know if he had a plan or just was hoping for luck. Two songs later, *Down On You* started. I grabbed her hand and went back out again.

I repeated with Carson's friend, Alix, to show I wasn't playing favorites.

Socializing is hard work. It's easier to get spread than have a conversation.

Two hours into it, I grabbed a crab cake sausage roll. It was a bit bland meatwise, but had enough wasabi I teared up.

There was actually a ladder up and then down across the grav center, right through that rock. I gestured to Roger, he agreed, and up we went following a line of other people. I didn't look up his kilt. I didn't need any distractions. There was a turnaround near the middle, crowded with bodies, and I got groped once. Some asshole. Then we climbed down the ladder, watching out for feet and heads.

On the other side of the core mass was The Club in the Hub. The rhyme was silly, but it wasn't bad. They had much better decor, but it was crowded and almost too loud.

I mostly danced while Roger milled about with a drink, seeming friendly, and apparently scanned a lot of chips.

That four hours was very, very exhausting. I was staggering as we reached the ship, and just fell into my bunk.

I woke and got breakfast heated. Jack and Mo had gone dockside to eat at one of the dives, but most meals were aboard even in dock. I did perch and eggs, bacon and ham for the others, and some chopped greens with wheat toast. I had rice ready if anyone wanted it, but no one did.

"This is good stuff," Roger said. "You do well even with prepacks."

"It's mostly keeping it moist and adding some seasoning," I said. "But thanks."

Really, what most people don't seem to get is the prepacks are just bases. You add toppings, seasonings, extra meat or green, and it turns into decent food instead of just edible fuel.

Jack and Mo came back, and decided to have second breakfast, I guess. Half the crew ate a lot more than I figured. They burned it all off in metabolism and exercise.

I was cleaning up when there was a buzz at the lock. Mo was closest, he went to look, then came back wide-eyed.

Behind him were three UN BuSec goons in half-suit, half-uniform.

"Who is the ranking officer?"

"I am, sir," Juan said. "May I help you?"

"We need to see all the crew."

"At once," he turned, spoke to the board, and the speakers said, "All crew to C-deck, now."

Bast and Teresa came from below. Everyone else was here.

"These are all the crew?"

"As manifested, yes," he said. "Same as we've had the last couple of years."

He glanced over Teresa, looked briefly at Mira, then at me. He flashed his badge again, and reached out.

Before I knew what happened, he'd swabbed me with a probe.

Oh, shit.

His terminal did something, and he said, "Angloyce Kaneshiro, you are under arrest. You are charged with falsifying ID, illegal immigration, trespassing, espionage, reckless endangerment by violation of quarantine, and unauthorized slidewalk transfer."

That made my blood freeze. They were going to arrest me. I didn't dare say a word, because I didn't want to risk the others.

Juan asked, "But . . . . really? You're arresting her?"

"These are the charges."

Juan gave me a look of confusion and anger.

I looked around as the rest backed away from me. They looked surprised, horrified and I felt completely betrayed. They knew all this. They'd helped. Were they just going to let me be carted off?

Of course they were. They had a mission, and they'd do their best without me. They were acting outraged to separate themselves from me.

They were right, too. The war was more important than I was.

I teared up and started weeping.

It was so fast I couldn't even follow it. I hadn't seen the other two cops come in. They were big, shaven-headed, wearing lots of gear. Each one grabbed an arm and I was turned and slammed against a dolly hard enough to sting my scalp. There were buckles around my legs under my knees, arms below the elbows, waist and shoulders, cinched down until they bit.

Then they threw the hood over me, and I thought I was being drugged. I wasn't, it was just antiseptic in the fabric, but it was black and I couldn't breathe without effort.

It was terrifying. They wheeled me out, and I couldn't tell where I was. I was helpless, and expected to be hit any moment. I was strapped down like cargo, helpless and squishy against anything. What if they tripped and dropped me on my face?

I was ready to throw up.

CHAPTER 19

⊕

I couldn't blame Juan and the others. They had a war to fight. I was a casualty, no different than if I'd been shot. Letting me go made them look more honest.

There were locks closing behind me, I was sure. Then I was stood upright, and the chest and arm straps removed. They were pulled, blood rushed back through the flesh, and I wobbled forward because my legs were still secured.

Then those were loose.

The hood came off, and I was in a small cubicle with the dolly blocking me in.

"Remove your clothes and put on the coverall," someone said. Everyone present were female. They were in shipsuits with armor and gear belts. The coverall was screaming fluorescent green, and thin paper.

I stripped. They didn't probe me, but I know I was ultrasounded. The coverall didn't help keep me warm. But I may have just been chilled from fear.

I decided I was going to do my best to resist

interrogation. Maybe the crew could get off the station, or at least into some hole somewhere and ask the habitants for help. If I was lucky, I was going to spend my life in an Earth prison.

But I was pissed as hell at their reaction. Yeah, it was necessary, but fuck, I felt like I'd been held up to block bullets.

The guards emptied out my wallet and imaged everything, then dropped it all into a bag. They kept my phone. I hoped there wasn't anything too incriminating on there.

I wasn't even sure how much damage we'd done to them. We'd slowed down some shipments, and killed a few control drones, but was it really an effective thing, military-wise? I didn't know.

They left me in that cell. It had water and a toilet, and a bare rack with no mattress. It was a featureless poly block with an overhead light strip.

I have no idea how long I was there. I didn't sleep and didn't get hungry, but I did feel dizzy. I may have been gassed. Or it may have been just fear.

I had no track of time, except that I knew I should be tired and hungry, even though I wasn't. I drank water because I needed to, and peed when I needed to.

Eventually, I heard steps outside, and a lock slide. The lock was much louder than it needed to be. Probably to scare prisoners.

Two guards in masks and armor motioned me out, and I complied because I knew they'd drag me if I didn't, and hurt me in the process. They threw a bag over my head and cinched it so I couldn't see and could barely breathe.

They didn't dolly me, they just cuffed me with cables and guided me along.

I went right, left, right, and then shortly left again, into a room. The door clanged. It was amazing how sensitive my ears were even through the bag, because my eyes weren't. I could smell my breath, though, and it smelled sour and scared.

The cuffs were pulled and I was guided to sit on a reclining bench.

"What is your name?" The voice was male and in standard English.

"Aonghaelaice Lillyan Kaneshiro." I was scared that was the wrong answer.

"Date and place of birth?"

I told them, in Freehold standard.

"What is that in Earth standard date?"

"I'm sorry, I have no idea."

"You don't think it's important to know the calendar of the parent planet?"

"I know Earth time and use it when traveling, but I was never told what the Earth date was."

Right then something punched me in the gut. I curled up and couldn't breathe, didn't dare puke and couldn't find a position that didn't make me feel worse.

"I don't like your attitude," the voice said. He sounded Earth American, in his forties, maybe.

I think he hit me just to establish the dominance he already had anyway, and I think the fucker enjoyed it.

"Well?" he asked.

I couldn't speak, just let out a moan that was more "eep" than anything.

Hands grabbed me from both sides, and someone started pouring water over the bag. It trickled over the coverall.

When I tried to inhale, the cloth bag came with it. I tried tilting my head, but they held me down and I got liquid in my nose and panicked. I tried to scream, and just barely managed to hiss out, "Please top ur rownin me."

"We'll stop when we feel like it. You are a filthy scum terrorist."

I couldn't breathe and couldn't not breathe, and was held tight so I couldn't thrash. I desperately tried not to inhale, because I also realized the wet fabric wouldn't let gas exchange. I felt CO_2 burn in my muscles and lungs.

I passed out.

I woke up mumbling, something about Teresa having nice hips, and Roger being in the shower with me. All dream.

"When did you first acquire false ID?" someone asked.

"When I was ten," I said. I had. I didn't realize they meant this time around. I was too disoriented.

"Why did you do that?"

"I wanted to travel. It's hard to get some places without local ID, so I got some, and I have real ID as well. I'm not trying to scam, just work and travel."

I was hauled off that bench, and tossed onto something else. Someone ripped the bag off and scraped my face in the process, then wrapped a blindfold over my eyes and cheeks. I still couldn't see, but at least I could breathe.

They were strapping me to a frame, and I felt very exposed. All of a sudden, every centimeter of me was twitching.

Then I felt something pinch my big toes.

Whoever was doing it wore gloves, and I felt alcohol wipes. They didn't feel like sensors of any kind.

The suit was ripped open, then they played gyno and slid something cold and hard up inside me. I didn't know what it was, but I knew it was bad. It wasn't surgery, but I didn't want anything touching me there. I had no choice. The fingers on my labia were cold. I mean, not only not romantic, but not hurtful. I was just a thing they were examining or probing.

I felt a really sharp tingle between the egg inside me and my toe. It went from buzz to tickle to a clench of excitement to actual pain.

"Ow!" I said, and regretted it. They knew how to hurt me.

"It's all up to you," he said. "You talk, nothing happens. You act stubborn, it hurts more."

Electric shock from cooze to toe. I understood it. It meant no current through the heart. So they wanted to keep me alive, and they did want to hurt me.

"I've told you what you asked!" I said in a panic. I didn't want to be zapped or worse, and I knew I'd tell them everything if they did. I wanted to comply with anything that didn't give away the team, so I wouldn't have to do that.

"Your answers were too cute. So, you have false ID. How many, and where?"

My Caledonia ID was real. My Freehold ID was real. My Novaja Rossia ID was a transient authorization, and real. I knew what he wanted, but those were easy to find and if he couldn't find the people who did it, I didn't want to burn them. The only fake ID I had was the one for aboard ship. So I had to tell them about that but make it sound like it was my idea to make it.

I tried to remember how someone had told me they did that.

I took too long. I think I felt voltage spark inside me, and it fucking hurt. I cramped up like an orgasm gone terribly wrong, and I could feel the muscles down my thigh rippling. I screamed and everything went fuzzy.

I heard blood rushing in my ears, and the lights came back slowly. I'd fainted. The mask was off now and the lights were too bright in my face, dark everywhere else.

"I needed to work and the war made it hard for Freeholders to sign on ships. So, I—"

"You will not use that term. You are a 'Grainne colonist.' There is no war, only a liberation action. It is important that you understand and use proper terminology."

"Fine. Either way, I needed work and couldn't do it on my real ID."

I guess he didn't like my attitude again. I got shocked hard enough I thought I really was dying, then realized I'd been hit on the cheek as well, with some sort of baton. It came back the other way and hit my temple.

I woke up again, gasping, cold and ready to vomit.

"Awake? Good. You will act in proper respect to UN authority. Is that understood?"

"Yes, sir," was all I could say.

"My chosen pronoun is xir."

"Sorry, xir." I hoped I got the pronunciation right, with that "zh" sound from Spanish. Gods, really? His voice was pure male. There was nothing the slightest bit trans about his presentation. If his psychology was that far off from his physicality, he either needed to fix his brain or fix his body. Maybe that conflict and anger was why he was taking it out on me. Or maybe he was just a fucker. Or maybe he was lying to try to confuse me and find an excuse to hit me again. That would make him a dishonest fucker.

"So, you created false ID to travel with."

"Yes."

"That is a felony offense with a stiff penalty."

"I wasn't doing anything illegal. All I've done is moved around systems. You can find a bunch of ships I've crewed on," I said.

"We have that. What we're concerned about is the information you've given to the rebellious factions, and the actual sabotage you've performed."

"I haven't sabotaged anything."

Something smacked my cheek and it burned and stung. I saw it in his hand. It was a flat rubber sheet, heavy enough to slap. It probably wouldn't leave any damage except a welt. But the pain made me cry. It hurt. I wanted to curl up and couldn't.

Then they ran current through the probe and out my toes.

For a moment it was the most amazing orgasm I've ever felt. Everything clenched down and my brain melted.

Then everything kept clenching down, and it was the worst cramps I've ever had, and it felt like someone was burning my clit off with a torch. My legs locked up, too, and I could feel those muscles pounding and cramping, down to my toes. It felt like they'd curled to my heels. I screamed as I peed myself, and that hurt worse because it let the electricity flow better.

"Hurts, doesn't it?" he said, smiling a creepy smile and running a hand down my side.

I wanted to throw up. I wasn't sure if they were going to rape me for real, or just torture me with the worst tingler in the world. I knew I was helpless, and I knew I'd say anything to make it stop if they did that again.

"Tell us where you hid out in Caledonia."

That really wasn't very secret among skulkers, and it gave me an easy out. If I could just talk long enough, we'd get through today.

"I spread for this guy in maintenance named Edwin Marrot. He was a Mechanical Rate Three, and worked in . . . I think it was the enviro section, but it might have been the utilities section. Whichever one deals with filtration, but also does routine deck duties. Smart enough, but no genius. He was very friendly. We had four regular cubbies we'd use, and it really was hot, having him shove me face first into the bulkhead. Gods, I love a strong man. He had a favorite spot . . ."

It worked. They let me talk. I slowed down after about a half hour, and I was soaking wet the other way, remembering how he'd handled me.

I stopped and said, "I need a drink, please, xir."

He nodded, and someone behind me held up a tube with real water, cold and fresh. I sipped, gulped and sipped again.

"Thank you," I said.

"Tell us about the hideouts, not about your boyfriends." He emphasized it as "*boy*friends."

"Right. Well, as I said, I have the code to that storage. It's only a temp and quickie, but you can hide there most of a day, and if you know the schedule, indefinitely, as long as you keep your gear tight. Even if they get off sched and find you, usually all that happens is they chase you off, and if you run fast, you're gold. There's lots of those. I can probably point to several on a blueprint. Do you have a blueprint? And I bet the pattern is repeated around the hub. I'm sure there's others."

"We'll come back to that. Where did you hide the stuff you smuggled?"

"Oh, the main corridor is easy. First, you have to enter the service corridor, I think it's Seven Charlie in Alpha Red . . ."

I talked for two hours. I told them everything I'd told Juan about those routes, because I assumed he'd consider them compromised anyway. I knew how often the dumpsters were emptied along there, and made hints about stashing stuff. I told them about the overheads, and the under-decks, and the power conduit last.

"Well, let's check some of those statements," he said.

Someone else shouted, "Not to fifty!"

Enough voltage slammed through my cunt to open a cargo hatch. I blacked out screaming.

I woke up panting, writhing, face covered in vomit. The idiots were lucky I hadn't aspirated it.

"It's what I told you," I said through tears. They were real. I was lost, helpless, hopeless, pissed the fuck off and disgusted.

"Keep talking," he said.

I talked for what I hoped was another hour. I made

up some crap about storing stuff in the warehouse behind Tad's Backy, because he tried to demand head for a short debt once. If they tossed his place, I'd laugh.

"I'm thirsty," I said.

"Keep talking."

"So thirsty. And tired."

I really had no trouble faking tired. That jolt had been stronger than most workouts, all at once. I'm sure there's thirty-fours who'd love it.

"What did you smuggle? We know there were weapons involved."

"I'm sorry, I didn't take any weapons. Tobacco and some leather is all." I hoped if I admitted to non-dangerous felonies of forbidden material, I could get them away from the terrorist thing they wanted to push. A criminal was much safer. They'd parade me for publicity and I'd stay alive, and maybe I could get a lawyer later.

"I want to know about the weapons."

The lights went out again, and my entire lower half went numb.

My vision came back in splotches, and I was in agony. It felt like I'd shit myself, but it might just have been sweat and residue and leftover paper from the coverall. The bench was really hard under my back and ass, then. I'd been there a long time.

His voice softened. "All you have to do is tell us. You're going to prison, but you don't need to suffer. Just tell us where the drops were made, who's hiding where, or who was hiding. We'll take it from there. You'll be jailed under the code for illicit information transfer, minimum security, nonviolent, and out in a few years. But if we have to dig, I expect we'll find you had an active role. At that point, you start getting multi-life."

I gave him a pissed-off glare through the blindfold. It was all I could do.

He said, "Look, you don't owe them anything. You're all going to wind up in jail or dead. You should choose jail." Bargaining, so earnest sounding. I knew he was lying.

I wanted to scream at him that he was a complete idiot, and already had real intel. I couldn't do that, and the rage mixed with the pain and fear.

I let my eyes slump closed and thought about cuddling Juletta to calm my BP and pulse. It must have worked. The tech on monitors said, "She's fading. You can keep her conscious, but I don't think she'll be coherent."

"Fine. Unplug this petty criminal trash and toss her in a can."

I forced myself to remain limp and not tense up as they unfastened me and pulled the wires. The scraped my toe when they pulled the clamp off and I let my foot jitter. It hurt, but not as much as anything else.

They grabbed me under the arms and it tickled. It took everything I had not to squirm. Then they had me under arms and by ankles, and just carried me like a sack for a few seconds, out a door, down a passage and into another door that was code locked. I wouldn't have risked looking even if I wasn't masked, but I listened carefully.

Another door opened, old style on hinges, and I was dragged past the frame. They didn't drop me on the deck, but they did just let me slump down, then pulled off the hood and locked the door behind me.

It was a different cell, and managed to be even less pleasant than the first one.

The deck was cold. There was a squat toilet at one end of the cell, and it was just long enough my feet didn't hang into it. This was a short-term sitting cell, not a detention cell. The light was directly overhead and bright enough to be annoying without being daylight. The air was cold, too. I was able to squat painfully, and there was running cold water and some astringent soap, but at least I could get clean.

I did nap at least, because I had no idea how long I was going to be there, and I had to recover however I could.

Some time later I woke up as something dropped through a slot. It was a food bar. It was both tasteless and nasty at the same time, but I made myself eat it. The only water was from the wash faucet.

I had no idea if I'd slept two segs or two divs. I was still exhausted and weak. I lay back down, twitching against the cold deck, waiting for body heat to warm it so I could doze back off. I put my arm up to block out the glare.

I did sleep, but woke when the door clanged. I wasn't sure if I'd be treated better if I cooperated, or presented as still dysfunctional. They answered that question by grabbing my arms and dragging me upright. I half-walked as they dragged me, while someone else threw a bag over my head.

I was taken to what felt like the same frame, and it was still sticky.

The hood came off.

An old bald guy said, "Welcome back. I'm Mister Jones. Mister Smith will be back later. We're not allowed to work more than ten hours each." He smiled a really, really scary smile, and nodded. The bag went back over my head and was rolled up past my mouth, then taped to my face.

They wired me up, something large and hard in my ass, probe in my vagina, sharp clamps on both toes, and there was a bare tingle.

"Contact," someone said.

Then I felt like I'd been hit by atmospheric lightning. My ass puckered, my entire guts clenched down into my cooze, my legs cramped and kept on cramping. I was fastened loosely enough that I was able to smash something with my toes, too.

I puked up nothing, just dry heaves that burned my throat.

"I will repeat that any time I am unhappy with your response. Do you understand?"

"Yes, sir."

I swear the local transformer overheated when they zapped me.

"'Yes, Mister Jones,' is the correct answer."

Oh, gods, he was some dom perv.

"'Yes, Mister Jones,'" I replied.

I must have sounded sarcastic. He zapped me again.

I didn't have to fake bawling. I knew I was going to be abused until they figured out I didn't know much of use, then they were going to stuff me out the lock. I cried and couldn't stop, so they tingled me just enough for me to focus.

"Tell me what you smuggled. Don't give cute answers, just be direct."

"When we got into Caledonia, someone swiped two boxes off a pallet from the internal bay. I don't know what they contained."

"Describe the person."

"Male. Average all over. Wearing a dull orange shipsuit. It didn't have obvious company logos."

"What did you take aboard that was noticeable?"

"We had something atmosphere sensitive, but I was told it was wine."

"Describe the container."

It went on and on. I told him everything. I figured Juan had everyone covered by now, and since we were starting with weeks ago, it was hopefully less critical. I needed to stay alive.

A huge jolt ripped through me, and it felt like I ripped tendons off my knees with the clench.

"Fuck, what was that for?"

Another hit me, only half as hard.

"I will ask the questions. You will answer. That was a reminder, to keep you honest."

He was going to do this for ten hours, then Smith was. Or, he said that's what they were doing. My sense of time was completely kiboshed.

He asked, I talked. A while later, wham, they juiced me again. I was lying in an oozing puddle of waste, and hopefully not blood from tearing anything. I was upright enough to remain nauseous.

I wasn't sure how much longer I could string them out. The jolts were every now and then, needed or not, to make sure I knew the fuckers could be fuckers. I got to dreading. I was terrified of dying, so I kept talking, and I was terrified of giving them something actually useful that would make them escalate, so I dragged it out as long as I could, but every little while, they burned my cooze, or my ass. The jolts there felt like a firehose enema. I expected they'd go with both again soon.

I lay there weeping. I couldn't last through days of this, never mind months. I was going to tell them everything just to make it stop, and they were going to vac me. If I never existed, there was no reason to worry or care. And after they won, who was going to call them on it?

"Well, I need a steak and a beer. I'm sure our guest would like a mango-spinach food bar and some recycled water."

They dragged me back to my cell again, and ripped the tape and hood off.

I crawled and heaved myself over the toilet, washed off and shivered from the evaporating water. I took a drink because my throat was parched raw. The food bar dropped through the slot, and I choked it down, then tried to lie down to rest.

I was in that state that's half sleep, half restlessly awake, and not at all restful. I had bad dreams, bad feelings and physical discomfort, outside, inside, hunger, sensory. Everything.

CHAPTER 20

⊕

I heard banging and sat up, but it wasn't my door. I slumped back down.

There was more banging, and it sounded closer.

It was right outside and turned to scuffling. I figured there was a fight of some kind. I silently cheered for the detainee, whoever they were.

Then a metallic voice shouted, "Angie, are you there?"

What?

"Here," I croaked, then I shouted back, "HERE!" and coughed through my gooey throat.

"Fire in the hole! Fire in the hole!"

It took me a half second to realize what was said, and roll over onto my face.

Which was when something exploded.

Metal and polymer whizzed overhead. I looked, and the door hung in twisted tatters. Something had splattered in a mess on the wall.

"Angie!" Juan shouted. "Function report!"

"SIR, THIS RECRUIT IS DISORIENTED BUT

FUNHCTIONAL!" I replied. He'd shouted just right to sound like an MI, and I'd responded just like in recruit training.

I was lying. I hurt all over. My head and ears rang, my skin stung, my limbs ached, my throat was filling with debris, but I was alive and in one piece.

"We are moving!" he said.

"Moving, sir," I said, just as if I were back in RT. I hunched, gasped, got to my knees, and tried to stand.

Roger and Mira were alongside and pulled me upright, smoothly but very quickly. It didn't hurt. But then we moved and it did hurt, and I couldn't balance.

"Step," Roger said, holding out pants. I stepped in, he pulled them up and fastened them around my waist as Mira tugged a polo over my head. Roger grabbed my feet and stuffed shoes on them as if I were a baby.

My brain tracked slightly. He'd had his hands on me and very close to . . . and I couldn't even enjoy it I was so sick and sore.

They held my waist and shoulders and pulled me out the shredded door.

Sebastian yelled, "Left!" and they drag-carried me that way.

Behind us there was another explosion, but it seemed smaller.

We passed another lockhatch, and holy hell, it was blown right off its seals. Had they done that to get to me?

My balance came back along with my hearing, but my ears still rang. There were klaxons all over, and I heard, "Fire in Administration Three! Fire in Administration Three!"

One of them looped a lanyard over my neck, with an ID on it. They were just in time. Around the curve ahead of us clattered a security team, who glanced at us for badges, and seemed to assume we were theirs.

Mira pointed and shouted, "They came in the back lock. Ten or more. They said they were the People's Right." Her accent was believably North American.

The lead man nodded, waved and they kept running.

I couldn't believe that had worked, but the UN troops were in a panic and we were fleeing the area in question, so I guess it seemed reasonable.

Mira grabbed my hand and shoved a pistol into it. I didn't recognize the model. It was probably for some non-military agency. The safety was off. I hoped strongly I wouldn't have to shoot it.

Juan said, "We have about fifty seconds before they catch on."

Sebastian suddenly turned down a side passage. There was a maintenance door there, and he had it unlocked and open in about ten seconds. We went through.

"Do you know where we are?" he asked me.

I looked around. I could almost see straight, but stuff still blurred a bit.

"Not yet. Help me out."

"Sector Golf, Third Level, outboard and behind the UN offices."

"Okay," I said. I knew about where that was from the map. "This way."

I hadn't been here in years and wasn't entirely sure where this access went, but it went the general way we wanted.

I asked, "Are we getting our ship?"

"No, but we need the dock, and a hole for a bit."

"Got it."

I could stagger at least, and stumbled along with them.

"You came for me," I said. I was crying again. My voice was a rough whisper.

Roger said, "The Regiment does not leave troops behind."

I expected he'd say something about the intel risk, but that's all he said. So I assumed they were Blazers, whatever else they were. They'd come for me, not the intel.

And they considered me worthy of effort.

Or not just that. I figured they enjoyed blowing stuff up, too. It also sent a message about retaliation, but it made them more visible. I didn't know how they weighed it all.

"Where can we go for a few hours?" Roger asked.

"Service passage behind the shops. There are several cubbies. Maintenance dolly bay below that. Or there was the Short Time Lodge. Very seedy. Pay by the hour. No questions asked."

Roger said, "Mira and I will go in the front. The rest of you come in the back."

A sudden joke occurred to me about how many times someone had come in the back there. But it had only been two, not four. The body has physical limits. Anyway, it had been a nicer place then. Also, jokes aside, I didn't want anything sexual for a while.

I felt weak and nauseous the whole way, down public passages, through the back "alley" passages, and through past the compartment lock, which was broken. This area didn't get well-maintained, because of a combination of bribes and neglect, and it was effectively abandoned by the habitat government.

We got into the room, and it was as bad as I thought it would be.

There was one bed, no sheets, with a peel-off sanitized cover. I didn't want to think about what might be under that, even in space.

Sebastian and Teresa laid me gently on the bed, and she went into medic mode. I hadn't even seen her arrive from wherever she'd been.

"Gods, lady, they did a good job on you. Where do you hurt?"

"All over. Electrical shock. Convulsions. I got beat with padded . . . things."

"I think your food was laced, too. Probably both disorientation and anti-inhibitors, and I expect something that was a mild poison or irritant. Did you feel better part of the time?"

"Yes, worse, better, worse, better again."

"Good sensation with the good interrogator."

"There was no good interrogator."

"Bastards. That was all kinds of illegal."

She shot me with something that felt cool in my veins, then in my head, then my guts. It helped.

I started babbling. "I said when I volunteered that they wouldn't let laws get in the way. Either they'd claim I was lying and have no evidence, or they'd just vac me." At least trying to hide the abuse made the former more likely. But what about the next bunch?

"Bathroom," she said.

I was able to hobble through. She closed the door behind us.

She softly said, "I deduce they used an electric probe internally."

"Yes," I said.

"If you feel any burn, I have some salve."

"Please," I said. "Should I spread or bend over?"

The look on her face was momentarily shocked. The idea of touching me seemed to agitate her a lot.

"If you can do it alone, I was going to let you."

"Thanks," I said. I was fine with medics handling me, but I'd been probed enough.

She left, and in privacy, I was able to squirt the goo in my rectum and vagina. They were both burned, irritated, sore, and it felt like they were scarring. The stuff did help. It was messy, and took a lot of wiping and rinsing. It hadn't felt at all sexual, and not at all like sexual assault. It felt like I'd been a medical experiment. Gross. Dirty.

By then, my metabolism felt better. I was sore from beating, but fit enough otherwise.

She handed me a bulb of soup, clam chowder. There was a half-sandwich of almond butter. I made them disappear. I washed them down with a liter of water.

"I can't give you more yet," she said. "You need recovery time. A couple more hours."

"Okay. I'll wait. Thanks."

I rejoined the rest. Despite the name of the place, it was almost a palace for space. We could stand, had room for all of us, and two chairs.

I felt the glance they all shared, and it was embarrassing.

I'd been exploited and assaulted, and everyone knew it. I didn't want to dwell on it, but I didn't want them . . . I didn't know.

Teresa asked, "Are you fit to move?"

"I think so."

Juan said, "Good, they'll start DNA sniffing soon. It won't work. They'll have to admit they fucked up, but they won't let that be a permanent block. We'll just have to leave them something else to worry about."

"Why won't it work?" I asked. I was surprised they hadn't DNA sniffed us already.

Bast said, "Our DNA is all over the station. I have two bots spritzing it anywhere handy. Anywhere we've crossed with other elements, we've swapped, too. All our DNA is all over every station. If you can't isolate it, spread it."

I wanted to get on with it. I wanted off this station. I was terrified of what Round Two might be if they caught us—me—again.

Juan and Mira were dressed in business wear— polos, jackets, pants and deck shoes. The others were changing.

Teresa handed me the same outfit in my size. She must have measured me at some point. They were exact.

Juan said, "Just follow our lead. If we need directions we'll ask, but I have your previous summary."

He and Mira carried boxes and had wrist scanners with phone mounts.

"Okay," I agreed.

He paid for seating space on the slideway. We were almost twenty minutes from the bay at that point. It was neat to watch our booth slow, wheel left and merge, then do the same up-ramp and right. It was faster than dollycab, though, and much more comfortable than foot travel.

We debarked and took a back way to a smaller lock that was crewed by only two agents. They scanned the ID he held and nodded, counting us off in mutters as we passed.

I wondered what we were doing, all here together. If they were hijacking transport, they'd want to send only the ones they needed. Unless we were skipping out at once. Well, I could replace everything except David's engagement necklace and Violet, my favorite toy. Why did I still have that necklace, anyway? The marriage had lasted a year. Earth year. It wasn't bad, but what was the point?

Why was I thinking about that now?

We entered the dock area, though it was hard to tell. Our route was all passages and hatches. They were low, only about two hundred and twenty centimeters. It's like being some rodent in a tube-trail enclosure.

Sebastian was in the lead, and flashed some sort of ID to a Leo we passed. She nodded and moved out of our way, avoiding eye contact.

A few frames more, and we came to the actual checkpoint for the bay proper. Behind it I could see the emergency pressure curtain and the bulk of ships on the docking rails.

There were people queued up, crew and service, passengers with luggage, some dolleys and lifters. We passed all the lines straight to a gate proctor.

Sebastian flashed the ID, said, "UN Customs

Authority Inspection Team. We're responding to a lead. I need admission at once."

He'd chosen someone young, who reached for a comm button, and he grabbed the man's hand.

"Even me talking about it is a risk. Scan fast, let us through. We can't delay a ship, but we have to inspect for smuggled cargo."

The man looked at it for anti-tamper marks, saw them, or thought he did, nodded and carded the gate open for us. We strode through acting determined, with scanners and a doc box, and he smiled uncomfortably.

I made a point to expand my chest a bit and give him a scowl. It wasn't hard. I was still in pain, still frightened, still very, very pissed.

We were through. Security for ports is almost silly. It's impossible to search everyone, there isn't time. They can scan packages, but how do you stop a bomb aboard a docking craft? Or toxic gas? Or vented engine plasma and radioactives?

We stepped aboard a slide and gripped the rails, and a little while later, stepped off near a cluster of gates. We plugged our ear protection in. It wasn't dangerously loud, but could get that way.

We approached a ship. I could tell from the umbilicas, the flashing light on the ram, and the initial warning flash above the out-hatch they were about to depart. Sebastian went straight to the omnilift for that bay, grabbed the controls as we crowded aboard, and steered it straight to the command deck. He flashed a strobe through the port near the hatch, and slapped a controller on it for commo and to open it.

With this equipment, I wondered why they bothered with a tramper. They could just steal whatever they wanted.

Whoever was in the hatch looked as if they were trying to avoid answering. They called for someone else. Another man came up and there was more showing of IDs and gestures. He seemed to protest, then shook his head, and held his hands up.

"Let's go," Sebastian said.

We went down, through a personnel lock, up and into the C-deck.

Juan said, "Good day. We're from the Customs Authority." He waved his ID toward them. "You are not in trouble, but we have reason to believe there is contraband in one of your bonded containers."

Sebastian looked at Juan.

"Ready, sir," he said.

"Start aft, check everything meeting description. Keep it brief."

"Will do," Sebastian nodded. He turned to us and said, "Get to it."

The ship's captain said, "I'm supposed to undock in twenty minutes."

"Don't worry, we won't delay you. If we do, you'll be covered."

A moment later they were covered, alright. Mira had the cargo crew at gunpoint. The other four were involved in prepping for shove-out and disabling some of the comm gear, and sweeping the vessel for any other crew. I stood there holding documents and trying to look mean.

"This is piracy!" one of the detainees hissed in anger.

Juan smiled. "More accurately, it's commandeering. But I'm sure your term will be used. Now, if you don't get in the way, you'll all get to live. You'll also have documentation for insurance."

In three minutes, the entire manifest of crew were in the C-deck.

Sebastian said, "There's a pressure hold at Frame Twenty, has recently been used for livestock and a passenger module."

Juan said, "Perfect. Put them there. Make sure there's good oh-two lines and sanitation."

I figured he was saying that on purpose to reassure them. I knew he wasn't going to kill any bystanders he didn't have to, but they wouldn't know that.

I just stood there, slowly recovering from two days of abuse, drinking water, watching five people completely bash a ship. Mira took the astro console and started keying and loading. Juan watched time and made notes. The others took the prisoners aft.

They were back shortly.

"Okay, let's do it," Roger said. He waved and I followed with the rest. Down two, aft two, out-starboard one. It was the emergency hatch.

Bast slapped some sort of mechanical linkage to a padeye and hooked it down. The other end connected to the hatch's grip handle.

I couldn't believe we were egressing through the escape hatch while in station, and that there wasn't some sort of alarm glaring on someone's board.

"And out we go. Angie, lead the way please."

I wiggled my butt into place and slid down the chute.

I landed between the ways under the ship, then had to move fast to avoid being squashed as Sebastian came down.

"Fastest way out, walking like we're on a bust," Juan said.

I gestured ahead and he did so.

He led, I was second and offered occasional directions.

"How long do we have?" I asked.

"About three more minutes before they lock."

Roger came alongside.

"You're still walking stiff. Okay for now?"

"I can walk, yes. I can't dance, lift loads or do anything complicated."

"Good." He stepped ahead of us.

"This way," he said, and he led the way.

I was jealous that he knew his way around. It felt like he was cutting into my job. But I couldn't know every route in every station, and they'd had time.

Shortly, we were at a standard docking ring. Jack attached some sort of device, punched a code, and the lock popped. Pressure was just different enough for a whuff of air.

I followed Jack through, and had a braintwist moment.

"This is the *Pieper*," I said.

"Undocking and departing in ten minutes," Juan said as he moved past me.

They were crazy fuckers.

"How?"

"Too long to explain."

I asked the next question.

"So why did we risk ourselves on that ship?"

"They're looking for us there now, and assuming we can't use this one. If we pulled the docs right, this reads as sold at auction. Actually, we sold it to one of our own cover outfits."

I said, "But anyone here knows it wasn't."

"Here, yes, but others might not."

"'Might'?"

"Nothing's guaranteed in war, lady."

Mira said, "And right now, our IFF is telling everyone we're a completely different ship, which was in airdock and was due out tomorrow."

"So you programmed . . . whichever ship that was to respond with passable comments?"

With a single shake of her head, she said, "Nope, not at all. They're running silent. That complicates their response."

"Hopefully they don't just blow it up."

She shrugged. "Unlikely, but if they do, it's not our war crime."

I guess I understood that, and it was war, but wow.

The rest of the crew came from somewhere. I gave Shannon a glance as he walked past, and he said, "Your cubby behind the Backy shop. I had to leave a couple of guns there. They're probably going to toss his place."

"Only if you left them in the open . . . how do you know about that place?"

"No, they're well-hidden, but I anonymously told the cops where." He waved a stick.

"Huh. He's an asshole anyway."

"You're welcome." He smiled. "I have the file of your

interrogation. I won't read it but it is stored for archive and we'll destroy it as soon as we can. I think Mo managed to wipe their copy before we left."

"Thanks," I said. But even assholes like Tad didn't deserve UN Fed attention.

I hit my rack and strapped down, and we were shoving off. I didn't know if they'd hacked a system or bribed someone, but we were out.

Only, ships don't move fast near stations. If they went to full drive, the distortion would really rip local astrogation, and get a real quick military or Space Guard response, and Sol Space Guard did mount cannon and missiles. I don't know if they'd used them in years at that point, but they could slag us to debris.

And if we moved slow, we were easy to intercept with that same response, once they figured out what happened.

Only, the hijacked ship, the *Montrose*, was keeping commo silence. First that confused everyone, then it got an emergency alert.

The commo was full of chatter, asking for data from any ship, asking *Montrose* to respond, calling Space Guard to pursue and rescue, reassuring *Montrose* there was help coming.

Mira had a disturbingly sexy grin.

"What did you do?" I asked.

"I think they're figuring out it's plotted for the military terminal."

"That's . . . about three Earth hours, right?"

She nodded. "So they'll be trying to reach it from both ends. That keeps them busy."

"If they don't decide it's a suicide run and slag it."

I didn't find that grin sexy anymore. She was aroused, and amused, by risking a shipful of innocent trampers we'd hijacked with false ID and guns. I guess they were my people, even if I didn't know them personally. To her, they were just a tool.

I knew, if the UN would tie me down, half drown me, zap me, club me and toss me in a cell, they'd blow those poor people away. That's if they even knew someone was aboard.

"This is wrong," I said.

Next to me, Teresa said, "Angie, it's war. I'm sorry it's hard on you."

"Yeah," I said. I guess it's useful to look at it like that. I was still struggling with it.

Shannon came on. "Departure plotted, we're in the slot, we'll deviate in a few hours but we're solid for now."

I unlatched, stretched, and lay there for a moment.

Teresa slipped across the deck and eased her way onto my rack. That was . . .

A hug.

"How are you recovering?"

I said, "Hell, I'm still in pain and feel disgusting. I need a shower."

"I don't think you should yet," she said.

"Yeah, you think they'll chase?"

"They will," she said.

I hadn't touched anyone in weeks. It did help. I gripped her shoulder. Her hair was rubbing with mine.

"You'll get grubby just touching me," I said.

"We're all a mess, don't worry about it." But she rolled to her feet and went off to do something.

CHAPTER 21

⊕

I guess I fell asleep. I woke up, checked the terminal, and it was an hour later.

The rescue bands still had talk about the *Montrose* but much less. There was a military gunboat shadowing them, and some sort of intel boat, and the Space Guard.

We were holding low thrust with intermittent emgee.

Shannon announced, "Rotate for food and hygiene. Keep it brief, buddy nearby. Angie, Teresa, go."

I grabbed a clean brief and coverall, and went to the head, Teresa following. She waved me in first, and I spent three segs getting really clean. It felt a lot better, and some of the ick washed away with the actual dirt. The drain bubbled brown with dust and crud. We'd done a job on ourselves.

I got out in the shipsuit, she moved right past me and in, naked. She didn't have the gym-rip Mira had, or the men, but she was still in really good shape. If I was more into women, and she wore skintight over that in a club,

I'd have thought about taking her home. I had with women, once or twice, if I was really tense. And once I was just really turned on. I thought about it, if we'd had privacy and she'd offered. I wanted human flesh, not synthskin toys, especially as all I wanted was human warmth.

I went forward and made up sandwich wraps in instant seal packs with heaters, and bulbs of soup. That would keep things safe from spills or burns even if we had to maneuver.

I delivered a tub of them to the C-deck.

Jack said, "And they've remoted into *Montrose* and have control Looks like they had a remora punch into the power section and backdoor it. They should be safe now."

I didn't feel good even then. I figured those poor crew were going to get interrogated until someone figured out they were victims. It wasn't us doing it, but that didn't make me feel any better.

Juan said, "So, they'll know where we are now, as in, which vessel. That's further than I thought we'd make it."

And I wondered what was next. If this was further than he thought, what had he planned?

"Well, we're queued to jump," Mira said. "In less than twenty minutes, it will get harder for them."

Just because UN BuSec could deduce which ship we were on didn't mean it happened at once. We made the jump back to NovRos, with almost empty racks, and then had the problem of what to do. Docking would mean we'd have to abandon ship and disperse. Not docking would draw attention shortly. I also wasn't clear on where we could go once positively IDed.

We hung back and boosted slowly, but that was only delaying the inevitable.

"What do we do when?" I asked Mira.

"That's why I'm saving reaction mass now."

"Ah. Got it."

We were going to run. The question was where.

And it was right then that NovRos Jump Control pinged us.

"*NCA Pieper*, please assume following vector." There was the beep of received nav code.

Juan said, "They have us. Prepare for silent running and minimal signature. C-deck, Galley, Head and Bunks. Everything else cold. Sebastian, can you hear me back there?"

"I got you, Captain."

Juan said, "As we discussed," then clicked for shipwide. "All hands to command deck."

The techs and Dylan came forward only seconds later. A disciplined crew was a good thing. I wondered what was going on.

A moment later, Mira and Sebastian had sidearms out. They were at opposite corners of the space. They were aiming at Dylan.

Juan said, "I need to be sure. Comment?"

Dylan looked at them, completely cold. "I don't think I have one."

"How long?"

"All along," he said. "The best way to fight a grossly unfair system is from inside."

Juan almost seemed angry. "Oh, god and goddess, not that crap. There's enough of it on the propagandacasts."

"Maybe you should consider that ninety-nine percent of humanity is right."

Juan raised his eyebrows and asked, "Anything else?"

Dylan said, "You do have to consider that—"

Juan gave a fractional nod, and they shot him, chest, chest and head. He flailed to the deck and lay in a puddle of lumpy blood.

"Shannon, Teresa, check his bunk, carefully. Jack, clear the deck. Angie, can you assist?"

"Yes," I said briefly. I didn't want to talk. I'd just seen a court martial and execution take place in twenty seconds. They'd rescued me. They'd shot him.

"UN plant," Juan explained, but I'd already guessed. "He's why we've had several targets displace. And how you got taken."

"Why are we still alive?" I asked, as I grabbed a sorbpack from a spill kit and kicked it around the spreading pool. It turned pink and the pool turned to trails of drops.

"I think they wanted to get intel on other units. Which is part of the reason why we generally don't interact with them."

"He didn't fight," I said, watching the blood suck up into the crystals.

"No point."

That was disturbing. He'd been completely fatalistic, and they'd wanted just enough confirmation to kill him where he was. I suppose he couldn't carry any obvious defense around his own buddies, and starting a fight wouldn't have made any difference with their training. He could have killed me in seconds, or any normal ship crew, but the team were as uber as he was. He'd have lost regardless.

It felt cold and vicious to stuff his limp flesh into a trash bag and haul it aft. Once there, Jack took charge. He stuffed the body into a fluid tub, went to a tool kit and pulled out a large brush tool, and started whacking off chunks of limbs. I felt nauseous and saw everything through a green tinge.

"He was how I got caught?" I asked.

Jack said, "We think so. First you, then the rest of us. They seem to have had several overlapping plans to either find if we have other elements, or to stop us if they didn't get better leverage."

"Do you need me further?" I asked. I wanted away from the scene.

He gave me a sympathetic look. "Just for washup. I'll handle this part."

"Okay," I said.

It was revolting, and I couldn't turn away. Hack, hack, hands. Hack, hack, feet. Forelimbs and upper limbs took the saw blade. His neck had to be chopped, sawed and pried to separate it. Each piece, Jack fed into the recycler.

I helped hose out the blood and some assorted bits of flesh, and some other, less pleasant fluids. Then I went to my rack and kept a light on all night. I didn't sleep.

I understood what had happened and why. It terrified me how matter-of-fact it had all been. Identify mole, confirm, shoot dead, dismember, feed into recycler, wash off, and get dinner. Jack had gotten dinner, that is. I didn't.

Then I realized Dylan had risked his own life to stop

us. Even if he was an enemy plant, he had guts. That, and staring down the guns that were going to end his life, and did.

Juan had even said, "We'll need to see if we can pick up a replacement on some leg. Make sure he's demanifested when we dock."

Teresa said, "NovRos, at least, makes that easy. I'll make his pay disappear from the account, we can cash it for extra goods, and he debarked to go visit family, looking for another leg. No, we don't know."

Wow. They were even going to spend his pay. Well, it wasn't really his pay, but . . .

Vicious.

CHAPTER 22

⊕

We were still wanted, though, and it's hard to hide a ship anywhere near other ships or habitats.

We'd ran dark. They knew we'd pulled out, and they probably had a rough idea we were "those" people. About that, I still had no idea why we were still in the same ship.

Shannon said, "Pressure protocols, there is some risk."

"What are we doing?" I asked. I was on my way back to my rack to strap in and watch vid until something happened. Or, I was going to pretend to watch vid so no one knew I was ready to scream about the likelihood we were going to be glowing vapor soon.

"Dead zone from a previous engagement. I've got the ephemeris. There's a bunch of debris from both target and intercept. We're going past it."

"Do we know who the target was?"

"No one you know, but yes, one of our other clandesties. They're gone. They did make the UN pay."

"Sorry to hear that," I said. They'd lost friends, I could tell.

"Thanks."

So we drifted through unsafe volume while wondering if we'd eat tungsten shot or gammas. I figured Earth was going to mine every approach that could be a problem. I just wondered what they'd do with all that loose debris later.

War got unsexy very fast.

"We have pursuit," Mira reported. "Astern, not crossing. Harder for them to catch us, easier to shoot us."

I felt what I call combat cold. It wasn't the first time I felt it, but it was the first time I noticed it. My mind, emotions and hormones just shut down. There was nothing I could do, and whether I lived or died depended entirely on what others did. So I felt nothing.

Juan kept up chatter about schedule and plans. I think it was to keep the rest of us occupied. He couldn't be that concerned with them like this.

We were under steady drive, at near-G acceleration. That wastes a lot of fuel, but it moves you places fast. I didn't think this old beast could do that for long, and it certainly couldn't go much higher unless we cut the cargo train loose.

Deep space combat can be slow. They didn't want to launch until we were positively IDed, or positively refused signal. They pinged and pinged, and we ignored them. It was three hours, us at 1G, them at more. First they had to match velocity, then they had to exceed to close the gap, then they had to plot intercept for missiles.

"*NCA Pieper*, you are ordered to cut thrust and cooperate with boarding for inspection."

Mira was all over her screens, both viewing and flat. Figures scrolled as she wrote across it.

"We're not going to make the Jump Point in time to slam them," she said.

Juan shrugged. "Well, it wasn't going to work more than a couple of times anyway. Plan B it is."

"On it."

He and Mira cut thrust and coasted.

"*NCA Pieper*, you are complying, but we are not receiving responses. If you are receiving this signal, please indicate with a double-tap of thrust, then resume free flight."

They sat and watched the seconds tick by. Three full minutes later, Juan burped the engines.

"*NCA Pieper*, understood on commo problems. Please continue to follow instructions and we will assist with repair."

"Are they Navy or Space Guard?" I asked.

"Navy."

It made a legal difference. Space Guard had law enforcement status. They had limited rules of engagement for shooting. A UN naval vessel could shoot under laws of war if they felt threatened for any reason. We needed to make them feel safe.

I realized later that everyone had been milling about prepping various things in their duty stations, and sorting gear. I warmed rat packs for everyone, and made sure they stayed hydrated. I even monitored fluid levels through the head usage.

"Juan, Mira, Sebastian, you all need to drink a half liter or better."

Juan looked at me.

"Thanks. I appreciate you monitoring. We're going for half that at present, but will catch up on the rest later." He grabbed the two bulbs I held, snapped the top off one as he handed the other to Mira, and sipped it.

It was another two hours before the UN craft was in proximity, and they did all the maneuvering, since they thought we were helpless.

"I think that's close enough," Mira said.

Juan said, "Then Plan B it is."

They cleared the deck so fast I wasn't even sure they'd all been here.

"What are we doing?" I asked.

"You're staying here," he told me. "Do you trust me?"

That was a silly question, but asked that way, was scary. "Yes?"

"We're going to have to confront them. They might board. Don't argue or fight. Try to keep them talking before boarding and after. Commo is about to function again. We'll be back. You're noncombatant," he said.

"Oookay."

Mira engaged some program or other, and they followed the rest aft.

I had no idea what was going on.

Warning buzzers sounded angrily. I didn't know what to do with them, and I got the impression it was planned.

There was a faint shift in the atmosphere, that you get in any small ship when there's bay or lock evacuation and transfer. Then I saw a very clear display that said the maintenance tug had launched.

I wondered who was aboard, or if they'd all tethered onto it. They wouldn't fit inside.

They wouldn't want me captured. My intel was important. I knew that. They wouldn't just leave me to die. I was a lot more use alive. Right?

I was. They'd even blasted their way in to recover me.

I fought off a wave of panic.

The ship was in trajectory, and there was nothing to collide with. Worst case, I could bleat a mayday and someone would salvage the ship and save me. Supplies on board would last me for months. Someone would want a half billion marks or credits of ship and cargo.

There was no reason for anyone to vaporize it.

I sat and shivered, and my eyes got wet. I had no idea what was happening.

Then commo came on. "*NCA Pieper*, are there any crew aboard? Emergency broadcast from *UNS Scrommelfenk*, over. Navire Commercial Alsacien *Pieper* . . ." the respondent repeated in dialect.

I found a headset, and replied, "*Scrommelfenk*, this is *Pieper*, Angie leBlanc, Officer on Watch, over." Well, I was.

"*Pieper*, do you need assistance? We show reactor irregularities and craft launch, over."

So, Juan had said to keep them talking.

"We're functional, over," I replied. I hoped it was true.

"Can you explain the EVA launch, over?"

"I really can't. That's not my department. Sorry. Over."

"Is your captain or engineer available? Over?"

"They are not available at present, over."

"Officer leBlanc, your responses suggest you're being

deliberately deceptive. Please tell me in clear language your ship's current status, or I'll have to treat this as a potential piracy. Are you under duress? Over."

I was definitely under duress, but not the way they thought. Still, I was to keep talking.

"I am not under duress. Our current status is in flight, in-system. I'm commercial crew, not rated for astrogation. We don't have a big enough command crew for that. Everything I was told to watch looks nominal. Over."

Nothing followed for a while. I grabbed a food bar and a coke, and turned on lights and music. I was alone in a ship I couldn't pilot with commo I could just barely use, in empty space near an enemy warship. How the fuck did I get here?

I sat there watching the chrono scroll, the trajectory numbers change, and the sensor screen show a large ship and a bunch of nothing. I was afraid to leave. I needed to use the head bad, but didn't. I was completely mentally numb.

I jumped and almost went bejeebus. There were clanging, clanking thumping noises from the crew lock, and a moment later, it cycled fast. Someone had dumped atmosphere to get in quickly. The hatch swung, and four troops in armored V-suits burst through looking like clowns, but I was sure it was an intentional maneuver.

One of them, I wasn't sure which, said, "Please keep your hands where we can see them. Identify yourself."

I raised my hands. "Angie leBlanc, Officer on Watch."

Then I was grabbed, twisted to the deck and bound in cuffs. They checked the pressure, checked me with a flash of light, and started doffing helmets.

One of them reached the commo console and started swiping buttons.

"Sir, this is Bernard One. We're aboard, over."

We were close enough for a video connection. Juan appeared onscreen.

"How convenient," he said.

"Who are you, over?"

"Juan Gaspardeau, Freehold Military Forces. I have seized this vessel in combat operations."

How the fuck had he done that? From a maintenance tug? Had he hacked their commo, or . . . ?

The lieutenant immediately said, "I have your crewwoman."

"I have your captain," Juan replied, waving the camera over. He held a pistol. The captain looked ashamed and livid. Behind him I saw Sebastian and Mira. "Are you seriously proposing to exchange a cargo-grunter for a ranking officer?"

The lieutenant flapped his arms in confusion. "What, then?"

"Surrender at once." Juan sounded so reasonable. God, I loved the man. Had he really captured a capital ship?

"I can't do that."

"I have not killed anyone I didn't need to. I would like to maintain that standard. If you harm her, you lose an officer."

"Sir, what do I do?" he asked his captain on the screen.

Juan answered him. "You have our ship. We have your much more valuable ship. We can destroy you in that ship if you don't comply. Per Geneva Conventions and Mars Accords, I am not initiating violence against anyone who has surrendered or been detained. If you initiate violence at this point, you're a war criminal, I can kill you out of hand, and I have weapons. You will surrender and return. If you run, I'll consider you a combatant."

The captain said, "You must surrender, for now."

The lieutenant wasn't done yet. He was twitching, furious as he replied.

"Sir, I will comply with your orders under protest. I want it in record that these pirates used a fake distress call to lure us into a rescue, as a way of hijacking us."

Juan smiled.

"When did we sound this alleged distress call?" he asked.

The lieutenant stuttered. I thought he was going to melt down entirely.

"But, your engines, and emergency pod . . ."

"Tug, not emergency pod. There was no distress call. We even deactivated the transponder on the tug."

On screen, the captain turned to Juan said, "Damn you, we acted in good faith."

Juan nodded. "You did, and should be commended for that. But we're still taking your ship."

He had no response to that.

In front of me, the lieutenant said, "If I surrender, how do we proceed?"

"Hand your sidearm to my crewwoman. Place the rest of the weapons where she tells you and follow her directions."

A moment later, he nodded to someone who unshackled me. He reversed his grip and handed me his pistol.

"Ma'am," he said.

Juan said, "Angie, lock them in the bunktainer. Make sure they have some rations. Unpower the hatch. We'll take it from there."

"Yes, sir," I said.

They did as they were told, the lieutenant waving his boarding party to move ahead of him. They were so-so in emgee. I had more practice. I made a note of that.

Juan kept the comm open.

He sent a very terse transmission to system control.

"Freehold officer reports capture of *Scrommelfenk*. Removing from system under neutral terms. No hostility offered. *NCA Pieper* accompanies. Respectfully request plans for priority transit."

A reply would take a while, and he gave orders in the meantime.

I had the detainees precede me through the passages. They looked pissed. Hell, I could feel it in the air. They didn't argue, though. We had a warship.

Over the PA and echoed through my phone, I heard him giving orders to the screen ships.

"Fueler, gunboat, EW boat, you are not engaged in combat and may depart if you do so at once. This is a neutral system. You know your way back to Earth, or you can move closer to Novaya Rossia support. Your command already violated neutral space once. Don't test me."

About then, something came back from system control that was like, "Did you say captured? *Yobannyj v rot!* How the hell?"

I heard Juan say, "Previous transmission is correct and complete. Please reply."

The boarding party entered the pod, and I kicked it closed, then locked it using a johnson bar from the tool mount. I was amazed they hadn't tried to swarm me, but I guess Juan having their captain worked. I locked the hatch again, with my pin. They couldn't open it from inside now.

"Uh . . . hold on, sir."

Another voice came on. "*Pieper*, are you reporting clandestine status as a warship, and capture of a UN vessel?"

"Yes. They attempted to intercept with threat of fire. I'm filing the usual complaints, as we were in transit and noncombatant at the time."

We were about thirty seconds round trip.

"Understood, *Pieper*, though you should have been identified as a warship."

"We didn't become a warship until they decided to attack us, based purely on our flight path. See previous tx about usual complaints. We've captured her and will depart system with prize crew shortly."

"How the hell did you manage that?"

"Through wit and skill. Please stand ready to clear both vessels for Jump Point."

"Angie, messenger line coming," he said to me.

"Okay," I acknowledged. I knew that was possible. I never heard of it being done.

There was a thumping on the outer hull, which I heard through the insulation and inner hull.

How the hell had they captured a warship, even if they'd boarded it? There were so many ways to evac passages, seal locks. I figured the UN had some sort of boarder repel protocol. We'd never used it that I know of,

except in an exercise a few years back that had cost lives.
So how had they done this here?

I was dying to know.

Through the commo I heard, "Inbound, it's us."

More mechanical noise came from the outer
passenger lock, and I backed through a separator so I had
a good field of fire. I had no idea if I could shoot anyone,
but I'd try.

Mira came through the lock, armed. She moved so we
had good separation, and then others came through. It
appeared to be most of the ship's senior officers.

"This keeps them out of trouble," she said.

It made sense, but a moment later, some mouthy
commander second class started complaining.

"Per Geneva and Mars, we're supposed to be provided
quarters matching our rank. These do not."

Mira said, "As circumstances permit, which they do
not. If you want privacy, you're welcome to pitch a
hammock in the engine room, or outside."

Someone else grabbed his arm and muttered to him.
He shut up.

"How?" I asked. They'd captured a capital ship.

"Later," Mira said.

The senior officers were followed by Sebastian and
Jack. I wasn't sure who was still on their bridge, of either
their crew or ours.

This group were split between the bunk pod and the
pressure section of the bay. We threw padding and
bungees at them. Mir said, "No, it's not comfy. It will have
to do. You're alive and will be repatriated in good time.
You, Captain Second, what's your name?"

"Monaghan."

"You seem to be in charge. I will meet with you twice a day to track the needs of your fellow captives."

He asked, "Can I get your name and rank?"

"Astrogator Mira. Yes, that is my rating. My actual rank would not make sense to you."

That matched my guess that she was a Blazer. In public, that's the only way they're called. They have a rank and rating structure, but in public, they're secretive. "Blazer Mira Zelimir" would be her ID.

He looked irritated, and I couldn't blame him. He'd lost his ship. That probably meant the career end for every officer, and might mean criminal charges. It certainly wouldn't make any crew confident of their ability.

I figured they were doing something, and it was a matter of a few hours when they started transferring more personnel over. I mean, they stuffed them in, and then pulled us out.

I guess it made sense. *Pieper* had no weapons and limited engines. Put all the prisoners in her, and we'd have them as a shield.

They were going to stuff all the non-essential personnel into a cargo hauler that was mostly empty bay.

When the third transfer came over, there were casualties, stuffed into body bags. I gather none of them were able to be saved, and there wasn't time for stasis and a trip to a facility of course. You need an Alpha Center for that.

I figured a ship that size had a crew of three hundred. At least half that many came over, including what seemed to be every officer and CPO. They were all sequestered into life space, but without any commo. It took hours.

Toward the end, Mira released their ranking prisoner and brought him forward.

"We will provide rations from your ship. Heating facilities are limited. Toilet facilities are limited. Shower facilities are very limited. We will attempt to find a way to furnish deck pads for sleeping, and additional wash water. Drinking water will be in drums and we can fabricate cups. You will need to save and wash them."

"Thank you. If that's the best you can manage," he managed to say with a condescending sniff.

I remembered a rescue run with half that many passengers stuffed on a similar class of ship. It was better than best.

Mira didn't faze. She just said, "This is a cargo hauler. It's what we have. We could have just slagged a breech in your hull. This works better for everyone."

He nodded and let it drop. I understood him being pissed, though. They'd done the impossible, and he was humiliated, as were all the crew.

He changed subjects. "Ma'am, I formally request permission to hold a memorial service for our casualties."

"Granted," she said at once. "We can arrange it in the forward craft bay."

"Uh . . ." the captain muttered. I think he'd expected to be refused. He continued, "What honors will you allow?"

She wrinkled her brow, and said, "I assume you want a firing party? We'll do that for you. Please make sure your people understand we'll have live rounds under the blanks, and no one is to get clever."

"Absolutely!"

So I wound up in the firing party, while she sat at the controls in a locked bridge, with hard vacuum holding the hatch closed, ready to seal off the entire compartment if someone did get stupid.

Their service is similar, since ours came from Earth anyway. They didn't do any religious stuff other than a chaplain reading from three books—the Bible, the Quran and the Book of Life. They carried the sealed bags of dead into a vacuum cell so they'd stay preserved for the duration home. Once they stepped back with one flag, we fired three volleys of blanks, "we" being me, Mo, Jack, Teresa and Roger. Mira was up front. Juan, Shannon and Bast had control of *Scrommelfenk*.

I hadn't done firing party before, but we'd rehearsed.

"Half right, face. Load. Aim. Fire. Aim. Fire. Aim. Fire. Half left, face. Present, ARMS!"

The blanks were fucking loud in that space. Then we stood at present arms while they played "Taps," the flag was folded and presented to the captain. They didn't play "Amazing Grace." I guess that's something we do.

When he received the blue flag, the captain pivoted, and ordered, "Firing Party, dismissed!"

As we marched out, Roger turned and backed into the hatchway. I followed his lead, as did the others, so we always had the prisoners in view. It felt like that.

But it did feel good to give them some closure and proper respect. It seemed to calm them down a lot.

Jack and Mira stayed aboard with me. The rest remained or went back aboard *Scrommelfenk*.

⊕ ⊕ ⊕

The captain and the engagement officer gave us no trouble. Whenever they were out, Roger followed them around, armed with a knife and a baton. They never argued with him once.

The crew, though, were determined to take their ship back. Roger and Mo had to reroute controls, and hard-cut several conduits. Then, they kept everywhere we weren't using in vacuum.

I got to suit through, alone, in an acquired UN V-suit, placing optical motion sensors in discreet places, and disabling lighting, even emergency glow. It was scary. Ships are never dark unless you have a private berth and choose it. But I turned parts of it into an airless coffin. Even the hatches were disabled.

The crew actually managed to cut between their powered sections and team up. We tried to keep track, as a lieutenant commander kept them busy with sanitation, cooking, exercise. That was good and effective.

But it didn't take all of them to do that, and they had a lot of down time. Some played games, but Teresa pointed out that a lot of them weren't accounted for.

"I think they may be planning to cut into one of the shorter passages and try to reach life-support from there," she said.

"They all die if they do," Mira said.

"Should we stop them?" I asked. I wasn't sure.

"We have an obligation to make sure they don't kill themselves through error. But, they know this is possible and they're taking the risk. I expect if they make a small hole and start getting a pressure drop, they'll seal it."

They were surrounded on six sides by hard vacuum.

We only pressurized the main passage when we needed to. Three times a day I rolled a dolly of rations down and left it in the passage for them. They returned it for the next meal.

Sure enough, they started cutting into hard vacuum and slapped a patch over it. It wasn't a very good patch, but we left it like that to keep them nervous and afraid of trying again.

I guess they hoped to complicate things if they got through, but really, where would they go? They'd have a cargo ship is all. Unless they figured to ransom us to the others in exchange for a warship? Hell, it would be a fair trade to treat the four of us as collateral and slag the lot of them, and keep the warship. I knew Juan would see it that way.

I worried about something else. There had to be an intercept en route. There was no way we'd be left alone with a ship, and why hadn't it had some escort boats?

When it was all over, I got to see the after-action review. At the time, I was just confused.

There were escort boats, but what could they shoot at? We'd effectively captured a squadron. Or, they had and I watched. Actually, I didn't even watch, I was just in the area. I wish the story was better.

The escorts hung out a few light seconds away, but when Juan explained that he could slag them, and NovRos wouldn't do much to interfere, there was some high-level discussion and they pulled back a distance. I guess they were waiting for backup and threat.

I wasn't sure they'd actually destroy the ship, though. Money, people, politics. They'd argue and send letters and try to rile up the public. Or, they might hide it entirely from shame. But it was trillions of marks, they had hundreds of people's lives at stake, there was no way they'd just blast it. Juan was going to roast anything that tried to close. So I didn't see a way out.

Their ships are different from ours, but not much. She was a bit older than *Mad Jack*, but both were older than our new ones that have phase drive.

We all transferred to *Scrommelfenk*, leaving *Pieper* under control of the prisoners. We sent more of the crew over there, until it was stuffed. They were advised to follow directions or be considered to have escaped and be combatant. We had the warship. The crew left with us were sequestered aft, too, vacwalled from us.

I got to see the damage, and I took a guess at what happened.

The reactor warble and pod jettison made them think we had an emergency. They'd sent a boat to meet the pod, but it was already inbound for them, acting like a rescue pod homing in. Our people came out of that tug and swarmed the boat crew. Mira must have had them back aboard fast.

Once they'd docked, it looked like the guys had blown the mount and lock, then blown a hole in the compartment. Then they'd blown a hole into the outer passage.

I figured that set off every pressure alarm in the ship, slammed all the hatches and got everyone racing for vac or rescue gear, and for secure space.

They'd blown the next hatch, then through a bulkhead and compartment. One was a bunkroom, and that's where the casualties had been. Back into passage, and forward. I could trace the holes.

It must have completely confused every system, because it wasn't structural failure and it wasn't a missile, so what the hell was it? And as they moved, the entire crew was panicking into vac gear and not responding.

Then they'd reached the C-deck, locked in, shot someone—there was still a blood stain on the deck—and demanded surrender.

The ship was a mess, but it was all superficial, not structural. Emergency repairs would take a few minutes with a spark welder. In fact, Mo fixed the lock nearest the C-deck exactly that way.

I was impressed.

To Juan, I said, "Of course, once the word gets out, no one can ever pull that off again."

"No, we'll do something different." He shrugged like it was no big deal.

"Like what? Do you have a list?"

"That's restricted," he said.

"What you'll do next is? Or the existence of a list?"

"Yes. Both. Neither." He grinned.

"Okay," I said. It wasn't my business.

"Of course, we did have some luck," he said. "That was our last charge." He pointed at the lock, or I guessed, the hole behind it.

It was all luck as far as I could tell. How could you move that fast through a ship?

Juan directed *Pieper* to make for the Jump Point, and sent a message to NovRos Space Control that we intended to jump.

They cleared us at once. I don't think they had an idea of anything else to do.

We were already boosting for NovRos JP3. At max G, no one was going to intercept us easily. Trying to stop us on an "approaching vector" would mean fifty-fifty odds of hitting us before we hit them, and way better than fifty that we'd both be shredded or dead. Once we had control, there wasn't much they could do.

It was really weird to have an entire ship to the nine of us. You can run one like that if you need to. My job was to keep them fed and watch gauges for anyone who needed a break. We ran two shifts of five and I covered half of second shift, too. I slept when I could. It was almost two days to loop around and realign. NovRos didn't want to be a belligerent, so they weren't going to lock the point. They were neutral, so any UN craft could follow, but not actively pursue or shoot. They wanted us out so it wouldn't be their problem.

And they'd already filed a huge protest with the UN and the Colonial Alliance over the UN chasing us, since we were not acting as combatants in their space. Of course, they'd also complained about us being suspected of transferring war materiel in their space, but it wasn't proven.

I didn't think it would be. This team was a group of devious fucking geniuses.

NovRos didn't complain about our response and capture. It had been legitimate self-defense. I also think it terrified the hell out of them.

Mira sent a signal to *Pieper* ordering them to queue, and with data for Jump. They were told to await orders on the far side.

Since we had the warship, knew they'd be there, would only be thirty minutes behind, and had active search that could roast them inside the shell, I figured they'd comply.

Thirty minutes later, we got our light, and were within three minutes of the point. Mira could astrogate even better than she could shoot.

Then we were through.

CHAPTER 23

I wasn't sure why we chose Govannon, other than it was close. We could have gone back home, and perhaps had a crew waiting so we'd have more firepower in our system. But I guess stealing it and going away kept them busy and wondering.

Govannon was also neutral, but sort of friendly. We bought a lot of material for our Halo, and even sold them some volatiles and quite a bit of organics and lithics.

Govannon was ideally neutral, though. The UN couldn't do much to them without being cut off from all that lovely metal. The equipment they use is highly specialized, and the technicians wouldn't be open to taking orders from bureaucrats.

When we entered Govannon's system, there was a ship waiting. The *Mad Jack*. Along with her was a mass transport.

Their Jump Point control told us we had ample time for our mission, which was repatriating all the prisoners we had into the transport, where they were even more crowded.

The nine of us had added a capital ship to our nation's forces. Well, okay, the eight of them had. I'd sat and looked confused.

For now I stayed solidly out of sight, with a hat low over my head in case anyone recognized me. Between my lips, eyes and figure, someone might, but I'm pretty good at evading notice. It would have been nice to say hi to the ones I'd gotten to like, though. Or to find out how they were doing. We weren't told, so we didn't have any information if captured.

The first thing was to set up a docking tube, and move all the POWs into the transport. Sorry, that was second. First we brought over enough security to ensure they wouldn't try a fight.

At once, the technicians started converting her over. All the software, some of the hardware, and any codes were changed. Panel markings and such needed adjusted. One of the good things about the UN is they require *everything* to be marked with safety tags and identifiers. Heck, even the wrenches warn, DANGER: THE METAL PARTS OF THIS TOOL ARE ELECTRICALLY CONDUCTIVE. CAUTION: THIS TOOL IS HEAVY AND CAN CAUSE PERSONAL INJURY IF USED INCORRECTLY.

Actually, that second bit is one of the great things about wrenches, when you on purpose use them incorrectly.

A couple of spacers definitely recognized me, and they made eye contact, nodded wisely, and smiled faintly.

Obviously, they thought I was some sort of technoninja like the others. I didn't speak, just gave slow nods back, and hoped that even that little leakage wouldn't come back to hurt me. I got more paranoid every day.

Once we had the UN crew off, a security team conducted a stern to bow inspection, of every rivet and space. They looked for recording and transmission devices, bombs, other sabotage, abandoned goods. Quite a few items were discovered, including several sensor suites or simple electromechanical personal toys, as they were referenced. There were random clothes, unmarked, and small amounts of cash and valuables. The actual valuables and identifiable possessions were sent to the UN transport. The rest was imaged and either kept or disposed of.

At that point we were released back to *Pieper*, which had had the same type of security sweep.

She hadn't been damaged badly, but they had tried to escape, and there was normal wear and tear times ten. She'd been crowded.

I wanted to sterilize my bunk before I took it back, just in case, and the airlocks would need to be fixed.

One spacer came aboard, about twenty G-years old, as fit as the rest, with brown hair and an olive tone. His ears stuck out, but just enough for grip, not enough to be ugly.

"Juan, is it now?" he said.

"Yes, and who are you now?"

"Glenn Malcolm, as always. Sorry to hear about Jensen."

Juan nodded. "Yeah. Any outcome?"

Malcolm shrugged. "Unless someone did a really good substitution, he was born on Grainne, one of us. Just went for the social statist mentality in a big way."

Juan looked disgusted. "Hell, he could have left. Earth would have been happy to have him."

"Yeah, but some people want to change the world, and that's the kind we get. He did some damage, but not a lot. We're in a decent position."

"Glad to hear it."

"Where do you need me? And who is our crewwoman?" he indicated me.

"Glenn, Angie leBlanc. She's loader, but trained as medic and cook as well. I need you in maintenance and second on engines and drive."

"Pleased to meet you, Angie," he said. I offered a hand and we shook.

"Likewise," I said. I assumed he was another Blazer or whatever they were. Some sort of very elite element I'd never be in.

"I'll log into my cabin and be in engines when you need me. *Bounder Dog* is a good ship."

"Are we changing names?"

He said, "On file, yes. Company investment, and the records on *Pieper* were scrambled. Of course, they may have images of all of you."

"Hats, masks and makeup," Juan said. "I hope the Aardvarks are being strip-searched on the way out, too."

"In a Faraday compartment, a few at a time, with no notice. Just as they'd do."

He nodded at his correct assessment. "Best we can manage, then. On with the war."

I got most of that. So the UN spacers, "Aardvarks," even if not all of them were from Earth, were being searched, as was their data, to minimize anything except verbal reports.

Malcolm took over second on engines and maintenance, and on life-support. I never knew his real name, either.

Hell, even my name on file wasn't real.

A short time later we had a debrief. Juan called us all to the C-deck.

"Here's the summary. Our hosts are graciously extending credit to us, and providing overhaul and upgrade, since this is a noncombatant ship as far as they officially know."

I guess technically it was. We had no mounted weapons and hauled civilian contract cargo.

"We're going to refresh on everything. Reactor maintenance and fuel, environmental filters, food, upgrades and updates on astro, proper blended patches on those holes, and even cleaning supplies."

Ships did that all the time. Few private vessels did it all at once.

I said, "Daammn. That's a lot of credit."

"Officially, it's on account to be paid later."

So really, it was a gift from the Prescots.

"Nice," I said.

"No. Doing it for us is 'nice.' Doing it for *Mad Jack* as well is bordering on alliance. But they're covering it up as 'necessary spaceworthy repairs.' And I don't think the UN wants to fight with them."

"I guess they have money, but that won't help if the UN sends a military force and brings its own engineers to run things."

He said, "And I'd guess the company that mined the entire crust of a planet using nuclear charges, and has enough energy to melt planetoids, might have some means of deploying them in-system at least. And they control Jump Point entry. It wouldn't surprise me if they've had charges sitting in place for decades."

"Huh," I said. I hadn't thought about it. I guess they could. They had ships, they had energy shields of all kinds, and they used fusion explosions almost like fireworks. In fact, they did occasionally have big blasts that tourists could watch. I hadn't caught that from orbit, but I wish I had.

Apparently, our prize crew from *Mad Jack* managed to irritate our hosts right after that.

They moved *Scrommelfenk* to the far side of the system to the Earth Jump Point, because that's where the gear for heavy ship repair was. Once on station, *Scrommelfenk* did a hard boost without clearing it with control. They ran silent and fast, jumped into Earth space, slagged the first warship they saw, lobbed several loiter missiles at the military terminal, jacked off over the entire approach to the Point on their way around and back, and jumped back into Govannon.

Technically they hadn't violated any neutral terms, but it didn't help relations with Govannon or Prescot.

We were sitting in what was now called *Bounder Dog*, listing repairs and upgrades and documenting modules, since most were nonstandard. We needed an accurate load to show our hosts, who were supposed to be sending technical help. We were heading down to their "capital," which is pretty much all habitat at the primary planet's L2 point and in stationary orbit closer in.

I figured at that point they were going to tell us to leave and take the war with us.

It had literally been a four-day max burn. We weren't close to where we needed to be.

Juan called us in for our evening brief.

"So, there was some excitement, and we're smoothing things over."

"That's putting it mildly," Mira said. "Though I am impressed. Earth didn't even have time to post action review before we hit them."

"Everyone is impressed, and quite a few are pissed. We toasted one of their picket destroyers and a hundred crew."

Roger said, "That didn't win any friends down there. That's why the regulars need to leave the clandestine warfare to the regiment."

Juan nodded. "Well, it's done now, but we're dealing with it. We're scheduled to arrive in a couple of days and they have a labor crew ready to help us."

I asked, "Still? Despite all that?"

"Yes, it's been defused and we're not to blame."

"Good."

"Also, we sold them *Scrommelfenk*."

"Uh?" I said it the same time as Teresa.

"Two billion credits, on account with them here."

I whistled. "That was nice of them."

"It would have been, if they gave us a choice. Prescot

really wasn't thrilled with the excursion to Earth. They bought her to prevent us using her, too."

Yes, the Prescot family could afford that. That was impressive. It was also cheap for a warship. They secured the ship and got it cheap, while extending us enough account to honestly say any non-military repairs were on contract. Everyone came out ahead except the UN.

It meant Earth could feel more secure, too. Prescot had taken the ship from us.

"They couldn't fight an actual war," he said. "But the cost to Earth of stopping them would be prohibitive. So they're loading us up on non-military gear and calling it humanitarian. They're doing the same for a UN system frigate. They're paying up front. We're on our account. But of course, the UN have stations and support boats they can use for R three."

I must have looked at him funny.

"Reload, refuel, rearm."

"Ah," I said. "And yeah, they have several positions in several systems. Even neutral ones."

Roger asked, "How are the locals justifying owning a warship?"

"Apparently, they claim they'll use the fusion warheads and beams for mining and slagging. They're commissioning it the *Cullan*."

Mira said, "So, they've upgraded force beams that can cut planetoids, fusers that can melt them and a-matter that can vaporize them with puny G-beams and missiles?"

"Using one of Earth's major warships, yes."

She asked, "Can we buy it back later?"

"I doubt we can do so with the weapons intact. But after the war, we might."

It was amusing, but at the same time, scary. Earth had a major ship for each system, which could lock a gate or bombard a planet. If you barricade the gates from the far side, a system would lose all its outer system industry, then its in-system. We needed to take out enough ships so they couldn't barricade us, and hope other systems would back us up against them.

At least that's what it looked like to me.

The money involved scared me, too. I had been able to help a bit with my cubbies and friends. They had other resources like this. It was amazing what you could do with almost no money if you were creative. I realized I was a small boat in this race. I could get or swipe enough to keep me going. They were getting enough to keep a ship going in a war. A small ship, but the operating cost per div was more than I'd ever earn, unless I did get paid for this at the end. But even that wouldn't cover more than a few days running.

Late that cycle, we docked at a skeleton frame far out from the Jump Point proper, and "behind" it for transfer purposes. It had obviously been built here to protect it from anything coming through. That was done some places, and it was always blamed on "safety" against runaway, out of control ships, which I don't think had ever happened.

As soon as we secured and connected to their power, we had movement. The outer lock was set on OWSO—Open With Safety Override. It would be open for passage unless there was a pressure drop on one side or the other. It wasn't long at all before chimes and lights announced visitors. I heard Roger's voice ask, *"Bounder Dog*, what is your business?"

"Ship maintenance, sir, request permission to come aboard." The man's voice was like honey.

"Permission granted, welcome and thank you."

I ducked my head around, and he had the face to go with it. He looked like some sort of aristocrat, very polished, clean, trimmed hair with a bit of wave. All he needed was a uniform with a high collar and epaulets instead of a shipsuit.

Behind him were a platoon of mostly men with a few women, who waited in the shaft and lock and fidgeted while he spent two segs consulting with Juan and Roger.

Eventually he turned and said, "Alright, people, fall to."

I stayed out of the way but watched. I'd never seen a crew work so fast. I would swear they were all raceboat maintenance crews for the Lagrange Rampage.

I shoved aside as five of them entered the galley and took a quick inventory. Then they ran scanners over all the equipment, and started pulling.

Ten segs later, we had three new cooking modules. They also cleaned the bay. I mean really cleaned it. I did my best, but there are limits on the chemicals you can use in flight, and only so much shift time. With the elements and ovens out, they were able to scrape off a couple decades of hardened crud. A couple of Freehold decades, I think.

I don't know what went on in control or engineering, but when I looked, everything was brand new, compact, with new touchscreens and plugs for remote mods.

They brought lunch with them, but I made up some

grilled cheese with jalapeños and ham. I started with the hot-looking guy in charge.

"Oh, that's decent of you, ma'am, thank you," he said. I made sure to offer him first. After all, he was the crew boss.

"You can call me Angie," I said. "You're fixing our beast. I can at least offer food."

He took one, and a bulb of soup. I'd zazzed up the tomato with some mild red salsa and a bit of onion.

"Mmf vish is gooth," he said around it. "Sorry. Thank you again."

"I didn't catch your name when you came aboard," I said.

"Oh, sorry. Ian. Prescot." He waved instead of shaking hands. He was holding food and hooked to a stanchion by one foot.

Prescot? "Oh, family member?"

He nodded. "Yes, but a distant cousin. I own stock, but I don't own enough to matter."

"I've been through here a couple of times. I wish I could see more."

He looked bothered. "I can't help you w—"

"Sorry, I wasn't asking, just noting." Crap, no, I didn't want him thinking that.

He relaxed and said, "Right. Well, I've been down to the domes twice. They are impressive, if you can drop kilomarks without blinking."

"Yeah, maybe someday. Your station is beautiful, though."

"Thanks. I have quarters there, when not out here managing refits."

"I spent a lot of time dancing at Dark Eden."

"I've been in it. I don't dance much. I have wrenches for feet."

So much for that approach.

One of the others said, "I've been there quite a bit. Jiggy lights."

"They do," I said. He wasn't bad looking, but he wasn't Ian.

"Thanks for these, too," the second one said, nodding around his sandwich.

"Sure."

The whole crew seemed pleased. Their rats looked okay, but had been packaged hours before. Mine were fresh. I'd kept the spice level mild for us, probably medium hot for them.

I gave Ian another warm smile, and decided to let it lie until dinner. I'd offer my code then if he hadn't asked.

There were fitters inside and out over the holes we'd patched. Someone even upgraded the head, including the shower.

When I crawled out of my rack in the morning, I was the last one in the female wing. As I cleared the hatch, someone asked, "May we work in there now, ma'am?"

"Yeah, sure. Need me to move anything?"

"We'll be careful, ma'am," she said. She looked about twenty-two Earth-years, but radiated confidence. She pointed, and two others hopped in with tools and gear. I had no idea what they'd do in billets.

The head was marked off. A sign directed me to a portahead set up in the dock tube. I took care of peeing and planned to shower later. Relieving yourself in emgee is a task. It takes a seal and vacuum, and feels really odd. By the time I had everything fastened, I felt like I was about to burst.

Ian not only directed, he did some of the work himself. He was spare hands if anyone needed something held, and inspected each job personally.

He seemed to be paused for a moment, so I swam up and said, "Thanks for the work in the galley."

"You're welcome. I take it you approve?"

"Yeah, it's plush. Feeding this crew was hard with the old stuff. There wasn't any room."

He seemed more attentive that day, and did eye my cleave a bit. I wasn't flashing it, but I did have enough showing. I hoped it was clear it wasn't an accident.

"It's a tight ship, but the design is sound," he said.

"Yeah, the shower was way too tight to do much," I hinted.

"Oh?" he asked, looking interested now.

"It was hard to reach everywhere. And even if I had help, there wouldn't have been room."

"Right. And you can't really do that with fellow crew."

"Not generally, no," I agreed. "I just wish I had time to club a bit while here," I said.

"Are you docking after this?" he asked.

"No, I think we're right back out."

"Shame," he said. "I could probably get a free pass to a club."

"I'll be back through again," I said. It wasn't likely, but I wanted him to think about it.

"Well, if you come in through this point, I may still be here."

He still seemed hesitant, so I stuck out my hand until he reached into a pocket for a card.

"I'll call if I do," I said. "I'll let you work now."

His crew were still crawling through the ship, and were even working on the cargo davits far aft. She looked twenty years younger and a much classier tramper, probably second class rather than fourth. It was an upgrade and a disguise.

Glenn, the new guy, was back in engines. There was a crew there, too.

I overheard one say, "Once we're done, you may find the engines can manage about ten percent over with safety, and twenty percent with risk. I really wouldn't go past thirty, but if the alternative is death, she might do thirty-two for a few seconds."

They definitely understood what we were planning, and were helping.

They even repainted the hull designators.

We had everything new and art state, just nothing that was actually military.

If you're not a spacer, I don't think you can understand what that meant. It would have been a lot of company or family capital in peacetime. In wartime, it was absolute treasure. As a private, hidden combatant, it was beyond price. We couldn't have gotten it anywhere. It freed us from any worries other than hostile fire. It even changed and reduced our energy signature, with the engine work we got.

It was a risk to them, and they'd offered it.

I offered Ian something else, and I even found a new favorite hideout.

It was a mechanical room, with firm foam insulation around the pipes. Two of them were perfectly placed for me to wedge my ankles in and arch them for grip, pumping up my calves, and a larger one where it could support my chest. That left him free to pump me, from behind. Low G meant he could reach around with both hands, one gripping my right breast, one cupped and rubbing me. I gripped my left breast and sucked my finger as he laid into me.

The humming machines covered my gasps, and I think I passed out for a moment. There was a long time of rushing noises in my ears and I couldn't think. The smell of metal and oil was a turn on. I hadn't done this in far too long.

I could tell he was a good engineer. He found the right resonance to drive it into me, rub my clit, grip me as I slid forward, and ride back out as my hips bounced. It was the best fucking I'd had in months. I got hickeys on the back of my neck, too. I had to keep my hair low for a week.

He'd never stayed in a bunkie. I dragged him into one and snuggled for the half the night that was left. My alarm was silent. When it tickled me, I stretched and gently detached, missing human body heat as soon as I did. Then I woke him up with my mouth. I gagged and damned near choked on his second pulse, but his convulsions were worth it.

No, Ian wasn't actually his real name. But he knows who he is. Thank you for all of it, Ian. I still owe you interest on the account.

Teresa eyed me as I made it back aboard. I winked and grinned and she gave me a thumbs-up.

"How'd you do?" I asked.

"Dinner, a nice walk, and I was the only one in the bay."

"Nice!" I said. It wasn't as nice as what I got, but actual privacy and a walk. That was a close second.

CHAPTER 24

⊕

Those three days did wonders for our morale, even without having an almost-overhauled and rebuilt ship. Then, the Prescots filled our train with processed raw metal—iridium, lanthanum, tungsten, platinum, gold, iron, cobalt, manganese. It was on "Account," and we'd have to find buyers, but that wasn't hard. It rebooted our capital and ready budget, too.

Once done, we pulled out in a long, slow orbit. I didn't know where we were bound.

It was marvelous to cook with modern gear in a clean galley. I even prepped stuff ahead of time so there'd be flash-heatable leftovers. The passages were clean and had new locks. The deck plates had modern magnagrip panels with padding for shlippers when under G.

The head had new fixtures, and the shower had full surround jets with interface for "audio." I tested that with my BodyBuzz. It still wasn't as good as live man and pulsing water, but it was as close as you could ever get with modern technology.

I've often wondered about sex toys. They manage to have not only different, realistic textures, but to shift between them much like real flesh. There's obviously serious engineering in them to make that happen. So how the hell would an engineer tell anyone about that? Did they also have medical degrees to understand the tissue they mimicked? I should probably ask.

It was ten days of system boosting when Mira announced, "There will be a lengthy flight delay, then we're going to pull serious G. Everyone take care of food, hygiene, strap in, report."

I figured it was best to toss rescue rats at everyone. They didn't complain, but Roger did grab an apple as well. I hit the head and pulled into the bunkroom. Teresa was there, Mira was on the command deck.

"Angie, I'm in," I called.

Then we sat, for entire divs, half a day. We had life-support at minimum, dark and cool. The powerplant was just barely humming. I knew we were in a shipping lane. I didn't know where or what for. I had a vid playing, but wasn't paying any attention. It was just movement.

Teresa had something playing, but would occasionally look over at me, and sometimes I'd look back.

"Any idea?" I asked at one point.

"Yes, but I can't say."

"Understood."

"Are you going to take me clubbing at some point?"

"Are we doing that? I thought we were keeping discreet."

"Sure, but isn't that one of the best ways to blend in?"

"We can," I agreed.

She was nervous, and I caught it. I had no idea what they planned. Launch a hidden missile?

All of a sudden, Mira announced, "Prepare for acceleration. Immediate."

The engines hummed, rose to a whine as we hit max G, and I gasped and panted. Breathing hurt, and when I turned my head slightly, my neck cramped up, pain stabbing up and down the tendons on the right side.

Then everything blurred and I knew we'd transited the Jump Point. G slacked off, and I asked, "What was that? And is anyone hurt? I'm minor but functional."

Shannon said, "We slammed the Jump Point. Stand by." He throttled us back down, and we rolled and changed vectors.

"Slammed it?"

"Yes, we were right up against it, cut past the *Ghali* and bang, we're through, and they've got twenty segs, thirty-odd minutes, before they can do anything about it. The only information on this side is that the point triggered. They won't be looking for us, and we're on a slow shifting course to make the search cone as large as possible. They will probably assume a drive failure and scramble rescue. They will eventually figure out what we did, but that search volume is getting bigger by the second."

"Where are we?"

"NovRos Three, again."

"That's far from anything." That one was in their way outer Kuiper Belt, almost to Oort distance. It was a smaller star than ours, so we were a bit closer in, but still. Light-hours if not light-days from anything.

But, we had legit cargo, a new ID, and should be good for now.

I wondered how long we'd have this ship, and how often we could change. I figured eventually, the ten of us were going to fit a pattern, or I'd be recognized even through my makeup.

There was one small thing to like once I synced my phone. Lady Alexia had a new vid-sensie out. I was definitely playing that.

I don't know if she's known outsystem, but in Grainne she's a torch. Shapely, enthusiastic, gorgeous eyes and lips. As much as I like men, I'd be hers in a moment.

It was a div-long scene with two men and a woman. My BodyBuzz had good goggles, a good probe, touch gloves and a torso pad. In the shower, with it on low pulse just above skin temperature, I watched and felt a little bit of what she had. Her first man was well-built, and large enough to make me pant, as well as firm and vigorous. He had very delicate fingers, though, and I shivered as well as clenched up as I orgasmed. I felt it all the way up my belly and around to my neck.

The woman was very sensual and gentle, almost teasing, and had Alexia, and me, very ready for the next man. They shared, both of them, with very nimble tongues and firm grips, then his cock and her tongue, then each of them in her mouth, and I wished they had an interface for that. I wanted to taste them both.

But as far as simsex went, it was mindfucking, and totally worth the cost. Her plays run from very nice to off-the-scale scorching. This was definitely more that way. I knew I'd be using that at least once a week on my current rotation, but damn I wanted some real flesh. Man if I could find it, woman if not.

But I was a spy in a warzone. Simsex was probably going to be my last thrill, and ratpacks my last meal, before I died in a glowing haze of burst reactor.

But it took the edge off.

And it felt so fucking good compared to being probed and zapped.

I missed Ian.

Despite it being a remote station, this was the way I'd come in last time, and I'd gone through a couple of times before that.

Roger and Jack went to sell metal. The others were doing stuff, and I stayed aboard to fix one of the new ovens. It had a connection issue of some kind. It was minor, just a dirty terminal, and the kind of thing that happens with refits. Mo had already fixed a nav sensor that wasn't quite tracking and didn't hold zero. Routine if you have a new ship, which we basically did.

Roger and Jack were back shortly.

"Good news is, we sold a bunch," Jack said. "Bad news is, the ship was through here previously. Whichever one they lifted the ID from."

"How bad is it?" Juan asked.

"I don't know. I think a bit of cash will fix it. But we should clear out and stay low until it does."

"Damn," Juan scowled. "Yeah, we don't need to have another inspection crew come through. I wish I could take the heat on this, but—"

"I'll hold it," Glenn Malcolm said.

"Thank you."

It made sense. Juan was the team officer. He couldn't sacrifice himself unless there was a good reason. Bad ID that might lead to an arrest wasn't good enough.

I also remembered Glenn was new, and covering for someone we couldn't trust.

Juan said, "If we can find a bolthole, then call the Port Authority. I'd rather go to them in a panic, worried about my ship and wanting to get things clear."

I said, "NovRos means you will need a bribe either way. Offer it as a reward for clearing the issue. Stress schedule time or something. Ask for help."

"A share of the profits we don't lose for keeping schedule?"

"Yes. Ask if a small percentage will work."

"How big do I have to go? I don't want to be obviously desperate, or cheap."

"I honestly don't know," I said. "But I know someone who might. Actually, he has an office we may be able to hide in."

"An office? That does business?"

"Sort of."

Yuri Molotin should still be in his regular place. I sketched it out, gave them the addy and said I'd lead. Yes, sketched. You wouldn't find it on a map. The station was old and had been recompartmented several times, then you're dealing with a lot of underworld types who like safehouses, and usual spacer attitude. Half the station wasn't properly mapped.

"I don't know if he'll be willing to take us all, but I have an idea. Can you follow me in stages?"

Glenn said, "Easily."

"Okay, about a seg apart, but make sure the passage is mostly vacant." I told them what order to be in.

"Got it." He grinned. I felt like I was telling him stuff he already knew.

Yuri consults for people. Most of the time, it's legitimate research on routes, markets and laws. Other times, it's slightly less legitimate research on routes, markets and laws.

His office is five rings in, off a second-flow passage, down a business way, through their door and into an office block, down the passage and around the back, behind the frosted door of a suite marked "C." There's no sign anywhere. You contact him by messaging his contact and he arranges to meet you. The only reason I knew where he worked was because I'd been in that office helping him with similar stuff to what I was doing now. And getting a shower with all the pleasures.

I pretty much walked straight there. It was evening by clock time and quiet, but the office block was still open. I went to his door and knocked gently.

Of course, sometimes he works from home if he doesn't have a pending client. I wasn't sure where his quarters were just then, and there was no answer to my knock.

I tried a second time. Two knocks.

Eventually the door cracked open.

"Angie!" he said, eyebrows raised. Then he smiled. "What's up?"

"Can I come in?"

"Sure." He opened the door and waved. He looked slightly older and had gained a couple of kilos, but still a good-looking guy and very responsive if you knew what he liked.

I said, "I happened to be on station and thought I'd look you up."

"Cool. You're tramping?"

"Yes, with a friend. Platonic only, though."

"Hah. They usually are except in your hot sensies."

"I know," I said.

That was when there was a knock at the door.

"That's Teresa now, if that's okay," I said.

"I guess," he said, and opened the door. "Hi, come in."

"Thank you, Goz," Teresa said politely, and took the chair next to me.

"So are you looking for work?" he asked, with an expression that was almost suspicious. But, he's always suspicious.

"Not exactly," I said. "I might have info for you, though. I've been on a long tour with a couple of friends since the war started. And we need some info."

"Oh?"

"Yeah, Teresa and I are bunkies on a tramper out of Alsace. The astrogator may definitely have some useful route updates for you, with all the missile exchanges going on."

"Oh, are those real?"

Knock knock.

"That's Mira now," I said.

"Fine," he said, and opened the door again.

Mira took a stool he offered.

I said, "I was just telling him about the missile exchanges."

"Yes," she said. "I've tracked several, and we went through a dead zone."

"I'd like to hear about that," he said. "How did that come about?"

"Well, the five of us are crew on this Alsace tramper," I said.

"How did we go from three to five?" he asked.

"Because Jack is in engines and Roger handles cargo, and you might want to know about that, too."

There was another knock, and it was the two of them. They leaned back into the corners, and I could tell Yuri was a bit nervous.

"So you're all crewing on this ship and have info on clandestine maneuvers?" he asked.

"Yeah," I said. "A month ago we were in Govannon, and Juan and Mo managed to arrange upgrades and refits. It's not even really the same ship anymore. That's part of our problem."

He said, "Okay. This is definitely useful stuff if you can give me details."

That knock should be Mo and Juan, and it was.

"How big's the fucking crew, Angie?" he finally asked.

"Just three more."

"Bring them in. And you're going to give me actual data, not teasers?"

"As best we can."

"Why?"

"We need crash space and to find out who can help us clear up a registration error."

Roger, Shannon and Bast came through, and his front office was packed. He looked put upon and nervous.

"I can hide a person here. Maybe two. Beyond that, it'll start to show in air cycle."

Juan said, "We can rotate. Our need is only intermittent, and not all at once."

"It's conditional on your data being stuff I actually need," he said. "We're not in the war, but, *bozhe*, are the cops getting snoopy."

"Everywhere," Mira said.

"Yeah. And I'd rather not be dragged in for suspicion of terrorism. I handle enough data as is, and I do my best to make sure they're just smugglers or tax evaders, not real criminals."

"I will make it very worth your while," I offered. He was clean and decent enough, I could get some touch, and I knew that kink he liked with a silk tie and brandy.

"We can discuss it," he said, blushing slightly. He wasn't at all a prude, but liked to be discreet, as with everything he did.

"You guys get food," I said. "Give me a couple of hours to fill Yuri in."

Actually, that was one of his kinks. I almost snickered.

I worked him over with my toys and his tie until his twitches told me he was near his hard limit. I wanted to push him but not hurt him. When he came he literally screamed and whimpered, and almost looked like he was having a seizure. I'd seen that last time, but it still scared me. That's what gave him the best release, though.

Once his eyes focused he grinned.

"Ohhh, *bozhe*, Angie. Almost no one can ever get me off like that."

"I like watching you," I said. It was partly true. I was

flustered and needed to be nailed myself, but this was work.

Once he cleaned up and redressed, we talked business in his back office.

"So what do you need?" he asked.

"The captain says there's an error in our registration. We show on file as a different ship of the same class, but we have the wrong dock histories on manifest."

"Ah, a manifest problem from discreet transport. These problems happen often."

I wondered how often from just errors, rather than smuggling or deeper stuff.

"Can we fix the manifest?"

"You can, but fixing it well is expensive. Just getting a short waiver is cheap."

I figured a better cover was what we wanted, especially as we might get into Earth space again. I called Juan to come back.

He arrived, and I was impressed how he looked us over, assessed the last two hours, and moved on with no comment or expression. He took a seat.

"Welcome back, Juan," Yuri said. "Angie tells me about your problem." He summarized back.

Juan said, "That's about it. Our logs have errors and with the current political climate I'm concerned about being hassled."

"Logs can be updated," Yuri said, "but it can be pricey." He leaned back in his chair with a glass of vodka. I declined. Juan accepted.

He sipped and asked, "How expensive?"

"What are you carrying?"

Juan had a printed page with no name or nomenclature, that listed metal tonnage.

"That," he said, handing it to Yuri.

Yuri read over it.

"Wow," he said. "That's a lot of cargo for a tramper."

I said, "Yeah. They're good at getting contracts."

"Very good," he said. "It would be smart to be a bit less good, to attract less attention in future."

Juan said, "Possibly. Business means money, though."

"May I destroy this?"

Juan said, "Please do."

Yuri fed it into a multishredder that turned it into fine dust, flash-burned the dust and soaked the ash. How many people keep one of those handy?

He kept talking. "You know how the UN frowns on money, while spending quadrillions."

"Yeah."

"I know the man to talk to in the Port Authority. But he will want more than just money."

"Like what?" I had a guess. This was NovRos underworld.

Yuri said, "It is a rule of his to have someone of the female crew. No permanent damage, but the women I've talked to did not enjoy the experience."

Yeah, some of the fucking mob were exactly that.

"Is he hideous?"

"No, he is quite attractive. Just very demanding and unpleasant." His expression didn't reassure me.

"I guess I can manage for a few hours. Will that be enough?"

"Yes. Though my people tell me those hours feel like a sentence."

"Good thing the others are away, then. Who needs to see him?"

"The captain, and the sacrifice, if that is you."

I understood he was using that word on purpose. "How much damage does this guy do?"

"Nothing permanent outside," he said.

"Can I get drunk first?" I was wondering about a Zap, some Sparkle and possibly Null before I went on this.

"He will insist."

"Oh, great." I was surprised I didn't sound sarcastic. I was going to pimp myself to a vor to get our Adminwork sanitized. Gods.

Yuri took me and Juan to see an Ivan Chesnikov in the Port Authority. His office read, "Records Inspector." He was tall and handsome, and he looked as cold as a fish. No emotion at all.

"Mister Chesnikov," I noted that Yuri didn't call him by his first name. "This is Mister Gaspardeau and Ms. leBlanc. Their ship's log has become disorganized and doesn't reflect their proper space history. I have told them you are an expert in correcting errors."

"Yes, I can do that," he said. "Do you have the archive with you?"

Juan pulled out a stick, and handed it over.

"Do please take seats," he said. "Thank you for bringing them to me, Yuri."

"Have a good day, Mister Chesnikov."

Yuri was gone.

The man was good. "Yes, I see discrepancies here. It

could be bad. Read without context, one might think this ship had disappeared off the books for a year, and changed systems to Govannon. Obviously, you went through . . . Chersonessus to Alsace to Sol to Grainne, which you were concerned about listing, then to Caledonia and to here, and from here to Govannon."

Juan said, "That is the route we took, yes. For some reason, it didn't log properly."

"Very good," Chesnikov said. "I can fix this from our files. There is a research fee, and it will require overtime on my part."

Juan said, "I'm happy to pay for your overtime, sir. I know you have a lot of ships to track, but the sooner we can depart the better. I understand work outside regular duties is a drain on your office budget."

"Exactly. Mistakes happen and can be fixed. We will work on it." He wrote a number on a slip of paper.

M70,000. Goddess.

"Of course, sir." Juan didn't quibble.

"I will work late tonight and tomorrow. Could Ms. leBlanc bring your payment then? And join me for dinner?"

I put on my bubbly club grin and said, "If that works for you, Captain, I'd be delighted to join him."

"That is excellent news that it's that fast a fix," Juan said. "Perfect, and thank you."

"I'll buzz for entrance," I said, wanting to sound naive for him. He probably liked that.

"No, call this number at the gate," he said.

The next night, I put on split panties and stockings

under a clingy black dress with a high neck and cleave window. It had a window in back, too, and thigh slits that didn't quite show anything. Slices of my ass showed through the drapes. I had black hair ticked with silver to match, and dark lips.

I arrived on time, with a half-dose of Null in me, because I was fully believing it was going to be rough.

He answered my call and said, "Come around to door two."

I could see that door, and went there. I walked in, and everything in the passage was dark except for one office.

And there he was. We didn't have dinner.

Chesnikov was a real bastard. He literally cut my clothes off, and that hadn't been a cheap outfit. Spanking I can handle, but he laid into me hard. My ass was nothing but tender bruises for three days. I could barely walk. He pissed on me, spat on me, called me names that didn't matter because this was business, but insisted I play along. I was a filthy whore. I craved his cock in my ass. Yes, like that. Hurt me.

I love roleplay, but this was work. Making it sound not like work was more work. Making that feel not like work . . . you get the idea.

I'll give him this, he kept to the safe signal when he choked me. Whenever my hand went slack, he stopped long enough for me to gasp.

When he got close, I arched my back, clamped down hard enough that I felt everything burn, begged him to choke me like a bitch, and demanded he pull my hair, daddy. He did, and that left bruises, too.

Then he got completely disgusting.

I felt satisfaction when he finally came, but it wasn't enjoyable, just, *oh, good, that's over, I hope.*

But he almost passed out himself, and admitted he was impressed.

"When you come through next time, you must look me up again," he said.

"As soon as I clear ship," I said with a wink, a glint and a grin.

Not for fifty K-marks, you disgusting perv.

That was one of the worst parts of the war for me. Fucking him was harder than shooting people, or getting shot at. I don't know if he's alive or dead now, and I don't intend to ever find out.

But he delivered the logs back, with corrections and a couple of small fines noted, and we never had problems after that.

I walked back to Yuri's in a schoolgirl outfit he provided. It was exactly one size too small all over.

Back at Yuri's, I handed the info to Juan, and sat very stiffly as everyone stared at me.

"How was it?" Yuri asked.

"I will not fucking talk about it." I said. "Ever."

He seemed sympathetic, but there was a curious bite to it I didn't like. The Null was wearing off, and I took another, a full one this time, and a glass of vodka with some banana juice mixed in. I needed to numb my brain.

"I'm going to use your shower," I said. I needed to wash piss out of my hair.

Teresa said, "I've ordered a coverall in your size."

"Thanks."

As I reached the door, Juan called, "Angie."

"Yes?"

"You have our very sincere thanks. That's the last that will be said about it."

I nodded and went in to get clean.

CHAPTER 25

◈

A few hours later, after I'd napped and swallowed some NanoGen for the bruising, and Juan and Mira had reviewed the corrected log, we were back aboard ship.

"I think it's safe now," Juan said.

Glenn Malcolm said, "I guess it's going to get tougher all the time."

"Yes," Juan said. "They'll change codes, policies, clearances. They'll piece together which ships were where. Even after we left, they can eventually pattern it all. Then they'll backtrack *Bounder Dog* to *Pieper*. Eventually they conclude we're the threat."

"What happens then? We die?" I was scared.

He was smiling confidently as he said, "Or we shift everything around again. We also hope the war is over by then."

"Do you think that will happen?"

He barely shrugged. "I don't know. But we didn't plan the mission to end with death. It might happen, but we plan to survive."

"Good."

"So, we're going low key for a bit, and will stick to lesser systems where fewer questions are asked. We can't do as much damage, but we can likely cause them to have to regarrison. That means shuffling more troops around."

"Is it worth it?" I asked.

"It's a bit late for that, isn't it?" His smile was amused and quirky.

"I mean, will that matter?"

"It all matters. Five percent here, a kilocred there, someone in tears inside their perimeter. It all adds to the effect. Eventually they break."

From NovRos we went across system, didn't do anything untoward, and jumped into Mtali. Mtali is a system so messed up the group who discovered it abandoned it in under a century, and it's fallen into tribal conflict. It's not as bad or as poor as Salin, but it's not much better.

They import a lot of metals and gases, and we sold the rest of what we had. They export mineral goods and artifacts. They have some stunning wood that was being shipped both as raw timber and in finished lumber and goods. There were coffee tables I'd have loved to have, if I had a place to put them and the money to buy them. I could get them cheap if I stayed here, but that was more expensive than paying for them. I mean, it was cheap to live there, but for reasons that made it a bad idea to live there.

They prefer to ship through NovRos, because Earth's rules are a pain in everyone's ass, and a lot of stuff leaves Earth semi-legally and then officially departs from Mtali. Drugs, weapons. Even though there's theoretically a UN office in-system, they know better than to interfere. There's one station in planetary orbit, and no one really docks to it. It's very bare. There are a couple of name hotels, some chain restaurants, a lounge and a government-run bunkie lodge. That's it.

We were back out of there, through Alsace, and to Chersonessus, which was remote but surprisingly wealthy. I'd never figured out why.

They have very little UN presence because they're a secondary system with no other breakouts yet, but they were tunneling to Earth and the Freehold then. The Freehold point was probably going to be a waste with UN occupation.

We loaded up on volatiles. There were short transits that weren't hugely profitable, but very reliable. Remember I said it's sometimes cheaper to get stuff from another system through the point, than fly all the way down the gravity well to get it in-system? This was that. Chersonessus had stupid amounts of gas giants and liquid dwarfs in the outer belt. That's where their money came from. Slow and steady but very reliable, because everyone needed them.

We went back to Alsace and delivered half, then across system to deliver the other half.

We had a briefing, and Juan thanked us.

The overhauled C-deck even had supplemental seats. The refit had shaved a few centimeters off consoles and such, and even that makes a space feel bigger. Modernizing had reduced mass, increased space and efficiency, and made our home much more comfortable.

Facing us, Juan said, "Thank you all. That was very smooth, and helps our cover and commercial reputation.

It should take a few scents off, especially as we now have a reliable fake last year."

"Was that reliable?" Jack asked.

"It seems to be. Nothing else has pinged."

"As long as he doesn't sell us in."

I said, "I doubt he will. It would compromise him. He'd have to try to cut an illegal deal with the UN, which they'd keep until it was expedient to burn him. Also, they hate the UN more than we do."

Juan said, "There has been a significant amount of moral support from NovRos."

Glenn said, "On the one hand, good. On the other, I might prefer a higher class of bastards as allies."

Juan said, "So we're going back into action, in two ways."

"First we're going to need to get more personal. All UN personnel are now targets and we'll take targets of opportunity. I'd like to minimize threats to families. It's not their war, and they pack a huge psychological footprint against us.

"Then, we're going to start running fake ops and false-flags both. In Earth space."

Mo said, "Damn, that's ballsy."

"We tried avoiding them, and it did keep pressure off home, but they've violated all the niceties, so we are, too. We have to scare them into withdrawal."

Jack asked, "Think it'll work?"

"If not, it will at least mess them up."

The news from back home was frightening. I hadn't been there in years, other than the Halo, but it was still my home.

Earth had occupied, but had destroyed the economy in the process. Everything was down and closed. Food wasn't a problem, with the huge agricultural sector, but no one had jobs to pay for it.

"So I'm going to translate," Roger said. "The 'offered' aid to farmers is mandatory oversight with a bunch of fees and adminwork to get the minerals they need for production, followed by mandatory inspection, tagging, et cetera of produce, and mandatory regulated packaging and transport, all of it billed back to the farmers. Large amounts are rejected, so the price goes up. In the cities, no one has any jobs because there are no imports, and the UN mandates a variety of 'free' benefits to employees that employers have to pay for, so a lot of them went broke and closed shop, which is now illegal, so they ran out at night."

"Wait," Jack cut in. "How is it illegal to stop doing business?"

"It's bad for the workers."

"But if you have no assets?"

"They consider that punishment for not being successful. And if you are successful, they tax you until you break that way."

He looked more disturbed by this than I'd ever seen him. "How can you be successful with all that management? And no customers?"

"You're trying to be logical."

"How does anyone make money in the UN?"

I said, "Mostly black market, and large corps with ties to the government, who use their reps to negotiate exemptions."

"'Reps?'"

"Their representatives in the General Assembly of Nations."

He looked even more confused. "I'd heard of that. How do companies have political representation?"

"I don't know, but it keeps them in business and the government gets a cut."

Mira said, "But there were small outlets on station."

"Almost all of those are owned by some larger conglomerate," I explained. "They use their own name, but they're sourcing someone else's goods and riding on their revenue ID."

"Gods."

I said, "I'd never imagined the UN would try to apply their system to ours. I can't even guess how you'd set it up. First you'd have to find everyone."

Teresa said, "Even then, you'd have to plow quadrillions into creating databases, establishing policies and offices. How can they afford this?"

"They can't," Juan said. "And it's our job to make it as much more expensive as possible, until they collapse. That's why we're heading for Sol system soon, too."

I wasn't sure space travel was going to survive this. Our system was dying fast, and how long could the UN afford to maintain troops all over the place and transit costs that weren't generating income?

If we went down, and someone else went down, Earth would go down for certain, and that was it for civilization. The number of people didn't matter. The costs and the fragility mattered.

I may be wrong. I'm a cargo handler. But I know what

it takes to run a ship and make a living, and how thin that margin is. Supporting another system, which is what they were trying to do, by remote, was like trying to fix a plumbing leak by setting your money on fire and flushing it, so the ash would fill the crack.

CHAPTER 26

⊕

Three jumps later we were in Sol system, and cleared for cross-system with a beacon. We finally arrived at Sol JP3 across from Caledonia.

I guess the reports of other "terror" attacks were true. The station was locked down tight. The engineers had built a jetty, and we docked to that. They sent a crew to detach the train, and a powered dock to take the onboard cargo. Some of the V-suits read "INSPECTOR" or "SECURITY." They ran scanners over everything, and I was worried we'd get nailed.

"Are they billing us for that?" I asked.

"Oh, yes," Roger said. "We're barely making a flip on this leg."

Pretty soon ships would stop calling if they did that.

"What are we loading?"

"Dried and nitro-packed food, sundry goods and administrative technical gear for the Freehold occupation forces."

". . . they're paying us to take stuff to our own system?"

"It's times like this that war is awesome. Now, if we can just get them to pay us to bring it back . . ."

They were still unloading, and charging us dock time for the time it took them to do it, even though we weren't docked.

I wondered how many of the other ships were somebody's spies only here for some leverage.

Roger said, "It'll be late tomorrow night before they finish reloading us."

Once the unloading crew had cleared ship, Jack and Teresa went aft with scanning gear.

"Look what we found," she said when they returned. She had a plastic jar with layers of gel padding and something inside those.

"I'm assuming that's a bug?"

"It was. It's now getting a lot of white and pink noise that sounds like engine testing and fluid transfer."

"Interesting," Shannon said. "Just us, all ships, random, or specific craft?"

Glenn asked, "And how much could it pick up from back there?"

"It would have taken a lot of filtering but anything in the bay would have been audible. It's isolated now."

"What about outside the hull?" Mira asked.

Bast said, "I ran a pretty strong microwave beam around. We'll want to check for intel, but I should have cooked anything."

Juan said, "Nevertheless, keep chatter even less than minimum, and . . ." he nodded to Mira, who did something with her console ". . . we'll continue this with audio jamming."

He sat back and brought up an external view of the station.

"We're trying to both have a logistical effect and a psychological one. We can't readily get through the triple gate they've got. So we need an alternate way into the terminal, via personnel lock. Inboard container C-five W has the stuff."

I remembered that one. It was one of the "rich people" stash of cargo we kept remanifesting with help from local shills.

"That stuff?" I asked. "It's recreational beach equipment."

"Which can hold pressure and supply oxygen."

I thought through the manifest I'd seen months ago. They were actually planning to use wetsuits for EVA.

"Underwater gear in vacuum?"

Bast said, "Dive tanks and fishbowls, with gaskets and harnesses. Jack will set you up."

"How reliable do you think that will be?" I was thinking they were going to use friction tape and insulation foam. That was spacer engineering.

"As long as it gets us in, and hopefully out, it's fine."

"I'm guessing you need a map?"

"No. Now you really earn your pay."

I gulped and my guts tensed up.

"I really don't know this station well." This was another one I'd visited once.

"We trust your knowledge of the stations generally, and culture," he said.

What they came up with was more sophisticated than

I expected. The bowls had foam gaskets on a yoke, and strapped and pilehooked to the top of the wetsuit, with oxy bottles on the back. The fittings for the oxy lines looked very professional, and professionally mounted into the helmet with bearing locks and gaskets.

"Can you get fitted?"

"Me?"

"We'll come back in and need to be out of sight. You've got to lead."

This was insane, and probably deadly. And I'd signed a contract for exactly that.

It was the most intimate, non-sexy thing I've ever done. Shannon, Bast and I stripped naked to get into the suits, and Teresa and Jack helped us.

The wetsuit went on over what felt like a gallon of lube. It was exactly the same lube used for sex toys. That made sense. Jack slathered it all over my back, I got my front, breasts, thighs and down, then he got my arms while I did my own collar. It was slippery and sensual, and damned cold in the air.

It wasn't even sexy watching them lube Roger up. This was business, and someone was going to die in the process.

I wiggled and pulled with Jack's help, getting the flexible membrane over me. The suit was a tight barrier. The boots were military-arctic-issue, solid elastomer, and then covered with polymer bags and elastic. The gloves were done the same way. The oxy and nitry hoses were clicked into the fish bowl, and I wondered why the hell I was doing this.

It was a vacuum suit. It had no heat or cooling, no

relief mechanism. There were no transponders or even latches for lines. The only gauge was a blood meter clipped to my ear, and I was expected to adjust the O2 feed with a knob on my left shoulder.

"Can you reach it?" Jack asked.

"Just," I said.

"Good. Keep your color above orange and below violet."

"Got it," I said. Yes, I wanted to keep breathing.

The maneuver harness was the most professional looking bit. I'd never used one, but it looked right. I don't know if they'd built those or bought them. Or stolen them.

We had a crew lock next to the rear cargo hatch, that was officially connected to the escape pod.

The others cycled through first, then greenlit me. I locked in, pumped down, locked out, and the pod had been shifted a half meter on its ways. I could just squeeze out into space.

I'm EVA-qualified and have used several crawlie pods to traverse a cargo train. I'd done it in a rated suit once, a few years before. In all cases, I had two tethers or a trolley cable to hold me in place.

Now I had neither.

I didn't have any commo, either.

I can't tell you how absolutely terrified I felt right then. We were unattached, in improvised suits with no commo. Any mistake would mean either instant depressurization or lingering hypoxia.

I climbed out and pointed myself toward the control blister on the hub. I was told the thrust vest should be aligned with my mass, close enough, and that I could make small corrections in flight. Shannon had been very specific.

"You eyeball with both eyes to make sure you're aligned, then just the barest gas, and repeat every hundred seconds or so. You don't want to hit at speed, and you don't want to ricochet or flyby."

"Have you done this before?" I asked.

"Yes, in training, never like this."

"Okay," I said. At least it wasn't just some clever-assery they'd come up with.

Very slow, they'd cautioned. We had divs. I stared at my target, checked with each eye alone, then took a deep, deep breath. It was almost too much oxy, and my head spun. I held it in until I leveled out, then did it.

I opened the valve just a RCH and closed it. I waited, counted a full hundred seconds, and looked around. I'd moved about fifty meters. The rough parallax scale I had, printed on paper, confirmed that. Yes, that was probably a good velocity.

It was hard to see any movement, and I was still twitchy with no line. I was in free space. The money wasn't enough for this, so, I obviously wasn't doing it for the money.

It was fucking cold. We were in shadow, and radiated heat. My hands and feet were numb by the time we were a half K along.

It was a half div before we reached the lock. It had apparently been either an emergency or cargo lock at some point. Now it was an inspection and maintenance lock with steady traffic.

As we approached the lock blister, I saw others EVA.

They were doing repairs and inspections of two ships brought to this end for close examination. I hoped they didn't examine us.

I wondered how we'd avoid attention. There were several other people pulling maintenance on the station hull and sensors, using crawly drones. I guess they were just too busy to pay attention.

No one gave us a glance. I figured it was three things. We wore V-suits, so we must belong outside. There are so many models and styles, no one would pay attention to one unless it was really sexy and techie. And even improvised, they were well-made and looked professional.

Besides, most spacers aren't familiar with wetsuits. Hell, I wasn't.

We locked through with several others and nobody gave any notice or said a word. I was sweating even though I was still shivering, and trembling a bit from fear of the outside, fear of notice, and recovering from it all, but no one mentioned that, either. The guy next to me looked pretty wiped out from whatever work he was performing.

Most of the EVAs had lockers inside the personnel dock for changing. A few did wear them all the way back to their ships. Juan didn't want us hanging out here. We planned to change elsewhere so we didn't leave a trail either way.

There were locker rooms, showers and dolly-boxes all the way through. We made our way, and were almost out when a guy looked up and said, "Hey, are those amphibious suits?"

Shannon said, "I dunno, might be. We got them used."

"Military surplus?"

"Dunno. Suit Cycler had them on special a few years back."

"Neat."

We kept walking, hoping for no more interaction with anyone. All the cameras and sniffers were threat enough.

I was on new deck here. I'd never been in any controlled areas off-dock. All the hatches in the passage were sealed.

But there was a vestibule around one that would give us room to change if we hurried. It had some stacked crates that weren't even dogged down, so it was probably not used much.

We all peeled and squirmed out of the suits. They clung worse than wet spandex, sticking then pulling loose, and the lube gel had dried sticky. Bast handed me some wipes that first made it all slippery again, then cleaned it off.

Not bad. He had nice tone, nice lines and I could definitely see him spreading me. It was a shame we wouldn't have a chance until this was over, if ever.

Shannon was also quite acceptable. They had intelligence, fitness from exercise and that emotional strength I could feel.

Shannon had shipsuits in his satchel, and slipper boots. We had no underwear. We had passes that were fake, but people generally don't look at them inside a perimeter. Bast had a tool pack across one shoulder. Hopefully with the pouches and suits we'd blend in enough.

Rolling the wetsuits was tough. There was no way they'd pack small enough. Even being modern ones, and I gather the old ones of rubber were huge, they would fill a fair-sized backpack. Bast used some line ties and turned them into discreet bundles. He ripped the tubes off the helmets and stacked those behind the crates.

We were on the night hours by system time, but it was getting close to morning. There are people up all cycle round, and more were going to be up soon.

CHAPTER 27

✛

As we walked out of the service passage into the terminal passages, someone challenged us.

"Hey!"

Sebastian said, "Sorry, we got lost. Thought there was a service 'vator we could use."

"No. This is operations only."

"I said we're sorry."

We made it out and into the station service passage behind that. We were still in restricted volume, even more so. This was the public access for the processors, not the underdeck for the maintainers.

Someone had seen or said something. A squad of security goons came at us from three sides. They had carbines out, and I was staring at a muzzle.

"All of you face down on the deck and do not move."

I raised my hands and puckered up, imagining interrogation Round Two.

I don't know who moved first, but it was suddenly a

melee. Sebastian had one guy bent backwards over his knee and his hand around the throat armor of a second. Shannon was on the ground with two others in a tangle.

One of the last pair waved his carbine around, looking for a spot to shoot, I suppose. The last one had me covered. I couldn't do anything without getting shot.

Then he turned his head a fraction to watch the thrashing legs in Shannon's fight.

I tuellered him. I have no idea why, I just shoved and sprinted. He glanced back at me, I heard the safety click, and why was his weapon on safe after a fight started? And I hit him, my left arm around a thigh, my right hand heel under his chin. He staggered into the wall and fell on me.

I tried to roll on top, then realized his buddy might shoot me if I did. I was safer here.

He was heavier than me, of course, and had armor. He broke my grip and struggled to get up until I thumbed him in the throat and squeezed. It was just above his armor, and he started choking and coughing.

Then a foot kicked him in the face and almost broke my thumb in the process. It was Shannon's.

"Let's move," he said, and dragged me from under.

I hobbled behind him as he pointed up the ladder. Sebastian led the way, applied a power shear to the lock and opened it. We climbed up and were in a ventilation and power conduit.

Those all look the same, and I knew what we needed.

"Over there, behind the plenum," I said.

Once there, I found the access door. You can actually walk inside them, and the engineers do, for maintenance. Sebastian cut it, Shannon opened it, and a gust blew dust all around. That wasn't good, because it would be a sign of us, but it also meant they didn't get back here for at least days at a time.

The airflow isn't fast because there's a lot of volume in there. It's a slow breeze. There is noise from the fans, but it's tolerable and not dangerous unless you wanted to live there.

"Did I kick your thumb?" he asked.

"Yeah. But you got him." Goddam it hurt.

He looked it over and had me wiggle it.

"Seems to be mostly soft tissue. Analgesic and a quick genstim when we get back."

"If we get back."

"It'll take more than a few of those dorfs to stop us," he said. He held up one of the carbines and a coder. They'd block signal on that soon, but in the meantime, we could make distance. On the other hand, they might try to track where it got used. I said so.

"Oh, I don't plan to use it," he said. "We'll pull some data, though."

"What will that do?"

"Maybe nothing, but it's all intel. This guy's movements, that schedule, some incident. Add it all up, pattern it all out, eventually some of it becomes intel for the fight."

I knew that was how intel worked, but I didn't see how this one would matter.

"Caught your breath?"

"Yeah," I said. "My thumb and my tailbone hurt." They weren't crippling, but they were going to be sore for a few days. I wouldn't be lying on my back comfortably.

I don't know what they did in there, but they installed some kind of small module.

Shannon had two carbines as well, and extra ammo sticks, and handed me one. It was easy to figure out. Insert, cock, release, shoot.

"Ever shot anyone?" he asked.

"Not yet."

"You will very soon. Are you okay with that?"

He sounded so matter-of-fact and educational.

"Better than getting shot," I said.

"Exactly. Don't shoot unless you need to or hear us, but then shoot fast and think later. Get past the hurdle. These people want us dead."

"I know," I said, gripping my bruised thumb for a moment.

Bast did something with the coder.

"General call. I'd hoped to avoid this, but we're going to have to shimmy as far as we can and shoot our way through, then get underdeck as soon as we're in another area."

Shannon nodded and boosted him up into the plenum. He pulled me up, then we both pulled Bast.

"I have no idea where this goes," I warned them.

"It goes toward main pressure," Shannon said. "For now, that's what we need."

"Will they figure out where we were?"

"Depends on if we get out unseen."

I said, "I won't know where we are until we get out, and I may not even then."

"We do what we can."

"Okay."

The duct twisted around in several long curves and dips. We slithered to keep quiet, and stirred up dust that blew behind us. I shifted sideways so Bast's dust didn't get me in the face, but there was still some. It was fluffy clumps, probably from static.

We came to a dip and had to slide down, the joints between sections caught and bruised me. Then we had to crawl up the other side using those joints for fingergrips. G wasn't high here, only about .3, but it was still tough to haul myself up by fingertips. Then the duct split three ways. They were secured with large metal mesh.

Shannon looked at something in his hand, pointed to the right and said, "Hub is that way." His voice was a whisper, and it echoed.

"Are you sure?" I asked.

He held up a clear disk with markings and a pointer.

"EM and grav compass. It's tracking the emergency nav marker, and the rotational G."

"Ah," I said. I knew what a compass was. I'd seen and used them in training, long years back. This was something different. "I hadn't realized the station had that."

"Most do, or else light beacons. If everything fails, emergency crews need to orient."

"Yeah," I agreed.

The echoes ran down the conduit and turned into scary feedback. I didn't want to talk much.

Bast pulled out a tool and tightened it around one of the bars, then kept cranking it with a lever. It was some sort of shear blade that wedged its way through a bit at a time until there was a loud pop, almost a bang, and the bar snapped. He repeated at the other end.

With a section removed, he whispered very quietly, "Can you fit through there?"

It was only two squares wide with sheared ends sticking out, but I got my head through, then one shoulder, and the other got stuck until I shimmied a bit. The sharp end at the bottom gouged me but I got past it. Then my ass required serious gyrations to get my hips through one at a time.

After that I was through.

I sat there while he cranked the wedge through another bar to create a V-shaped hole that he could get through, with difficulty. Shannon slid right through.

Then it was back to crawling along ducts and watching the dust blow.

After a lot of that, we came to a grating over industrial access.

"I vaguely know where this is," I said.

"Good, get us to the ship."

Why hadn't we come in this way, I wondered?

Bast had a tool that reached through the grating, around, and undid the fasteners from the outside. Shannon caught the mesh as it came loose, and hauled it up.

"You're down first, Angie. Shoot anything you see."

I gulped. "Okay." That order seemed to be a complete violation of the Law of Armed Conflict, but I realized it was probably the only thing we could do.

Bast dropped down next to me, Shannon stood on his shoulders, and reattached the grating.

I stood there sweating, with my pulse racing. We were standing in a passage, and there were cameras somewhere around here, and sensors that would want to see ID chips we didn't have.

Nothing happened, and we moved at Shannon's gesture. We were clear for now. His tracker told him to turn right, which was spinward, then left again for south.

We came around a passage bend and ran into an entire squad of police in riot gear. They were about ten meters away and closing in our direction. Eight of them. They'd obviously been alerted because they were moving in leapfrog and cover.

They started pointing weapons at us, and it was obvious they weren't in any doubt as to who we were. It took me only a moment to figure out I should be shooting at them.

Shannon already was. He caught one right under his visor, above the neck armor, and right through the chin. That spot is barely a couple of centimeters wide. He nailed it. While advancing.

Bast had hit one in the thighs, one shot each, right above the knee armor where there's a gap. The guy staggered and fell. He screamed and convulsed and screamed more from the damage.

All I managed was suppressing fire. I buzzed a burst and watched it ricochet off walls and visors.

With three down and two limping, they started to retreat, falling back in echelons in good order.

Then Shannon threw some sort of grenade. The bang was deafening and the walls flexed. Two more of them flailed. I watched their limbs flop like hoses. The human body doesn't bend that way.

He led, Bast brought up the rear, prodding me along

as they went. I figured whatever we'd wanted to do was wasted, and we were just trying to unass the area as fast as possible.

As we passed the downed wounded, one of them pointed his weapon at us. Before he could shoot, Bast swung, fired and kept moving. The guy was dead, hit in that hollow near the throat.

Klaxons and sirens started, and we were at a run.

We reached a marked entry point just as four more cops did. I butt stroked the nearest while exhaling in a "Yah!" I followed with a kick to his shin, one to his knee, and basically stomped over him as he went down. Screwing up my face, I smashed the edge of my foot down against the throat joint of his armor. Then again. It hurt. He flailed and tried to grab me, then clutched at his throat.

Bast just stomped on one as he ran over him and beat the next into the bulkhead. Shannon damned near ripped the fourth's arm off, twirled her like a dancer, grabbed her head and pulled. I heard the neck bones crunch and the girl dropped, twitching like she'd been shocked. Residual neural impulse, I was sure. She was dead.

I was pretty sure if mine wasn't dead, he was going to be in critical support unit for days.

I'd followed their lead and not opened fire, so I'd kept noise and sensor tag to a minimum. I was proud of that at least.

The door blinked and slid open and we were out.

There was someone at a reception desk, and Bast shouted, "Get down!"

The guy did.

We were out the next door and into public area.

"Lead, Angie," Shannon said. He reached out and gestured for my carbine. I handed it back.

We were still in government cube. I slowed to a walk, and waggled my arms down and away. As we passed a recycle post, I heard one of the guns go into the waste can. I turned to keep us moving south on the station axis line, toward commercial space.

I know we were being watched on camera. I had no idea what to do, but I got us into back commercial passage. There was a rear employee's exit for something, and someone just coming out. We went past them, I grabbed the door and held it.

The woman coming out said, "Hey! That's—"

I winked at her and said, "Shhh!" with my finger up over a coy grin as the guys went ahead of me. She looked flustered and embarrassed and said nothing.

The door latched behind us.

"We're in the Hilton," Shannon said.

He peeled out of his coverall and tossed it into a rag bin. Bast and I did the same. We were naked, and needed to dress up if we were going in public.

Bast pulled three vacbags out of his kit. One of them had a blazer and tie for me, the others had jackets and pullies for the men. I found someone's brush on a shelf, and hoping it was clean, dragged it through my hair.

Then he went to a trash can and dumped three severed hands into it. They had patches over the stumps. I'd completely missed where he got those.

"Biobatteries," he said when I looked at him.

"Is that how we got through the checkpoint?"

"Yes."

Fuck. If we got caught at this point, we'd killed cops, mutilated bodies, violated security, and goddess knows what sabotage was about to happen. If we were lucky, they'd just space us.

We walked through the doors to the rear of the public area, and there was one guest by the slide pod.

I improvised, "I think we'll need to move some of the tables from the middle."

Bast got it at once. "How many guests was it?"

Shannon said, "Forty-three."

"That should work, then."

By then we were around a corner and out of sight.

"I have an idea," I said.

I found a door that I was pretty sure went to table and chair storage. I pointed to the lock, Shannon whipped out some small tools, and in five seconds the door was open.

Yes, that's what it was.

"We can hide here for a few."

"Only a few," Shannon said. "Breather, water, keep moving."

Bast pulled out a ProTeem bar and took a bite, popped a water bulb and swigged. He handed them to me and I took a bite and gulped a couple of gulps. Shannon finished them, crushed the bottle flat and stuffed it and the wrapper in a pocket.

Shannon also had an actual comb. I cleaned up my hair a bit more and rolled the back. He straightened his. Bast combed his luxurious wave over his right ear.

"Okay, where to?" he asked me.

I led us out the front in plain view of everyone, toward

a restaurant I'd heard of, because I knew they had a back entrance into maintenance space. We were able to go to the restrooms then out the back.

"How are we going to avoid alerts since we don't have any chips now?" I asked.

Bast was the bag of holding. He handed me a visitor tag from a faramesh pouch.

"Damn."

"It's clean," he said, as he grabbed two more. "We'll need to change appearance."

"That's why you wanted makeup."

"Yes. Make me swish," he said.

Which was silly. He was more masculine than anyone I knew, and none of my makeup would match his skin tones.

I did what I could with some violet and a touch of glittergloss around his eyes. A dusting. He pulled his hair back and swept it over his ears with a bit of lift in the middle.

"Thank you," he said, and it was uncanny. He did swish.

Shannon had already flattened his hair, run a dark streak through it, and slouched. He presented totally differently.

I squeezed a green dye on top of mine and rubbed it through. Bast had a towel for me to clean up with, and I suddenly looked younger and poutier after I did my lips. I love that combo in the themed clubs.

From the Hyatt, we went across the main passage to the Vista. We went into one of the family restrooms, changed again, jimbled our way through the dance club and took a side exit to a cross passage.

From there, we hit another club and joined a glitter parade, which I figured would screw with any sensors. From there to another, then I found an entrance to backspace. We made it around unhindered.

The dock, though, was buttoned down tight. They'd already had an alert, which was why we'd gone the way we did.

They were swabbing every person.

Right. We'd left unmistakable DNA in those suits. It wasn't just residue, it was very clear evidence.

"Can you get us around, Angie?"

"I haven't been here recently, and not in detail. I'm sure there's an access tunnel, but I have no idea how it's secured or controlled."

"If you can find it, we can crack it. We have a few hours."

I had to think. Those conduits came from main power directly to the dock. They probably had interfaces outside the dock, so they could be cut and revert to emergency power. "Where's the emergency plant for the dock?"

"Radius forty-three."

"We're at fifty-two."

We made our way around, and it wasn't a straight shot. Older stations like this one have longitudinals more than latitudinals. We had to go back and forth, and up and down.

I found it at .25G, level three, radius forty-one.

"It should be this," I said. "But I don't know if we can get into it."

Shannon said, "The lock is well-used and has scratch marks around the latch."

He went at it with a toolkit while Bast and I stood there and tried not to appear suspicious. Three people went past, but none of them gave us a second look.

I was sure there would be an alarm, but he opened it and nothing happened.

"Disabled," he said.

"Probably too many panic responses to nothing," I said.

We slid through and closed it behind us. It latched, but we could get out. They're always one way to allow trapped workers to escape.

We needed to move north longitudinally. Shannon's indicator showed us that way, and I was glad, because I'd gotten turned around. We went in that direction.

"Dusty enough I don't think anyone's been here recently," Shannon whispered.

"You're right," I said. I was still in a burning overload with my pulse hammering. It hadn't stopped. I was exhausted from sheer mental tension. When were they going to catch us and how were we going to die? Because I knew we were going to die. Even if we weren't spies or clandestine combatants according to law, we were incredibly dangerous to them.

I still wasn't sure what they'd actually done back there, and couldn't ask yet.

There were air breaks every hundred meters or so—like airlocks, but they just latch rather than locking. There was a spot where someone had been working.

"Looks like he came from that lateral," Bast said, pointing at a cross-passage just ahead. Even his whisper carried.

As we reached it, the maintainer came around that corner. We were face to face for about a half second before he clutched for his phone.

Bast grabbed the phone and the guy's neck, Shannon stuck a knife up inside his skull from behind the ear. I watched his eyes twitch and roll as his brainstem was scrambled, and he died in a gooey mess of shit, piss and blood.

"Fuck," I muttered.

"Sorry, dude, you were in the way," Shannon said. "Let's move."

I ducked under some hanging cables and banged my head on an access panel door I didn't see. I saw sparkles and my head throbbed. I made a loud "eep" noise and kept it to myself, but fuck, it hurt. It should have been funny when Shannon did the same, but it wasn't.

And then I saw the exit hatch ahead, marked with reflective symbols. I waved my hand and pointed.

It was ironic. I'd just found the right exit when the alarms started panicking.

I mean every alarm there was. Fire, vacuum, toxic leak, power failure, collision warning, everything.

"I think they found our package," Shannon said.

I didn't ask. We got the hatch open, and took a careful look, but everyone in UN uniform was in a freak and running off the dock.

We walked straight across to the tram and took it to our radius, then a cable dolly down the gangway.

I was wondering how we were going to bull our away into a ride, but there was no need. Everything was unattended. Bast grabbed an inspection tug and we crowded into it, greasy and stinky and close enough to really notice it. He burped the jets manually to get it out of the bay and across to *Bounder*.

With no way to actually dock that thing, Roger opened one of the bays and Bast maneuvered us in. Pressure-balanced, we debarked. Shannon grabbed an oxy bottle and glue-stripped it to the side of the tug. That done, we left the bay, depressurized it, and shoved the tug out into space.

"Did you mean for that to be a navigation hazard?"

"Absolutely."

We got into departure track and waited. There was nothing from jump control for an hour, just a warble of "All controllers busy, please stand by."

The news covered it. Twelve people were dead from toxic gas inhalation, and two others from anoxia. The atmosphere distribution blowers had been sabotaged. Additionally, several bombs had gone off, fifteen (!) police had been killed, along with a maintenance worker and two Hyatt employees.

Jack asked, "Are they exaggerating, did you get lucky, or have they pulled some of their own people and are blaming us?"

"Unknown."

We weren't killing them in large numbers, but their efficiency was badly damaged and their morale had to suck. We kept getting closer to Earth, and I wondered how many other operations were doing similar things.

Eventually, Jump Point control came back on air. "All craft will stand down and await inspection by fisheries patrol."

"'Fisheries patrol'?" Glenn asked.

"Ah ha!" Juan grinned back. "They're conducting shipping inspections. That's way old legal code from Earth for inspecting fishing vessels for contraband."

"So why here?"

"Because they haven't got a code for mandatory manifest inspections."

They were all smiles. I asked, "What the hell do we do when they search us and find DNA traces and everything else?"

Juan said, "We'll bluff our way through, or we kill them and run. It's going to get interesting."

He had a different definition of interesting than I did, but I had signed up, so it was my fight, too.

No one was going anywhere, and that was a massive problem for their outer economy. They needed those metals and volatiles. They didn't need the higher end foodstuffs or luxuries, but the people who wanted them might not like the delays.

They started searching ships, using the four boats they had. Anyone connected to the dock got a hands-on inspection at once, which is why we'd pulled out.

Jack and Teresa came forward from the maintenance bay and handed each of us a pistol.

"Where did these come from?" I asked.

"Made them."

They looked like standard issue, but I realized they had no marks of any kind. They'd just cranked them out on the fabmill from whatever specs they had.

"We're going to fight?"

Juan said, "That depends. If they are doing a cursory

hands on, no. If we can bull or bribe our way through, no. If not, we try to take them out, or at least take them with us."

I felt better that if I was going to die, I was going to have a weapon in my hand.

We talked tactics. Who was going to be in where during boarding, and who was going to move where if it turned to a fight, where the guns would be, and who would move to support whom. I was going to cover the second rear passage toward engineering, and back up Bast if it came to that, and he'd be my backup.

It was all day waiting and we didn't eat. We heard rumors and then news. They actually apprehended three crews in-station. I don't know what happened to them. They worked through the big corporate ships first, because it was easier. They blew vacuum in all uninhabited spaces to ensure they were empty.

Then they moved to the trampers, but they still had ships coming in, and prepping to depart, and no way to move anything. It turned into a snarling jam.

Just as I was prepping myself for a firefight, because I was not going to be a prisoner again, they called it off. They said they'd do random searches of luggage and goods. They pulled out and told jump control to start queuing us.

I stayed nervous until we actually joined the queue and reached departure.

CHAPTER 28

They changed the rules again, and wouldn't let us deliver to the Freehold directly. We stopped on the Caledonia side and disconnected the pods, and had their own people take them through on a military tug.

Only, Bast and Jack had spent most of two days inside those pods, and had fake seals to put back on. I could only wonder what fuckery they committed on the contents. I'm assuming it made them less than spec, whatever they were.

We kept moving, just like any other tramper. It seems obvious that the number of decoys, false departures, fake manifests we could use was limited. Also, if something happened every time we docked or undocked, it would be obvious what we were. So most of our runs were legit cargo or passengers. We took a lot of relief runs to Mtali and metals from Govannon to Earth and Caledonia.

During this, a cargo pod in Freehold space burst open, and discharged loiter missiles that took off and then went silent to lurk. I never heard if they were found or not, and no ships were reported damaged, but it certainly ate up search resources looking for them.

I knew even then that eventually someone would find a pattern in what we did. We just needed the war to be over before they did, or enough warning to scram and try something else, or to make sure we did enough damage.

I had no idea what we were accomplishing. A lot of it seemed small stakes. Though, capturing a capital ship had to count for something just by itself. It wasn't planned, though, so I don't know if we'd been tossed out on some off chance, or if there were plans underneath.

They kept escalating, which I figured was partly from getting to know the risks and responses, and partly from needing to do more damage.

I wondered how long we could get away with it before we got caught again. Would they get some or all of us?

At this point, I figured they'd just space us or shoot us. Holding us was dangerous and didn't get them any intel, and trials would take time. We also might get away. They could legitimately call us terrorists, and would do that instead of acknowledging any movement, which we didn't belong to. They'd already denied our nation existed.

I have no idea how I managed. Every jump, every dock, I expected to get grabbed.

We were also getting intel from the UN, watching how the troops reacted, what their mindset was. They were as tense as we were.

I'd hear about other attacks or sabotage, and I don't know if that was other Freehold action, or just random dissidents and rebels, or just disgruntled residents.

A couple of months later, with no activity I could tell, we wound up back in Sol on the Salin side.

On the C-deck, Juan said, "Intel this time. We're going to pull as much data as we can, so we need IDs. Angie, we need a club where lots of them will hang out, and you have to help bait them."

"Just dancing, or how far do I need to go?"

"Dancing and drinking for certain, after that, it depends."

"Can we sit apart? Having a male nearby is a block in Earth or Caledonia. In NovRos they might think you're a pimp. Back home or Meiji, they don't care."

"What if you went with a woman?" he asked.

"I haven't before," I said. "But I could."

"Are you comfortable doing that?" He asked it completely matter-of-factly.

I replied the same way, "Sure."

Teresa said, "You might have to act out to keep the cover solid."

I looked at Teresa. "As long as you brush your teeth and don't get food stuck, I can manage."

"Well, of course," she nodded and smiled. "Business can be dirty, but if it doesn't have to be, clean is better."

"Good," he said. "Then we'll send the two of you as a distraction while we procure resources."

"What type?"

"Data off phones, chips and ID. Same as last time."

"Those are shielded, and I thought they updated their protocols against intrusion again." And we were in their home space.

"Yes, and we can crack them in a minute or so. You just have to keep the subject busy."

I said, "I'm going to get a reputation as a titch like that, but okay."

"Are you known here?"

"Not well, but word does get around here and there, and we can't do it more than a couple of times in any window. Not more than two clubs or two nights, or they'll suspect something."

"Which 'they?'"

"Sorry. Clubbers, possibly management, possibly cops. Best case, they think we're trolling or just pros. Worst case, they think we're mob bait."

"Can we risk two nights and two clubs each?"

"Probably."

"Then whichever clubs will give us the best hit on intel types."

I looked at Teresa.

"Been clubbing much?"

She said, "Not really. A few weekends in training. I've been busy since then."

"Okay. Do you know how to do makeup?" I asked.

She said, "For formal events, yes."

"Ah. Let me teach you anti-formal. Can they watch?" I asked her. "They might need to seduce someone, too."

"Sure," she agreed.

"Good," Juan said. I hadn't been joking, and it hadn't fazed him at all.

I went to the bunk and grabbed my new dress-kit from my personal crate.

"Okay, light, clean foundation," I said. "Just to smooth out pores and give the rest something to stick to." I dusted her all over. "Line the eyes to match your color. We're going light metallic blue. Pencil right here."

She said, "Ack!" and twitched. "I hate having my eyes touched."

"Sorry," I said. "It only takes a moment. Now, two swipes of liner, one lighter than the other, and blend with your finger. Drag it out past the corner to make your eyes look wider. You don't need mascara."

I tilted her head up slightly, and highlighted her cheeks with a couple of puffs.

"Make sure the base color blends on the ears and throat," I said. "And then just a faint contour along your jaw." It surprises some people how fast you can dress up. I guess some women take hours doing it. I learned how to do it fast so I could maximize my port time.

"Now, lips. Yours are thin, so we want to widen them slightly, but not too much. Outline here, color fill. Glitter or gloss. We're going with glitter. And a topcoat."

When I was done, her lips were noticeable, but not quite garish. Men would see them, though.

"Change bras," I said. "Show some stack and cleave."

"These are all I have." She indicated her briefer. Good shipwear, not great for clubbing.

"Well, that's practical, but not what we want here. Mine is probably a little large, but . . . try this one." I pulled one from my "skinny" compartment, when I'm off ship and lean from working out.

She pulled it on and I tightened the shoulders more than they should be, to give her some lift.

"There. Go with that sleeveless tank tunic and the tight slacks. They do good things for your ass."

"You think so?" she asked. "They're not too tight?"

"Too tight for anything practical, but they'll work to distract a man."

She blushed a bit. It was cute.

I didn't go all out, but I wore stockings, open panties, a medium skirt with a quick release back slit, a tunic that flared over my hips, and a choker. I tied a blue bandana in a triple knot to make it clear I was looking but not promising. I wanted to look right for the part.

Before we left, she motioned me into the bunkroom.

"How far can you play this?" she asked.

"What do you mean?"

"Are we supposed to be a date?"

"We can be. Played right, two chicks can get most guys. Either back and forth, or together."

"That's what I mean. Are you able to get physical to maintain that image?"

Ah. It was good to ask that, but no worries.

I said, "Yes, I can dance with you, kiss you, feel you up, and act like I really mean it."

"Good. I don't want to overdo it, but a little makes the lie work. And a little more keeps people from noticing us directly."

"I've done that before when I needed to get past a pay gate," I said. "I like girls okay, just not as much as guys."

"Hah. Got it."

I looked over the loads about the local clubs. We wanted the two that would appeal to spook or techie types. I chose Avant because it had Neuro Dance Night.

Neuro was bound to get nerds who liked it and others who wanted to analyze it. Halfway Inn had a heavy singles clientele who were into mystery fet. They wouldn't even ask who we were.

Juan said, "I'd deliberately avoid a place like that for that reason."

"Which is why the ones who will be there are the ones you want."

"Valid," he agreed. "You're on."

"How will you get them?"

"All you have to do is get them into a cubby or a dark booth or some passage alley. We'll do the rest and you won't even see it."

"How long?"

"Five minutes will get us everything. Three will get us a lot. That's the minimum."

"Okay."

We walked off the dock followed by the gaze of every male at work. They knew where we were going, hoped what they thought we were going to do, and were jealous. I bet none of them could describe our faces, either, just the outfits and makeup.

Twenty minutes and three tram rides later, we had a room at a Hansa hotel. It was across the promenade from Avant. It was major Neuro music. I could feel the tremors and some sort of phase shifts. It panned around and through my head as the MJ mixed it and moved the epicenter. Yes, he knew how to hit those low freqs you can feel in your cooze and nipples. I wonder if men get some similar effect?

I got into the groove and started flexing. If I was going

to be here, the first thing was to look and feel like I belonged. Teresa got behind me and bumped me now and then. I leaned back to rub shoulders and shimmy, then back to flexing limbs.

I turned to face her and pumped my ass out for bait. I wasn't looking on purpose, but I knew guys were watching.

She leaned in and said, "Kiss me a bit."

She was touching me anyway. I ran my lips along her jaw, brushed across her lips and felt that tingle I always get. It's part first kiss, part surprise because I almost never have women. Her lips were soft and relaxed, and her tongue rather naughty. She either liked it or was a really good actress.

It was a really good kiss. Damn. My brain started wondering about her and Roger or Sebastian. That would make for an amazing session, and I might have to play that out later.

I pulled away, winked and turned back around. We shifted across the floor until we had a booth and flicked the light so it said we were available to talk only.

We had images of some of the potential targets, but I couldn't remember who they were and didn't dare get caught looking. Teresa found someone, though, and smiled and waved.

He came over and waited for her to pat the seat.

I slid out with a wink and let her get to work while I went to get some cold water and dance some more.

Five minutes and a song section later, I took a look and she was busy with her mouth on his and her hands in his hair. Then he slid out and she followed.

I guess that was a score. They went toward the back exit, either to lurk there or find a passage with a nook.

I didn't recognize anyone, so I floated around the dance floor waiting for someone to ping my phone and let me know I was near one. The music was very inspiring and my pulse hammered.

In my ear I heard, "Get her out."

I did a slow nod and moved my steps toward the back.

She was there, in a corner, in the walkway behind the booth, being passed by occasional servers who paid no attention to them. The place was discreet.

She was still making out with him. He had hands under her tunic. Juan had what he needed, so I went to rescue her.

"Hey, girlie!" I said cheerfully. "Oh, I'm sorry. I'm always interrupting." I giggled and winked at him.

"Oh, that's fine," she said. "Sorry, I got distracted." She pulled her tunic back and ran fingers through her hair.

"You should," I said, then moved in as if to poach. "Nice shirt," I said, running my fingers along his shoulder. I slid them down his side with my other hand and she pulled it away.

"Dammit, stop doing that, Hazel!" she snapped at me.

"What?" I looked at her, then back at him, running my eyes up and down. "He's cute. I just was complimenting him."

He looked at her, then at me. He muttered something and stepped back. She'd played perfectly, and he was smart enough to get away from what he thought was going to be a bitch fight.

And she'd slipped his phone back into his pocket as he paid attention to my fingers. I'd barely seen it.

We went back to the booth and then to the floor. I found a guy who was cute, but not on the list. I let him give me a good rubbing and necking in the booth, but blocked his hand when he went under the skirt. I made a point not to rub him or tease him, and eased him back onto the floor after a couple of songs. He actually was my type, but I had work to do.

I danced with two more and Teresa made out with another, back in the booth, eyes closed and panting. She was tense, and I wondered if he was good enough to get her off.

"Hey, can I try?" I asked, and she let him go.

He wasn't sure if he should be glad for another woman, or sad at not having her. I put a good liplock on him and got my fingers on his neck and shoulders.

He was okay. Nice looking, interested in what he was doing, trying really hard, but it was obvious he was trying. I gave him a minute or two, and she'd left the booth by then.

We didn't find anyone else, and after two hours she leaned over and whispered, "Let's move."

She knocked back a shot of something and we headed for Halfway Inn.

I'd thought it would be a meat market. Godsdamn I was right. I think ninety percent of the cooze was for hire, and at least twenty percent of the cock. The rest were all trying to give it away. That really wasn't safe, even this distance from Earth proper. I'd bet someone here had had an Earthie grounder or six, and someone had a disease from it. Most of them aren't lethal, but they are nasty.

They did have the spy theme, even calling the servers "agents." But it was over the top and not real. I now knew what spies were actually like. They weren't like this.

Still, we played along.

We got a booth as far back as possible, which in this place meant as inviting as possible.

A guy came by and nodded. I nodded back.

"How are you ladies this evening?"

"Passable," I said. "And you?"

"Quite well. Would you like to dance?"

"In a bit," I said.

Teresa added, "We just got here."

"Can I order you a drink?"

Right then the server showed up with drinks we hadn't ordered, but Teresa jabbed me with her thumb under the table and said, "We already did, but if we're here later, we'd enjoy that."

He bowed marginally and strolled away, to the next table with more women than men.

It wasn't long before another guy came by, stood facing away, and said, "I'm looking for Sasha."

He actually looked pretty good in a dinner jacket, mandarin collar and fitted pants.

"I'm Sasha," I said. "Sasha Godentyt."

"I'm Rod Stouffer."

It was pretty clear what he wanted.

Teresa said, "I'm Mitzi Graben." That wasn't bad. I thought we were doing okay.

"Do you have the goods?" he asked.

I wasn't sure if he was playing a role or being direct.

"Do you have the password?"

"Legs," he said.

"Legs?"

"Yeah. That's the word. Help spread it."

I didn't roll my eyes.

Still, I got a buzz on my phone that said he was on the list.

"We have a safe house nearby," Teresa said, getting into the theme.

"Take me to the safe house," he said.

We went back down two levels to our room, giggling all the way. Once inside, we each took a side of his neck and started kissing, and I felt his whole body arch. I got my mouth on his and an arm around his middle and steered him to the bed. It was big enough for three.

Teresa came back over with three drinks. "Sasha, you wanted a light Sparkle, right? Do you want anything, Rod?"

"What is it?"

"Just spiced ginger ale. I'm not mixing Sparkle with booze."

"It's fine plain." he said.

But he put it on the side table and didn't drink it. Smart man.

I tried mine. It had the barest dusting, just to give me a hint of how to act silly.

I went back to necking while she clutched him through his pants and rubbed his chest. We had him panting. He had a hand down the back of her skirt and was trying to wiggle up mine.

He was a bit rough with his fingers, and the sudden touch made me jump. He liked that.

I let him finger me, though I did grab his wrist to slow him down. He took the hint.

I gathered he needed to be drugged, so I did a lot of open mouth kissing. It took about ten minutes, but his mouth dried out enough he grabbed for the glass. I sat back and let him sip.

Then I went back to work on his neck, because I had no idea how potent that stuff was.

I could feel him start to get woozy and slow, and he began slurring his words.

"Can I halp you take the shkirt off?" he asked.

"Sure!" I turned so he could pull the zip, and let him get a good view of my ass. He had us side by side, fingers in each, and I tugged at his velcro and belt, teasing him along.

He was nodding off, but I kept squirming, and so did Teresa. Then he slipped and his hands fell on the quilt.

She bounced off the bed, grabbed something from her bag, and squeezed another dose between his lips.

"Okay, move fast. We have about fifteen minutes." She got his phone and dropped it into a shell that I assumed imaged it. His ID all got scanned, and his right hand for his chip went into the same scanner. This was a lot more detail than the previous ones.

"What do we do after that? Slip him in the alley? Wake him up and finish?"

She winced. "I'd really rather not finish him, but I guess we have to so he doesn't think he got rolled and reports it."

"How does that drug work?"

"It's a neuro inhibitor. Memory processes and prefrontal awareness are down, but everything else works."

"Okay."

I got his pants off, and the trunks he had for undies. He was still stiff, and a few seconds of mouth got him wet enough I could start stroking. He reacted just like he would awake, and I followed the twitches to find the best spot. I dribbled and stroked and in about three minutes he gushed pretty well. I wiped my hand on a towel.

I left him like that. "When we wakes up, make a show of kissing me and we'll get dressed." I finished pulling my skirt off and pulling the tunic halfway around my waist. She nodded and followed.

When he started twitching and blinking, I grabbed her shoulders and went for a vigorous kiss. She muffled and panted and gripped me back.

"Oh, damn," I heard him mutter.

"Hey! You're awake. You came pretty hard."

"I guess. I'm sorry. I didn't think I drank that much earlier."

"It's fine, you gave us what we needed." I handed him the towel.

I squirmed a bit and sighed. Then I made a show of sucking her nipples for a few moments as she hissed.

He reached up, and she said, "Well, hell, we're back on shift in an hour. You want to shower before we do?"

"I'll be okay," he said. "I can go home." He lowered his hands and looked sad.

He was disappointed at not remembering it, and seemed a bit more disoriented than the drugs would make him. Probably wondering why he'd blacked out, but I didn't think he'd tell anyone. He'd gotten off and had two women making out, so he had a story to exaggerate for his friends.

We each kissed him off, waved and smiled, and closed the door. We cleaned everything up, and she sprayed some bottle of stuff.

"DNA mask," she said. "It's got about fifty people's traces and this is a nano to break them down into fragments. Ours and his." She held up another bottle. It went all over the bed, the carpet around it and the door and bathroom.

We left with our stuff, and I followed her onto another tram, around about ten frames of radius, and we got out at a Claremont. I followed her past the desk and down a passage to a room. She knocked, it opened, we went in.

Mira and Jack were there with gear. They took the module from her and started processing.

I was a little bouncy from that hint of Sparkle. She was definitely not. She had been holding something in and now looked ill.

"Stressful?" I asked.

"Gay," she said.

"Eh?"

"I am completely femme. Men creep me out," she said.

"I'm sorry," I said. "I didn't know. You acted it perfectly."

"Yeah. I can act. And I hate myself when I do."

Jack handed her a bottle of rum. She eyed it, tilted it, and took three measured swallows.

"Thanks. I was afraid he was going further than the hands." She shivered. "Eww."

Well, that explained the kiss. She'd presented as all duty, but that had felt real, and apparently was.

So that's why she'd kissed me so well. That hadn't been an act at all, or not nearly as much of one.

I remembered Chesnikov on NovRos. Then there was the interrogation and overall stress. You don't have to get shot to be a casualty.

CHAPTER 29

I wasn't sure how many IDs we had or from what sources. All I know is we had a variety that could get us in a lot of places, but not everywhere.

The next day a bomb exploded outside a monitor station. No bystanders were hurt, but three cops took frag and died. I had mixed feelings about that. These guys hadn't been actively hostile, but their government sure as hell had, to me personally.

That was followed by a stack of printed sheets left in several office kiosks.

THE INDIVIDUAL IS THE GREATEST MINORITY.
The state does not control the individual. The individual controls the state. When the state refuses to serve, it must be made to comply. You have now been shown the penalty for failing to serve the individual. Lessons will be repeated as necessary. The individual must be shown due deference and respect.

It went on for four pages of ranting. It came across as someone megalomaniacal.

Then there was a list of demands. They were ridiculous on purpose.

Badges will refer to individuals as "sir" or "ma'am." Badges will be identified by name, and will identify themselves by name when addressed. Badges will not demand ID from sovereign individuals who are not engaged in crime."

Then there were ten more pages, some of it C/P, some of it original, some referencing what I think were obscure theses.

"This is weird," I said.

"It should be," Juan agreed. "All nine of us worked on it."

"So they won't be able to identify a single individual," I guessed.

"Yes, and went for narcissism, high-functioning sociopathy, paranoia and depressed inferiority. They'll be analyzing for days."

I wondered where you went to school to learn to fake all that.

At least I hoped they were faking. They seemed normal.

Mo mailed it in from a cafe through some source strippers or something to all those kiosks. Another copy was messengered to monitor central station. I think they stashed a few at checkpoints.

The next day they had a fuzzy safety cam image of Juan, and an APB with a reward of M100,000.

He chuckled over it, and said, "If I didn't think they'd backtrack any informant and try to take them out of the picture to avoid paying, I'd have you turn me in and take the cash. But since we can't do that, let's play through."

A div later, he and Mira, Sebastian and Roger followed me down the ramp and along the convolutions of the inner pressure wall of the dock. I was looking for one of the conduit accesses.

I wondered why they weren't better protected. Maintenance didn't go in more than once a week most of the time.

Roger answered that when I asked him.

"If they use a standard code or key, there are so many out there, locking it is pointless. You're not the only girlfriend or slooz to meet people back in those. Even then, a lot of guys won't lock it because they don't want to have to juggle keys. It gets worse if each one is a different key and has to be signed out or remoted. They probably all locked at one time, but people stop bothering. As long as the homeless don't steal or damage stuff, they'll roust them occasionally and ignore them otherwise."

I guess it made sense. I know a lot of maintenance gals used a screwdriver to pop a latch instead of a key.

I found one that was a crawlway, and thinking about it, only someone homeless or really wanting to fuck in private near the docks, or for a thirty-four, would go there.

It was a literal crawlway, dusty, dank, unlit because old lamps had burned out, and very tight. That eventually led into a main tunnel that did have proper locks and even scanners. It also had a maintenance crew on one of the power conduits, though they were a couple of hundred meters down.

We got behind the pipe, and there were braces and cross-feeds to hide us. This area had some recent wear, probably a lurker's den. I gestured and we moved about fifty meters the other way, past a huge waste pump that would give IR and noise cover.

Sebastian had a rough map, and I pointed where we were.

"Okay," he said. "We're good. You need to get back to the ship so we have you later."

I wanted to stay, but my job was to be the guide, and I didn't have their training. I knew it was important, but it was less satisfying than working in an infirmary, or even a rec center.

"Understood," I said. "Take care. When will you be back?"

"We have our schedule aboard," he said.

Right. They weren't going to tell me.

I was loitering in the galley and not-watching vid when Glenn stuck his head in.

"Abandon ship, grab a change of clothes and some sanitary kit, move."

I sprinted to my bunk, grabbed my overnight and joined him and the rest at the forward lock.

"We're going wherever you took them. They said it was a good spot."

"Got it."

I went there, followed by them about fifty seconds

apart. I had no idea how they did that, but they said not to worry. So I walked and they followed at a distance. Distances.

I got there and the hatch was locked.

Jack came up behind me and I pointed at it. He nodded, reached down with tools, and a few moments later it was open.

"Go, wait inside out of view," he said.

I took that to mean I should watch for them. I ducked inside, found a spot behind a power box, in shadow, with a stack of polymer panels, and waited in a squat.

The rest came through in intervals and I motioned them into the shadow with me.

Now I had to find a place we'd fit.

I really hadn't spent that much time in underpassage. I tried to keep jobs and savings. But I did spend about a month in one in Caledonia, and it had been as old as this place. They ran main power through here, and water for ballast. It also served as a main air return to the plant. It was stale and dirty smelling, like a shipsuit after sweaty maintenance and loading.

I led with them following the same way. I was looking for something we could hide in that wasn't taken, and wouldn't get a lot of traffic.

It was almost a kilometer before I found it.

It was a large electrical transformer cabinet, and I'd seen one like it before. The dead space behind it was what I wanted. I wasn't sure if I could squeeze through the access, but Jack came up and slid something into the lock and popped it.

The gated hatch was still barely wide enough for my

ass, but the others were skinnier or male. We made it through.

When they'd upgraded to a smaller, more efficient setup, they'd stuck this in place of the old one. It left a gap behind it just under a meter wide and eight meters long.

Jack went back the way we'd come, and returned with two of the cover panels that were stacked near the entrance. Two shots of AdhereHere cement fixed them on the inside of the gate and the rail at the far end.

We had air and a livable temperature, indirect light, and a little space to stand or sit in.

"How long do we stay here?" I asked.

Glenn said, "Indefinite, unless you can find a larger one."

"Can we rent a lodge?"

He shook his head. "Not at this time."

"Then this is it. It's not going to be comfortable."

"It'll do."

It was most of the day cycle before the other element caught up with us. They wore clean shipsuits but were filthy underneath. It wasn't just from the conduit.

"Here's the vid from their feed. It'll be on the news soon," Bast said.

He plugged it into his phone and let the file play.

I didn't know what I was looking at at first. They showed a replay. Then I got it.

Juan had presented himself for them to arrest. They'd moved in with the whole dolly setup.

Then from the surrounding crowd, Mira, Sebastian and Roger stepped out, fired guns, and stepped back.

Three cops fell down, bullets through their vertebrae at the joint of armor and helmet. Then smoke bombs billowed up.

Then the rest of the cops opened fire in a panic.

Juan grabbed one, yanked and wrenched his arm out of place, then shoulder threw him while holding his head. I saw the cop's neck snap.

He went straight through another, kicking him in the chest so hard the guy bent double, then landing feet-first on the guy's ribs, and smashing a boot down into his face. His jaw mashed flat. I didn't think that was deadly, but it was viciously violent and I figured regen and restruct would take weeks.

More smoke and Juan was gone.

I realized I actually enjoyed watching them kill. Part of it was that they were so efficient, so fluid, so deadly.

The other part was that I wanted the people who hurt me to suffer. They really hadn't hurt me as much as they could have, and they didn't kill me, which they could have. It was war. I was a spy. I didn't get any LOAC protection. But they'd hurt me, and I wanted to see them suffer.

"How many did you get?" I asked.

"According to their reports, we killed five and injured three more escaping."

"Good," I said, and meant it. They were cops, not soldiers, but they were still combatants to us, and to them. But I didn't think it was a very efficient way to fight a war.

Then more of the story came out.

The cops shot twenty-seven people. Four of them died. The station was locked down in complete panic. They put up checkpoints everywhere, demanded ID or chips for access to anything even semiofficial. It slowed down departures for as long as we were there and beyond. They wanted to stop civilian ships entirely, but couldn't. The bottleneck on those slowed down the military ships. Every time a military ship bumped a civilian ship, there was annoyance, and vice versa. It was a complete mess.

I realized that had a huge economic effect.

Then a freighter bound insystem for Earth blew up. It was reported to be sabotage with a bomb on board that had managed to crack a bulkhead to the engines, wreck the controls, and let it run away. The ship actually melted, and the cargo had to be abandoned as contaminated and unretrievable. The crew got out by evac pod, except for one engine minder.

The smiles and glances I saw made me think Mo and Roger had put that together. We'd delivered quite a bit of cargo. Had they built a bomb into one of them?

Hell, the fab gear we'd gotten in the upgrade had made the pistols they used. I assumed we could have all kinds of weapons as quickly as we needed them.

I know it's not hard to make any item if you have the blueprints or code, and guns are very simple mechanical things. But they came up with several different ones depending on what we did.

But that was days later.

Right after the police attack, Roger took one of the acquired ID tags and went back out that night. As he passed a checkpoint, he left a small bomb. It blew a cop's foot off. He tossed the ID and came back on a spare.

After that, no one wanted to be near a checkpoint.

In three days, this entire Jump Point transit station

had been reduced to a panic, all shipments either way stopped, and everyone pissed off and scared. I realized that had a lot of military effect.

Billions of tons of supplies would have to go around other routes to get insystem, and everyone in this station would miss resources. It wouldn't be much. There was enough locally produced food and power. But it would get less comfortable.

"Not only that," Teresa said, "It won't have any effect on Earth. It's going to piss off everyone in habitats and alt-environments, and give them more social distance from Earth."

"Won't they hate us for doing it?" I asked.

"Some. But did you notice how many are claiming it's all false flag by their own government? It's easier to hate the big one. And they want Earth to fix it, who really can't, and won't anyway. They can't get anything through their own bureaucracy."

I realized there was a lot more depth to blowing things up than I thought. It could be why I'm not good at chess or Go. They were thinking months ahead here. I just wanted to know when I would eat and get laid. Which made me average.

The next two weeks were boring. More than boring, tedious and aggravating. We were stuck in the cubby, cooking field rats over a tiny resistance heater. The troops kept one on watch at all times. I was a contractor, so I wasn't assigned, but I did some anyway. There wasn't much else to do. We played quiet word games and puzzles. I'm not good at chess, they were brilliant. I did okay at memory games, but they were perfect. We exercised standing up, doing isometrics with the bulkhead and the back of the transformer. The bulkhead had old access holes and some cable conduits we could hang from, and buzzed constantly. We had limited phone access, and sleep hurt, on bare plate with rolled clothing as a neck pillow. We had to sneak out for latrine use, but there was a bucket at one end for emergencies on waking.

After three days of not finding us, the cops were in a complete panic. I guess someone told them to deliver. They started rousting homeless people and transients, going through cubbies one by one, checking occupants. It tied them all up. They went past several times but never tried to enter, and I was in a panic each time. Then there was a run of hobos trying to boost rides on any ship going anywhere. The ships reported this, but then got delayed for more searches, so they stopped reporting it. Then the customs and transit agency started visiting ships at random, then visiting all of them.

Everyone was pissed off, everything moved slow. The cops were busy dealing with starving dropout families who didn't have chips or papers and had to be placed in inflated shelters in park space or in empty cube wherever they could be stuffed. Those homeless people sometimes had mental issues or were low-grade crims, and broke stuff.

Every ship was delayed hours or days.

I wasn't as sure as Teresa. I figured they'd beat or kill us if they figured out we did it.

I think Juan agreed with us. We stayed in our crawlspace, taking a few minutes twice a day to stretch upright in the passage. Mo charged our phones and comps at a terminal a distance away, and we used them on very narrow local only, burst loads. Teresa kept taking our phones, running ware through them to sanitize them and recode them.

Three days in, I took Roger with me to shop for food.

It was harder than I expected. They were requiring ID chips to get groceries. We were almost into a store when he suddenly took my arm and said, "Oh, wait, we need something from Climan's first."

Once past the entrance he said, "Find a quiet corner now. We need to camo."

He actually found it before I did. A jog into a passage that had some sweepers and spare rollers for the walk.

"Take this," he said, as soon as we were behind a shelf and out of view of any fixed cameras. He slipped the tags into my hand while pulling me in close and kissing. I got my hands around his neck and his tag went on as I did.

He was such a gentleman, mashing lips but keeping his tongue back. It was a kiss. I wasn't having any of that halfway act. I clutched him and probed his tongue and raised a leg over his hip.

Whew. That was better, and even worse for frustration. I coaxed his hand to my tunic collar, wiggled until he was feeling me up, then reached up gently and pulled his hands out. Damn.

I giggled a bit, and straightened my collar while looping the tag around my neck. It was a guest tag, not an implant, but it would work in this area of the station. Get into the habitat area and they expected implants and would start scanning and questioning visitors.

The poor man was obviously tense after that, and straightened his collar. He should have straightened his crotch.

But we looked like a couple having a quick tease, and were out of there in thirty seconds. We both had the tags we needed, and could shop this area until someone flagged them, which might or might not happen.

Food was rationed. We followed the signs, bought as much protein as we could, and some of it was canned chicken. I was amazed there was any left, I don't know why there was. Fish was on stock. The rest we filled out with starches and reconstitutes.

The checkout scanned his cart and flashed. The supervisor came over.

"Sir, that's more than you're allowed I'm afraid." His English was good. There wasn't much of an accent. It wasn't his first language, though.

"We're both shopping," I said.

"Oh, then please scan your ID, too."

I did. The machine was happy. Then it pinged something else.

"Are you recently arrived?" he asked.

Roger nodded. "Yeah, not long ago."

"Okay. Our system doesn't show a record of you."

"We haven't shopped yet."

"In two weeks?" The man looked suspicious.

"We had a lot of stuff aboard. I travel with foods. Religious issue," he said.

"Ah, okay."

I was glad that worked. He could have asked which religion and checked against data. They have freedom of

religion in the UN, but only certain religions are
recognized. The rest are free to operate within regular law
but aren't tax exempt and don't get protected speech. I
sort of belonged to two churches, and neither was
recognized by the UN.

It wasn't much food. It was adequate for two people,
but we had ten, and four of them couldn't risk being
seen.

I said, "We'll need to dumpster dive for some."

"Safely?"

"Yeah, it won't be very nutritious, but it will be filling."

"Okay."

We dropped off the stuff we had, then with a couple
of satchels, went down the access behind Breadbar and
Kenniwick's.

Behind Breadbar I found several loaves set out on a
rack for homeless people to take. Some had faint mold
rings. Others were just stale enough to use as clubs. I
grabbed a handful. There was also a box of beignets.

Kenniwick's had some bags of tuna salad and some
fruit. We could rinse the fruit off. I still wasn't keen on it,
but this was war and we had to eat. Two of the tuna bags
were definitely off. I had Roger sniff the other.

"I think it's still passable," he said. "Barely."

"We'll eat as soon as we're back." I figured it hit toss
temp and they tossed it. It would be okay for a couple of
hours longer.

Hopefully we wouldn't wind up with screaming shits
and nowhere to go.

Back in the nest, we scraped off the surface mold,
spooned tuna on the spread, and ate. Jack rinsed off the

fruit and I made myself eat an apple. We passed around the packaged stuff for later.

Then it was back to standing watch, keeping hidden, and waiting for some set of actions Juan wanted before we moved. I had goggles without sound, or ears without vid. I couldn't shut everything out. So I listened to music and wished I could dance. We took turns with one peeking out, another ready to move, and everyone's bags slung to go.

I needed an orgasm like you wouldn't believe. But I wasn't alone, it wouldn't be fair to tease them with the show, and I couldn't use them. The dynamic was all wrong. I was contractor, not staff, not contracted for sex, and unless I did them all, it would cause tension. Even if I did do them all, and by that point I would have, even both chicks, I wasn't a professional. That would mess up the separation we had.

So I gritted my teeth, sweated in the dust and dark, and tried not to clench my legs and grind. I managed an occasional rub in a stall when we went out to wipe down in lieu of real bathing. My hair was nasty. I was sweaty and slimy.

The station was effectively shut down. I assumed they were searching in detail, and eventually they'd find the hideys.

I spent a lot of time listening to trance and staring at the inside of the brim of a hat I'd acquired. It blocked the light and I had nothing else to do. It was almost worse than being shot at. We barely talked in case we were overheard. We used whispers in ears when we did. The transformer hum was driving me crazy.

After two weeks we got out. It was only two Earth

weeks, not ten-day Freehold weeks, but it felt like being released from prison. I guess in a way it was.

We cleaned up with bleach wipes and Roger handed us fresh coveralls that said we were crew of the *Copperly*.

CHAPTER 30

⊕

We walked directly from our hide, to the main passage, to a mid-price hotel—the Баспана, I think. I kept a frozen calm expression on my face. We didn't have chips and I was waiting for the monitors to jump us at any moment.

Nothing happened. We checked into an econo-suite with four private berths and a common room. Jack ran some kind of sensor around, thumbed up, and said, "Nice place." He flicked on a device I figured was some sort of counter scrambler and said, "We're clear in here."

"Even without Ident chips?" I asked.

"I masked us from the sensors. I can't do it often or they'll see the hole in the grid, but it got us here and we're going to fake it from here."

Juan said, "Everyone take a couple of divs to unwind, shower, eat, and grab a medicinal drink if you need to. Next stage starts then."

"What are we doing?"

"Stealing our bonded ship back from system security monitors."

I was sure they could do it.

He said, "To bring you up to date, we left the ship unattended. They're not positive we're connected to anything, but we are 'persons of interest' and they are holding it. So we're going to break it out and tie them up more. Go clean up and get ready."

I wasn't able to do much in the shower. I got clean fast, and hot water beating on aching muscles felt so good. I followed that with a cool mist and dim light. I felt a lot better when it was over. It was five minutes. I wanted fifty.

After that, I had crabcakes and rice from the pile of delivered food, and a drink of a cane sugar rum. It was stronger than beer or spritzers, but it was drinkable and did help calm me slightly.

It wasn't enough. Juan, Mo, Bast and Roger were the biggest four. They came back in with large rollerlockers.

Mo said, "We have chips. The rest of you will pile in these, and we'll head for *Bounder*. If an altercation actually starts, you can bail out with the lever here." He pointed at a pull loop mounted inside. "Yanking that pops the hinges and you're out. Don't do it without a real fight or you'll blow our cover."

"How will we know?"

"Gunfire, case getting slammed around, one of us yells."

That wasn't a thrilling idea. Claustrophobia and a firefight.

It was tight in the case. I was in a half-squat with my knees up and head down. I spread out as much as I could, and tried to find a squat that didn't put all my weight on my ankles.

"Ready?" Mo asked.

"No."

"Good!" he said, and sealed me in.

It wasn't totally sealed. There was a small vent at top and bottom so there was circulation. I hoped it was enough. CO_2 asphyxiation isn't fun.

It was worse than the dolly I'd been strapped into when arrested.

I tried desperately not to panic. I didn't want to get everyone else killed. When we started rolling, I started crying, as quietly as I could, tears dripping down my nose and lashes where I couldn't touch them.

It could be an hour or more, and I had no way to track time. I was squashed, and my feet started cramping and aching with the position.

I was rolled along. I couldn't tell exactly what route we took, but I felt the joints, the changing G, and the surface as we neared entry control for the dock. We stopped, there were voices I could barely hear, and shuffling. I tried hard to breathe while not making a lot of noise. I had to suck air through the case shell, then exhale down and hope the vent at the bottom was enough.

This was ridiculous and dangerous and no one sane would do it.

Which was exactly the point.

Then I was tilted over and there was grunting as the case slapped down on a table hard enough to knock wind out of me.

The seal popped, glaring light and cool, fresh air hit me, and a voice said, "What the shit?"

"Portable dishwasher," I said. He looked at me funny.

I couldn't stand or do anything complicated, but I could reach his throat, and did. His body armor meant I didn't get much of a grip, but I held on tight.

Mo hit him from behind with something. It might have been a lock pin. Whatever it was, the guy's head whiplashed, his eyes rolled up, and I heard the sound of a cracking egg.

Near me, Mira had swarmed out of her case and was beating someone savagely with a small baton.

Mo pulled me to my feet and half-dragged me.

"We want to get under faster than they can see us, move, then come back up somewhere else, doesn't matter where. In the dock. Can you lead?"

"I think so. That strut fan should have an access." I pointed.

"Go."

Behind me I heard more shouts, more screams, and stunner fire. The team was breaking people with mostly bare hands.

Then I heard what sounded like grenades. Three shockwaves passed me one after another.

I didn't look behind me because it would slow me and I trusted them. I cleared the nearest strut and skidded around, even with grip shoes on textured deck. I made a note to replace them if they were getting that slick.

The hatch was locked and sealed. I had no code and no idea how to open it.

Jack came around and started poking at it. The rest ran block, and I mean "ran." They went in four directions, came back, crossed on the far side of the struts, and generally kept monitors busy. There were only three monitors anyway. Sorry, I mean two, or apparently, one. Bast clobbered him and he went down. It was a savage beating. That man could hit.

Jack ripped the lock and I hit the ladder. I'd expected that. This should go straight down to the underdeck.

I gripped my insteps around the outside of the ladder and slid, using friction as brakes. I hit the bottom and it tingled the leftover pins and needles until they stung.

From here we could go hubward or out. I chose out.

"Is the ship docked close?" I asked.

Jack said, "No, it's anchored out. We're taking a shuttle again, if we can find one."

"Shuttle at the dockmaster's office. A six-boat."

"Crowded, but doable."

I said, "As long as someone is there with it." I was making it up as I went along, because I'd never been in this design of station, nor in this part of this one. I just figured there would be a power conduit to the Dockmaster's office, and it would be walkable.

I found it near the inner hull skin. It was mostly walkable. I had to hunch down. Teresa was smaller, everyone else was larger. I heard quiet grunts and hisses behind me, as we scrambled over bolted section joint and bends in the conduits. It was only notionally a passage. Over the years, pipe and conduits had been run through and across. We had to weave and squirm in spots. I ached in my back by the time we reached a ladder going up.

"Locked and probably sealed," I said.

Bast said, "That's me," and squeezed past. Really squeezed. This section was manhole tight. "Fire in the hole now. Move back."

I scooted back with the others behind me. I heard him futzing with something, then he suddenly dropped down and fell flat. He clapped hands over his ears, so I did, too.

The bang was really sharp and loud, and bits of stuff pinged and rattled down behind him.

I got stepped on.

Bast threw himself upright from a pushup, grabbed the ladder and jumped. Mo went over me, almost stepping on my fingers. I yanked everything in close to my body, as Roger said, "Excuse me!" and followed.

The three techs were last, and I brought up the rear.

I climbed up, still a bit dizzy from the blast, and my ears rang. I threw my arms out of the hatch and pulled myself up.

I was in a power cabinet, and that hatch was off its hinges, too.

The office was a bunch of small rooms along a passage, with an airlock at one end with the boat. The inner end had an emergency lock in case of pressure failure. The surviving dock crew, all eight, had been stuffed in there, and barricaded. I wasn't sure how, but they weren't getting out and were beating on the port.

Juan and Mira had the lock to the inspection tug open, and I stumbled through. I banged an ankle, an elbow and the side of my head, and dropped to the deck crying.

Someone pulled me clear of the LZ and stuffed me into a G couch.

I didn't feel that hurt, but I barely tracked until G went away. We'd undocked and departed on a centripetal line, whatever it's called.

Up front, I heard Mira say, "I think that's close. I don't

see anything in position to intercept, and I'm pretty sure they don't want to toss beams or missiles around this close to the station."

Jack asked, "How did you calculate the trajectory?"

"I just sort of guessed and unlatched when we hit that point. It appears I did it correctly."

Several segs later, a voice started shouting at us through comm. She ignored it and started maneuvering thrust. She made one shot that tapered off at an odd angle, but killed our rotation and apparently brought us right up to *Bounder*'s passenger lock.

Teresa and Jack helped me to my bunk. I thought I was recovered, but I was still a bit out of it. I'd hit harder than I thought and not felt most of it.

Mira's voice said, "Boosting max. Stand by for G."

It ramped up from a hiss to a rumble in the frame, and the lights dipped to emergency levels. I guess she fed everything from the plant into thrust. It felt about 3G standard, but might have been a bit more. In a cargo hauler with a train that was a lot of power.

Juan said, "Everyone stand by, we're going to try to slam the point. Timer." A countdown showed on my phone, stowed in place above my bunk. Had I done that?

Teresa came over, slapped a patch on my neck and handed me a bottle with a straw. I sipped, and felt a cool wave, then throbbing warmth, then my thoughts cleared up a lot. She looked tense. Then I realized she was standing at triple G. She collapsed back into her own bunk.

I was mostly back on track as we neared Jump.

Mira came on air again.

"Just an update. We're looking good for position. There's one hauler that could beat us if they pulled harder, but they don't want a thrust-measuring contest. Apparently, I like thrust more than anyone else."

I wasn't sure about that, even knowing she was making a joke. I do love good thrust.

"If they're not fighting us, I believe we have it. There's a Space Guard ship in pursuit, but they're far behind. Even though they're pulling a lot more, we had a substantial lead. They won't get us in range. However, we may have been reported on the last jump, it just depends on if Earth is willing to admit they fucked the dog on this and ask for help, or will try to bury the bone."

It was the first time I'd ever heard her swear.

The timer adjusted several times, shorter and longer, as we got closer. I believed her that there was no effective pursuit, and I was quite calm when we hit the tick.

CHAPTER 31

We were in Salin space. There was so little here, I wondered what good it would do.

We were still thrusting, though slightly lower.

Mira said, "I have reduced power to one hundred twenty percent of Never Exceed. We hit one thirty-five for a bit there. Prescot's engineers are phenomenal."

Shit. We were still twenty percent over danger level? And had exceeded their "even the goddess won't save you" emergency level?

I wasn't calm anymore.

I wondered what we were doing here, still at overmax boost.

Shortly, Juan announced, "I'm putting it on shipwide. We have pursuit from their Jump Point patrol. They don't know who we are yet."

"Unidentified ship, if you cease flight immediately, you will be captured and held for trial. If not, you will be destroyed."

We didn't respond.

I unbunked and carefully stepped up the main passage to C-deck. The C-deck wasn't my place, but I was fascinated. What was the plan?

Juan said, "You know there's a large KBO not far from the point, right?"

"No?" I said.

"A frozen gaseous dwarf planet. It was conveniently near the point's breakout, so they used it for grav slings and other astrogation, and as a grav anchorage."

"Okay."

Mira said, "So we're heading that way. At this vector, about a standard hour will do it."

"Isn't it dangerous to Jump at that kind of speed?" I asked.

"Yes," she said, and shrugged. "It's what we had to do."

Juan put magnification on a monitor and zoomed in. There wasn't much to see. The planet was white and off-white and gray with a few bits of brown. It had a slight but visible equatorial bulge. Tags blinked on screen, showing a couple of ships in orbit and some sort of small station. It was really just an oversized ship with no main drive, only maneuvering thrusters for orbital correction.

"I have to drop thrust to one-ten," Glenn announced. "Really, we must."

"That tightens the window but we should still be safe," Mira said. "Do it."

G slackened slightly more. I still felt huge with all that acceleration, and I had no idea how we were going to brake.

I forced myself to go to the galley and warm up some

food. We were eating a lot of soup from bulbs, and wraps, more than just during cargo handling.

I took some aft to the guys there, and forward to C-deck. Glenn and Mo thanked me with big smiles. I think they were hungry. Everyone went for the soup. It was warm. For some reason we were all chilled, even though volume temp showed normal—25C.

We ate, I cleaned up, used the head and came back.

I was just in time to hear Mira say, "I think we can have them in position in about a seg."

Juan asked, "Are you ready?"

"Absolutely."

Everyone got silent again. I watched the scale that showed their range against their weapon range. We'd be in that shortly.

"And . . . volley one," she announced. "We shouldn't be a target for them now."

I felt jolts and G increased.

I looked the question to Juan, and he said, "We just dropped some pods. We gained acceleration. They have debris in their path."

"A couple of pods are easy to miss."

"Not when they explode into chaff, frag and jacks."

We'd just jacked off right where they had to pursue. That would slow them down.

It looked like we were approaching the planet on a tight pass.

"Unidentified ship, we now identify you as *Bounder Dog*. Item One: Drop thrust and stand down to be boarded, or you will be destroyed.

"Item Two: You missed. Try again?"

I wasn't sure what we could do, but I didn't think taunting Mira was smart.

She spoke to us only as she said, "Volley two."

We were definitely pulling in tight enough to rotate around a barycenter as we came past this nameless snowball of a planet.

I felt more jerks and figured out they were additional pods detaching. G rose again, and I hoped she'd accounted for that in her astrogation.

Of course she had.

We were going to pass awfully close, though.

I didn't realize Teresa had come up and was next to me on the remaining couch.

"There's negligible atmosphere," she said. "We can get in pretty close. And it's largely frozen ices. Not much in the way of mountains."

Just how fucking close were we going to approach?

"*Bounder Dog*, we are about to open fire. There will be no warning shot. Drop thrust and assume orbit. You also missed again."

Mira said, "Volley three."

This time there was a significant change in thrust and a lot of clattering. We'd dropped something big.

Juan was busy with a headset and hush hood. He was talking to someone, I figured one of the guys aft. Whatever it was, he looked serious, and pleased. That was a good sign.

I was trusting them again, because that iceball was now visible and huge on a *normal* view. We were within a few thousand kilometers of it.

The Space Guard commo tech called again.

"*Bounder Dog*, you missed again," she taunted.

"Did I?" Mira asked, sounding innocent. I realized she'd opened a freq and actually talked to them.

The response was shouted noise for a moment, then, "You goddamn fucking whore! I hope they rape you over a fire! You fucking—" it went on, furious, incoherent. Then I realized they were terrified.

"What did you do?" I asked.

She drew something at her station quickly, and an animation popped up.

"Those are our bombs. That area I lit is the only safe place for them."

"Okay?"

"That's too low in the gravity well. They won't be able to pull out of it."

She'd boxed them in, and they were going to burn in.

"Hmm," she muttered.

The boat tried to lift out of that orbit, I guess. They ran right into whatever we'd scattered as our own area denial. That seemed fair.

"There's a lot more sharpies there, and closer separation," she said. "They can't do it."

It didn't seem to actually destroy them, but they stopped calling, and were obviously in panic mode about the debris.

Then they did call.

"Mayday! Mayday! Mayday! UNS *Hammerskjold* in critical danger. Hull integrity breached. Powerplant damaged. Drive damaged. Astrogation and helm damaged. Atmosphere integrity lost. Critical emerg . . . Mayday! Mayday! Mayday!"

A few second later, it was, "Please, any ship respond! Crew are on emergency O-two. Life-support failure. Containment failure imminent. Anyone. Please help!"

The two ships at grav anchor responded. I heard one offer, "—we can thrust to reach you. Can you decelerate? We can match trajectory in approximately four hours."

"We don't have four hours! Attempting deceleration. Astrogator and helm are dead. I am the systems officer."

They weren't going to last four hours.

The sensors twitched.

Juan said, "Looks like they had a short overload on that attempted thrust."

"Blew up?"

"No, but screwed up their vector."

Mira swiped her screens and read numbers.

"They're going in. They lost enough velocity they can't make it. By the way, we are at periapsis."

I had no idea how close we were and didn't want to. I swear I felt centripetal, acceleration and natural G all at once.

But we were obviously retreating. We'd made it. Though I did hear some creaks in the train.

Hammerskjold's screams kept going, shouting for help that couldn't reach them. They were leaking atmosphere, had lost engines, and were going to bore into the snowball anyway. It would have been a cleaner death to go right in.

We'd taken out another warship. A small one, but in actual combat.

With a fifty-year-old tramp freighter and cargo pods.

The planet blocked the view of them crashing, and I think I'm glad.

Everyone wanted us dead, though.

We even heard that.

"General bulletin. A million mark reward is offered for the confirmed capture or destruction of NRS *Bounder Dog*. Do not attempt pursuit, but all UN military ships are advised that weapons clear and pre-emptive fire are authorized. All ships report on sensor track."

Juan pulled off his head gear.

"Angie, how fast can you have your personal effects packed?"

"Uh?" I was confused. "I can have both my bags ready in a seg if it's an emergency."

"Assume so. Go." He pointed. "Everyone else, we are offloading now."

I bounded through the way to my bunk and started stuffing my backpack with essentials. Comm, clothes, makeup, toys. The rest of my loose stuff went into the carry bag.

"Good, you can board," he said as I returned. He indicated the emergency lock.

I wondered what the hell was happening? Was a slow missile inbound? More ships? We couldn't really fight them.

I got into the lifeboat, which was both very old and very updated.

Roger was there already, a bag under him and one in his arms. I started buckling into a harness and did the same with my stuff.

"What's going on?" I asked. If it had been an imminent disaster, we wouldn't have personal gear.

Shannon boarded, followed by Mo and Jack. Mo filled

the hatch and had to squeeze. Sebastian came next and barely made it.

Roger said, "We're swapping ships."

Teresa, Mira, Juan.

"This one's been made," Juan said. "So we're moving."

Something happened, and the klaxon bleated. I heard umbilicals pop, and bolts blow.

We were in emgee and floating.

Then the klaxon bleated three times, and on number three, the escape thruster kicked in. The harness cut into me tightly, and I winced. Then I gasped.

"Ouch."

"Are you okay?" Teresa asked.

"The web's cutting into me."

"Thrust ends in a few seconds," Juan said. He sounded pretty strained himself.

Then it did, and we were in emgee again.

The webbing stopped cutting, and I gently pushed to shift into a different position. It had left welts and numb spots.

"I hope we have a pickup," I said. I didn't see many positives to sitting here waiting. We weren't going to get found by friendlies.

"We do," Shannon said. "Soon."

We sat there in silence for a bit, before Jack started talking about one of the games he played. I don't game. It meant nothing to me.

Teresa asked, "Angie, what's the load you got you've been paying so much attention to."

"Uh . . . intimate."

"Ah. Any good?"

"Alexia is always good." I don't mind sharing with friends, but not in public.

"Oh! I've heard of her."

"She does amazing things."

"Hmm. Can I check it sometime?"

"Sure. But here is probably not the best place." The head was a toilet with emgee seals over a vac-extraction bucket, with a curtain to wrap for privacy. If we were here more than a few hours, there'd be smells, then someone would have to seal and empty it.

Mira said, "We have our ping. It won't be long."

That reassured me.

"Who's getting us? Neutral? Ally?"

"One of our stealth boats."

"Ours?"

"Stand by."

I waited.

Mira added, "By the way, in case you're curious, periapsis was sixteen thousand meters. We could have gone closer, but I was worried about possible terrain features."

Yeah. Ice mountains could easily be that high on a distant snowball.

Goddess. Sixteen kilometers close approach. Atmospheric craft flew higher than that. That explained the clanking from the train. It had pulled taut on centrifugal force as we whipped around.

There was a soft thunking sound that rang like a synth tone. Then the sensation of motion changed.

After a while there was thumping and bouncing. We were against some kind of mating harness.

The hull buzzed, and said, "Codeword Victor." It was metallic sounding even though it was a composite hull.

Juan said, "Anna."

"Welcome, friends."

After a bit the voice said, "You'll need to inflate rescue balls. We can't dock."

We went aft to the lock. I let Mo and Glenn zip me into a ball. Jack and Bast wrapped all our gear in a mesh net. Juan punched for depressure and open, then jumped into a ball fast and zipped up. I felt my ball swell in the vacuum.

As soon as there was room, three ghostly figures came through the hatch opening, and as soon as it was at full width, started dragging us across. Whatever the ship was, it was completely matte black.

Their bay was smaller than ours, and I sensed it was under, not side. I felt someone next to me, our balls all crunched up. Yes, I know, there's a joke there.

Someone must have EVAed to the tug, because our personal gear came over as well.

The bay closed in complete darkness, and the ball softened again as atmosphere increased. When the hatch finally snapped tight, dim lights came on, but I could see.

There was a bomb in front of me.

I wasn't sure what it was, but it was some sort of weapon. I recognized the warning tags.

The bay was long, narrow and tiny. We were stuffed in with no room between.

A rescue ball has a release you can only open under pressure. In vac, internal pressure holds it closed. I tested it, and it popped loose. I felt a slight pressure change to their vessel, which was lower than the ball's, or at least, it was in a recently open bay.

Someone in a V-suit came over and pulled me free.

"Welcome aboard the *FMS Selous*. We're informal here. I'm Dick."

"Thanks. Angie." I took his hands and shook, and he helped me upright.

I stretched and wondered what the heck we were doing.

They brought me up to speed.

Selous was a stealth boat on a J frame. It looked black outside because it had no color, and the outside of the hull was coated with fractal gel. Inside, everything was minimal signature. They didn't even use much light.

"We're a black hole in space," Dick said. "Nothing reflected or emitted."

Their crew was about our size, and they were in theory a war boat. I've been told not to give further details. I never learned their names, barely saw them, and mostly lived in that hold, which was chilly and spare and not at all hospitable. I'd gotten used to living like that. Bunks were luxuries, and I was tired from that chase and the massive adrenaline release from it.

I was still gulping at the dead *Hammerskjold*. Instant glowing vapor was one thing. Sitting in the leaking cold knowing you were going to die had to be a lot worse.

The crew brought food back to us. It was heated crew-packs, not much for flavor, but they did bring a small spice bar we could use. I may be the only vet who actually liked the tuna with noodles entree.

"I'll take any seafood or chicken you have," I said. "I really prefer not to eat mammals. I'll swap."

Glenn said, "I think Angie becomes more awesome all the time, with that attitude." He grinned.

I shrugged it off. I don't like eating mammals, and people who do are happy to swap with me. It works both ways.

Bedding was limited, but we weren't under much G. A thin pad and two blankets worked okay. Teresa showed me how to fold them.

"This one has two layers under, one over, and this one has two layers over, one under. Then you have the pad underneath. Gives about three centimeters of cushion and three layers for warmth. Almost as warm as an Arctic bag, so you can open the top for ventilation."

"That looks rather comfortable," I said. I used a rolled towel for a pillow.

It was odd. We were billeted in a cargo bay, but still had all our personal gear from *Bounder*.

I guess Mira and Juan had to be debriefed. We didn't see them for a while.

I looked at Roger and said, "I take it no one is going to tell me how one of our stealth boats got into this system undetected."

With mock cheer he said, "You're right! Besides, it's not important right now." Or maybe it wasn't mock.

"Are we docking at some point?"

"Sort of. We're passing by."

I said, "Docking control doesn't like that. But I guess they can't see us."

"That's the plan."

Mira came back and said, "We're going to unrein a pod and toss it at them."

"That'll break some surface stuff."

"And then explode mightily, if I did my job right." She was always so perfectly collected.

"When did you rig that?"

She said, "Ongoing. You remember certain shipments stayed with us and just changed manifests."

"Ah, yeah. How big a blast are you talking?"

"Hopefully enough to cripple the station. Evac will tie them up."

"Was something like this behind the evac on Station Ceileidh?"

"No, not sure why that one happened."

Mira and Shannon went EVA over to *Bounder*, which was in a parallel orbit, drifting in-system. She'd managed to steer that way on the planetary maneuver, barely skimming the surface, while arranging a gravity kill for the UN ship. I can't even imagine the math that goes into that.

"They can't see us, but why can't they see *Bounder*?" I asked.

Juan said, "Powerplant is at idle, it's in free trajectory, and the close approach and changing thrust gives a huge cone of possible vectors. They also have no reason to think we'd go anywhere near a station, now that we're identified and wanted. Also, politics dictates they search the volume around the point and planet first, to ensure we don't attack another vessel. Every seg they don't catch us is several more in which they won't. This is going to be a long flight."

Mira and Shannon went EVA several times over

several days. They started detaching pods and shoving them around with a pneumatic jack. They also equipped some with maneuvering jets.

Shortly we were in a formation of pods and loose cargotainers, our own little flotilla.

It was a long flight, as Juan said. We had a very respectable vid and music library. There was a small but effective gym and we had room to spar. We actually went on a schedule a lot like recruit training, reveille, PT, breakfast, minor chores and maintenance, lunch, any necessary shipboard drills and ongoing training, along with whatever news we could pull from *Selous'* sensors. After dinner we were free for a couple of div and a bit. I hated being regimented like that, but it probably kept me sane. I wasn't as tense and aggravated as I had been behind that power panel.

The head was small, but did have a shower pan big enough to sprawl in, and we all took turns cleaning it. I expect everyone else was using it the way I was, too. I know how people look when sated. No one was physically frustrated, but I really could have used human flesh. But we were at war.

Some of the boat crew went out with Mira and Shannon. Then Jack and Teresa went along. I knew something was up.

Teresa wouldn't say much.

"We were making changes and repairs to some of the 'tainers, and to *Bounder* itself," she said.

"Can you tell me? I'm bored and dying to know."

"You'll see when it happens."

Shannon came over and handed her a bottle. She

measured three shots into a squeeze tube, said, "Thank you," handed him back the bottle, and started sipping it.

"What's that?"

"Medical tequila."

"'Medical?'"

She nodded. "We can choose our flavor. It's partly to aid as a vasodilator to improve circulation after EVA. Between radiating heat and the suit tension on the skin, you get a warm core and cold extremities."

She took a long, slow drink, and took a deep breath.

"Second is because floating in complete darkness outside the range of any safety line is terrifying to some people." It was obvious she included herself in that. She was still more calm than I had been.

She finished it.

I said, "Yeah, I like space, but from a loader or station shell, not from floating in it."

She shrugged. "Our training isn't as intense as the Blazers' training, but it was pretty rough in spots. We never did anything like this, though. They did, and they said to expect it. I never thought we actually would."

"I never thought being a flaky tourist laborer would pay off, either," I said.

"What's your favorite station?" she asked.

"Breakout always was. Partly because it's home, you know? It's our oldest, so it's got the best facilities and a lot of traffic, so there's a lot of culture. There's a lot of beached spacers and dropouts, though. But that's where I learned about underdeck culture."

She said, "It's been useful. It's amazing how many

variations there are, little microcosms in each station or even section."

"Yeah, you fit to your surroundings. I guess any engineering plan assumes a bunch of people who aren't accounted for."

"About twenty percent," she said. "Higher back home since we don't track anyone, but even Earth admits they can't actually do anything about a lot of them."

"What could they do?" I asked. "If they spaced that many people, it would be noticed. If they tried to account for them and feed them through official channels, it would take more infrastructure."

"There are scholars who study it," she said. "We couldn't get any of them who we could trust. They either weren't available, or from other systems, or questionable as to loyalty."

"A lot of them are Earthies," I agreed.

"Or elsewhere. Being from the Freehold doesn't make them more trustworthy of itself, but it means skin in the game. Anyone else starts off with questions."

I wasn't clear on what the "technicians" were, only that they weren't quite Blazers themselves. Either that, or the six teammates were something more skullkicking than Blazers. From watching them fight, I could believe that. Their movements were explosive, almost like acrobatic dancing. Then someone's shoulder was dislocated, or a neck broken, or ribs crushed. They didn't have any problem killing people. I did notice they tried to avoid civilians. They seemed to genuinely like killing cops, though. More than they liked killing enemy troops.

I wasn't sure I blamed them.

The gym was a small unitized component. You climbed in, strapped in, and grabbed the handles. It felt your leverage and adjusted resistance to match. I chose from the existing programs, and it worked me through legs, back, arms, core on a daily rotation. I'd do two sets taking ten segs. Then I'd shower while the next person lifted, then I'd clean our area, then I'd catch up on briefings. It worked. We kept moving and didn't crowd each other too much.

CHAPTER 32

It was twenty-three days before anything happened.

Juan called us to informal formation.

"We are back in combat, though mostly we'll be observing, Mira and the boat's cargo specialist, 'Jerry,' will take charge of maneuvering *Bounder* remotely. We get to watch. If this ship gets detected, there will be emergency maneuvering. Everyone remain fastened for the duration. We start in three segs."

That was just time for a head call. I didn't really need to go, but if we were going to be strapped down, I didn't want to be uncomfortable later.

I strapped to padeyes on the deck and waited. We got a flat image projected on the forward bulkhead of the bay, broken up by a strut, but adequate for our needs. We weren't doing it, just watching the game.

A tag showed up from the status identification transponder, but it was for a completely different ship name, the *Umara*, registered out of Mtali.

The track shifted, and Juan explained, "We are doing a slow maneuver to place us in the sensor shadow of our decoy. It's not really a secret that this ship uses string drive."

I didn't know they could fit one that small. This thing was a boat, not a ship. There are rescue cutters larger than it.

We did move into the shadow, and ahead another SIT identified the station. It was tagged *Salin Port of Entry*.

"That's entirely a UN station," I said. "It's barely even local on paper, and only as a territory. This place has never managed a stable government."

Juan said, "Right. It's also distant from us by a fair piece, which means in response they'll have to disperse their forces even wider."

Mira apparently sent an automated request for trajectory plan and approach. Scrolling data showed next to our tag, and I had no idea what any of it meant.

Juan said, "Rest break, ten minutes."

Yeah, it had been a full div, almost three hours Earth, and we'd been staring at the screen.

We used the head quickly. One of the crew handed us each a protein bar and a Neurade, and we fastened back down.

After that, it got interesting.

Control called and said, "*Umara*, you appear to have loose cargo. Please verify train integrity."

I could just see Mira in the compartment ahead, which seemed to be for electronic warfare and payload control.

She sat there, wearing a mic, not answering.

We were about five light-seconds out, I think. It was over twenty seconds before they sent again.

I could see what they meant, though I'm guessing our display was built from passive sensors. Several tainers seemed to have separated and were loose. A slight deceleration had let them move ahead. There wasn't much separation yet, but there was going to be in time.

"*Umara*, we must have a status report if you are functional. If not, please use flares, engine flash or some other signal."

This time she responded. "Control, we are operating within parameters."

Lightspeed lag pause.

"*Umara*, we show debris or separation. It is imperative you correct any discrepancies at once. Extreme danger."

"Control, we show everything where it should be, over." She still sounded calm.

I realized she was being completely truthful, with different definitions.

"*Umara*, our impact defense system will fire on anything that poses a collision threat. Can't you see the clutter around you? It looks like several large pods or a broken one has spilled cargotainers."

"I see something now, Control."

She waited five seconds before responding further.

"Control, we have a loose pod. We will attempt to secure or jettison. We are engaging per your instructions now."

She did something, and *Bounder* shifted slightly, but her velocity increased more.

There was a flash onscreen and one of the pods disappeared in melting globs.

But the one right behind it blew through the cloud.

"*Umara*, please declare your status and intentions. Imperative. If you do not, we must treat you as a threat to life and astrogation, and fire to destroy you. *Please* communicate with us on this."

The tech genuinely sounded distressed, not scared.

The loose 'tainers were pulling ahead, but *Bounder* increased thrust again.

I heard Teresa mutter, "Looks as if I wired everything right."

Bounder ran at them, engines at max plus the thirty percent we'd been told they could handle in an emergency, and a bit more.

Pieper. Her name was *Henri Pieper*. *Bounder Dog* was just a cover.

I guess it didn't matter. I had no idea which name was real, or if either was. She felt like *Pieper* to me, though.

There was another deceleration, then a long, slow roll that changed attitude slightly, without changing heading.

The station beamcast and we caught fragments of it even with the debris in front of us. They were in a panic, and we watched, as invisible as one could get. We had it on five screens in five spectra, from UV to IR to Commo.

"*Umara*, you must respond at once. We are going to be forced to fire. Perform a yaw maneuver, a pitch maneuver, use flares or engine flash. Please indicate you are in danger, or we must consider you an intentional threat."

Behind *Pieper* now was the lifeboat and cargo tug, in

free flight and trailing, along with all her pods and more loose cargotainers. The connections to the train cable came loose. Everything started to spread out behind her.

Then she retro-braked, and the pods closed the gap and moved ahead.

Control said, "*Umara*, our automated defense will fire in twenty seconds from this message. You are ordered to engage maximum retrothrust and course change. We have ruled your intention hostile."

Mira fluttered her fingers over the screens, and did something. I couldn't tell what.

Station Control fired something, particle beam or laser, and the first pod burst into bright flashes. I figured it was foil, to create a cloud in their sensor images. I know there are ways to defeat that, but they take time.

They caught a second pod, which broke into several large sections. The struts had been pre-cut. Now they had several large decoys, and hundreds of bits of chaff. In vacuum, they didn't scatter much other than from a little internal turbulence. They made a large, slowly dispersing screen with the rest of the mass hidden.

Mira said, "That's titanium and aluminum powder, which we were transporting for electrically isolating paint for components. Now it's a cloud that will ruin their sensors and coat everything with dust."

Pieper kept closing, with her escorts.

Mira said, "They've got a parallax image, either civilian with good sensors, or they managed to launch a boat."

"I'm on it," one of *Selous'* crew said.

A pinpoint flash turned into an accelerating trace of a small missile. It didn't launch from our boat. It came from some drone somewhere. Long seconds later, possibly a seg, another flash.

"Got them," he said.

It was fascinating to see a space battle fought by proxy. Some systems were self-guiding, others were remote, so there were long delays. We, meaning Mira, had some control over the maneuvers.

The beam fired again, so hot it was visible. There's always atmosphere residue and chemical leakage around a station. Then there was all the dust we'd thrown. That all turned to plasma as the beam front hit it.

Pieper became a glowing dot, then trailed like a comet, then broke into pieces that continued to glow.

And that was her end. She'd gone from being an in-system cargo hauler to a trans-system tramp, and now she was a missile. She burned in the dark.

The station recharged their cannon and aimed it at the first cargo pod. It took only a hit to flash into vapor, but it glowed a lot brighter.

"What's that?" Glenn asked.

"Zirconium and cesium. You know those containers marked 'mill shavings for recycling'?"

"We've had those a long time."

"Yes, and now they have that flash, the decoys and *Pieper*'s guts and reactor core fogging their sensors."

I saw what was happening.

The next canister burst, and it fluttered into a cloud of fog.

Mira said, "Uranium dust and oxygen. Deflagrates rapidly in plasma."

I don't know what else we threw, but the pods kept

bursting into clouds of debris, creating more and more chaff cloud, which would coat every sensor and mess with mechanicals.

They got several pods, but then the first one slammed against the shield. That was meant to stop particles and gammas, not multitons of mass.

They got another one, but two more sailed through the vapor and crashed.

Then the next one started tumbling from all the debris impacting it.

I don't know what the guys put in the lifeboat, but when it hit, the explosion damped the display.

The rest of the containers tumbled into the fireball. It might not destroy the station, but it was doing all kinds of havoc. Structure, hull integrity, sensors all took a beating. The shock would travel along struts and crack rivets and joints. There is no such thing as "minor damage" to a habitat that can't put everyone into a suit plumbed into life-support.

That was a lot of damage. They might not need to evacuate, but they wouldn't be docking or transshipping anything large for weeks, possibly months.

I said, "She was old, but I'm sad to see her burn. She was only a cargo hauler, but she was my home longer than any other ship."

Mira replied, "She was a warship when she died."

I guess that was so. She'd done well for a merchant ship.

We were behind and closing, though we were changing course slightly. I saw the explosion for just a moment in the screen, even as the view pivoted. We passed over the scaffoldock fast. It wasn't functional, the control dome was destroyed, and I could see atmosphere leaking. I could tell from the dust and trash blowing out with it.

We'd openly attacked them now.

There was complete panic on comm. I heard begging, pleading, crying, shouted anger, every negative emotion.

"Congratulations to Mira and Hank," Juan said.

"I thought his name was 'Jerry.'"

The guy turned and said, "In another three segs it'll be JR."

I did laugh.

Something scrolled on screen and one of the crew said, "Oh, shit."

"What?" from the captain and Juan together.

"Ionization trace. Our drive, all that plasma and dust. If they see it—"

I hoped they were too busy with their on-station disaster to do anything. I didn't want to eat a missile.

Jerry/Hank/JR said, "They have something online. We're being actively probed and they probably know we're stealthed."

Acquiring tracking in space is hard. Keeping it is easy. We'd been seen, and enough resolution should show our power levels, that ionization, and there are a range of possible trajectories.

I said, quietly, "Thanks for being a great bunkmate, Teresa."

"And you," she said. "I don't think we're dead yet, though."

I was pretty sure we were. It might take a while, but

they had time to let every Jump Point know to be waiting for us on this side and the other, and we couldn't stay here forever.

Juan said, "Head break, fast."

I waited in line, zipped suit and drained fast, got back to my improv couch. I was just glad I didn't die sitting on the commode.

"We do have a missile," Jerry said, and I gulped and clenched eyes.

The captain said, "Full evasion. Decoys. Chaff. Flares. Dazzlers. Counterfire. A-rad. Emergency boost."

As he said it, I heard or felt it. We suddenly shifted on three axes. Thunks indicated stuff being deployed, and I saw the view fuzz and flare and twitch. Something launched because I felt it blow out by pneumatic. Then we hit G. I mean we really hit G. It was six or eight. Ours, not Earth.

It immediately stopped.

There was a large, bright explosion aft.

"Hopefully that did it. They shouldn't see anything for a while."

I understood. A short, heavy burn in all that crud right after hitting them should be hard to find even on review. The explosion was a decoy, and there had been others. I wonder if their missile had hit one.

Jerry said, "Pity we can't do that to ground-based targets, but they've got so much sensor suite they can see dust specks, and enough counterbattery they'd have cooked us before we got into approach."

I said, "I understand even an accident would be devastating."

"Yes, if you call several gigatons 'devastating.' You'll never see a ship impact a planet. Meteor guards were adapted to make sure."

The station, though, was apparently less critical, even with all those lives aboard.

Juan said, "This will obviously dictate a change in our operations. Either we find another ship we can use or borrow, or we resort to passenger status and do what we can."

They'd lost their ship and still planned to attack. I had to respect that kind of balls.

"Unrelated question," I asked. "Assuming this boat doesn't have phase drive, how do you get in and out of systems? Our fleet carriers are obvious."

"We can't answer that," I was told.

I still don't know if they'd been in-system that entire time, slammed a Jump Point, piggybacked on another ship, or actually had a billion-credit phase drive.

My immediate worry was staying alive. Our diversion worked, and we moved outsystem, with less and less likelihood of them finding us in the volume.

The station was critically damaged. The passive sensors on that boat were amazing, but I assume they were built for intel scooping. We caught local news, outsystem news bursts, and apparently decoded some scrambled intel signals.

They brought in engineers and modules and set up an emergency control center, but the ships couldn't dock. That meant they had to borrow lighters and shuttles, transport them in-system, and use those for unloading. Then there was some political argument over whether the ships should pay for that as a cost of doing business, or the government should underwrite it as a catastrophic event.

When it was made clear that no one would bother shipping if they had to pay for the unloading, they threatened to criminally charge ships that didn't for "war profiteering." How were they going to identify which ships? There were probably a couple on contract schedule runs, but most were now and again, or even one-offs.

I've never known politicians to make sense.

After two weeks, they came around to the UN paying for the loading and unloading, but had a huge list of requirements, even more than the ones we'd had to deal with.

I could see how a handful of ships doing our kind of thing could utterly crash chunks of their economy. I just wasn't sure that would stop them from destroying us in the process.

I said two weeks. We were around longer than that. We kept going, outsystem. I got concerned. It was quiet and dark out there, and no stations.

Fifteen-day cycles along, thrust came back online and we moved out of emgee into .5. Given the time and trajectory, we had to be out of the gravity well of the star and in the right range for a Jump Point, but there was no way it was unguarded for us to get through.

We kept going.

No one else seemed scared, so I tried to assume they knew what they were doing. I was sure they did. I just couldn't feel secure when I didn't.

We had no news out here, either. No one could

beamcast us, and broadcasts for local space were too weak even for the sensors on an intel boat.

It was as alone as I've ever been in my life. Despite the "depths" of space, most people stay near habitats or planets, or routes with regular traffic. Or else they take large survey ships in pairs. We had fifteen people in a boat the size of a ground-based house, and most of that house was engine, powerplant, sensors and oxy production.

A ten-day Freehold week after that, there was activity up front.

"Contact. Positive ID on the *Serang*."

I recognized that. The *Serang* was one of our destroyers.

Eventually there were bumps and clangs and we were docked and attached.

I felt a lot better.

"How far out are we?" I asked.

Juan and the captain exchanged looks and shrugged before I got an answer.

The captain said, "We're out by the astropause."

"That's outside the outer Halo, yes?"

"Kuiper Belt and Scattered Disk, yes. Typically it is. With the smaller star, we're actually still within those. Slightly."

Damn. That was actually the deepest into space I'd ever been.

It's deeper than almost anyone got to go.

I said, "I don't recall them updating to phase drive."

I got no answer.

I found out much later that officially they hadn't upgraded. Brandt had a couple of units ready to go when we got attacked, stuck them on a ship and donated them. They were concealed and dragged out of system, and then installed. The UN didn't even know *Serang* still existed. Supply boats fed them, they fed us, and they hadn't been in any system for the duration. They'd been astrogating in deep space, alone. That had to be a hell of a story.

They spent half a day fastening us to their superstructure. I don't know the physics, but you can't just tow a ship, apparently. There's an envelope around the structural mass based on some sort of submolecular shaping of space from it. There has to be complete contact and only certain overall shapes work.

It was my first time in phase drive, and it was neat. There's no whomp upside the head. Everything gets really fuzzy for a bit, almost like being drunk, then it fades back to normal. We were elsewhere.

Once again I found out a lot later. We were at an actual interstellar base our engineers had built. Our phase drive ships were here, dragging the others with them whenever they could.

Churchill had been destroyed. I didn't have any close friends who'd been aboard, but they were mostly good people and they'd fought bravely. I felt like crap for being here.

Teresa supported me again.

"Don't feel that way. Death is something that happens, and dying there wouldn't have allowed you to help us. You've done a lot more here. You couldn't have saved the ship."

"Yeah, I know," I said. "Survivor's guilt."

"You have nothing to feel guilty over. It's perfectly

natural, so I'm going to offer you some medical rum and thanks, for getting us where we are." She had a selection of bottles in her gear crate, all labeled with stock codes that declared them official issue.

I tossed the rum back and grimaced. There's a reason I drink fruity drinks.

It didn't help at once, but I did eventually accept it. It still sucked to know they were dead and I couldn't have done anything.

"You couldn't have done anything if you'd never been aboard," she said. "They'd just be names then."

"I can't detach myself from people like that."

"It's tough. It takes time. Should I leave you alone to meditate? Or do you want company?"

I shrugged. "Hanging out is good. I won't talk much."

"That's fine."

I avoided that by thinking about what was here. Actually, the one led to the other. Our warships weren't fighting. One on one, they could fight UN ships. What they couldn't do was resupply. Once low on fuel or ammo, that was it, even if they didn't lose, which they would some of the time.

Instead, we had them running supplies. They were faster-than-light, go-anywhere transports that could haul multiple cargos. They moved fuel, people and intel where it could be used to strike at UN operations. I didn't realize at the time how much influence I had. I was one small part of a team of ten, but that team reduced UN operational effectiveness by several percent in several systems. Add in the actual battles we'd fought and the skull kicking was all out of proportion to the size of the boot.

Regarding the station location, apparently, the astrogation crew had coded and locked instructions they accessed in flight, and not even the captains knew. Since there was no Jump Point to that station, the UN couldn't even get there, even if someone who knew told them where it was. It was literally impenetrable until the UN finished outfitting a phase drive ship, then they'd have to either know where it was or do a lot of searching, then they'd have fewer ships for that battle than we did.

As far as the smaller ships, they couldn't fight us if they couldn't find us, and if they found out we were inside their borders, they still couldn't really fight us without hurting their own people and infrastructure, though it was clear they didn't really care about the people. All the resources they put into protecting their systems, stations, people and equipment was resources not in our system. We wanted to avoid fighting there for all those reasons.

"*Churchill* did their part by delivering you to us," Glenn said.

I looked up. I realized I'd been muttering and blushed.

"Angie, a lot of people go through life wondering if they matter. None of us have that problem. You shouldn't either."

I nodded with damp eyes.

CHAPTER 33

◈

Yet another tramp showed up, towed by another ship. This one was newer, registered out of Caledonia. It scared me how many ships with false histories and registries seemed to be floating about. It was the *Camby*.

"Are the logs correct on this one?" I asked. I didn't want to pimp myself to a perv again.

Juan said, "They are, because several of our residents have been running it the last decade. Those residents retain Caledonian citizenship because they planned to retire to our system. They were made very comfortable in an alternate retirement."

That sounded disturbing.

"What does that mean?"

"It means they were given a lot of money, new ID and a quiet place to live to enjoy that money. What, you think we killed them?" He gave me an odd look.

"I, uh, wasn't sure."

They gave me a Look.

I thought it was a fair question, but obviously I'd made a social error.

I asked, "We're just going to do the same thing as last time?"

He said, "Not quite. We will still engage in clandestine combat as dictated by mission parameters and opportunity. However, we're moving more toward intelligence gathering for others to use."

I hoped that would be a lighter load than we had. A year and a half of this was wearing. Days of boredom and real work done for fake reasons, followed by segs of terror and panic and divs of fear of getting caught, rinse, repeat. We all have our limits and I was near mine.

At least there was room aboard. She wasn't as nice as *Pieper* after upgrade, but she was better than a lot I'd served on. I had my own small bunkroom with a rolling hatch. I could be out in seconds, and private when I needed to. Talk about luxury.

I was stowing my gear when an All Hands klaxon sounded. It was a military klaxon, and I made a note to tell them to change that if this was supposed to be a civilian vessel.

I reported to the C-deck. There were MPs there. Ours.

The warrant leader in charge of the element was talking.

"Captain Gaspardeau, can you fully vet and account for your crew?"

"I can. Angie is an attached asset who's been with us for several months, and is absolutely reliable. The rest are members of my element and we have trained as a unit since before the war, in preparation for it. We had an infiltrator whom we identified, court martialed and executed before we captured *Scrommelfenk*. What specifically are you looking for?"

"We will need to search the ship in a full showdown, sir. I apologize for the necessity."

"Fair enough. But are you able to answer my question?"

"After we search, sir," the warrant said.

One by one, we went to our cubbies and opened every container of everything. Teresa and I went together as chaperon for each other. I opened my roller and my bag, laid out everything down to my toothbrush and epi cream. I put my BodyBuzz on the bunk, then my wigs and dyes.

The female MP asked, "Ma'am, are the cosmetics professional or personal?"

Not "lady" but "ma'am." She didn't know my rank equivalent and was making sure to address me as an officer.

"I use them for both. We frequently change appearances."

"Fair enough. Stow that and show me the bunk, please."

I put everything away and peeled the bedding, the gel mattress, lifted the springs and opened the underbunk storage.

We swapped while they had Teresa toss her stuff. She had no cosmetics to speak of, more clothes, minimal toys.

Cleared, we went back to the C-deck with our belongings stuffed into our luggage, while the MPs plus a ship maintenance crew started there and worked aft. I went to the galley to monitor while they pulled every pack, opened all the heaters and the fridge, everything.

It took all day.

Outside there were sounds of hull techs doing yet more searches.

It didn't stop there. They went over the capital ships the same way. They had two crews on each checking each other. Stem to stern of every craft, then the station.

It turned out that nothing is one hundred percent secure. There were a handful of UN infiltrators who had good cameras and old-fashioned parallax gear to measure and determine the station's location. Then either we would have a phase drive ship, or perhaps just a huge warhead or a bunch of generators to scramble space and destroy any ship trying to precipitate (as I found out the term is) there.

Two of them had been caught talking and swapping data on paper. Very secure, until someone sees it. The other two were found in the sweeps. All four were given quick but fair court martials, then shot at the base of the skull and spaced. The recovered bodies were recycled for minerals and hydrocarbons.

I guess the court martials might have been a bit abbreviated, and the UN complained about that after the war, but they were caught with the gear and enough evidence proved they were plants. And I guess we didn't shove electrodes into them and torture them, so I wasn't very sympathetic.

We put everything back together, and our host pulled us out. This time, phase drive went on for longer. Apparently, that's not related to distance, but is related to some complicated energy expenditure based on the structure of space.

I still have no idea where that station is. I'm not sure anyone does. But I bet it still exists.

CHAPTER 34

⊕

When we precipitated, we were in Mtali, or near it. Far outsystem. We had an extra fuel bunker in cargo, and a feed mechanism to get it into the powerplant.

Juan said, "Now, if we're lucky, Mtali won't ask too many questions about why we've been here a month and not done anything. We have a backup plan of claiming repairs and can limp in if needed."

Mtali runs their own point, though they have a lot of cultural arguments over who does it, so they rotate. It depends on which group you get how well they do. The Sufi and Sunni aren't bad. The Amala and Shia are terrible. The Christian Coalition are in between. The other groups aren't big enough to involve. Yes, they divide by religion, not nation or industry. It's a mess.

That worked for us, though, since it was a different group on departure, and they don't like to talk to each other, so no one questioned when we'd come in or who through. We officially came from in-system, didn't dock, queued up and Jumped.

That put us back in Alsace.

This was a station I wasn't very familiar with. I'd been here twice about five years before. All we did was eat and sleep out, though, and pick up legit cargo.

Then we went across system to where I knew. It was the station on this side of Earth.

We were very clean. We dropped cargo there, picked some up, logged an "irregularity" in Mtali space, then jumped through to Earth.

I realize they were the enemy and our main target, but I hated being in that system, every time.

It was another old station, a long cylinder with hub and crossing center spokes. They're not all the same or evenly spaced. They kept building off the end away from the dock, then built another dock, then added struts for volume.

We docked, and called for estimates on repair for the powerplant feed regulator management.

Glenn asked, "I know you don't work with engines, but any idea who's good here?"

"I've always heard good things about the Rocket Surgeon—Le Chirurgien de Fusée. He's upper end, but not the most, and very professional. He provides detailed reports on his work for log."

"Who's good and cheap?"

"Carrie the Fixer. Avoid the Duct Tape Engineer. He's for people who need to get to a real outfit and don't want to spend money here, but why would you do that? I guess they'd rather get to the Freehold, but it's a long trip with failing equipment."

"Will any of them be able to tell we broke it?"

"I don't know. Possibly. I guess it depends on how well you did."

"We'll risk it."

They got estimates from three shops, and took the Rocket Surgeon on my recommendation. Then Juan asked if they could get a discount by not being in a hurry. Some math suggested waiting three days would save enough to justify waiting, but it meant not earning meantime. Since the money was from our government and we didn't need a haul for income, we waited.

We actually did need regular hauls to offset expenses, but we did have some budget for military ops. The whole thing was largely self-funded, though, and there were no official records. It was brilliant. I wonder who came up with the idea originally. I'd at first figured to take ones or twos through to hide and look for intel, not to crew a ship and blow things up using the profit margin.

In the meantime we did more spying.

We split into singles and pairs, got bunkies and rooms, and split up.

I carried some sort of passive sensor around in a purse. It felt weird. I hadn't carried a purse since tech school when I was ten. I've used a shoulderbag or backpack ever since, but they wanted something smaller for even better concealment.

You can't get into the government sector easily, though I knew these guys could if they had to, but there's a passage of bonger clubs, pizza joints and soup cafes literally one frame away. We rotated through there, carrying our sensors. I had some okay clam chowder and decent garlique baguette, made with Russian wheat. That seemed weird.

I don't know exactly what they were looking for, but I'm guessing phone signals, and possibly any kind of coding or traffic analysis from the control center. Yes, I'd started learning about types of intel. It was hard not to.

We weren't doing any HUMINT, just hanging out, getting known and getting passive SIGINT.

Still, if you hang out, you get HUMINT. We learned who the bouncers and owners were, and we listened to people bitch about their jobs. That can tell you a lot, too. Their own security protocols were slowing people down, pissing them off, and making work harder.

I still didn't think this would win the war, but I was sure it helped. That encouraged me.

I was out in a club, listening to Undertoad, when I got a ping.

I let the message scroll across the hat I was wearing. It had a screen on the brim.

"Emergency. Find us a place."

That wasn't what I wanted to hear.

I checked the time, swallowed my drink, tossed a chit at the bar, and walked out muttering, "Fuck work," in case anyone was listening.

I was sure it was bad. I thought about places I knew here from the one time I'd been here. How old was this place? Right. So they should have engineering crawls on the outer hull, and I did mean "crawls." What was closer? There was a large volume in Frame 60, Radius 40 that was a homeless camp. We'd have to spread out and act the part, but it could work.

I got onto a slideway heading axial north, and moved

across to the express belt. Then I walked back over to the slow belt, because 60 came up faster than I expected.

They'd given me an encryption program for my phone that they said they trusted. I shot an image of the Frame number as I reached it. I went a bit further and got off at 62. It was quiet, which wasn't what I wanted, so I worked back on foot through stores, trying to look like I was browsing when I was trying to relocate.

At 60, I got on a local slideway and went counter. When I reached Radius 40, I sent another image. I went past and backtracked again.

The problem was, there was still a homeless camp, but it was a lot smaller than last time. It had held a couple of hundred. Now it held about thirty in eight boxes and sheets. Ten of us would show. I figured I'd stick two "couples" here, and the rest of us would go somewhere else. But where?

There was a spot at 85/26/1. Outer hull. It wouldn't be pleasant, but we could hide.

I sent the message with first initials only. "J&T, M&M, here." I'm sure Mo had a tarp or something they could sleep under.

As they started arriving, I made distant eye contact. Mo was first. I watched him sweep his vision across the volume, stretch and make an "ok" with his right hand. He'd take it from there.

Roger was next. I turned with a bit of emphasis and started walking. I figured the rest would follow.

I took slow slideways and stepped off early this time. It was an enclosed passage with an actual stop. We were near the industrial section for station maintenance, storage and support.

I faked it with my phone as I got closer, talking into the air with my bud in.

"I understand his schedule, but if he wants this delivered he's got to respond. I'm going to try to get a count now, so they can be on pallet at the site when the crew arrives. We may have to bring some from the other stowage, and if there isn't enough, there's going to be a delay, so we need to start ASAFP."

There was hardly anyone around, and a woman in a coverall talking about a late project was nothing anyone would pay attention to. I walked right past a lone monitor. Lone. This was a decently safe area. Though I figured the team would fix that problem in time.

There wasn't exactly a hatch here. There was an expansion joint with a pressure curtain. The curtain closed with a magnetic airtight seal which had two gaskets that interlocked. It was cheaper and I guess easier than having a separate lock.

Behind that was dead space to the outer hull. It was pressurized, held in place with crushable columns in case of impact, and pretty much empty, because it was black, cold and had nowhere and nothing to use for shelter or concealment once inside. I'd found it when one of the maintenance guys thirty-foured me into going there. It was neat to feel warmth on one side and cold on the other, but it got unsexy as soon as the thrill ended. I didn't know if we could stay long, or if we needed to, but Juan had said, "Now."

I stood with my back to the curtain and waited.

Roger came up and asked, "So what's the problem?"

I understood he was covering and said, "The pallets

were short. Someone miscounted. I've called Mathews and told him to grab a couple of spares from stock, but we may need to pull some from the other project. This has the shorter deadline."

While I talked I indicated, and he eyed the joint. When I finished, he said, "Yeah, we've got until Tuesday, right?"

"Monday."

"Crap. Let me think."

Then he muttered, "I guess if that's all there is, but that's going to be fucking cold."

"He said fast."

Bast arrived then, pulled out some small tools and ran them over the joint, while waving his phone around in between like he was doing some sort of inspection. I hoped he didn't take long. We were cool for now, but eventually someone would start asking what we were doing.

He got the gap open and shimmied through. It was about a meter overlap, and there were cold breezes as he shifted. And I mean cold. Holy hell.

We kept up the chatter as Shannon, Juan and Glenn arrived. Shannon was through and Juan in the joint when that monitor came back.

The first thing he said was, "Someone better have a work order. There's no orgies in the connectors."

I said, "Oh, sorry. We didn't mean any harm."

"Messing with those is considered sabotage. Get your buddy out of there, I'm going to have to arrest you all."

I'd never seen Glenn fight before. Glenn moved so fast I barely caught it, and kneed the guy in the chest so hard I thought his lungs were going to come out. He dropped and curled up and started twitching. He obviously couldn't breathe.

Then he twitched a lot more. Then he stopped.

Glenn had fucking kneed him into a cardiac arrest.

"Get him in there," Glenn said. "We'll find his chip later."

We stuffed a dead, oozing body into the gap, then went through behind him. There weren't any actual smears, but there were wet streaks. Uck.

I got inside and it wasn't quite black. Someone had a light set on a low lumen level so we could move about. I took the ladder down three steps to the outer hull, and had to get into a crawl.

The body was down here with us, stuffed against a support pillar. Someone had cut open his hand and pulled his ID tag, and then ripped open his shoulder for the monitor ID.

It was cold enough that we weren't going to smell that body for a while. I had a thin jacket in my pack, with really good insulating properties, but that meant ten degrees difference, not twenty, and it didn't help my head, hands or feet. I huddled as best I could. I tucked my hands and shoulders up, and let my hair fall over my ears. I exhaled warm air down my collar.

Once everyone was accounted for here and above, Juan got our attention.

"UN intel caught up with us. It seems one of Chesnikov's people informed them on our ship logs. We have a reasonable guess who, because that person was killed in a creative manner. They were given an oxygen mask and then exposed for slow vacuum trauma. So it wasn't Chesnikov, as best we can tell."

Wow. That was worse than being spaced, and probably worse than being zapped.

"However, that let them confirm our presence in Salin. Then they must have checked out all vessels of similar size and class. They've seized *Camby* and you should assume anything aboard is compromised or confiscated. Which is why no one had anything of relevance to intel there, right?"

I thought about that. I had my phone. I had the chips for all my personal files. I didn't think anything aboard had my name on it, other than initials to ID them in transit or laundry. Those were my cover initials, not real.

I shook my head, and no one confessed to anything.

"Good," he continued. "So everyone kill your phones."

I'd already done that as soon as everyone was accounted for.

"It's fucking cold down here, but we need to hold out as long as we can, unless we can find somewhere else. Then we have to see about transport."

Glenn asked, "What type of transport?"

"Anything that lets us continue the war."

He was crazy. At this point, it was likely the next raid would ID us personally. We were going to keep at it until we died.

I realized I had signed up to save myself and others. They'd signed up to save others and themselves. It made a difference.

I really, really needed to talk to someone for emotional support. I knew the best way to survive was to win, but I wanted to fucking run. Fake another ID with their help, and just disappear, and wait for things to die down.

But we couldn't. We had to keep the pressure up, even if we died.

I didn't want to die.

I didn't realize Teresa was near me.

"Scared?"

I wasn't going to even pretend to be brave.

"Yes. Gods, yes."

"It's all we can do, Angie. No matter what, we need a ship."

She was right.

"I'm not sure I can get on that ship," I said. "I know I should. I also know I can hide pretty well here, and get onto something else later. Except I probably can't anymore."

"You said it yourself. If we lose, all that goes away. They'll tag everyone everywhere, and track every movement. Everyone will be a ward of the state, working for it, not themselves. Disposable."

I was starting to wonder if it was so bad. Earth managed with a population of billions. People survived and existed. Was it really that bad? Were we really right?

It didn't matter.

Either I kept going until we won or died, or I gave up and I was likely to die.

I was disposable.

But not everyone had to be.

CHAPTER 35

My choice of the shell had been desperate, after my first choice wasn't available. It was definitely secure, but it was terrible otherwise. It did keep us out of sight, but our only latrine was a bucket someone had grabbed outside, and the overhead was barely enough to allow room to squat. My shipsuit was in the way. It was nasty.

We waited, shivering, through an entire day cycle.

Not just shivering. We sat in a huddle, between the next person's legs and holding them for warmth, and changing every few minutes so the outside people moved inside. We could babble jokes to each other, and not much else.

Mira was ahead of me at one point and said, "We did things like this in Blazer training. I never figured we'd do them for real."

"I guess it came about from somewhere," I said. "Or we're just lucky."

"Some of each."

Every couple of hours we took a break to use the bucket, then we exercised and ate a bit of food. "A bit" is all we had—some energy bars. It was two bites each, but it helped keep us hungry, not ravenous.

When day cycle ended, Mira and Glenn snuck out. I wasn't sure what was going on. I felt pretty damned low, between our situation, my crappy attempt at cover, the cold, short food and the long day.

I mentioned it and Teresa shrugged. "We lost a ship due to planning errors. You found us a slightly-less-than-perfect hiding spot."

I guess.

When Mira and Glenn came back, they had clothes.

"These should fit everyone pretty closely. Get dressed and we'll relocate for the evening. We'll have time to find another spot."

Roger asked, "Where are we going?"

"An astrophysics conference."

That was a new one.

I lay on a frigid, dusty surface and pulled on a skirt suit. I'd never worn one. The shoes were glossy on top, but still shlippers underneath. I could walk. Mira actually put on heels. So did Jack. He had a nice set of boots under a twill kilt.

I was amazed we got out unchallenged, with all the foot traffic and a dead cop underneath us, but Mira went out first, then poked a walking stick through to indicate safe times. I came up third and she handed me a phone, with a map showing.

I glanced at it and started walking.

Along the way, Glenn came up and said, "Oh, hello,

Researcher Kiro. Here is your notepad. It's been updated and the files cleared."

"Thank you," I said. Behind it was an ID badge with a picture that could be me. It said I was from the University of Machlan, Caledonia and a visiting researcher. My other ID said I was from a habitat around Meiji, and originally from New Liverpool, Caledonia. I could fake all that believably.

If they thought I could fake any knowledge of astrophysics, we were all in trouble.

It was clever, though. We were all in suits. We all were supposed to be ranking professionals. We shouldn't get too much attention in public, as long as we stayed in the right crowds.

There was a manual ID check at the conference hall. They glanced at mine and let me in.

Mira and Jack signed us in, and she had a card from somewhere that was apparently legit.

Soon, we were gathered around a table near the rear, and several of them had larger data screens plugged in. I messed with my phone and notepad and tried to look like a professional. That kind of professional.

We even had a catered supper, with soup, fish and rice cakes. I guzzled about three pots of hot green tea with honey, to warm up from the day in a freezer.

I kept my thoughts to myself and ignored the lecture. I didn't have a clue what any of those equations or images meant, but I pretended to whisper and nod to Glenn and Jack from time to time.

Mira actually pinged in and asked a question.

"In your transfer equation you reference an oscillation

ratio. Do you yet know if this is related to the mass or diameter of the particle? If it is, what form does the relationship take?"

"Excellent question!" I heard. "We have found the ratio follows two curves, one for mass and one for diameter, which matches optimal particle size as shown on page four. Interestingly, the ratio does not seem to . . ."

It still meant nothing to me.

"What about you, miss?" he asked, highlighting me. "You've been quiet. Any feedback?"

I slung words. "Right now I'm just taking notes. It seems very well supported, and I'm looking forward to the follow up and any refinements of the numbers."

That was odd. It was almost as if they were testing us.

They might actually be testing us.

We had lunch together and hung in the back, as a small group, chattering about these other people we knew outside the field, and keeping to ourselves.

It worked, though I spent the entire day staring and nodding, and faking making notes. I had not a clue what was said or if it was feasible or complete BS.

Then we went to a floor suite at the Hotel Obernal.

Mo rolled in with an entire dolly of sandwiches, soup, baked chicken and fish for dinner.

Juan briefed while we ate. I understood that most of these briefings were for me, but they did clarify points for the others.

"So, the ship is gone. We're unhurt and unhindered, and they're looking for 'leads,' which suggests they don't have much. It could be they don't want to share what they have in case they give intel to us, but it doesn't seem that

Mil Intel is involved, just BuLaw locally. I'd expect them to try to scare us out or into hiding, and have rewards out, So they don't seem to be sure. It's noteworthy that Angie isn't mentioned, despite being a previous detainee. They may think they killed several of us during a previous attack. There's no mention of the attack on the Salin station. They've kept that out of the news."

That seemed positive, sort of. It wasn't negative. We were hiding for our lives and didn't have a ship, though. That didn't seem to bother them. It was almost, "Yes, I lost a hand, but I have a spare," attitude.

"At this point, we have to escalate to a level I'd preferred to avoid. We'll need to actively hijack a ship."

"We commandeered one before," I said.

"This time we need to keep the ship, and not have it discovered."

"You're going to kill civilians," I said.

"Yes." He nodded firmly. "If I could think of a way around it, I would. The only justification I can offer is that ending the war will mean less collaterals, and that we're doing so to save our own lives."

I didn't know how to respond. We'd been a gray area for so long, since we were non-identified combatants, but there was no way to do what we did while identified.

At least he wasn't claiming it was a good thing. Just necessary.

I stared at the floor.

"Angie," he said. I looked up. "If you can think of any way at all to acquire transport without killing anyone, I'll take it. A ship in repair that's unoccupied, except that we need to put it in service. A crew we can detain, except we can't risk a port inspection that way. We have to do what we're doing, and we can't buy one or I would. But even that would be noticed. If we acquired a ship like the one we commandeered, and could smuggle their crew elsewhere, I would. If we can smuggle a crew onto another ship, I'll take it. I can't find a way to do it."

I shrugged. The responsibility wasn't mine.

Except it was all of ours.

The next morning, I was dressed down. Way down. The clothes I wore were dusty, stale, musty, had been well-sweated into and even had some urine sprinkled. I even wore a well-used briefer underneath, and it felt disgusting and my skin crawled. Mira had dusted my hair with deck sweepings after I worked up a sweat.

I looked like the complete bottom echelon of humanity.

I had a couple of food bars, and the wrappers were mashed and stomped. I had a water bottle with coffee stains on it. I had a shredded backpack with a collection of bits and stuff in it. The only worthwhile thing I carried was my phone.

We all had different covers, but at least Jack and Bast were also made up to look like dregs. We walked on foot, slowly, from near the homeless camp all the way to the docks. It took most of the day.

The dock security wouldn't have let us in, but there was a power conduit. It still amazes me how many of those we used and no one ever caught on. We met up, Jack shagged the lock, we all went down, then we staggered back out a half hour apart. I mean actually staggered.

I didn't know what ship we were taking. I just knew to

be ready to get to it, that I might have to fight my way aboard, and that innocent people were going to die.

I just hung out where Juan had said, and looked helpless. I felt it. I knew sooner or later the cops would round us up.

My phone buzzed and I read it as a scroll on my hat brim.

Move toward SCS Prophet's Glory. SCS was Salin Commercial Ship. That didn't mean it was local, it was using their registry as a convenience. It probably couldn't pass a modern spaceworthiness test, or they didn't want to pay higher fees or reveal personal info.

Did we have a ride? I glanced around slowly, and there it was. What a piece of crap. But if it got us out of here, it was worth it.

I saw Bast lurching toward it, trying to look fat and out of shape. He did okay, but he had a lot of muscle to hide. I gave him three segs and moved generally that way, trying to plan for moving transports.

I did okay, but was next to a marked lane when a jenny hauler went past.

"Outa the way, you burned-out trash whore."

That was nice of him. I guess he'd never actually been a transient, never mind homeless.

But a while later, I was loitering at a strut near *Prophet's Glory's* lock.

I saw the crew muttering. They didn't want anything to do with me, even to get rid of me. They were embarrassed and ashamed that I existed, and they'd have to deal with me.

I didn't get any closer, and they kept watching me

but didn't approach. I mumbled to myself and shook my finger at the strut now and then as if I was schizophrenic.

Their cargo arrived, and we weren't in the way so no one said anything. Actually, I wasn't in the way. Bast was elsewhere entirely. I didn't even know where the rest were. If I got taken, they were clear.

They had two loaders, old Dash 2s. As in, first generation, not even upgraded. Everything about this bucket was worn out. I was surprised it still flew.

Still, the crew were decent at operating them. One took a load, the other came around and reached for another.

The takedown was brilliant. As the loader rotated, Roger appeared, sprung and yanked the operator off. Bast caught him and applied a chokehold, then laid him gently down. Mira swabbed his nose with a sponge and I guessed he'd be out for a while. It was probably Ruff or some similar knockout.

Mo, Teresa and Jack rolled up the ramp using Roger's loader as concealment, and disappeared inside. The command crew hadn't seen anything.

Roger delivered the cargo, rolled back out, and this time, Glenn, Shannon and Juan went inside.

That left me to follow with Mira and Bast. I lost the homeless ghillie, and strode up the ramp in my standard shipsuit.

"There's another one. Hey, chick, who are you?"

Mira was on him with the Ruff and down he went. Roger sprung off his loader and took a second one out. Bast just grabbed one and gripped. That was enough to disable the man before he was drugged, too.

It looked like we controlled the internal bay. I

wondered if anything had been caught on vid, or if anyone on this ship even cared. C-deck should at least have monitors for the bay.

Maybe that's why they'd picked this ship, or maybe it was chance.

The ones they'd disabled were here, and alive for now. That was a mixed thing. I guess they might be allowed to survive, and this was a chance. But if something went bad, someone was going to choke, shoot or space them, while they were helplessly trussed.

"Aw, *shit!*" I heard Glenn swear.

I looked back toward the main passage.

Kids. They had a baby and a boy about ten.

"They weren't on the manifest I saw," Juan said. "We don't have time to divert."

"What do we do?"

That was a good question. Killing adults was one thing, and still bad. Kids, though.

"Truss everyone, we'll sort it out after lift."

The ten-year-old struggled. Bast clobbered him hard enough to stun him, but not enough to kill him. They and the baby went into the passenger stateroom with the others. That made sense. Passenger rooms couldn't reach any control functions.

Roger and Jack were parking the loaders when the next thing happened.

Down at the bottom of the ramp, Bert sat, waiting for permission to board.

On the one hand, I didn't want to ignore him or leave him in Sol system. On the other, I had no idea how long we were going to stay alive.

"This isn't the best ship, Bert," I said.

He wagged his tailed and yipped, because he recognized me.

Godsdammit.

"Welcome aboard, Bert." Maybe we could drop him fast.

He trotted up the ramp and headed for a bunk room.

We sealed up. There was some confusion outside. Someone from another ship was near the ramp looking curious. Bast and Mo at the top shrugged and gave him a thumb's up. He waved and left, looking unsure.

Juan asked, "Do we have to note the Admiral is aboard?"

I said, "Ordinarily, I think so, even in Earth space, but I don't think they know he's here."

"Good. The less interaction the better."

Mira was talking to control with a breathy rasp.

Whoever was in charge of departures said, "Damn, Valerie, if you sound that bad, you should be in your bunk and let Rich handle it."

This crew were on first names with the control office.

Almost nothing had gone right.

"I'll be fine," she said.

"Valerie, just to make me sure you're not under duress, please tell me who you're talking to. My nickname."

She looked up as Mo started frantically pulling up data on personnel, and it wasn't public, so he was digging. She opened the channel and started coughing hard.

After four seconds, Mo had the name, pointed to the screen, and Juan leaned over her.

"Controller Ambril, I must officially ask you to lay off. We need to minimize talking." He cleared his throat slightly, then said, "Maven, Mav, please, we're fine."

"Sorry, Lou. I needed to check. You're cleared for departure. Have some honey tea and get better."

"We will. Thank you."

Pneumatics started shoving us off.

Juan said, "I'm not assuming they're convinced. Ultimately, the live crew might save ours, though I'd rather we all got away than wound up prisoners."

"Where are we bound?" I asked.

"We're going from here to Alsace and Chersonessus to continue bonafides, then resume combat if we can. If not, the backup is to cause minor mayhem wherever possible, disrupting operations, until caught, and beg for status."

I was trusting them to make that unnecessary, because I couldn't think of a way that didn't result in our deaths. Then I realized I was completely over the fear. Either we died or we didn't. It was just the nature of things. Then I was scared that I wasn't scared.

I remembered when I was young and tried to have the longest orgasm I could. After a couple of segs, I could still feel vibrations and neural response, but there was no more cortisol in my system. It was just an irritating buzz. This was like that.

There was another brief run-in connecting the train. It was automated, but Roger had to be out to sign off. The station crew didn't recognize him. He pleaded being a sub on contract. They seemed to accept it.

We got under way, with a bunch of Mo's hand-built

sensors giving us every spectrum possible. If someone came at us, we wanted to know.

With all the post-launch taken care of, we had to try to create good relations with our captives, and find a spot for Bert.

I found a chunk of foam and a box I could insert it in for Bert to dump in, and he was quite happy at the foot of my bunk. The little snit was getting a touch of gray at his muzzle and eartips. I wondered how old he was and how long he had left, assuming we didn't blow up together.

That really didn't take long, and I wandered aft. Shannon and Mira had C-deck, Bast and Mo had stern, the rest of us were freeish and went to check on Juan's discussions with the former crew.

He unlashed them and had them sit on the bunk and the deck.

"First, let me assure you of your safety at present. We have tried very hard to avoid collateral casualties, and would prefer to avoid them now. You will be fed and kept safe for as long as our resources permit, and transferred offboard as soon as is feasible. I apologize for any roughness in our transition, and our medic will be happy to treat any injuries or discomfort you have."

The guy I figure was captain-owner said, "This is still piracy, sir."

"The last time it was only commandeerment. This time it most . . . likely is piracy. I will make no apologies. You can assume our origin and purpose. We hope and intend to all come through this alive, with the ship intact. We do not require your cooperation to achieve that, but we recommend not trying to hinder us. You are not combatants. We are. If you act as partisans, then you can be treated as hostiles. Your position is not great."

The captain asked, "And what is your ultimate goal? Be specific, sir."

I liked him. He might be our prisoner, but he was still captain of his ship. Good man.

"To continue our operations. Had we been able to just take your ship without you, we would have. It would have been simplest to space you all on departure, but I would prefer not to kill civilians. Please accept that and act with grace."

The woman cuddling the two-year-old and ten-year-old looked like they were all cried out.

She said, "I want my children to live. Whatever you need . . ."

He said, "I want them to live, too, Ms. Keral. It wasn't our intention to take children. The manifest we had didn't show them."

She and the captain exchanged looks. They were still scared, but it was true—if we needed them dead, we would have done it already.

Juan said, "I will place a vac gap a frame forward of here. Please don't attempt to cross it. Food will be brought to you. Engineer, vac gap a frame forward."

Bast replied over intercom. "Yes, sir."

Flight through to Alsace was unhindered, but the ship was a relic. I almost thought they'd be better off if we put them off and scuttled it. Half the kitchen elements had taped repairs. I felt engine rumbles now and then. Mira cursed something in another language. There were deep scratches near my bunk where years of stuff being moved about had worn away at the bulkhead. One of the locks had a non-standard replacement switch. It worked, but it wasn't able to be secured. But that's why I carried a lock pin. Although I'd rarely used it for its intended purpose.

I took food through to them personally for breakfast and dinner, and made sure they had cold goods for lunch and late night. I rationed out sweets for the two children.

My first trip, dinner, they thanked me but ignored me otherwise. At breakfast I asked what they wanted for dinner, and they settled on beef stew. I asked about breakfast when I took that.

They liked the stew. "That was good," the captain said at breakfast. "Thank you."

"You're welcome. I'm sorry you're stuck where you are."

The boy asked, "When are you leaving our ship?"

That was a tough one, and I really didn't want to disappoint him.

"I don't know. I'm only crew, not in charge. I was with another ship before this."

"Are you a prisoner too?"

"No, but I'm noncombatant. It's complicated."

I left, because I didn't want to let anything slip.

CHAPTER 36

◎

By the time we reached Alsace JP1, Les Atterissages, they were in decent spirits and seemed to accept that we weren't a threat to them.

But I remembered the plan had been to kill them as needed.

When we arrived, we had contracted cargo and loaded it. Juan made specific inquiries with the real crew.

"Is there anyone we're supposed to know, or names we're supposed to use? Your safety depends on this as much as ours."

Captain Lou said, "There's a list of ships who know us. You'll need to avoid them. I don't think anyone at control knows us personally."

"Can you tell me which ships?"

"You tell me, I'll check them off."

I really hoped they weren't going to try to be heroic. I wanted them to live.

We pulled out with no trouble, but we were a bit low

on load. The contracted stuff was aboard. We hadn't stuck around to try to fill capacity. We did the usual news/data transfer as we jumped through.

Two Jumps with no action did reduce my stress level. Just because I'd accepted impending death didn't mean I liked it. I felt much better after those Jumps.

Then we docked at Pyli—Gateway, in Chersonnesus, brand new on their only Jump Point, though a direct one to Earth was due to open in a few months.

There were cops and inspectors waiting as we locked.

In what seemed like ten seconds, Teresa and Jack handed us pistols and ammo. He also handed me a scarf.

"If it's legit, we'll take those back at once," she said.

I wrapped the scarf over my head and loaded the pistol.

Juan asked, "Do you know a safe hole outside entry control?"

"I think so." Again, I'd been here rarely.

"I hope so."

He went to the lock personally, and I heard the ranking woman present him with a warrant to inspect, for both contraband and standard safety requirements. That seemed like something we could argue our way out of, if we didn't have a kidnapped crew aboard.

He stepped back and ushered them in, turned, took a pistol that Teresa held ready, turned back and started shooting.

It was so eerily like the previous fight, only out of the dock, not in.

By the time I reached the lock, all six were dead and I think it was Juan who got them all—headshots.

I ran to keep up with the team, and I've never seen anyone move so fast. The techs and I brought up the rear. We bounded down the ramp at .7G, went past another lock, and someone rolled a smoke grenade into it. We kept going, and it turned into a huge, confusing mess for everyone else.

I'm sure some of those grenades killed bystanders. It was a panic evacuation and they were using it to create more mayhem.

I wondered later if that was the primary intent at that point. We probably could have made it off the dock before anyone really noticed. The shots weren't that loud with the loads we had, and industrial noise is common in docks.

Twenty seconds in, though, there were several explosions, three ships with smoke and a couple of other things smoking. Then I saw a fire flare up on a tug, from an incendiary.

They were just unloading ordnance as fast as they could.

I have no idea how they ran that fast. I was last and gasping as we reached entry control, and the monitors there were dead. At least one had a broken neck and the rest had been shot.

"This way," Jack said, and pointed.

They had scattered into a crowd that didn't yet know what was happening. The alarms finally started going off just then.

They were still wearing hats and scarves.

As we rounded a corner, Roger, next to me, peeled his jacket, wadded it and stuffed it into a trash can. I was only wearing a shipsuit, no jacket.

Then Teresa pulled my scarf off and handed me a poncho. I shimmied into it. It was a brown that went well enough with the coverall, and made it less obvious it was a coverall.

There was a maintenance room here, or should be. I didn't have a code for it, but I figured Jack did.

There was. I turned to it and barely pointed. Jack came up and went to it, and had it open in moments. It wasn't majorly locked.

I went in first and almost ran into a pair of maintenance guys. I stopped and stared, they stopped and were about to say something, when Roger and Glenn came past me and put them on the ground, unconscious but probably still alive. Probably.

Shannon asked, "Does this go anywhere?"

"Into maintenance space."

"Not ideal, but lead us out to main passages."

Everyone was changing. Mira yanked off my poncho and handed me a stylish turban. She then started spraying a dye that turned my coverall a dull purple. That was one of the service colors.

I turned, she finished spraying. Teresa slapped patches on the two unconscious workers to keep them out. The guys were mostly changed into casual business wear. I hadn't seen a bag.

I led the way, they all had viewplates out. I made up some dialog as I went.

"The conduits are one of the items on your list. I'd like your opinion on them, so please note them for followup. The locks and latches are functional, but an upgrade wouldn't be a bad idea . . ."

I took a cross passage, then turned north along the axis and found a door to main passage.

Shannon had a sterile phone out—either we had a crate of them, or acquired lots as we went—and said, "There's a Shelton sotel not far from here." He increased his pace and pulled ahead.

By the time the rest of us reached it, he'd logged into a room. He left some kind of sign and Roger took me to the room. The others arrived a few minutes apart.

It was a king suite with a second parlor, big enough to hide us for a bit.

Food arrived by delivery. There was stir fry, sausages, burgers and crab cakes. I started munching because I suddenly realized I was hungry. The guys and Mira were voracious. Those insane sprints had taken a lot of energy, I figured.

The news mentioned us, but the images they had were terrible quality, and didn't really show us. They had some older pictures of us, but a bit of hair and makeup work would fix that. They admitted to having no clear DNA signatures. Their descriptions came down to us looking like average people. They called us, "Notorious terrorists with professional training from the Grainne rebel paramilitary."

They claimed twelve of us.

Juan clicked on a noise generator/damper field of some kind and started briefing us.

"This is as far as we go with ships. They've cracked down to where we can't effectively do anything. From here on, we will travel independently as crew and passengers. We have less than a month to reach several locations. Angie, I'm including you in this because you'll be acting as courier. Also, as commander, I want to officially thank you for your support and assistance. I would estimate you personally made us at least fifty percent more effective, and we learned a lot from you in the process. You were absolutely critical to the missions."

"Thank you . . . sir."

"So," he said, "we have orders for a pending major offensive. We've got a short time to reach three of Earth's jump stations if we can, and we're going to dispatch personnel to each."

"Alright. And no ship?"

"No, it's no longer safe. We'll either fly contract or pay funds out of pocket using emergency IDs."

"So what are we inserting for?"

"You're not. We are. You will courier information home. Our orders are to disable the stations to hinder logistical lines."

I chuckled. "I can't wait to hear how two or three of you are going to disable a station."

No one laughed back. Juan just stared at me, while the others looked around at each other.

I realized I'd make a really bad joke at a bad time. How were two or three people going to disable a station? They were going to render it uninhabitable . . . while aboard.

"Goddess, you're not serious."

"You've seen images from back home," he said. "You know some of what ships we've lost. There isn't much left. Either we stop their infrastructure now, or we go under."

"So you're going to . . ."

"Render their infrastructure unable to transfer materiel, or to process Jumps."

I didn't know how they'd do that, but I knew what the result would be.

"Gods dammit, you're all going to die!" I shouted at him.

"We know," he said. "I am so sorry we find ourselves here."

"I'm coming along," I said. I was terrified of dying, but more afraid of leaving them. They were my people, the only people I'd had in a decade.

He said, "Your offer is appreciated, but I need you elsewhere. You will help maintain crew manifest and manual operations. You will deliver our post action reviews."

I was relieved he said that, but wanted to argue, but didn't really, and felt sick and cowardly for being relieved, and angry that I wasn't included, and angry with myself for being all whiny when they were the ones on a suicide mission.

Teresa handed me a flask. It had some strong liquor in it, and I took a gulp and choked.

Juan said, "I think our odds are good for the mission, and for the war concluding. We actually have acceptable odds of surviving. We're not just blowing the stations up."

He was trying to reassure me. To take down command and control with all its redundancy, emergency power and O2, and hinder the docks, meant bombs and structural damage with air leaks. If they actually took a station down . . . I'd seen what happened when a habitat tried to evacuate. If the Jump Point was down they were going to swim around, because not all those ships are in-system capable. Even if they were, those are long trips. That's assuming they were able to undock, or had enough time to board evacuees. They probably had to just slam locks and blow out before they got caught in the failure.

There are no small disasters in space.

Then, every UN troop and monitor would be looking for them, hard. I figured they'd snag anyone the slightest bit questionable. Even if they didn't space them all immediately.

I nodded, though, lying that I believed his lie, so he could lie to himself that he'd reassured me.

His plan called for two each of the main six to deploy to each station. Mo and Jack would set up on the NovRos side of that point. Teresa was going to Caledonia, and would go somewhere then. At that point, I was released from obligation and could report back if we won or go obscure with a sanitized ID if we didn't.

He was completely calm. They were going to blow up chunks of three stations, damage two others, kill hundreds of enemy personnel, a lot of them noncombatants, and probably collateral some civilians. Even if they didn't die, if they got caught, they weren't going to get a trial. They'd be "lost during the attacks they caused" or something.

But he sounded like he was discussing dinner plans.

The evening was spent drinking strong liquor. No one got drunk, but they did drink enough to act as a tranq. There was Sparkle in use, too. I took a dusting, because I knew more would be bad.

Honestly, I was surprised we'd lived as long as we had.

We . . . they, had really torn up some infrastructure for the size of the group, and for very little money, since we'd done it around shipping contracts that offset some of the cost and neutralized all the transport expenses.

I went into the back parlor to collect my thoughts. I'm not religious, but I needed to center, ground and meditate.

I was on the couch. A bit later, Mira came in, quietly, gave me a questioning look, nodded and folded out the bed. She took one side and lay down.

I heard her sobbing. I wasn't going to say anything, if she didn't ask. She didn't.

I lay back on the couch and dropped a Nitey Nite. I wasn't going to sleep without one.

"Lights ten," I said.

I slept badly. They weren't nightmares, but they were weird, ugly, shapeless dreams, and I couldn't wake up.

When I finally did jolt awake, I looked around in ten-percent light and Mira was already gone. Teresa was in the bed, sleeping and twitching and muttering. Poor woman.

There was a note on my pillow, handwritten on a piece of food box.

Thanks, Angie. You were professional and courageous beyond your calling, and a fine shipmate and friend. Make sure you destroy this. Mira.

We'd never interacted much off duty. I really wanted to keep the note as a souvenir, but it would be a bad idea. She was right.

I tore it into tiny shreds and pocketed them in three napkins to drop into trash later. Then I thought about it and chewed and swallowed them in a handful of water.

Teresa woke up with a stiffening twitch.

"Morning," I said, to reassure her where she was.

"Hi," she replied, and rolled out. She went into the bathroom. I needed to go but I could wait a bit, and we'd always been good about not hogging time.

I opened the door to the main parlor to check on the guys, and saw they were pretty much ready. I realized that everything had been left on the previous ship. The only gear we had was those things we'd picked up or acquired on this leg. Packing was depressingly easy.

They looked up, I nodded and closed the door to leave them to it.

"I'm out next," Teresa said.

"Good luck. Really, really good luck."

"Thank you," she said very seriously. "I want to ask something before I leave."

"Go ahead."

She blushed and shifted.

"It's not appropriate. Never mind."

"How long have we been around, Teresa? I've done your makeup and dress. You patched me up after I was beaten and naked. Hell, I've kissed you."

"Yeah. That was good, actually. I . . . one for the road?" She blushed even more.

Oh.

I asked, "What, kiss? Or bed wrestle?"

Her eyes flared and she heaved her chest. She really was interested in me. I was flattered, and if she wanted to, sure, I would enjoy it well enough and she deserved it.

"I better stop with the kiss," she said. Then she stood there, hesitating.

I pulled her shoulder, and she clung to me while locking mouths. She really did want more. But we didn't have time and she had her reasons.

I think it was the closest embrace I've ever had. I could feel her pressed against me from knees to head. She felt tiny like this. And warm. Her hands gripped my shoulders, then ran down my back and over my ass. She settled them on my hips.

The kiss was warm, wet and very deep. Though I would have enjoyed finding out what else she could do with that tongue. It moved like an electric eel on stim.

We broke for breath, she pulled back, looked at me, looked away, and said, "Thank you."

"Good luck and safe flight," I said. "You should look me up afterward."

"I'll try," she said. "But that's a long way off."

She grabbed her bag, clutched my arm and said, "Thanks for everything, Angie. It was good to have you as a friend."

I saw her out into the main room, and I was sure I was blushing, too. She shook hands and hugged shoulders as she passed through. No one said anything. Then she was out the door, carrying a backpack and a rolly.

Mo was also gone. There were fewer of them all the time.

I hoped nothing happened before we all split. Jack was the only one left to handle all the improv.

Two hours later, Roger, Bast and Jack were also disappeared. I hadn't seen them go.

Then Glenn left.

Juan handed me a small insert for my luggage.

"Cash, a credit line, two IDs if you need them. They're real, our people maintain them. If you want to get cleaned up, I have all our files for you to courier for us. They'll be sub-Q implanted."

Yeah, I needed a shower. I was drenched with sweat, most of it mine.

When I came out, Shannon was gone.

Juan said, "The shielded shirt is your size. Teresa recommended under your right breast for the chip. It should be hard to find there, and out of your way."

"Okay." I peeled my shirt up, feeling a bit shy, which was ridiculous. He'd seen me every way possible already. I think it was the fact this was intel.

He placed a small tube half under my nipple and clicked it.

"Ow!"

Damn, that hurt. But I could tell it was well under and not likely to be found unless someone was getting very friendly, and even then, lots of women have medical implants.

I pulled the shirt down and finished dressing.

The rest were gone; it was him and me.

"Wait at least ten minutes before you leave," he said. "The suite is paid out through tomorrow. We've coded for privacy."

"Got it."

"You have enough cash for a month's lodging, food and local travel. You have credit for two Jumps. I figure you should do fine getting where you're going."

The ID had overlapping quals with my real ones.

"I can make it work."

He was so calm, but I was sure he wasn't tranked. He was just that focused.

He said, "Don't go back insystem until the war ends."

"When is that going to be? A year?"

He twisted his mouth. "You'll know when you see it. It shouldn't be long."

"It's not looking good back home."

"It's not. Do you trust me?"

Of course I did.

"Without reservation," I said.

"Head that way in a week. Hang out in Caledonia until it's done."

"I understand."

"I have to go. Good luck, and thanks. It was a privilege to have you with the team."

He shook my hands and bumped shoulders.

He turned and walked out.

There was nothing for me to do but putter around and then follow after fifteen minutes.

I was still worried about DNA or face recognition, but those scarves and hats had worked amazingly well, and whatever they'd done with the pheromones was secure. No one questioned me. I walked through passages, free of any kind of interference, not carrying obvious contraband, and with no ill intent. My war was over.

A war isn't over when it's over.

CHAPTER 37

✛

I made a recon survey of the dock before I went back. First I identified as many conduits and accesses as I could. Then I found three that might be passable with a lock pin and a butter knife. Then I walked past entry control several times, making sure they could see more of my face each time. No alarms. That took an entire day cycle.

I walked through the crew lounge and nodded to a couple of people at random. That afternoon I went back and had a soda and a sandwich.

The next morning I showed up and looked for transit across-system. I was way behind enemy territory, and I expected something to explode in vapor before this was all over. I'd been given a mission, and it meant getting out of here.

No one was hiring across system. That required special clearance, and they weren't allowing transients, only existing in-system craft. They all had local crews.

I shopped around until I found a good rate for passenger space.

Then I had a travel interview.

"Marie Shinabe," the interviewer said.

"Yes, sir."

"From New Skye."

"Well, I live in New Skye, officially."

"Yes, I notice you have family in Meiji and in New Liverpool."

"I got sick of space and wanted land, but then I keep getting called away."

"This says you're a chef."

"Not officially. But I have a fan following. For some reason, rich people like having a private cook."

"Do you have a channel or load?" he asked.

"'Private,'" I said. "Word of mouth."

"For . . . cooking."

"I really do cook," I said. "Presentation matters, but I do an amazing crab bisque with a toast point island and roe clumps."

This ID allegedly had a background that said that.

"What about your veal carbonara?" he asked.

"I'll tell you it's amazing, but I don't eat it myself. Religious reasons."

He nodded. He suspected I was half escort, half cook, and he wasn't terribly far off. He just thought I was in a much higher echelon.

"Good luck getting home," he said, as he cleared me on screen.

"Thank you," I said, gratefully. I pointed at the fridge behind his desk. "By the way, if that tomato cheddar soup is for lunch, add a sprinkle each of smoke, pepper, cayenne and cream. You'll like it."

"I'll give that a try. Thanks."

He seemed to believe me, and glad of the food hint.

Cleared for boarding, I fumbled through the gate like I hadn't done it a thousand times, then walked slowly to my ship, reading berth numbers as I went. I made a point to take my time. If they caught me now, there was nothing I could do, and I'd be in their system for another three weeks in flight, so there was no reason to rush.

I'd gotten pretty good at reading threats and slinging bull to cover my ass.

Araminta was a middling old carrier. She was blocky and functional. I found my way to the hatch and buzzed for the purser.

"Ms. Shinabe?" he asked.

"Yes."

"Welcome aboard. Your berth is on the far side of the center passage, third back."

"Thanks very much." They had four cabins free. I had no idea who was in the others, if anyone.

I had only one bag, almost no possessions. Most of what I had here, Teresa had bought for me to make me look like I was a traveler, not the refugee spy I really was. I stowed the bag, plugged my phone in so they could see I was aboard and ready. It was amusing having instructions on how to dock my phone to their net. I'd done that almost as many ways as I've had sex. When I got aboard a ship, I docked my phone. I never thought about how.

I waited in my cabin, watching a classic vid—Kylo versus Kirk. It was okay. I guess I was too concerned with waiting to leave.

They cut in with a standard safety briefing for passengers. Egress instructions, emergency sounds, lock and head discipline. I paid attention to their egress, ignored the rest because I knew it.

Then we shoved off.

I felt safer aboard ship because I always do. I was still as far behind lines as it was possible to be. If they IDed me at any point, I'd be picked up as I debarked.

I started wondering if I should have a final option plan to kill as many as I could before they took me down. I had my lock pin and all the training they'd given me. I figured I could take at least one with me, maybe two or three. If I could get to underdeck, I might manage a couple more.

I was still thinking about that as I heard the chime for chow and walked forward to the galley.

I entered the galley and froze completely.

Bast and Roger were aboard.

They looked at me and nodded as if they had no idea who I was. I shrugged and nodded back and checked the food line to see if they had anything I could eat. They had shrimp salad. I loaded up a bowl and pretended to watch vid while I ate. It was a *Spacewrecks* episode, showing a ship in far worse need of overhaul than *Prophet's Glory* was.

"God . . ." I'd almost said "gods." "How do they fly in that thing?"

"It looks pretty bad," I heard Bast say. "Hey, spacer, what's that about the engines?"

He was pretending to not know anything. That amused me. I didn't understand even a layman's explanation of how a string drive works, other than it apparently could be very inefficient and overheat the stinger.

I knew I was supposed to interact casually. Either too much familiarity or too much distance would be suspicious.

I said, "I guess I've made tens of trips and never thought about the engines. I know they're important, but that's all I know. What happens if they fail?"

I nodded through a summary of reactor, transfer and drive, which I did know as far as summary went. Then as Bast and Roger asked more questions that were very layman, I excused myself and went back to my stateroom.

I wondered if they'd already set some sort of device in action and were en route to another. Or perhaps they were going to live. I really needed to know, and I couldn't. So I mostly kept to myself and made sure I had vid streaming in the stateroom to prove I was "busy." I exercised enough to avoid getting twitchy, and tried to keep my brain numb. I used a bit too much Sparkle and a couple of Violet Zaps. I had some coconut and pineapple rum punch. I couldn't focus on anything, and fifteen days felt like months. I wanted off.

I'd already made my goodbyes with them, and here they were. It was painful, and probably more so for them.

When we arrived in Alsace, I debarked and thought about working a route, but I'd established this ID and was leaving the system. I coughed up funds on my account and took another leg over to Caledonia.

I didn't see the guys on this leg. I never saw them again.

I had funds for lodging and was in no hurry to cross

the system. I was waiting for news of . . . something. I rented a bunkie and stocked some food.

The further away I got, the safer I felt. I realized now how absolutely on edge I'd been, and with no chaplain or emotional health branch. We'd been in combat, or movement to combat, nonstop for almost two years.

I kept an eye out for potential transport. I found schedules for the expected ships. Tramps could show up at any time, but they had to work around the bulk carriers and military ships. There were less of those though. The UN was consolidating all its stations in every system. They were going to choke down all of humanity the same way they did Earth system. No one was going to be allowed to move freely.

If they won, I was going to be stuck on a scheduled run between systems, and they'd all look the same. There'd be no point in bothering.

I ate well enough, and it was easy to cook for just me. I kept to myself. I wanted to club, but I needed to not.

CHAPTER 38

Then I woke up one morning and the war had gone bugfuck.

Earth was in flames, literally.

I saw the news loads and felt weird. I had a very small part in setting this up, and it had been tough and necessary. So I felt good we'd struck back. But the damage was gut-churning.

Entire cities *glowed* from energy release. Or what had been cities and were now craters. Huge chunks of their space assets were disabled. They had the one functional Jump Point. Several production facilities around their gas giants were shrapnel and rubble. So much infrastructure was down there were billions of people killing each other for food, even in ration lines.

I don't know how many troops we used, but it seemed like it was an entire legion of people like my crew, and several starships. You hear the phrase, "Bombed back to the iron age," but this almost actually was.

There were guesses all over the place, but the opening suggestions were five hundred *million* dead. That raised to a billion.

We know now that after what they call "second- and third-order effects," which I guess I understood but I'd never heard the terms, they'd lost six billion people, twenty percent of their population.

They were dying for weeks after the surrender, because you just can't move that much food onto a planet, even if the food existed in space. It has to come from other planets, come out of the gravity well, get sorted and processed. The only people who could do that might be the Prescots, but it would have taken weeks to convert from ore to food, and Earth needed food in hours.

What got sent was experts, in cybernetics, medicine, biosphere engineering, and whatever could be thrown. The entire grid converted to moving stuff in toward Earth, not fighting anything.

Earth surrendered. They had no choice, they were terrified, and they wanted it to stop.

Then they wanted us dead, but no one else was going to say a word against us.

I thought about destroying all my Freehold ID. First out of safety. How well could I fake a Caledonian Looper accent to avoid angry mobs? But I was also horrified.

Then I saw images of Jefferson on Grainne, with the UN facility and its dead zone, and the buildings that were obviously abandoned because no business had happened in months. We had craters, too, and there were lots of reports of bioweapons and other nastiness loose down below.

Then I just hated everybody.

I crawled into the bunkie, and alternated booze, Violet Zaps, sleeping through vid and music, and getting out just enough to shower off the sweat. I was there for a week. I thought about a whole bottle of Sparkle, a roll of Zaps and a bottle of vodka and checking out.

But I remembered I still had a mission.

It wasn't until then that anyone knew what had happened to the stations. The only word was explosions, loss of containment, astrogation webs down, Jump Points working on a timed emergency schedule set up after a Space Guard vessel popped through to NovRos—their only functioning connection. All they could say was that Lucashab was on emergency lockdown with many casualties.

I knew what had happened. My six closest friends, yes, even Glenn, had gone in with violent intent and succeeded.

I wondered how many of our specialists it had taken to do that? I figured less than a battalion. It turned out it had taken less than two hundred and fifty. To destroy a civilization.

I did have to report in, and it was suddenly safe to travel to the Freehold. Completely unrestricted, with the understanding that we were doing background checks now.

I needed to find transport, and I didn't have enough for paid fare.

Luckily, a lot of ships were moving back in. We needed supplies, and had open routes.

It took another two weeks, but I found one heading in

with gas for Ceileidh. The leak had been fixed, structure was under repair, and they were reoccupying in sections as pressure and atmosphere plants came back up.

They weren't paying much, but that wasn't a problem. It was going to be a problem if it continued after I went back to work.

There was one bright spot. As I reached the ramp, there was another crewman waiting to board.

"You know who that is, don't you?" I asked as I strode up the ramp.

The purser said, "We've never met, but I know who he is. Welcome aboard, Bert!"

The little fellow yipped and trotted up the ramp, rubbing his head against my legs.

"I'll take care of him," I said.

"Understood." He turned front and shouted, "Admiral aboard!"

I had no idea how the hell he'd gotten here.

Logged in and stowed, I helped secure the cargo, and it felt good to do my job again, without some government stooge billing me for it. That would have killed industry long term, too. Eventually, the UN would have had an entire administration doing all the cargo transfers.

Which had been part of their point. Complete control of the human race.

I was pissed again, because we shouldn't have had to fight over that, and hurt so many in the process of stopping them from hurting us.

I took out my aggression silently, in a V-suit I'd paid too much for, while taking a tug back to connect the cylinder train.

A week later we were warping into Ceileidh. It was about fifteen-percent functional, up from zero. They figured another year to get to fifty percent, and three to fix structural damage and get the rest up.

I grabbed my bag, shook hands with the crew, took my pay draft and headed for the military detachment.

But first, I actually did wait in line, where the UN had demanded I wait, for our people to scan me through. I had my legit Caledonian ID, and my expired resident ID.

It took ten segs of discussion, but they let me through, and I found the military office. It had at least three rings of sentries.

I approached the first, pulled out the ID I had, and said, "Angie Kaneshiro. Contracted intelligence asset to a Blazer element. I need to report in on our missions."

"Stand by, please, lady."

It took another ten segs to get admitted. They searched my bag, and secured it in a bomb-proof locker.

I was escorted to the Intel office, with one alongside and one behind, weapon drawn. I didn't blame them.

Yet another reception desk, but it was labeled "INTEL," and I approached.

"Good morning, Senior. I need to report in from my operations."

"ID, please."

I passed it over.

"Ms. Kaneshiro?"

"Yes."

"This is not where you report. You should be reporting to Troop Operations."

"I was assigned to intel."

"We show you on the *Churchill* for a while. After that the records are `. . .` incomplete. You need to be debriefed."

That could be a problem.

I reported to Troop Operations, who took my ID and told me to, "Wait there."

I waited for a div and more. At least the seat was comfortable.

There were a handful of others, some of them talking to each other. I got snatches of conversation.

". . . so there I was, in UN space, hoping they didn't ID me. I have no idea how they never found me. I missed the entire fucking war."

"Yeah, Caledonia granted me asylum, but wouldn't let me leave the surface."

"I actually made it to the embassy, but then the embassy just assigned me security duties. That's all I've done."

I didn't belong here. These were displaced troops trying to get home. I was . . .

I wasn't a combatant, really, but I'd actually managed to engage. But I was displaced, too.

The waiting room cleared. More of them left than arrived, being logged in and accounted for.

I wondered what they had on me, when my name was called.

"Kaneshiro!"

"Here, Warrant," I said, to be polite. He was fit, shaven bald, looked bored and irritated, and waved me back. His office was private, but just big enough for two

chairs and a desk. The walls were bare. I gathered he
hadn't been here long.

He showed me his ID, Warrant Leader Gestang, and
pointed to a lengthy advisory that glowed on his desk. He
read it aloud.

I understood I was identifying myself as a Freehold
Troop. I understood there were no implied promises until
identification and investigation. I understood that all my
statements would be taken under advisement and crosschecked. If I had any information on others, I should
furnish that for cross-check.

"Where are you coming from?" he asked.

"I was all over, but just arrived from Caledonia."

"Can you summarize your circumstances?"

I gave the base date. "I'm a veteran. I volunteered and
took passage on the *Churchill*, came in-system during the
battle, which I understood was with two UN craft. I was
billeted as medic primary, services secondary and tertiary.
Then I transferred to Intel and was assigned to support a
Blazer detachment as a consulting contractor. I have
access to files to furnish to Intel."

"I'll forward that."

"I'm afraid I can't, Warrant. It's restricted NTK."

His expression was condescending. He thought I was
some sort of faker looking for headlines.

"Then let's stick to what you can document. How long
were you aboard *Churchill*?"

"Twelve days."

"That's it?"

"I told you, I transferred to Intel when she ported in-
system."

"Ported where?"

"Some rock they wouldn't ID for us."

"You realize *Churchill* was destroyed in-system?"

"I heard."

"So we have very few records. That's inconvenient for us."

He thought it was convenient for me.

"I am who I say I am. You can check my vitals. I have no reason to lie."

"I'll assign you a billet. Stay there, and don't go looking to sign up with Intel."

Actually, that's exactly what I should do, but I wasn't sure what kind of reception they'd give me.

It was a basic billet, roomier than a ship billet or a bunkie, smaller than a hotel room. My bag was waiting for me.

The grub was okay. It was spicy enough, they had chicken and rice and some fruit. I tried watching vid and couldn't. I wanted to dance and that was out. I just listened to Martinus and other techmento bands and zoned out.

I spent a lot of the next day sitting in the same office. There were another few displacees.

I heard one say, "So I didn't officially fight, but I did manage to sabotage a crapton of navigation gear, before I got fired. It was the fourth ship that got me."

I was glad others had managed. If he was telling the truth. It felt like he was, and I silently wished him luck.

Gestang called me back in.

He introduced Special Agent Morgan, who showed his ID.

"Please elaborate on your intel activities."

"I was aboard *Churchill*, went stationside at whatever secret rock we docked at, spoke to an Intel agent about my civilian experience. I knew, still know, where a lot of cubbies, back passages, access ways and flops are. They assigned me to a team of what I think were Blazers, with a ship acquired from Alsace, the *Henri Pieper*. I am certain we smuggled, but not entirely sure what. We sabotaged several ships, information systems, docking equipment. We had one mole. We captured the *Scrommelfenk*, took it with us, and did a refit in Govannon. We took out the station at Salin, which sacrificed the ship. After that we masqueraded as contractors for a while, then we acquired the *Camby*. Last month they all debarked, and I know they were all involved in that mass attack." My voice cracked and I teared up.

"I have the PAR, but I was told to deliver it under specific circumstances. I was listed in a document named 'Angeleyes,' based on my name."

The two of them looked back and forth.

Gestang asked, "You don't have any reference to an Agent Angeleyes?"

Morgan said, "I do not."

"I was transferred off the *Jack Churchill*."

"We show you AWOL. You were upgraded to presumed desertion."

I had a lump in my throat and couldn't swallow. This was very, very bad.

"Sir, I left the ship, logged in with Intel. They transferred my possessions after me. The agent I spoke to marked a file as 'Angeleyes'. She said it would be kept compartmented for my safety. And the mission."

"Do you remember this agent's name?"

"I . . ." I didn't. It had been more than one of our years, almost two Earth years, and I'd been . . . everywhere. "Jeanette, was her first name. I remember that."

"Garfield?"

"Maybe," I said. That might have been. I wasn't sure.

"Or Garweil?"

"That's it! Yes, Garweil. Blond with gray. Slim build. About thirty-five. Her voice was low and clear."

"Unfortunately, she was killed in an attack on the station."

"I am sorry to hear that," I said. Shit, I was fucked. "Did her records . . . ?"

"If they did they were on an encrypt wipe. Any files not tagged for transfer are gone."

"There was a lot of money, I—"

"Money is not your problem, Specialist. Disciplinary action is." He was suddenly very unfriendly.

"I was going to say the money is of less concern than reporting in and getting you the intel I brought."

"I can take whatever information you have," he said.

I didn't trust him, at all.

"Sir, I need an acknowledgment, a signed paper receipt, and neutral territory for this. Or at least a citizen's office."

He shook his head. "If the data is what you say it is, I'm not letting anyone see it."

"If you're not guaranteeing I get a fair challenge to a capital charge, I'm not telling you what it is."

"I will have to consult on that. In the meantime, you will be confined to your billet for security. Food will be brought to you."

He had the MPs waiting outside already.

They were totally professional. I walked ahead of them to my billet, coded in, and I heard the door lock cycle behind me.

At least I wasn't interrogated with a transformer up my ass or my cooze. But sitting there was terrible.

Had they all died for nothing? Well, it was for something, but if I was the only witness, they'd never be remembered. That made their deaths even colder.

Then I realized I was facing a desertion charge. It was the only crime I knew of that actually carried a confirmed sentence. Death by firing squad.

I really hadn't thought about it, but I was being dumped just as badly. My contract money, gone. My honor, gone. My life, gone. I'd risked my life and everything else, and I couldn't prove I'd done anything.

I don't know if I slept. I sat on the rack, head against the wall, chewing on the inside of my cheek until it was raw, banging my head. I didn't bang it hard, but I guess a thousand of them was enough to cause a bruise.

After what felt like days I was brought breakfast. Morgan brought it personally.

"Okay, Ms. Kaneshiro, I decided to take this further."

"What does that mean?" He was unreadable, but I thought I was about to be dragged in front of a court.

"You believably knew Ms. Garweil. I knew her slightly, I believe you met her. We had several clandestine teams out. A UN ship was captured, and they never admitted it.

It actually never made the news, because we weren't going to say anything. So I'm withholding any action until you produce the PARs, or don't."

"I said—"

"Yes, citizen's office. We can do that after you eat."

"And shower," I said. "Turn the monitors off." If I didn't relieve some stress, I was going to be a wreck. I don't mind a private show, but I didn't want the guards eying me taking care of business.

"Our appointment is at three fifty. It's two fifty-four now."

"That will be fine. Thank you, sir."

He nodded and left.

I used the shower. I couldn't orgasm, but I needed some kind of contact, touch, focus to get my mind in order. I often wonder if I have a hormone imbalance for male hormones. I always get wired when stressed.

I got clean, put on my shipsuit and pulled my hair up, and paced until they came and got me.

Morgan walked with me. The MPs stayed back.

I hadn't been in a citizen's office since I took the residency oath, and it wasn't a spaceside one. This one was bigger than my billet, but not huge. Even citizens were limited in available cube.

There was a reception desk, but it was empty. We walked past that into an open rear office.

The citizen was there, standing and waiting. He extended hands and shook.

"Lady, I'm Citizen Drake."

He was forty or so, gray, handsome, calm and not at all unfriendly. That helped.

"Aonghaelaice Kaneshiro," I said. "Thank you for seeing me, sir."

"I hope I can help," he said.

He took a seat, gestured for us to do so, and then referenced his screen.

"So, in summary, you report being a contract guide for one of our Black Operations elements, but all records have been destroyed, which is understandable, but puts you in a very delicate position."

"Yes, sir, that's the summary." Oh, good. He was fair. I felt a huge wave of relief. This might not be the last day of my life. I'd had too many of those lately. And yes, it was a very black operation. That was the first time I'd heard that name, and about then was the first time their existence was made public. I leaned back in the chair and relaxed slightly.

"What length of service was your enlistment?"

"It was a standard four-year, from when I was twelve to sixteen." I gave the dates.

He shook his head, "No, your new contract on *Churchill*."

"I . . . didn't sign one, sir."

"You didn't sign an enlistment contract?"

"I locked aboard right as they buttoned up, and they put me to work. I was assigned duties, but never actually put it on file, no."

"We don't have any records of that, either. That would tend to make any charges of desertion a problem, then, if you weren't enlisted. You'd be possibly a distressed spacer, or possibly a veteran on space available transport. I'd have to research it, but I don't think that's relevant to the core problem."

I had never even stopped to think about the legalities, and apparently no one on *Mad Jack* had, either. He was right. You can't go AWOL if you're not actually in the military. I never signed a contract and hadn't been conscripted.

"So," he continued, "you say you have post-action reports that will help clarify your statements."

"I hope so."

"You don't have them? Or they're not available easily?"

"No, sir, I have them, but I haven't looked at them. I told Juan, the element commander, I'd courier them home. I don't know what he actually documented."

"Understood. Well, assuming the documents check out, you are to be commended for your attention to duty."

He waved at his phone, which beeped.

"If you don't mind, I'm going to invite another party into these proceedings."

Morgan said, "I'm very uncomfortable with that, Citizen, but I'll of course go along with your guidance."

I said, "I guess it depends on who it is."

Drake brushed at his desk console, the door to the right opened, and a uniform came in.

It took me a moment to read her. General. Five battle stars. Citation for valor. Space, air and ground qual badges. Mobile Assault and Blazer tabs, and a command badge.

I was on my feet at attention.

"Ma'am," I said, and almost saluted.

"Please, relax."

She was young, too. I put her at twenty, maybe twenty-five. She was my age, and a fucking general.

Then I realized that was probably because she'd survived the last two years.

Then I realized that was a pretty high qual all by itself.

"I'm co . . . General Sansing. Second Legion command."

If things hadn't changed much, she was probably the third ranking officer in the Forces. She might be fourth if there was someone older.

"Pleased to meet you, ma'am," I said. Hopefully this wasn't all for nothing. I had as much attention as it was safe to have.

Morgan said, "If this suits your need for witnesses, I'd like to see the PARs, please."

"Yes," I said.

I continued, "So, the chip is implanted, but I'm told the right kind of scanner will read it."

Sansing reached down to her satchel, rummaged around and pulled out a monitor wand.

"Probably this one," she said.

"That could be it." I paused for a moment. "I will need to remove my shirt."

"That's not necessary," she said. "This can read through fabric."

"My shirt is made of faramesh." It wasn't as if we hadn't thought of things reading through fabric. I'd alternated the pair of these under my other clothes since . . . then.

"Oh. Then go ahead."

I took off my jacket and hung it on the chair, then zipped down my shipsuit to my waist and peeled the shirt over my head. The men did look, but they were discreet.

"Right here," I pointed at a spot two centimeters below my right nipple.

I'll give Sansing this, she didn't twitch. We're pretty casual people, and spacing makes that even more so, but actually getting close and touching a stranger like that still takes effort.

She pointed her scanner, moved it around slightly and said, "I have signal. And I have files."

Citizen Drake said, "I didn't know they could secure information like that." He was trying to smile politely without being informal. If I'd been an actual nudist, he could have ignored it. As it was, I was half-dressed with tits jutting out.

I said, "They said no one would be looking for it there, and it would be easier to hide than hands or butt."

He said, "Yes, faramesh shirts are easier than pants."

But Sansing was reading the files and not paying attention to us. I took that as permission to cover back up. The men tried really hard not to watch.

Nothing happened for half a seg. Then she said, "Citizen, please release this detainee. Specialist . . . Ms. Kaneshiro, thank you officially and personally for bringing this information. I wish it was under better circumstances."

"So do I, ma'am. Uh, what do I do now?"

"Oh, by all means stay here for now. I'm sure we'll have more questions. Agent Morgan, can you move her into accommodations of her choice? If the Hilton has space, book her in there."

"At once. Ms. Kaneshiro, I'm very glad this worked out. I hope the intel is useful."

"Thanks. Really, knowing their story is safe is the big thing."

That was the first time I'd heard of Black Operations. I now know they're their own element of Special Warfare. There are all kinds of rumors and war stories about what complete wizards and brutes they are. I can swear the stories don't even come close.

I was moved into officer lodging, which was a bit roomier and more comfortable, and given a chip to access the exchange and contracts. I pigged out on chili tuna and rosemary salmon and garlic shrimp, and buzzed my brain with a Violet Zap and some beer. I finally felt the war was over.

But it wasn't. The next day I was back in Morgan's office. It was down the passage from Gestang's.

"The files have been read and filed," he said.

"Oh, good. Do you need elaboration? Holes to fill?"

"We will. That's not the immediate issue."

I realized he looked very uncomfortable.

"What's wrong?" I asked.

"The report details their operations, and them meeting up with you in Earth space before the final push. You were furnished the intel and given transit funds back here."

"That's . . ." What the hell?

Morgan said, "So you were only a courier."

"I don't know why I'm not there. I should be." This just kept going.

"Lady, you're free to go. I wouldn't make any kind of fuss. You get veteran status for your very brief service, thanks for couriering the intel, and you're as free as the rest of us. Don't blow it out of proportion. And don't take it personally."

He paused for a moment, and I was still swimming. How did they manage to erase me from all that? How was that possible?

He said, "You're probably aware there's a lot of troops here who couldn't get into the fight, or had to go underground. There's one young man who managed to take a spaceside job and claims he sabotaged the UN astrogation on several ships. Hard to prove, but we know he took the job because he needed cover and funds, and it's true none of those ships fought their best. We also know *Scrommelfenk* needed a major scrub and rebuild of astro software, and some sensor refits. He gets the benefit of the doubt, too.

"Please understand I'm not calling you a liar. But we can't credit anything we can't prove, and we don't need a lot of grandiose stories cluttering the actual investigation. Thank you for your service."

That was it. He gestured at the door.

I left, wondering how much longer I had in lodging, if any time at all. I might have to start looking for cubbies and flops at once.

I'd trusted Juan. I wondered if he expected I'd get captured, and wanted to keep me out of it. If the UN got the intel, we might eventually steal it, or maybe already had plans in place. But if I was mentioned, there I was facing the death penalty again.

I knew whatever happened he'd had a good reason. I decided I'd keep quiet.

It wasn't the money. Okay, part of it was. It was a lot

of money. Mostly, it was my integrity. "We can't prove you're a cowardly, deserting turd, so we're going to say you served acceptably."

It wasn't acceptable.

The code showed I had two more days of lodging. I figured I should use a fair amount from the chip to stock my ruck with work clothes, food and some accessories. I'd be back on my own funds later, which were the leftovers Juan had furnished me, then back to my own savings. I ordered for delivery, and left everything there to go walk about and get my head clear.

I was in the exchange passageway when my phone pinged.

"Report to Morgan at once," it said.

Gods, wasn't this ever going to end? I hoped it was just for some details to fill in. Though what details, I wasn't sure, since they thought I wasn't even involved.

When I got to Intel, a specialist was waiting and directed me right past the screen to his office.

I knocked, the door opened.

I stepped in, and stopped.

General Sansing was there with him.

"You were on contract," she said without even a greeting.

"Yes."

"A substantial one."

"I didn't say that, but yes." What did it matter now?

She held up her phone. "Crypto found a secondary code that opened up a modified file. Warrant Leader Schulman actually wrote two complete and distinct logs. The second one includes you, confirms everything you said."

"Lady, I am very impressed by this report. There will be entire Military College studies done on this, all over space, not just us."

"All I did was act as guide."

"The black ops teams found guides to be essential. And you came to us, with a huge wealth of information. Then, you took active part in the missions. Really, you should be proud."

"Well, thank you."

Proud? Less than a day after I was supposed to be ashamed and keep my mouth shut?

She said, "I apologize for the complicated circumstances of war. Please accept my apologies on behalf of the Forces and myself. You will be credited with all the relevant service, and I'm sure we'll consult further on the events."

"Sure," I agreed. I didn't really have a choice anyway.

She had a wide-eyed expression as she said, "Which doesn't mean it's not going to be painful to authorize a draft for this amount. That is a lot of zeroes."

CHAPTER 39

So I have an award called the Intelligence Cluster. I'd never heard of that. I have a POW medal. I have a citation for Courage for volunteering aboard *Mad Jack*, and a star on it for volunteering for my mission.

Then two weeks after that I had to report to the UN consulate, which was three small offices guarded by a squad of Blazers, because people are still angry, and the UN can't afford better.

I wasn't sure they were "just" Blazers.

I stood at attention while I was awarded the UN Humanitarian Action Medal, for rescuing the crew of *Scrommelfenk*. We could have blown her, but they say we risked resources in combat to save their people. I received nine more, on behalf of the team, to deliver to their families.

The elderly colonel awarding it was very serious, even in a room with just himself, a lieutenant, and myself and one of our sergeants assigned as my escort.

He presented me with mine, shook my hand, handed me nine more for "the crew of the *Henri Pieper*" and shook my hand again.

He concluded with, "I wish all our engagements could have been under such honorable circumstances."

"Thank you, sir," I said. "I will make sure these reach their families."

"Thank you. I'm sorry for the loss of your comrades."

I think he actually was.

Then my pay. It was a huge draft, based on time, number of actions, risks. The actual military pay I got for the handful of combat I was in looked sad and trivial in comparison, which wasn't fair, because that was real money I'd earned.

I didn't feel like a failure or a traitor when accused of it, but now, I don't feel like a hero. I did what I could and what I had to.

I know who the heroes are.

It took me a month to realize I could follow up with their families. I'd had the UN medals shipped, but I could visit in person, except it would take months at least.

But I verballed them all, and we shared tears. I'm not going to cover that here. That's private and personal and not mine.

Recovering from a war takes longer than the war itself. All the existing routes and routines were a shambles. People were dead, missing, injured. Civilians had lost wealth and livelihoods. What had been the point of all this? Was it just jealousy on an interstellar scale? Is that what it all came down to?

They'd wrecked our system. We'd ruined theirs. At the end, neither of us owned any space we hadn't owned before. It was a total waste of resources.

A week later I was called again, though it was unofficially official. I reported to the mildock and joined a formation in uniform, with me still in work clothes.

I stood to as we officially commissioned four ships, including the FMS *NCA Henri Pieper*, which sounds so odd. A chime sounded, and she was officially listed as "Ship, Cargo (I supplement), Acquired Asset."

Then "All Hands" sounded, and another chime. Her status changed to "destroyed in combat with the enemy," and she was stricken from the active list. Mira had been right. She'd been born a freighter, but she died a warship, and deserved the mention. I cried.

Alongside her name were two and a half stars for engagements. One kill, one capture, one damage. She ranked higher than quite a few actual warships.

She'd been a grand old lady and I still missed her, too.

CHAPTER 40

Station Breakout, across from Earth, was useless until the destroyed Jump Point could be reconstructed. With phase drive to astrogate between the points, they said it could be up again within the year.

There were ships there, though, older and in need of refit, and the work was cheap because it took effort to go there. Their economy was a mess, too, and we'd done that one ourselves. One of our scientists had collapsed the point from inside. He was assumed dead, scattered across two levels of space.

I had a large bank balance, and there were ships. I found one a bit newer than the *Pieper*, similar class and capabilities, and then had a dealer help me put out a request for venture capital.

The problem was, I wasn't an astrogator, so I was going to have to hire crew. I put out word for that, and juggled the request for a ship for a crew I didn't have with the request for a crew for a ship I didn't have. The dealer didn't seem thrilled, but I had enough money to interest him so he kept sending requests.

I had no idea how to interview an astrogator, and I didn't even have a ship type to tell them, or even a drive type. That would matter to engineers as well. Cargo handling was less of an issue, and I figured I could fake purser duties if I had to.

Two weeks later I suddenly had backing.

Ms. Kaneshiro:

I am delighted to be able to return, in some small part, a favor you did for us. I was able to assure the investors of your sound judgment and determination to succeed. I wish you well in your endeavors and hope you will remain in contact. Juletta, especially, would like to see you again.

—Mark Parkerson

I had to wonder at "sound judgment," but I appreciated the favor more than a lot of things. I still wasn't sure what context to put money in next to torture, impending death, and dead friends. Juletta, though, was alive, and I missed the little weasel. I'd have to plan to go in-system as I went across to an active gate, and at least drop down to visit. I made sure to stash funds aside for that.

Yes, I plan to continue spacing. It's what I do. The system is a mess, but it's free and I can haul stuff for us and others. Phase drive makes it cheaper and easier to travel and the prices were coming down. As soon as I could, I should see about funding one.

I named the hauler *Teresa Kusumo*. I'm captain-owner, but not master, because I don't astrogate. I don't trust myself to even try to learn. I found an engineer. He'd crewed on one of our destroyers way back, and was a tattooed, cursing longhair who was actually really educated and nice under the asocial outside.

Astro was going to be the tough slot. Anyone who can do that can get their choice.

I own my own ship. Well, with the investment firm. So few people, so few spacers can say that. I have the freedom to go anywhere I can make a heading, and leave when I wish. All I have to do is make it profitable.

But I'd trade the awards, the money and the ship to have *her* back, snuggling me, or in the rack next to me, or just in the back of my own ship, keeping things together. And the rest of them. They felt like more than family, like the only family I'd ever had.

But I have to look at the future.

I had *Teresa* fitted out. I even had some potential connections for cargo. I was trying to find someone for astro, and knew that would be my biggest expense after fuel and dock fees.

I roomed aboard, since I had no reason to waste money stationside, and I had a very comfy captain-owner's stateroom.

I bought a loader that had once been on *Mad Jack*. I'd start with one and run it myself if I had to. Even that large amount of money was shrinking fast. I had usually managed to budget enough to keep me moving, but this was entirely different. I didn't dare run out of funds. I sat in my cabin cutting items to fit the budget and allow for some wiggle room.

I got a chime from the lock, and rolled out to see what it was. I rolled the station shield open.

The woman standing there said, "I understand you need an astrogator."

It was Mira.

"Please come aboard," I said. I was amazed at how calm I was.

I needed a drink. I knew she liked vodka, but I had rum, and fruity mixes for me. I just poured us a snifter each and invited her to sit in my cabin.

"I'm glad you're alive," I said. I was, and that was the most important thing.

"Thanks," she said. "I can't tell you what I did, but I did survive my mission. As far as I know, none of the others did. We weren't expected to."

"I still hate that. Wasn't there some way to end it without us losing our best and Earth losing . . . everything?"

She shrugged. "Maybe. I guess the historians will tell us in a few years. For now, I'm just glad we're here." She raised her glass in toast. "To the guys," she said.

"The guys," I agreed, and felt them again—ghostly, sexy shivers that were happy tinged with sadness.

She added, "And to us. And to *Pieper*."

"It took them days to figure out where the backup log was," I said, and told her about it.

She said, "I guess I should make sure they do that with all files."

"Yeah," I agreed. "How many other ships?"

"One that I know of and mentioned," she said. "I couldn't talk about others if I knew, and I don't anyway."

I figured she'd give that same answer if she did know.

We finished our glasses and I poured one more.

"Thanks," she said. "So you came out well ahead."

I flushed.

"I honestly never thought I'd live to see it, and never figured the prize money would pay off."

"Oh, it's fine," she said. "We couldn't have done it without you, and you took more than your share of it."

I had compared to some, but not against their tally. It wasn't fine, either. She was jealous and bitter and should be.

I wished all the money could go away. All the pain. All the destruction.

Amidst the rum, I rummaged in my cabinet and handed her copies of her decorations.

She looked them over.

"Ah, they still don't have my real name," she commented.

"No?"

"It doesn't matter. I'm Mira now."

She kept staring at them.

"I guess I earned them," she said. "They just don't seem to mean much, with everything else, you know?"

"I do know," I said.

"I found you because you named the ship after her."

"Yeah." I figured.

"You know she had a crush on you, yes?"

"I figured that out eventually," I said. "If we weren't crewing in wartime, I'd have said yes."

Mira said, "She was always shy. Even in training."

"How well did you know her?" I asked.

"We were the equivalent of bunkies for several weeks of hard training. Pretty well."

We were so calm, even after everything.

"Yeah?" I half-asked.

"Very good at math. She was an emergency backup for me. You still don't know how good she was with tools. She could make or wreck anything, while being stressed to the extreme."

I said, "Heck, I watched you wreck a ship and a station with cargotainers. The ship's awards are mostly yours."

She shrugged.

"I prefer flying them to smashing them, when I can."

"Then I guess I better let the crewdogs know, and start calling for cargo." A moment later I added, "Oh, you're hired. Lead scale plus twenty percent."

It was the least I could do.

EPILOGUE

Our shakedown cruise was interesting.

Honestly, if I hadn't had Mira astrogating, I don't think I could have done it. She took us mid-system of Caledonia on our first transit, and we were in planetary orbit in eighteen days, not twenty. She was that good, when she was allowed to be.

There was a dark irony to taking relief supplies to Earth, after we'd helped destroy the entire system. I guess some of it was survivor's guilt, some of it was embarrassed self-righteousness, and some of it discomfort over taking money for the purpose of helping refugees. Still, we had to be paid for work.

I just wished we didn't, and it wasn't us doing it.

The accounts stayed positive, though, even with huge fuel costs. Mira did an amazing job of plotting routes to save time, fuel and distance.

It was almost a year later when I actually put foot on

dirt. I met with the families of the crew, and felt guilty all over again for being alive. None of them showed it, but I was sure there was a feeling. Why was I here, and their men and women not?

I checked in with Mom. She hadn't seen Dad since before the war started. He'd skipped out with a woman a decade younger. I wasn't going to take sides in that. They'd had issues for several years. I was glad she was alive, and she was happy I had a ship. Then she tried to tell me how to run it.

Mira went to see her family. I have no idea what went on there. I wasn't going to ask.

I'd been invited to be a guest speaker at a memorial service.

There are memorials all over the place, and there'd already been a mass award, but there were a lot of little teams who hadn't been mentioned, because they'd been that clandestine. We were one of them. I hoped anyone else who showed up got taken more at their word than I had. Being accused of lying had hurt more than torture, or almost-death.

This presentation was just a plaque with names, including my crew. Two other people spoke about elements who'd been insystem in gunboats. Two crews had provided a lot of our intel, and taken out two warships and some remote unmanned stations. Reactor explosions don't leave much question of bodies, though.

I sat back and listened to the others. They were very heartfelt, and I knew all the things they wanted to say that wouldn't fit in words. Some of the audience did, too. A lot were in uniform.

I'd have survivor's guilt my entire life. But I knew what I'd say when it was my turn. I'd worked really hard to turn my words into actual prose.

That was when my escort touched my sleeve.

"It's time, lady."

It was my turn.

"Yes, sir."

I mounted the podium, still feeling unsure about the uniform. In seconds, complete attention was on me. I took a long, deep breath. This was almost as tense as combat. I didn't want to say anything wrong. I'd run the finished speech past Mira, who'd approved it with damp eyes.

She was listed there, too, officially dead, and I wasn't going to deny her that. Her past was her own, as was her future.

I took a deep breath, and glanced at my notes.

"Ladies, men, soldiers, Blazers, good evening. I am Aonghaelaice Kaneshiro. I am honored to be here this evening. I am here to speak about an element who crewed a clandestine ship they acquired under mysterious circumstances—" there were a few chuckles "—the *Henri Pieper*.

"We all served in some way, some more than others. I was proud to serve my system, and have been rewarded for it. Despite that, there is a hierarchy to heroism. It's not one we seek, or that can be bought. It usually happens by accident, and someone is called upon to do more than they ever thought they could.

"But there are those who know they can. They don't seek to pay the ultimate price, but they know, quietly, confidently, that they have that strength. Few of us ever meet anyone that strong. I had the opportunity to know nine of them well, and to meet several others."

"None of us can ever repay what they did for us during the war, and during the terrible final battles that freed us. We are here now, and our system exists, because of their unmatched courage, dedication and determination. We're here in memorial to them.

"I would like to mention those nine I served with and supported.

"Seth Jonathan Schulman,

"Robert Andrew Dupree,

"Peter Isman Tchayo,

"Marcus David Pond,

"Thor Eric Kessman,

"Astrid Iliana Venkov,

"Zev Theodore Ramovich,

"Evangeline Casey Laksa Spencer

"Addar Benton Falk."

I only knew their real names from the awards I'd transferred, and Mira said hers was still wrong. Those sounded so odd to me. Yet I knew the real people underneath, and they were the kind you trust with your life, and I had.

It seemed tragic that they were only known after death. And Dylan . . . Actually Karl Jensen . . . was not mentioned. He'd been as brave in his own way. He was as honorable an enemy to us as we'd been to him.

"Oh, my friends. I will always miss you. What we had in those months can be had by no one else."

Tears rolled over my cheeks, but there was still complete silence. So I forced control into my voice.

"But I read something in a history text that applies now, even more than it did then. I choose not to mourn that these heroes of our system died.

"Instead, I'm going to celebrate that men and women of such character *lived*. And, that for a brief time, I was allowed to know them."

I shivered and cried in thunderous applause. It wasn't for me. That was how it should be.

END

DID YOU KNOW YOU CAN DO ALL
THESE THINGS AT THE
BAEN BOOKS
WEBSITE?

* Read free sample chapters of books

* See what new books are upcoming

* Read entire Baen Books for free

* Check out your favorite author's titles

* Catch up on the latest Baen news & author events

* Buy any Baen book

* Read interviews with authors and artists

* Buy almost any Baen book as an e-book individually or an entire month at a time

* Find a list of titles suitable for young adults

* Communicate with some of the coolest fans in science fiction & some of the best minds on the planet

* Listen to our original weekly podcast, The Baen Free Radio Hour

Visit us at
www.baen.com